Mommy's Top Drawer

A romantic lesbian MDLG and ABDL
novel collection of 6 in 1 kinky BDMS
age play stories

By Tina Moore

Table of Contents

Nancy's Little One

A Lesbian Mommy Domme trains her baby girl in the MDLG kink

By Tina Moore

Chapter 1

Loren was not like most girls her age. At 25, she had no interest in getting married and starting a family. Loren didn't care about where her friends went on holidays, and she certainly didn't care about what was going on in the world around her. She was content living her predictable life while feeling so dangerously lonely it made her heart hurt. Loren worked as a real-estate agent and spent her week showing wealthy couples around luxury mansions she knew she would never want as her own. With the marble baths and indoor swimming pools, gardens greener than one in central park and more tech than she truly knew what to do with, these mansions were divine but soulless. They reminded her of herself. She had been working for the company for five years, and within those five years, she had learned one thing. Rich people liked expensive price tags. If a mansion was selling for 15 million, she would bump the price to 20, if a property was selling for 35, she bumped it to 40. Due to her excellent selling style, she had made a powerful reputation in the real-estate game, winning countless awards and enjoying the high commission. However, her success, she suspected, had nothing to do with her sales pitch. Her clients didn't need convincing to buy the mansions. The decision on the property was already made, that was not what they desired. It was her.

With a girlish vulnerability yet eyes that screamed use me, there had not been too many clients which she had not fucked. It wasn't that she was a slut. It was that she couldn't feel the world. She used these clients as much as they used her. The game both were trying to win, the prize, power. She wasn't even straight, but that didn't matter to her. Sex was sex. She would let a husband fuck her arse from behind while he choked her as she was cuddled and lovingly teased by a wife. An exciting mix of hate fucking and motherly love was the closest thing to what she truly desired, and although it never lasted more than a night, it was all she had.

As she showed a new client to the open air cinema, she felt a hand gently stroke on the small of her back.

"And from here you will be able to see the ocean," Loren explained as the hand reached under her skirt. Loren spread her thighs slightly to encourage the groping hand of the rich women. The woman moved in front of Loren. Her eyes sparkled with desire, but Loren's were dead. The older woman didn't seem to care as she began to stroke Loren's warm pussy through her satin panties.

"It's unusual for me only to show a property to one party. Will your husband be joining us?" Loren asked the woman 15 years her senior.

"Not unless you want him to," the woman replied, moving Loren's panties to the side and sliding a finger into her aching wet cunt. Loren moaned and buckled over, holding the taller woman's shoulder for support.

"There, there little one, come over here," the woman said as she felt for the chair behind her and sat down. She pulled Loren on of her lap, making the younger woman straddle her womanly thighs as she was fucked. Enjoying the breathless moans of the compliant girl, the woman leaned back and took in her beauty.

"You're going to be a good girl for me. You'll enjoy the commission you receive from my husband buying this house," she said as she pumped her fingers inside Loren harder, rubbing her thumb over her clit and making her rock her hips and grind down on the woman's hand.

"That's it," the woman coaxed as Loren leaned forward and wrapped her arms around the woman's neck. Loren closed her eyes and gasped as she came, cum dripping down her thighs and over the woman's hand.

"My my you are a dirty little girl," the woman said as she slowly took her fingers from Loren's juicy pussy and began to undo her blouse.

"Do you know what dirty little girls need?" She asked Loren who was enjoying the sight of this woman's breasts too much to bother replying. Slap. The woman hit Loren's face with a force that sent her head falling back. The older woman had held Loren in place with her other arm as she slapped her, clearly aware of her strength.

"I'm waiting for a reply sweet pea," the woman said as she unclipped her black lace bra.

"Um, no, I don't know what dirty little girls like me need," Loren said, playing the woman's game.

"They need a Mommy," the woman replied, grabbing the back of Loren's hair and drawing her mouth to her nipple. Loren could feel the sun burning through the back of her light pink blouse. It was her favorite one. Something about this blouse drove women wild. She had worn it on purpose.

"Do you want me to be your Mommy baby girl?" The older woman said in a friendly voice, Loren had not heard from her before. Loren didn't know what she should say. She was happy her mouth of full of this woman's nipple because it meant she didn't have to respond. She just nodded her head and continued to nurse.

"Yes, good girl. I knew you needed me," the older woman said as she gently rocked her, stroking her hair while Loren closed her eyes and suckled. She hadn't even realized she'd fallen asleep until she woke up. She was not outside anymore, and the woman was gone. She recognized the room, though. It was one of the rooms in the mansion. Loren looked down and saw her clothes were still on, but her heels had been taken off. Beside her on the nightstand was a glass of water and a note. It read, 'Thank you for showing me the property. I'll be in touch'. *Doubt it,* Loren thought. *Now I have to explain why I was so long with one client. Usually, this shit happens the first night they move in.* Loren was happy she had not scheduled any other appointments for the day. She checked her phone and saw that it was 4:30 in the afternoon. She'd hit traffic getting back to the office, and it would take her an extra half an hour to get home.

Chapter 2

It was a week after she had shown that woman the property she woke up suddenly as her phone rang. Loren looked at the name on the phone and rolled her eyes as she answered.

"What the hell did you do?" Came a screaming woman down the phone. Loren's eyes popped open from the sleep she just ripped out of and looked at the clock. *5:30 in the morning, this bitch is going to ring me at 5:30 in the morning?* Loren thought as she played dumb.

"What are you talking about?" She replied, trying to wake up.

"I'm talking about the fact that you, I can't even believe this!" Loren's boss exclaimed.

"That I what Jen!?" Loren shouted back down the phone angry her boss wasn't getting to the point.

"That you closed the deal 15 mill over the asking price!" Jen stated happily. *15 mill over the asking price. She wasn't lying; I'll enjoy this commission very much*, Loren thought to herself.

"Yo, you still there or have you died of shock?" Jen asked.

"Yeah, I'm here. Holy shit. Fuck yes. You better give me that pay rise now, lady!" Loren said, laughing.

"How much money do you need, you just landed the biggest fish we have ever caught. You'll be looking for your department soon!" Jen replied.

"I'll talk to you about the details later. I'm going back to sleep, and I'm not coming in today," Loren stated before she hung up the phone quickly as to not hear Jen's rebuttal.

Loren lay in bed. She thought about the woman. She couldn't even remember her name. *Suzan, Sharon, Sandra? Who the fuck cares, I just got paid*, Loren thought as she rolled over and took out her notebook and pen.

Ever changing nature and forced normalization silences scream in the throes of torturing stillness. To look upon a dancer so graced and elegant as she moves on broken legs yet only to her ears, the sound of crushing bone can be heard. How wonderful a sight she must be with her form and expression, oh but the unwavering admiration that is laid around her neck only serves as her collar and leash. The pulling from another, she moves into the positions they desire and kept there with a promise of...love. It's beautiful they say as they watched her fit into their boxes, pushing her shattered limbs into the shapes of their cages.

She read over her work and smiled a sad smile. That woman had been the closest thing to kindness Loren had felt in a long time, and she couldn't even remember her name. Deciding to go to the gym, she got up and walked over to her cupboard. Looking through her clothes, she remembered the first time she had bought a designer shirt. Five years on and designer clothes weren't exciting anymore. She found a pair of navy track pants and a white crop top. She laced up her newest pair of runners and put her hair up in a messy ponytail. She looked at herself in the mirror.

She ran her fingers over her abs and tweaked her hair so that it fell more to the left side. She liked that her tits were small enough only to need a sports crop; at a B-cup she didn't have to worry about much bounce. She walked out of her room, grabbed her gym bag, and walked down the steps of her home and on the street.

The street always made her heart happy. The smell of hot dogs and the flurry of birds as they fought over a piece of scrap a child would undoubtedly be throwing. The trees which dotted the sidewalks littered the ground. Mostly she liked how invisible she could become. No one knew she was there, and no one would notice if she were gone. It was a comforting thought.

When Loren got to the gym, it was unusually quiet.

"Slow morning Rach?" Loren asked the girl who checked in everyone.

"Yeah, I don't know what's going on. You're looking ripped!" Rach replied, taking in Loren's body. Loren looked down; she knew she looked good.

"Thanks," she said, laughing as she walked into the changing room. There was no-one else in the changing room as Loren put her bag in her locker and stretched on the bench. Her toned legs extending elegantly and her arms reaching over to hold her toes made her feel flexible even though she wasn't.

"I thought I might find you here," said a voice behind her. Loren quickly turned her head to see that the woman from the mansion, the one who had given her a noteworthy commission was standing in work out gear behind her.

"Mo — um, Hi," Loren said more excitedly than she would have liked. The woman smiled and stroked Loren's cheek, making her blush.

"Sweet girl, you can call me mommy if you like," she replied, making Loren blush harder. Loren looked around anxiously; hoping no-one could hear the other woman. She didn't know what to say, so she just looked down and toyed with her shoelaces.

"My husband would like to meet you. He is

very grateful you found such a wonderful home for us," the older woman stated. *I don't want to meet him. I don't care how fucking happy he is. I want you*, Loren thought to herself.

"I can't, I'm busy," she said when she finally spoke. The older woman sat down next to her and pulled her into her arms lovingly.

"Not right now silly, tonight," she said as she kissed Loren's forehead. 'This is too much. I'm done', Loren told herself as she pushed the other woman away.

"I said I'm not interested in your fucking husband," Loren half shouted as she walked to the door and out into the weight room.

"Rich people are the worst. They are all fake, and none of them even care about you. It's like you're just a thing for them to use and throw away," Loren said to Nancy who was wondering how many more times Loren, and she would have this conversation. Nancy owned the trendy café across the street from Loren's apartment, and ever since that first day she moved into the neighborhood she had come to Nancy's. The pie was all she was after on those bad days. Nancy would always find a way to break through Loren's cold, distant eyes and soothe the little pieces of a broken heart that Loren tried so hard to hide. Nancy was born to Latina parents who gave her the whitest name they could think of before adopting her out, or so said Nancy. But her name suited her. She had the whole motherly thing down, and her cuddly body with wide hips and full heavy breasts often made Loren wet just sitting in her spot at the counter sharing her problems. But it wasn't just Loren who got excited by Nancy. The way she wore her long thick wavy hair made most people who came into her diner stay longer than they needed too. Taking in her full lips and eyes that could melt a cold heart in moments, Loren looked at Nancy for a reply.

"Well yeah, you've been saying that for years," Nancy said as she poured Loren another coffee and wiped her hands on the apron, she had tied to her waist over her ripped jeans. Despite her 45 years of age, Nancy looked no older than 30. Her fashion sense of urban cool and timeless class often made Loren wonder just how successful she indeed was. From the stories Nancy had told Loren, Loren wondered why she would still be working five days a week.

"Why do you even mess with them? What are you looking for?" Nancy added. Loren wished she could tell her what she was looking for.

"I don't know Nancy, nothing I guess," Loren lied. Nancy suspected as much, but she ignored Loren's attempt to mask a blindingly obvious truth and tried to turn the conversation homebound.

"I'll leave in about an hour. If you want, we could hang out at mine. I've got movies and popcorn?" Nancy said as she smiled kindly at Loren. *Fuck it,* Loren thought to herself.

"Alright," she said as she took out her phone and waited for Nancy to finish work. Inside Nancy's living room Loren sat nervously.

"Your home is charming," Loren stated, looking around. With white wooden floorboards and white walls, the house looked light and airy. Nancy had a wall length wooden bench on one wall and a thick black fake fur rug covering the better part of the living room floor. Colorful artworks hung from the walls, and her TV was mounted to a wall. Loren was sitting on a dark green suede couch and thought the color combination of match black armchairs on either side where cool. *Coming here was a mistake, fuck, where am I going to get pie now?* She thought as

Nancy came back with the popcorn and handed a bowl to Loren, noting the fear in her sweet eyes, Nancy sat away from her.

"Don't worry, I'm not going to get too close to you," she said reassuringly as if reading Loren's mind. Loren just smiled and looked down, embarrassed that after four years of talking to Nancy, she had her figured out. The movie started, and Loren was hooked. She loved that film did that to her. She got completely drawn in and felt as though she was experiencing what the characters on the screen where.

"Um, where's your bathroom, Nancy?" Loren said, breaking the silence between them.

"Oh, it's just down the hall, to the right," Nancy replied, giving hand directions. Loren smiled and got up and followed the instructions. As she was coming back to the living room, she noticed something that caught her eye, a fluffy pink rug. Loren walked into the room carefully, not to make the door creak and was overwhelmed. It was a nursery and not a nursery you'd find at a baby shower. There was an adult sized cot, a rocking chair that looked custom-made for two adults and a bookcase filled with the kind of books Loren never let herself read. Toys in a toy box in the corner of the room and handcuffs bolted into the wall. She was so overcome with what she saw Loren didn't hear Nancy come up behind her.

"This isn't why I invited you around Loren. Let me shut the door," Nancy warmly said as she took Loren's hand and gently led her out of the room, shutting the door behind her. Loren didn't know where to look she certainly didn't want to look at Nancy.

"Are you alright?" Nancy asked tenderly, still holding Loren's hand. Loren just nodded her head and walked back to the living room and sat on the sofa. Nancy sat in the same chair she had previously been sitting in and turned the movie back on. Loren wasn't interested in the film anymore. Her breathing was shallow, and she was almost in tears. It was too much to know that Nancy was some sort of caregiver. It was too much to know that Nancy knew Loren wanted it. It was all just too much. The kindness Loren had been looking for had been in front of her the whole time, and she never knew. Nancy never tried anything, and god knows the times Loren had turned up drunk at the café Nancy could have had full access. But she never did, she would always just give Loren something to eat and walk her home, tucking her in and stroking her forehead as she fell asleep.

Loren looked at Nancy, who was already looking at her.

"So, what's that about?" Loren asked nervously.

"I'm into kink. I identify as a Mommy Domme. I like to have a submissive who I can take care of," Nancy said in an almost clinical way as she tried not to scare Loren off. Nancy was already surprised at how long Loren had stayed after seeing the nursery. She knew Loren was a runner. From the stories Loren had shared with her over the years, Nancy was sure she would have been out the door by now.

"Oh. That's cool," Loren said nodding as she spoke trying to be at ease.

"Loren. You don't need to feel uncomfortable; it's not meant for you. You should know by now you can trust me. As if I'd do anything to you," Nancy said as she stood up and paused the movie. She came over and sat next to Loren, happy she didn't flinch at the closeness but very aware she was forcing herself not to.

"Am I not what you like? I get it, like, not many people want me like long-term," Loren asked, looking down, wanting more than anything for Nancy not to say it was because Loren was unappealing. Nancy took Loren's hands in hers and kissed them, meeting her surprised eyes and holding contact.

"You are stunning, but I'm not a monster sweet girl. I can see you're hurting and I wouldn't get off on using your pain just to get what I want," Nancy said as she stroked Loren's hands with her thumbs.

"I wish you would," Loren said quietly as a tear rolled down her cheek looking away ashamed. She looked up at Nancy with her aqua green eyes filled with tears.

"I wish you were a monster like everyone else and I wish you would just take me how you wanted to," Loren repeated as she broke away from Nancy and walked out the door.

Chapter 4

Loren stayed away from the diner for months. She would see Nancy as she crossed the street to walk to work or when she came home, but she didn't go into the diner. She had lost a bit of weight since she stopped eating pie and decided that it was for the best. Nancy had seen her too. Out the back of the diner where she would occasionally have a cigarette, Nancy could watch Loren work out in the park. Her healthy, slender body dripping in sweat glistening in the midday sun made Nancy wet thinking of what she would do with her.

On a cold winter's afternoon, Loren had left work early to come home. She was frustrated with how the clients treated her and decided to go for a run to blow off some steam. Turning the corner towards home, she noticed a large group of men walking towards her. As she was about to pass the diner, she put her head down and hoped they wouldn't say anything to her.

"Oh hello beautiful," one man jeered, grabbing his dick and biting his bottom lip.

"Give us a smile," another one said as he blocked Loren's path, refusing to let her pass. They began to circle her, and as she frantically looked for an escape, she locked eyes with Nancy. Nancy saw Loren's scared eyes through the frosted window, and it made her blood boil. She came storming out in the middle of winter in just her gray woolen dress, her 6'4" height taking the men by surprise. She grabbed the closest one she could find and pulled him back, making him fall onto the cold hard ground.

"Get the fuck away from her," she yelled as she reached in and grabbed Loren's hand, pulling her into a warm embrace before turning her around and pushing her into the diner. Nancy didn't say a word but led Loren to the back room and wrapped her large jacket around Loren's shivering body.

"Thanks, it's OK, I'll go," Loren said as she stood to leave.

"Sit," Nancy commanded in a voice Loren had never heard before. Wide-eyed Loren involuntarily sat.

"You aren't going anywhere you hear me. We have played this game long enough. You said you wanted me. Well, you've got me, which means you're going to do exactly as I say, understood?" Nancy said sternly as she handed Loren a cup of warm cocoa.

"OK Nancy," Loren said softly, looking into the cup at the small pink marshmallows bobbing in the warm liquid. Nancy smiled in satisfaction and came to sit beside Loren. She wrapped her arm around the smaller girl, and Loren sighed and gave in, resting her head on Nancy's full breast.

"I've missed you," Loren said quietly, surrender in the voice, melting Nancy's heart.

"I have never...it's only ever been bad... I don't know what I'm supposed to do. I don't want to make you mad," Loren nervously stammered.

"I know you've been a big girl for so long, but Mommy's here now, and I'm going to take care of you," Nancy reassured Loren as she stroked her cheek with her other hand.

"I've read about contracts and stuff," Loren tried to say as Nancy gently placed her thumb in Loren's mouth to silence her.

"Didn't I just say to let Mommy take care of it? We are sitting in a broom cupboard baby, this is not the time to be writing contracts," Nancy replied, getting wetter than she had been in months.

"Sorry, Mommy," Loren softly replied as she continued sucking Nancy's thumb. Nancy smiled with satisfaction; it hadn't taken Loren any time at all to start calling her Mommy instead of Nancy. *She just needs love; she's perfectly trainable*, Nancy thought to herself.

"Drink that, and I'll take you home. I've finished for the day," Nancy said, taking her thumb out of Loren's mouth so that she could drink the last of her cocoa.

Nancy loved that Loren reached for her hand as they made their way to Loren's apartment. She let

Loren open the door and followed Loren inside. She had been inside Loren's apartment multiple times before, but never like this. Seeing that Loren didn't know what to do or what headspace to be in, Nancy called her over. She patted the spot on the couch next to her and tilted her head, telling Loren all she needed to know as she quickly walked over and sat down.

"So here it is sweetheart. I know you have your big fancy job. I respect that. Hell, I'm glad you've been able to support yourself for so long and so well. I'm not going to uproot your whole life, just yet. When do you think you could stay at my house? I want to start with making sure we want the same basics," Nancy said while holding a shivering Loren. The house was warm, but Loren was nervous.

"I finish work at 6. I don't do anything after that. Sometimes there's a gala or something, but I've gotten out of going before. I can stay tonight, what basics?" Loren said cautiously.

"You don't have to get out of those events

unless you want to. Work is work, sweetheart; everyone's got to eat. OK good, we can see how tonight goes and take it from there. Basics like, make sure we want the same things dynamically, sexually, and emotionally. It's just like a trail to see if we mesh," Nancy explained.

"OK, Mommy," she said as she melted into Nancy's big loving arms. Before jumping up suddenly as she had a thought.

"So, sex?" Loren asked.

"What about it?" Nancy laughed.

"Well, do I still get it?" Loren questioned.

"I'll fuck you when I want you. If you're lucky and you do what I ask, when and how I want something done baby girl I might even use it as a reward. Your pussy is mine now, and if I'm not happy with you, you can stay in chastity all month-long for all I care," Nancy answered, rubbing Loren's pussy through her workout tights. Loren made soft, breathless sounds as she closed her eyes and let Nancy continued to rub her, feeling her caress get firmer and a finger poke her pussy through her tights made Loren flinch backward.

"Don't run from me baby," Nancy said lovingly but with a clear warning. Loren held her breath and slowly moved back to where Nancy's hand was, letting her touch what she wanted to touch. Before long Loren was breathing shallow and fast. Just as she was about to cum, Nancy stopped, and Loren opened her eyes, compliant written in her eyes. Loren had already learned it was better to stay quiet than to complain to Nancy.

"You aren't allowed to cum just yet princess," Nancy said as she got up and pulled Loren up with her. They went into Loren's bedroom and packed the clothes she would need for the night and next morning. Nancy opened Loren's pantry and looked at the sugary foods she had stockpiled.

"How you keep that little body of yours while pumping it with this shit I will never know. You're going to be very moody as I wean you off this crap," Nancy said, looking at Loren and reaching out to feel her little waist.

"Well, yeah. I don't know. I eat what tastes good," Loren said. Nancy looked at her and smiled wickedly.

"No, you haven't, but you're about to," Nancy said as she leaned against Loren's kitchen table and slowly spread her legs.

"Here, now," Nancy commanded as she clicked her fingers to the floor where she wanted Loren. Obediently Loren knelt before Nancy and ran her hands under Nancy's dress.

"Make Mommy happy baby girl," Nancy said as Loren pulled down her panties and saw Nancy's perfect pussy for the first time. Her lips were full and puffy, with a thick strip of black hair that stopped just before her clit which pushed out eagerly. Nancy watched as Loren took it all in and smiled with satisfaction and desire.

"Kiss me there, baby," Nancy directed, mesmerizing Loren. She quickly dived on Nancy's pussy and kissed her lips, parting them with her tongue as she breathed through her mouth. She sucked on her clit and felt Nancy's hand come under her dress and hold Loren's head there. Moaning and gently fucking Loren's face. Loren flicked her tongue over Nancy's flick and then sucked it hard, enjoying the feeling of Nancy becoming wetter as juices pressed against her mouth. Nancy was right; she did taste sweet.

"Yes, good girl," Nancy moaned as she came loudly, shaking as she squirted into Loren's mouth, making her choke at the unexpected liquid flowing down her throat.

"I'm sorry little girl," Nancy said as she heard Loren coughing.

"Did Mommy cum down that pretty little throat of yours?" Nancy asked as she picked Loren up and made her straddle one of her thighs. She rubbed Loren's back and patted her firmly, and Loren snuggled into Nancy's breasts and sucked her thumb.

"Yes, Mommy," Loren said, trying not to cough.

"I liked it though Mommy," quickly followed as Loren became nervous she would upset Nancy by coughing.

"Good sweetheart, Mommy liked it too," Nancy said, picking Loren up like the baby she was and carried her to the couch. She sat down and placed Loren on her lap.

"I hope you've got a hungry tummy baby girl," Nancy said as she took off her dress revealing two massive breasts. Loren's eyes grew wide as she saw Nancy's breasts overflow out of her bra and was even happier when Nancy took her off. Her nipples were hard and thick, perfect for sucking. Loren nodded and smiled as Nancy took her thumb out of her mouth and replaced it with her nipple, pushing into Loren's mouth by the weight of her heavy breast.

"Suck little one, let's fill that little tummy of yours," Nancy said as warm milk flowed into Loren's mouth much to her surprise. She tried to pull away surprised that Nancy's breasts were full of milk, but Nancy held her breast firmly to Loren's lips, keeping her head in place with her other hand.

"Don't get fussy now baby girl. Mommy doesn't want to have to spank you," Nancy said warningly. Loren stopped squirming and opened her mouth wide as Nancy squirted milk into her pretty mouth. After a while, Loren held Nancy's breast in her hands, and Nancy stroked her tummy, enjoy seeing the slight swelling of it being filled. The night was setting in, and Nancy knew she wanted Loren in the nursery before she got too sleepy. She could see Loren's eyes fluttering shut as she looked up at Nancy who was aware there was still the matter of bathing and diapering Loren before she could let her fall asleep.

"That's enough, sweetheart," Nancy said warmly as she took Loren's hands off her and put her dress back on. Loren frowned slightly, her lips forming a cute pout. Not the bratty kind Nancy hated but the sweet, sleepy kind. She picked up Loren's bags and led her out the door.

Chapter 5

"Go to the bathroom baby, Mommy will run a bath for you in a minute," Nancy said as they entered her home. Loren nodded sleepily and headed to the bathroom. After Nancy put her bags in her room, she walked down the hallway and saw Loren was standing in the middle of the room, sucking her thumb and clutching her bunny by the ear.

"Come here, baby," Nancy said as she opened her arms to Loren who practically fell into them. Nancy held Loren up as she undressed her and ran her a bath. Nancy liked that Loren became doe-eyed and non-verbal when she was sleepy rather than the bratty hyperactive girls she had in the past. She washed Loren's small, thin body and made her giggle when she rubbed her between her legs. Helping Loren out of the bath she dried her. Nancy led her to the nursery and felt her hand being pulled back as Loren stopped promptly.

"What is it little one?" Nancy asked, slightly concerned. Loren looked as afraid as she had the first time she had seen it. It had not been six hours since Nancy had claimed Loren as her own and the thought that maybe she was rushing Loren only crossed her mind now.

"I don't think I like this. I don't want to dress in lame baby clothes. I'm too cool for those; it's not my style," Loren whispered into Nancy's ear.

"No? What is your style then baby because you haven't even seen what I have for you," Nancy asked as she sat down on the floor and pulled Loren down to sit in her lap.

"Wait, what, you've got me things? You've planned this?" Loren asked as she stopped playing with Nancy's hair.

"Ever since you walked out on me little one, did you think Mommy was going to give you up that easily?" Nancy asked, holding Loren's hand firmly in place, making Loren's stomach tighten. Loren thought back to that day and remembered how Nancy said the nursery wasn't for her.

"But you said it wasn't for me," she stated, looking at Nancy for an explanation.

"It wasn't, but it is now," Nancy replied, rubbing over the front of Loren's sports tights.

"Please, can I just have a t-shirt and panties?" Loren asked, her eyes begging.

"Please Mommy," Nancy corrected patting Loren's pussy firmly making her jump.

"Please, Mommy, just a t-shirt and panties," Loren begged.

"I'll compromise on a t-shirt, but you'll wear a diaper pretty baby, you don't wear big girl panties when you are not at work," Nancy said as she stood up and lifted Loren on the changing table. Loren looked around trying to focus on something, on anything. She wanted this, badly. But how could she give in to it? It was like Nancy knew what she was thinking about as she soothed Loren's worried mind.

"You will love this little one. I know you will. You'll be Mommy's cute little girl, don't you want that?" Nancy asked stroking Loren's forehead until she stopped frowning.

"Yes, Mommy, but what if I feel silly," Loren asked honestly.

"No one is going to see you, baby, no one is going to think you look silly, I certainly don't think you look silly. You don't like to be picked on, do you, sweetie?" Nancy asked, noting that humiliating Loren was off the table. Over the years, she had learned a lot about the type of things Loren liked; the concept of humiliation never came up.

"OK, Mommy," Loren replied nervously as she scrunched up her toes. Nancy gave her a fluffy pink blanket to snuggle into and pushed a white pacifier into her mouth and kissed her cheeks before she powered Loren for the first time. Tightening the diaper around her small waist, Nancy felt proud to have a baby girl as adorable as Loren. 'Mine at last,' Nancy thought, remembering who she had watched Loren over the years and pictured her just like this, lying there finally dependent on her. Sitting Loren up, she looked down to touch the diaper, running her hands over the crinkly plastic material. Nancy smiled as she walked to the cupboard and let Loren choose out of two t-shirts, something she would never have allowed another baby do. But she figured if allowing Loren have half a say in what she wore was going to keep her happy and Nancy's baby, it was worth the compromise. Loren smiled and pointed to a dark maroon shirt, and Nancy took out a plain white cotton diaper cover and black knee-high socks. She liked how tight the diaper cover was and rubbed Loren's pussy through the padding admiring how sweet she looked as she squirmed with the new sensation.

"Give me your little feet. I don't want you to get cold leggys baby," Nancy said as she rolled up the socks.

"There, come here, princess," Nancy said as she opened her arms and lifted Loren on the changing table. At 5'6" and only 60kg, Loren was easy for Nancy to carry. Nancy patted Loren's padded bottom as she took her to the living room floor. She placed Loren gently down, passed her her blankie and bunny and turned on a movie she knew Loren would love before going to have a shower. When Nancy came out of the shower, Loren was wrapped up in her blankie and fast asleep, her paci lying next to her. Nancy smiled and went to the fridge to make something for dinner. As she cooked, she looked over at her sweet girl stirring in her sleep. *Probably getting used to the new noises and the smell of a real meal,* Nancy thought to herself. She brought her dinner over to the sofa and picked Loren up and placed her on the couch. Nancy turned on the TV and rubbed Loren's back while she ate. Just before Nancy finished her meal, Loren sleepily stirred and woke herself up with a fright.

"It's OK baby girl, you're safe, you're at my house," Nancy said lovingly as Loren looked around the room almost teary eyed. She turned her head until she found Nancy and crawled to her.

"You want to cuddle with Mommy?" Nancy

said she put Loren's pacifier back into her mouth. As Loren nodded yes, Nancy moved her plate out the way and wrapped Loren in her arms as Loren's tummy grumbled.

"I'm hungry, Mommy," Loren quietly stated.

"What are you eating? Can I please have some Mommy?" She asked sweetly.

"It's only spaghetti baby. Do you want me to make you something else?" Nancy asked.

"Nope, I like sketti Mommy," Loren replied as her tummy grumbled again.

"You'd probably like anything right now," Nancy said as she got up and served Loren a bowl of pasta.

"Thank you, Mommy," Loren said as she reached for the bowl. Nancy had every intention of feeding her, but Loren had instinctively thought she would feed herself. *In time*, Nancy said realizing Loren had not done it on purpose, only out of habit.

"Yes, baby girl," Nancy answered, turning the TV off.

"It's about work. You know what I've done with clients. What happens if someone tried something?" Loren asked as worry spread across her face.

"Princess, when have you ever wanted to be with any of them?" Nancy asked in return, already knowing the answer.

"Never," Loren said, looking down at her bowl.

"Well, then. Don't let them," Nancy replied.

"I don't know how to do that, Mommy," Loren replied helplessly. Nancy thought, *that is true. I don't know how many times I've wiped her tears away after she let someone fuck her.*

"OK, tell you what. If someone tries something, ring me, straight away. Do you even need that job? Maybe you should find one a little less, tactile?" Nancy said.

"No I don't need the job, I have enough savings to not work for years. I don't think I even like the job, I just do it because, well, it's something to do," Loren replied honestly.

"Yeah I know baby girl, come here," Nancy said as she took Loren's bowl and opened her arms finding Loren in them within seconds.

"Can we just try it and see what happens? Maybe because I have you now it'll be different," Loren stated.

"It better be. I'm not sharing you with anyone. That's a big rule for me, Loren. You're my good girl, no one else's," Nancy said, making Loren's tummy churn. After an afternoon and evening being called her baby girl, hearing Nancy call her by her first name sounded awful.

"I don't want to be anyone else's, Mommy," Loren said as she fell asleep again in Nancy's safe, loving arms.

The next morning Loren woke before Nancy and got dressed in her work clothes. She looked in the mirror and felt her headspace shift into the mindset of an independent woman. Walking out into the living room and around to the kitchen, she made herself a cup of coffee and walked out to the veranda. Below the world looked like it did every other morning, but for Loren, it couldn't have felt different. She felt different. Nancy was different. Hearing footsteps behind her, she turned around to see Nancy walking over to her. Her black satin pajamas shining as the light touched them.

"Good morning," Nancy whispered into Loren's ear as she kissed her cheek. Nancy took the time to look Loren up and down, noting that she was far from the sweet baby girl who fell asleep in her arms last night. Loren's tight egg-shell blue dress and her cream pump heels complemented her light skin and white blonde hair. Her baby blue eyes sparkled in the morning sun, and the wind made the stray hairs in her ponytail fly.

"Hi," Loren replied, unsure of what to do or say next. Turning to face away from Nancy Loren sipped her coffee and walked back inside. Nancy followed her, wondering if she had pushed Loren too far the previous night.

"Hey," Nancy affectionately said as she grabbed Loren's arm. Loren looked at her blankly before pulling away and looking out the window.

"I hope you don't mind that I got dressed and stuff. I just wasn't sure if you were working today or like, what your plans were and I didn't want to wake you if you weren't working cause like, it's your sleep in but I have to be at work in like 35 minutes, so I just thought I'd go. And am I allowed just to go. I don't know what I'm doing Mommy. Nancy? What do I call you during the day? Is it OK if I call you Mommy during the day?" Loren tumbled her words out in one highly stressed breathe, and Nancy leaned against the kitchen counter and folded her arms across her chest, getting comfortable while she listened to Loren's long rambling. As Loren noticed Nancy's amused look on her face, she stopped and bashfully looked at Nancy wanting all her questions answered.

"Are you sure that's everything?" Nancy laughed leaning forward to take Loren's hand and pull her into a loving embrace.

"Yeah, for now at least," Loren giggled as she kissed Nancy's lips.

"You can call me Mommy or Nancy during the day sweetheart. If I call you and you are with a client or colleagues, I don't expect you to call me Mommy. But the minute you walk into that door regardless of what you are wearing, you'd want to be calling me Mommy. In the mornings, of course, get yourself dressed, get whatever you want to eat for breakfast and do whatever you need to do to get into the headspace for work. I think it is important for you to keep some of those things to do for yourself, if you feel like you want me to do them for you, let me know. But for now, you've been taking care of yourself for so long; it would be way too much if I took over everything," Nancy replied while stroking Loren's freshly straightened hair.

"OK, Mommy," Loren said, taking a moment to take it all in. As her phone alarm began to ring, signaling she needed to leave for work, Loren looked at Nancy, aware she was not meant to pull away from her.

"Go, sweetheart, don't be upset if I don't message you during the day, I'm going to the spa today and then having a friend over for coffee. I'll see you sometime before 7?" Nancy asked gently squeezing Loren before letting her go, following her into her bedroom as she collected her bag.

"Oh, have a fun time! It sounds like you've got a great day planned Mommy!" Loren exclaimed as she headed to the door.

"I liked kissing you, Mommy," Loren whispered as she opened the door to leave, looking back at Nancy expectantly.

"Are you trying to get me to kiss you now, baby? I wouldn't recommend you try to tell me what to do young lady; it won't serve you well," Nancy corrected making Loren blush and her stomach churn.

"Please Mommy, can I kiss you goodbye?" Loren said, begging this time instead of trying to manipulate.

"Better. That'll be something we work on," Nancy said as she patted the side of Loren's face, slightly frustrated she couldn't punish her that very moment. Holding Loren close, Nancy kissed her full on the lips. Impressed with herself when she felt Loren's legs buckle underneath her, Nancy quickly wrapped an arm around Loren's waist to hold her up. Nancy ran her fingers through the smaller woman's hair, causing Loren to moan and push herself harder into Nancy's enveloping body.

"Go to work baby girl. Mommy will see you later," Nancy said, breaking the kiss and watching her princess walk away. Closing the door behind her, Nancy sighed. She had not had a full-time baby in years and had forgotten how challenging developing a routine and dynamic could be. It was different when a girl had come over to be babied for the evening. That was all the same excitement level. This type of domination was different. It was highs and lows, exciting and boring. Nancy looked to where Loren had left her coffee cup and frowned. *The dishwasher was only 3" away Loren*; Nancy thought to herself as she took out a pen and paper and began writing a list of things she needed to teach Loren. It was hardly Loren's fault, and Nancy knew she wouldn't punish Loren for things she had not even informed her.

Focus, Loren said to herself as she walked a new set of clients around the indoor pool area of her biggest deal of the week. The couple, somewhere in their 30s, had told Loren they had picked her as their contact after being recommended by a couple she closed a deal with last year. She had tried to smile at their comment, knowing that this would probably not end well.

"Show us the bedroom again Loren," the

stern-voiced man commanded. Knowingly, Loren led them to the master bedroom, which overlooked the city. She opened the door to them but stayed in the corridor. Watching as the man and his new bride walked circles in the room, pretending to look at its features.

"Won't you join us? I have a question about the ceiling," the man said, his hands shifting to the pockets of his tailored trousers. Loren slowly walked into the room, and the woman circled behind her. The man stood firm in his place, next to the bed and looking up at the high ceiling.

"What would you like to know about it?" Loren said, trying to sound professional and not afraid.

"I want to know if you like the look of it," the man said as he grabbed Loren's wrist and pushed her onto the bed. Jumping on top of her quickly and pinning her hips down with his, pushing his hard cock onto her silk panties as he pulled up her matching colored dress.

"Get the fuck off me," Loren yelled as his

bride came over to the bed and began caressing Loren's breasts.

"We were told you like it. That you're the filthy little slut who puts out to make the deal," the man said as he wrapped a hand around Loren's neck and squeezed.

"Stay nice and quiet for me, bitch. Or I'll fuck that pretty mouth of yours until your jaw hurts," he added unzipping his pants. Pulling out his hard cock, Loren could see the pre-cum dripping onto her panties. As he forced her legs apart, his wife began to kiss Loren, biting her lip and making her pull away in pain. The man ran his wet cock up and down Loren's panty clad pussy, pushing it into her pussy and arse.

"Mm, which one first," he mocked as he rubbed her mound firmly. Loren stopped fighting and became still. She closed her eyes and thought of Nancy as tears rolled down onto her cheeks.

"Open that whore mouth of yours bitch, I'm going pump you full of cock, and you're going to be my cum slut," he said taking his hand and forcing

Loren's mouth open.

"Um, they never said anything about her crying," the wife said to her husband as she stopped kissing Loren's neck and looked at her face.

"I don't want this," Loren whispered, her eyes still shut and tears again rolling down her face.

"Oh, fuck. I'm so sorry; they just said you liked to be taken like this. Fuck, sorry," the man said as he put his dick back into his pants. The woman grabbed his hand and led him quickly out of the room.

"We'll buy the house, don't worry. You don't need to go to the police or anything," he said as they left the room. Loren waited until she heard the front doors slam and their car drive away and slowly opened her eyes. She took her panties off and pulled her dress down, not wanting to have any trace of that man on her. She went to the bathroom and looked at herself in the mirror. Her makeup was smudged beyond repair. Her hair was in disarray, and she had dark red markings around her throat. Her lips where she had been bitten were also red and swollen, and she only had one thing on her mind, Mommy.

As Loren strolled towards Nancy's house, she thought of the one rule Nancy had made crystal clear, she was not to be shared. Did this count? It's not like Loren had encouraged it. *What am I supposed to say to her? Did I fuck up the on the first day? Was it even my fault?* Loren asked as she disappeared into the crowd of people exiting the subway. As she approached Nancy's building, she took her panties out of her bag and threw them into the trash and headed inside. The foyer was quiet, and for the first time, Loren felt a warm feeling about going somewhere, which felt like home. *For how long?* Loren thought as she climbed the two flights of stairs and rummaged through her bag to find the keys. Opening the door and walking inside, Loren knew Nancy wasn't home. She put her bag neatly in the corner of Nancy's room and took off her dress, making a mental note to burn it. Walking through the house naked, she found her phone and called Jen.

"Hi, it's me," Loren said plainly.

"I quit," she added quickly.

"What?" Jen half shouted down the phone.

"I quit. Pay me what I'm owed, I can't do this anymore," Loren said as she hung up the phone and deleted Jen's number. Throwing her phone on the couch, Loren walked into the bathroom and turned on the shower. Letting the hot water burn her skin, she thought about how she was going to tell Nancy what had happened today. Loren sat on the couch for the rest of the day and watched as the hours ticked by, hoping that Nancy would come home early. To her surprise at 4:15, she heard the key in the lock open, and Nancy walked in, surprised to see Loren as another woman followed her inside. Luckily for Loren, she had decided to put clothes back on an hour earlier. Her white short shorts and orange singlet caught Nancy off guard as Loren's nipples were visible through the thin material.

"Oh I'm sorry, I didn't know you were having guests, um," Loren said, unsure if she should call Nancy Mommy or not. They hadn't talked about what happens if other people are in the house.

"Mommy?" The other woman knowingly suggested to Loren. Seeing Loren's eyes go wide and her head spin, Nancy smiled and walked over to her. Kissing her deeply and cupping her chin, Nancy made Loren meet her eyes and raised an eyebrow expectantly.

"Mommy," Loren half whispered, her voice suddenly hoarse.

"Sweetheart, this is Steff. We have been friends for years. She has a baby boy who is a bit older than you," Nancy said as Loren's neck caught her attention. She looked into Loren's eyes, and their broken stare was all she needed to know.

"It wasn't my fault, Mommy. I said no, nothing happened. I even quit my job. I'm never going back there. I never want that to happen again," Loren said as Nancy listened, Steff coming over to where they stood, curiosity on her face. Nancy looked furious, making Loren unnerved and tears well up in her eyes.

"Tell me what happened baby," Nancy said sternly making Loren confused, unsure of where Nancy's anger would be directed. Loren explained what had happened, looking from Nancy to Steff. Steff took Loren's hands in hers, but Nancy was not so expressive. She just sat there, listening to Loren's story as rage boiled inside of her. *How fucking dare they*, she said to herself as Loren told her how the man had choked her, his markings still clearly imprinted on her neck. As Loren finished the story, she looked nervously at Nancy. Then to Steff who gave Nancy a look, Loren didn't know the meaning of.

"I hope you're not mad and don't mind I quit Mommy, I just really don't want to go back there," Loren added for the fifth time, worried Nancy would be mad she had made such a rash decision.

"I'm not mad at you at all. I'm mad at them. I'm more than mad; I'm livid. I don't care if they buy the house or not, we are going to the police," Nancy said as she scooped up Loren and held her tightly, rocking her in her arms.

"But they'll just say I had a history; it'll get out that this was something I did. They'll say it's my fault. It'll get twisted," Loren replied as tears rolled down her cheeks for the fourth time that day.

"I don't want to have to relive it, Mommy," Loren said through her tears. Steff understood what Nancy had told her about Loren at that moment. Over lunch, Nancy had explained how fragile Loren was, how untrained and independent she was. How she would make decisions for herself and not be simply led.

"I'm glad you quit. The money wasn't worth it. We can talk about going to the police later. Right now, do you need Mommy, or do you need to go for a run?" Nancy asked, wanting to make sure to give Loren what she needed. Loren turned to Steff who smiled, almost reading her mind.

"You haven't ruined anything, sweetheart," she kindly stated. Looking back at Nancy, Loren began to suck her thumb and reached out for Nancy.

"I want you, Mommy," she replied, feeling Nancy tighten her arms around her. Nancy put Loren on her lap and turned her around to face Steff.

"She's adorable Nance," she said, wishing her baby boy was in her arms.

"She's a good girl," Nancy replied, smiling like the cat who got the cream.

"Steff is going to stay the night baby. Maybe Phil wants to come over for a play?" Nancy asked.

"Phil wants whatever I tell him he wants. He will be here in an hour," Steff laughed as she took out her phone while stroking Loren's cheek making her giggle. Steff was sterner than Nancy. She had an angular face and eyes that meant business. Loren wondered if it was because she had a boy baby and not a girl, making a mental note to not get on Steff's angry side.

"Let's get you out of this princess," Nancy said as she carried Loren into the nursery. Nancy laid Loren on her back on the pink mat, and Steff played with her on the floor while Nancy took out the things she needed.

"You know, we have never had a play date," Steff said as Loren reached for the toy she was holding high in the air.

"I know. That's because I've never had such a sweet girl," Nancy said as she came over to where Loren was playing and picked her up, carrying her to the changing table. Loren obediently lifted her bottom and let Nancy take her shorts off. She blushed as Steff came close and put a pacifier into her mouth and Nancy noted Loren was pushing through her comfort zone to let another person see her like this.

"She's a good girl for Mommy," Nancy said to Steff as Loren began to squirm, settling her with a warning in her voice. Nancy powdered Loren's pussy and added another layer to her diaper, making it thicker than the one she had on the previous night. She tightened it in place before holding up two choices of diaper cover for Loren to choose from.

"Oh wow, she had you wrapped around her finger!" Steff exclaimed upon witnessing Nancy, allowing Loren to choose what she would wear.

"She knows that if she isn't good, this will be taken away. Mommy doesn't mind treating her princess, but if she thinks she can be bratty afterward, all Mommy's treats go," Nancy said, putting on the tight fluffy leopard print diaper cover. She looked into Loren's eyes lovingly as she rubbed the diaper against Loren's pussy firmly making her giggle.

"Does it feel nice pushing against your pussy baby," Nancy said as she looked down on Loren.

"Yes, Mommy," Loren replied with her pacifier still in her mouth.

"Oh she's cute," Steff said as she ran her hands over her diapered sides through the fluffy material making Loren squirm as she felt another person touch her. Nancy watched as Loren's confused face went from Steff to her, wondering if it was OK to let Steff touch her. Nancy smiled and turned back towards the cupboard and took out a tight white t-shirt. After taking Loren's orange singlet off, Nancy pulled the t-shirt on and grabbed a pair of knee-high black socks.

"There baby," Nancy said as she took a pink blanket and wrapped it around Loren. Nancy carried Loren back out to the living room and put her on the couch. Steff tickled Loren as she rolled on her socks while Nancy fed her a bottle.

"No you can't have these right now sweetheart, they are for night nights," Nancy loving stated when Loren pushed her bottle away and reached for Nancy's massive breasts as a knock came from the door. Steff jumped up to get it, excited her little prince was here.

"Hi, baby boy. I have a new friend for you to play with," Steff said, taking the bag the man was carrying, holding his hand and walking him into the living room. Loren shifted uncomfortably in Nancy's arms as she began to blush.

"Hi Nancy," the man said in a small voice.

"Hello Phil, have you been a good boy for Steff?" Nancy replied, rocking Loren.

"Yes, Nancy," he answered, looking at Loren.

"This is Loren Phil; she's Nancy's baby girl. You'll have to play gently with her; she's not as big as you," Steff said as Phil got on his knees and crawled over to where Nancy was holding Loren. Phil reached in to touch Loren's hand, and Nancy wondered what would happen. *Either she'll pull away, or she'll be excited to play with him*, she thought to herself, smiling at Loren and Steff when Loren pushed off Nancy's soft stomach to touch Phil's nose. Squirming to get down to the ground, Nancy carried Loren to the middle of the large living room and watched as Phil showed her his toys. Loren spent her time, biting all of them as he passed her one after another.

"This is crazy, she had made so much

progress," Nancy said as she and Steff watched their babies play from the kitchen.

"Yeah, I don't think I would have handled her as well as you have. I love how dependent he is on me. I find it hard giving him his one a week of complete independence," Steff replied praising Nancy.

"I have known her for five years, though. I already knew who she was when she's Loren. Who she is, is just amplified when she's in her little space. I already knew she was fragile and a runner. I already knew she wouldn't respond to an overly firm hand. And I only give her a choice because I want to know the type of thing she likes. She's got a cool style I must admit. I want her to be more dependent on me sure, but that's a process, and I'm quite impressed at the progress we've made so far! I mean look at her, she couldn't even look at me when she first saw the nursery, and now she's openly diapered and playing in her little space. This is huge," Nancy replied as Steff passed her wine, and they made their way back to the living room. Phil had begun to draw a picture of his toys, and he gave a crayon to Loren who started scribbling on the piece of paper he put down for her.

"Has she wet her diaper yet?" Steff asked as she took off Phil's shoes. Making Loren's head snap around and look at Nancy.

"Not yet," Nancy said in a voice that made it very clear it would be something which was going to happen.

Chapter 7

Steff and Phil had stayed in one of Nancy's spare rooms that evening. After hours of playing of giggling, Phil and Loren had fallen asleep watching a movie and Nancy had gently picked Loren up and brought her into the nursery, placing her in the cot.

As Loren woke in the morning, she panicked searching for Nancy, who was nowhere to be found. Realizing she was in the cot, Loren climbed out and slowly walked out of the room where she heard Phil's voice.

"Hi Loren," he excitedly said upon seeing her watch him. Loren shyly smiled as she watched him play with a train set.

"Wanna play?" Phil was still in his train pajamas, and Loren made a note that he loved trains. Nodding, she dropped to her knees and crawled over to him. Phil gave Loren a train and moved her hand over it on the train tracks, showing her how to play. Giggling, Loren bent over the train set and pushed the train around the tracks. Phil watched her.

"You're good at that Loren," he said still in his little space.

"Thanks," she replied as Nancy walked up to them.

"Oh hello there miss," Nancy said as Loren reached up for her. Bending down, Nancy picked her up, and Loren giggled as Nancy kissed her cheeks.

"I escaped Mommy," Loren said proudly.

"I can see that baby girl. Are you playing with Phil's trains?" Nancy asked, putting her back down on the ground and roughing up Phil's hair.

"Yes Mommy, Phil showed me how to do this," Loren said as she moved a train around the tracks.

"That's my boy, always trying to impress the pretty girls," Steff said, coming around the corner.

"Morning," Nancy said as she turned on the

coffee machine.

"Phil, did you forget what day it is today?" Steff asked as she began to put the trains away. He thought for a minute before looking embarrassed, he forgot.

"It's my big boy day Steff," he said excitedly. Loren looked at Nancy for an explanation, but she was busy in the kitchen.

"What's a big boy day Steff?" Loren asked curiously.

"Every Saturday, Phil gets to do all the things the big boys do. He can do whatever he wants and doesn't have to ask me for anything," Steff said taking the trains Loren was handing to her. Loren crawled towards the kitchen and waited for Nancy like she had been told to do.

"Let me guess," Nancy said knowingly as she looked into Loren's overly excited eyes.

"My baby girl wants a big girl day too?" Nancy continued, walking past Loren and handing Steff a coffee.

"Yes, please Mommy," Loren eagerly

replied, following her back into the living room.

"Well, I don't see why that couldn't work. But look at you baby, I don't think you look like a big girl at all," Nancy stated as Phil walked back into the room. Loren hadn't noticed his broad back and muscular arms before, but as he strutted into the living room in well-fitting jeans, a designer polo and smelling of expensive cologne with all confidence in the world, she saw a completely different side to him.

"What do you guys have planned today?" He asked in a deep voice, making Loren's eyes wide with amusement; it was very different from his baby boy voice. Steff looked playfully annoyed at his bravado as he opened a red bull.

"Nice breakfast," she commented. While Steff and Phil spoke, Loren had crawled to the couch and climbed into Nancy's lap, hugging her tightly and sucking her thumb.

"Please, Mommy, I'll do anything you want," Loren begged.

"That is the most dangerous sentence you

could have used my sweet girl. I'll hold you to that," Nancy said as she rubbed Loren's pussy through her fluffy pants and diapered pussy. Steff smiled at Nancy knowingly and went back to talking to Phil.

"I don't know what you guys are going to do, but I'm going to find out just how badly my baby girl wants to have a grown up day," Nancy said as she took Loren's hand and led her into the nursery.

"Lay down sweetheart," Nancy said lovingly as she snapped her fingers to the pink rug in the middle of the room. Loren obediently followed hoping that whatever Nancy had planned it would go fast. Her mind was racing with all the things she could spend her day doing.

"You only have to do one thing for me," Nancy began to say making Loren smile.

"Wet your diaper," she continued, watching Loren's smile turn into shock.

"But Mommy, I know we talked about it, but we didn't say when," Loren began to complain as

Nancy took a pacifier and stuck it into Loren's mouth. As Loren reached up to take it out, Nancy turned around swiftly as if knowing Loren would try to protest further.

"Don't you dare," she commanded in a voice that made Loren drop her hand and shift uncomfortably.

"This is what I want. You said you'd do anything I wanted. This is it baby girl. The faster you wet your diaper, the faster you can go out and do all the big girl things you want," Nancy explained.

"I don't have to tell you that if you don't give me what I want and waste my time you won't enjoy the outcome do I, sweetheart?" Nancy asked as she pushed Loren back, making her lay down on the floor and stood over her. Loren shook her head no and began to squirm as Nancy pressed her foot onto her stomach.

"I know you haven't been to the bathroom since last night princess. I don't fight Mommy. I'll always win," Nancy continued as Loren fought not to wet her diaper although she desperately needed to. Loren held up her arms to Nancy, wanting to be cuddled.

"Oh I think the baby is trying to control Mommy," Nancy said, taking Loren's hands and slapping them, making her bring them back to her chest. Nancy bent down next to Loren and ran her fingers through Loren's messy ponytail.

"Are you nervous baby? You want Mommy to cuddle you and make you feel safe while you wet your diaper?" Nancy teased as Loren nodded her head, her eyes beginning to well. Nancy had never been so lenient with a girl before. She would have usually tied a girl to the cot and kept her there until she had wet her diaper, but Loren was different. It wasn't that she was naughty, and Nancy knew she wasn't trying to control the situation. It was that she needed more love than any girl Nancy ever had before. Most new situations scared her regardless of how much she wanted or liked it. This was no different. Nancy sat down and patted her lap and enjoying seeing

Loren eagerly crawl into her arms.

"Good girl," Nancy cooed as she rubbed Loren through her diaper. Kissing the top of her head and rocking her gently.

"Wet your diaper for Mommy baby," she continued as she kept on hand on the front of Loren's diaper, feeling her relax and begin to push against the hand Nancy was using to groped her.

"Mommy," Loren said softly as she turned her head and breathed into Nancy's ample cleavage. Nancy smiled triumphantly as she felt Loren's diaper become warm in her hand.

"Good girl baby," Nancy continued as Loren's face went red and her head bent in shame. Nancy kissed Loren's cheeks, and the top of her head as Loren continued to wet her diaper.

"Doesn't that feel better baby girl?" Nancy asked as Loren reached for her bunny.

"Yes, Mommy," Loren replied as she was handed bunny by Nancy. Loren looked down and tried to move away from her wet diaper, not enjoying the feeling of being dirty.

"You want it off, baby?" Nancy said, enjoying Loren's apparent discomfort.

"Yes please, Mommy," Loren forced herself to say loudly although wanting to whisper. She didn't want to give Nancy any reason to keep it on any longer.

"Lucky I'm such a nice Mommy then isn't it baby?" Nancy asked as she laid Loren on her back and began to take off the wet diaper. After wiping her down, Nancy left her on the floor to dry while she went to her room and chose panties for Loren to wear. Loren clapped her hands excitedly as she saw what Nancy was carrying as she came back into the room. Nancy stood over the top of Loren once again, shooting fear through Loren that something else would happen.

"Take that off," Nancy commanded, pointing to her t-shirt, Loren quickly followed Nancy's instructions and passed the shirt to her receiving her panties in exchange.

"Well, don't you want them on? I can easy diaper you again if you'd like to go out wearing your baby clothes?" Nancy mocked, making Loren laugh as she put on her panties.

"So," Loren said hesitantly, unsure of what do now.

"So? So now you can do whatever you want," Nancy replied as she watched Loren. Standing up, Loren walked over to Nancy and looked her up and down.

"Can we talk about how this is all going?" Loren asked. Nancy laughed and nodded, shutting the door to the nursery behind Loren and following her into her room. Nancy walked to her room and sat on the bed, watching as Loren got dress.

"So like, you're my Mommy, and I call you Mommy when we are in the house regardless of what space I'm in and who is here, I've got that," Loren stated to speak, looking at Nancy for confirmation. Nancy nodded her head and watched as Loren continued.

"But on Saturday's I can have a day where I do whatever I want. And during the day I am a big girl, but after the day is done, I'm your baby. Are you like my girlfriend on Saturday and during the day?" Loren asked, sitting down next to Nancy after she pulled on her ripped jeans and her favorite old band, singlet.

"OK. So, yeah you can refer to me as your girlfriend for convince sake if people ask you about me, you know, like friends or whoever. But I'm your Mommy, not your fucking girlfriend and there's a big power difference in those titles which I don't want you to get confused. Like we've said previously, this is a non-negotiable monogamous dynamic. It would be cheating if you were to be with someone else even on Saturday's. I can be your "girlfriend" as in we can do fancy dinners and romantic things together. You can get dressed in the most beautiful outfits, and I'd love to take out and paint the town, but I am your Mommy. So if we go to the movies for example and I say you've had enough candy or whatever and you don't either give me the bag or you just ignore me, that's still punishable. You're not just my baby when you're in diapers sucking on my milky tits; you're my baby full time, the rules we have don't change, only your headspace and outward expression changes," Nancy explained.

"Oh OK, that makes so much sense. So if I found a job and was like, 'Can we go out to this event', or something after work spontaneously, you'd either say yes or no, and then we'd go and if you said that I'd had enough beer for example and I keep drinking, I'd be in trouble," Loren said confirming with Nancy.

"You got it. Don't get me wrong; I'm not interested in locking you up every night. I want to do fun things. Still, I'm so happy you're finally mine but when we get home from doing whatever you're my little girl, and I'll treat you that way," Nancy said pulling Loren in and kissing her deeply.

"This is the best thing I've ever done," Loren said as she broke the kiss.

"I know," Nancy replied, reaching into Loren's pants and biting her bottom lip feeling how wet Loren was.

Chapter 8

Nancy and Loren slowly developed their lifestyle, going to gallery openings and bespoke bars. They blew cash on expensive shopping trips and ate out at the best restaurants. They added toys and clothes to the nursery, and Loren found a new job that paid less but was fewer hands-on experiences. Loren loved the way Nancy took the time to teach her what she wanted instead of punishing her for things she didn't know. After the three months, they had spent together, Loren had a handle on everything Nancy expected of her. Nancy had specifically told Loren that she would begin punishing her for forgetting a rule, and they had bought the paddle Nancy would use to hand out the punishment.

On a sunny Saturday, Loren had decided to go out with her old boss Jen, day drinking and shopping, throwing money around a casino and dancing with strangers to the street bands playing down alleys.

"I've been so worried about you," Jen said as Loren broke away from dancing and walked back out onto the main street.

"Why?" Loren asked in a drunken haze.

"Um, hello? You just up and leave one day over the phone and I don't hear from you for like two months, and now we meet up, and you're the happiest I've ever seen you!" Jen explained.

"Hmm," Loren sighed contently.

"It's Nancy. She's amazing," she added as they walked towards the subway.

"Café Nancy? Like, significantly older than you Nancy?" Jen asked, surprisingly.

"That'd be the one," Loren replied lovingly.

"OK, wait like you guys are fucking or dating or what?" Jen questioned, confused as to what Loren was talking about.

"Jen. I'm with Nancy, we fuck, we go on dates, we do a whole lot of what and it's awesome," Loren said wanting to end the conversation.

"Right, well I'm just surprised," Jen said

defensively.

"That's fine, be surprised, turns out I'm very surprising," Loren teased as she hugged Jen goodbye and entered the subway, heading back home. Loren pulled on her headphones and was whisked away into a world of carefree bliss, almost skipping her way home.

Opening the door to Nancy's apartment, Loren dropped her bag at the door and connected her phone to the Bluetooth speakers, pumping music through the house. It was 5:30 in the afternoon, and after ordering a pizza and opening a beer, Loren danced around the living room until her pizza arrived. She heard a knock at the door, tipped the pizza boy more generously that required, and slammed the door behind him. Taking a slice, folding it in half and moaning in appreciation, Loren made her way to the kitchen and flicked through social media on her phone. In her heightened state of bliss and drunken haze, Loren didn't hear the front door open, and Nancy walk in. *What the actual fuck Loren*, Nancy playfully thought as she saw Loren at the kitchen bench dancing in her seat. Seeing the shopping bags at the door, the pizza box and beer bottles on the kitchen table, Nancy smiled, happy Loren was enjoying her day.

"Hi baby," Nancy whispered startling Loren who jumped. She turned the music off and turned around, shocked to see what Nancy wearing. A low-cut almost see through light blue blouse which exposed the front of her breasts and dark denim jeans which held to her curves.

"Damn, Nancy. You look amazing," Loren slightly slurred, her eyes glazing over making Nancy tilt her head.

"Mm, what did you just say?" Nancy asked, wondering if Loren in her drunken state would warrant forgiveness. Deciding she most definitely wouldn't let Loren off the hook, Nancy tried to suppress an excited knowing smile.

"I said you looked amazing," Loren said, unaware of how much trouble she was in.

"I heard that. But I didn't hear Mommy,

what did I hear instead?" Nancy questioned, raising an eyebrow in satisfaction as Loren's grew full with the awareness of what she had said.

"Well?" Nancy stated.

"I um, called you Nancy," Loren said, sobering up very quickly.

"Yeah, you did baby. What was my rule on that?" Nancy asked, drinking Loren's beer.

"Not too," Loren said, realizing she was fucked.

"Yeah, so guess what sweetheart, Mommy's going to punishment for not following my straightforward rule," Nancy said as she finished the beer and slammed it down on the bench making Loren jump.

"Good, be scared baby. That would be wise," Nancy said as an evil smile spread across her face. Grabbing Loren's hair, she pulled hard, making her stumble to her feet and wince in pain as she was towed to the nursery. Nancy didn't speak as she pushed Loren against the wall and cuffed her wrists in place. She went to the changing table drawer and took out a pair of scissors and walked over to a scared Loren.

"No Mommy," Loren begged, fear escaping her voice.

"No, Mommy? Oh, I'm Mommy again? Funny about that," Nancy said, ignoring Loren's fear. As she roughly pulled on Loren's shirt and began to cut it off. She cut off her bra next and violently threw the material to the other side of the room.

"I'm sorry, Mommy," Loren begged.

"Oh, you have no idea how sorry you're going to be little one. What's my name, baby?" Nancy asked as she undid Loren's denim shorts. *These are too cute to cut*; she thought as she wriggled them down Loren's thighs.

"Mommy," Loren said, pulling away from Nancy who was cupping her pussy.

"That's right baby," Nancy said as she began to rub Loren's pussy, firmly squeezing her making her pull away again.

"I thought I taught you better than to pull

away from me baby," Nancy said as she cut off Loren's panties.

"Stick it out for me," Nancy said while walking to the cupboard. Loren obeyed and swallowed hard when she saw what Nancy was holding in her hand.

"Oh, baby, you look scared. Are you scared of what Mommy is going to do to you?" Nancy teased as she pushed a pacifier into Loren's mouth and covered it in tape.

"I don't want to hear you," Nancy said as she pinched Loren's nipples until she heard a muffled cry of pain.

"You should be scared, little girl. You've made Mommy very angry, and I'm going to take it out on your pussy," Nancy whispered in Loren's ear as she pulled hard on her nipple. Whack. Nancy struck Loren's pussy with a paddle making her gasp in pain and double over.

"I wouldn't move if I were you, baby," Nancy said as she readied her paddle.

"Wider," Nancy commanded, pressing

Loren against the wall with her other hand. Whack, whack, whack. Loren began to whimper but held in place.

"Good girl. That was for pulling away from me. You made yourself get double the punishment, wasn't that silly baby," Nancy said as she paddled Loren's pussy three more times, each time hearing Loren whimper louder than the last. Her pussy began to get tender and swollen, and Nancy rubbed it with her warm hands as she spoke to Loren.

"What's my name, baby?" She asked, trying to catch Loren's eye.

"Mommy," Loren said through her gag as she looked down, a tear falling to the floor.

"Look at me baby," Nancy gruffly ordered as she wiped Loren's tears away.

"What is it?" She pressed.

"Mommy," Loren repeated, looking Nancy in the eye. Nancy smiled, whack, whack, whack, whack, whack, and stopped once Loren's legs gave way, and she fell. Getting to her feet as quickly as she could Loren spoke as tears ran down her face.

"Crying will get you, nothing, sweetheart. I know you want this to stop, but it doesn't matter what you want. You're Mommy's baby girl and you'll be punished until I'm satisfied," Nancy said as she pinched Loren's nipples.

"I don't want this anymore," Nancy said as she put away the paddle and took out a butt plug and lubed it slowly in front of Loren.

"This will look so pretty baby," Nancy said as she poked Loren's arsehole with it, pushing it in while Loren winced in pain.

"Why are you fighting it? I told you, Mommy, always wins," Nancy said, laughing as she forced it inside of Loren and began to finger fuck tender pussy.

"I'm going to force you to cum baby. I know you're not wet, I don't you don't feel horny, but you're my baby, and when I want you to cum, you'll bloody well cum," Nancy said as she continued to force two fingers inside Loren's tight and ever increasingly wet pussy. As Loren began to moan and grind down on Nancy's fingers, only causing Nancy to use her harder.

"That didn't take long," Nancy stated as Loren covered her hand suddenly. She took her fingers out of Loren's aching pussy and wiped her juices over her stomach, drying off her hand. Nancy un-cuffed Loren's wrists and ripped the tape off her mouth, making her eyes water. Loren's legs buckled underneath her and Nancy lovingly carried to the changing table and rubbed soothing cream over Loren's red pussy. She cleaned Loren's stomach and sprinkled the powder on her so that she wouldn't chaff and put her in a diaper. She picked a light grey onesie with matching with light pink knee-high socks. After Nancy put Loren's hair in a messy ponytail, she placed a light pink bowed headband in her hair and gave her a pacifier, her blankie, and bunny and carried her to the living room. Cradling Loren in one arm, she undid the blouse which had caused all Loren's problems and began to nurse her.

"Good girl baby," Nancy cooed as she

rocked Loren while she nursed.

"You've been such a good girl for Mommy, taking your punishment. I don't like having to punish you, sweetie. But we have rules, and they will be followed," Nancy explained. Loren nodded as warm milk flowed into her mouth. Nancy placed her large hand on Loren's tummy and gently patted her.

"You're not going to forget Mommy's name again, will you?" Nancy asked, already knowing the answer. Loren took Nancy's nipple out of her mouth, and milk ran down her cheek.

"No Mommy," she replied quickly before Nancy filled her mouth once again, cleaning the side of her face with her blankie. Smiling, Nancy held onto Loren and watched as she rested in her arms.

Chapter 9

A month later the café had been booked out for a function that night, and Nancy would be staying late, and Steff had offered to have Loren over, so she wasn't alone. Loren had initially told Nancy that one night without her wouldn't be a problem, but she liked that Nancy had ignored her. Nancy, Steff, and Loren had come up with an agreement for what was OK and for what was simply not. Steff could put Loren in a diaper when she got there, bottle-feed her, kiss her cheek and cuddle her but anything sexual was strictly off the table. Loren would sleep in Steff's bedroom if she felt tired instead of Phil's and would take her toys. She would feed herself anything but her bottle and would use the bathroom if she needed to go. Steff had some rules that Loren had to follow, like waiting until she had finished eating dinner before Phil or Loren could have theirs. Staying on the floor, not the couch and strictly crawling on the carpeted surfaces. Any rule breaking or complaining would result in a firm bare arse spanking Steff assured Loren would not stop until she was crying uncontrollably.

"She's a quick crier Steff. If she's naughty, let's wait until Mommy is there, so I can watch her be spanked, so disappointed in you after Steff has been so good to have you," Nancy said as Loren looked at both of them nervously.

"I won't break your rules, Steff," Loren said reassuringly. Steff smiled kindly, half hoping she would.

"You'll be punished even if you break them by accident, OK sweetheart?" Steff more stated than asked a nodding Loren.

"Good, we'll see you then," she had added as she left Nancy's apartment. The day had arrived where Loren would go to Steff's after work.

"So baby tell Mommy again what the plan is," Nancy said as she cut up Loren's breakfast.

"I'm going straight to Steff's after work and

staying there until you pick me up. Maybe you'll be late, and I go to sleep there. Steff is in charge, and I can trust her to be nice," Loren said by heart before she ate a mouthful of bacon and egg.

"Good girl," Nancy said.

"I'm serious about not breaking her rules. She's a lot meaner than Mommy is. You won't like her punishment, and she won't stop just because I'm there, you know what you agreed to," Nancy warned, worried Loren might try to test Steff's boundaries.

"I won't be naughty Mommy, I promise. I don't want her to punish me. Phil told me not to mess with her either. He said she put a vibrator in his arse and kept his cock locked for a whole weekend once," Loren replied knowingly. Nancy lowered the spoon, shocked at the words Loren was using.

"Baby, Mommy doesn't like you using such foul language. Don't speak like that again, alright?" Nancy said in a loving but deadly-serious voice. Loren blushed, she knew that if she spoke like that again, she would be punished, and she hated being punished.

"Sorry Mommy, I won't," Loren said as she ate her last mouthful. Loren finished getting ready, kissed Nancy goodbye, and headed to work.

For anyone looking at her, Loren would have appeared to be a typically beautiful woman with possessions worth envying and a devil may care attitude that had people falling for her without her trying.

As she finished work and headed to the subway to Steff's house, she looked longing into her bag as she saw her bunny and pacifier. Jointed out of her train of thought, she felt the knee of a fancy business-suited man.

"Mind if I sit?" The man asked. Loren looked up annoyed, but her annoyance quickly fading when she realized who was standing in front of her.

"Phil?" Loren asked with a smile.

"Hi," he replied, nodding to her bag.

"Excited?" Phil asked.

"Nervous," Loren answered. She looked at his debonair appearance and wondered how he and Steff had met.

"Don't be, just," he cut himself off and looked around the carriage. Leaning in, he whispered in her ear, "Just be a good girl for Steff, and she'll love you." Loren leaned back blushing. Phil had used his little voice, and he giggled slightly and looked down bashfully. Clearing his throat, he readjusted his shoulders and gained the all-powerful glare he wore so well, making Loren laugh.

"Don't even pretend," she said as he grinned at her. Stepping out of the subway, Phil led her to Steff's.

"Why do you call her Steff?" Loren asked while they walked down a quiet street.

"The same reason you call Nancy, Mommy," Phil replied, whispering the word Mommy.

"I was told to," he added, looking at his watch.

"Don't you ever want to call her something more, I don't know, Mommy like?" Loren asked unsatisfied with his answer.

"Not really. We've been together for six years; she's Steff to me. I guess she's a different version of Steff to me than other people, but it's never really crossed my mind to question it," Phil replied honestly.

"Wow, six years," Loren stated in awe. She and Nancy had only been together for just over six months.

"Yeah, it goes fast!" Phil said as he pointed to a house in a leafy suburban street.

"We're here," he added, checking the mailbox and walking up the front path. Loren wasn't lying when she said she was nervous. She began to wonder if this was the best idea to have agreed to come here. It was new and therefore, scary.

"Hi guys," Steff said, opening the door before Phil could find the keys. She stepped aside and let them in. Loren looking for carpet, stood in the entrance way until Steff took her hand and pulled her indoors, shutting and locking the door behind her.

"Phil, I expect you to do what you know you need to do while I settle Loren in," she said in her no-nonsense manner. Phil nodded and walking up the wooden hallway, turned into a room and disappeared. Steff took Loren's hand and bag off her shoulder and led her to a room on the other side of the house.

"Kneel," Steff commanded clicking her fingers to the floor. Loren obediently knelt, as Steff put her bag on her bed and took out Loren's shower gel, tooth-brush, and pajamas, diaper and pacifier.

"Come with me," Steff said, holding out her hand to Loren who took it and stood back up. Steff took her into the bathroom and ran a bath.

"You're a very quiet girl, sweet pea. Are you nervous?" Steff asked as she began to undress Loren, running her hands over her body, enjoying how smooth her skin felt.

"Yes, Steff," Loren answered as she began to suck her thumb. Steff shook her head and took Loren's thumb out of her mouth.

"You're not clean yet baby, here," Steff said, putting the pacifier into Loren's mouth. Steff held Loren's hand as she helped her into the bath. Loren loved the bubbles Steff had put in the tub and played as Steff ran warm water over her body and washed her clean.

"There," Steff said when she was satisfied. She held out a towel and dried Loren, cuddling her and making her giggle. Steff laid Loren down on the towel in the bathroom and put on her diaper.

"These are cute," Steff said as she held up the diaper cover Nancy had chosen for Loren, a thick, white fluffy material cover with pink rabbits printed on it. Steff put the cover over Loren's diaper and rubbed her hands over her thickly padded bottom.

"Oh, doesn't that feel good little girl," she said lovingly. Taking a light pink long sleeve, Steff gently pulled it over Loren's head and continued to dress her, adding matching grey knee-high socks.

"You're the sweetest," Steff admired as she looked at the baby girl she had before her. Leaving Loren's hair in her signature messy ponytail, Steff led Loren back to her room.

"Do you want your toys, baby?" Steff asked nicer than Loren was prepared for. Nodding yes, Loren took out her paci and replied, "Yes, please Steff."

"Then crawl to me," Steff replied, eyeing Loren in a way that made her nervous. Loren began to crawl to Steff who handed her her bunny. Steff ran her fingers over Loren's head and smiled when Loren cuddled her legs.

"Come on, baby, let's see what Phil is doing," she said to Loren, who followed her back out into the living room where Phil was already playing.

"I drew a picture," he told Loren as he held it up for her to see. Loren smiled behind her paci as Steff looked over from the kitchen.

"Don't let her have the crayons, Phil, I need

to give her a bottle, and I don't want her hands covered in crayon," she called. Loren sat down and remembering she wasn't allowed on the couch; she waited as she watched Phil do another drawing.

"It's a fire truck," Phil explain coloring it in red. Steff came out from behind the kitchen bench and sat on the couch, patting her lap while looking at Loren.

"Come here," she said in a stern voice. Loren quickly crawled to her feet where Steff picked her up and cradled her in her arms. Steff was slender, and her thin arms were boney. Loren squirmed uncomfortably, missing Nancy's more full and thick-set curvy body.

"Stop fussing," Steff plainly said as she gently slapped Loren's upper thigh making her stop. Steff took Loren's hands and held them down as she took out her paci and pushed the rubber nipple of the bottle into her mouth. Loren instinctively began to drink the warmed milk in her bottle, and Steff relaxed back on the couch.

Phil looked up at Steff, who smiled back at him.

"You don't need a bottle; you're a big boy. Loren is a baby," she stated as if reading his mind.

"But Steff," Phil began to complain only to be summoned to Steff's feet.

"Kneel," Steff commanded waiting until Phil was in front of her before backhanding him across the face making Loren nervous.

"When did I say you could talk back to me?" Steff said, half yelled.

"Never Steff," Phil said, looking down, trying to hide his anger.

"Don't start with me, boy. I will not have you play up just because Loren is here. You should be showing her how well-behaved you are not a naughty boy for me," Steff said as she rubbed his red cheek affectionately. After Loren finished her bottle, Steff put her back down on the floor and went to order dinner leaving Phil and Loren alone.

"Do you want to play wrestling?" Phil asked. Loren shook her head no.

"You're no fun," he said bitterly making

Loren look around uncomfortably.

"Do you want to play with bunny?" Loren asked hopefully handing Phil her bunny. Phil looked at it and threw it down the hallway.

"No," he said, making Loren frown and pout. Loren began to crawl down the hallway to collect her bunny when she saw Steff coming out of her bedroom, hanging up the phone.

"How did this get here?" She asked Loren playfully. Loren looked back at Phil and pointed.

"He didn't want to play with bunny, so he threw her away," Loren said as she cuddled bunny.

"Oh I think somebody is a little jealous they have to share," Steff said, walking into that living room.

"I am not," Phil spat out as he scrunched up his drawing and threw it at the wall. Steff lifted her white pullover revealing a big silver belt buckle and brown leather belt.

"Oh boy I'm not even going to ask you to try that again, get over here," Steff said, aggressively making Loren's mouth gaped open. Unbuckling her belt, Steff removed it in one sweeping motion. Loren watched as Steff ripped down Phil's flannel, train-print pajama pants and pulled him onto her lap. Striking him without warning, Phil cried out, making Loren uncomfortable. Steff continued to belt Phil's arse until it was so red that Loren thought for sure he would pass out from the pain any minute. Steff didn't speak a word for the whole time, but Phil made enough noise for the both of them. Howling and crying he stayed as still as he could as time after time Steff belted his arse raw.

"You can sit there and think about how you should be behaving," Steff said as she put Loren back on her lap and cuddled her in front of him making him pout and frown jealously. Loren buried her head into Steff's model like neck and tried to relax. Her heart was racing, and Steff felt it against her chest. Patting Loren on her back and rocking her soothingly Steff felt her begin to melt into her. Smiling wickedly at Phil, Steff snapped her fingers to her feet where Phil quickly crawled to.

"Are you going to be a good boy now, or do I need to belt your little arse again?" Steff asked, putting a calm Loren down on the floor.

"I'll be good; I'm sorry Steff," Phil replied as a knock came from the front door. Loren looked excitedly to the door, making Steff laugh.

"I don't think it's Mommy Loren," she said, getting up and going to the door, paying the delivery guy and coming back with her order. Steff laid the food out on the table and began eating as Phil and Loren drew pictures and played with his train set.

"Can bunny play?" Loren asked, hopefully. Phil looked at her and then looked at the bunny. Hearing Steff clear her throat he reluctantly agreed and put Loren's bunny on top of a train letting her push it around the tracks.

By 11:30, Loren had been put to bed by Steff. Steff watched as Loren fell asleep admiring how sweet she was as she held her bunny and sucked her thumb. Phil and Steff began to watch a movie and Steff let Phil rest his head on her lap as she stroked him to sleep. At 1:30, a knock came from the door, and Steff carefully put Phil's head on the floor as she opened the door for Nancy.

"Hi, sorry it's so late," Nancy said as she came inside, greeting Steff in a warm embrace.

"How was your night?" Steff asked, shutting the door behind her.

"Long, my staff got put through the wringer. How was Loren?" Nancy asked as she looked around the living room for her.

"She was perfect; she's asleep. Phil got so jealous. He threw Loren's bunny up the hallway and back chatted me. I belted him in front of Loren; I think she'll be OK, I cuddled her afterward until she calmed down again. Easily scared. I think she was worried I'd spank her next," Steff said, offering Nancy a beer. Nancy laughed she had thought Phil would get jealous; she knew Loren would be jealous if her attention were on someone else.

"Yeah, she'll be fine. Oh! I needed that," Nancy said as she downed half the beer.

"Mommy?" Loren said as she sleepily rubbed her eyes, crawling out of Steff's room.

"Hi baby girl," Nancy said, turning around and walking over to pick her up.

"Where you a good girl for Steff?" Nancy asked, holding Loren with one arm and drinking the rest of her beer. Loren looked at Steff and smiled sweetly.

"I think so," she replied. Nancy began to rub Loren's padded bottom, enjoying how soft and think it was and making a mental note to buy more diaper covers in this material.

"You think so?" Nancy teased, raising an eyebrow.

"Well, I didn't get spanked like Phil," Loren explained. Steff laughed as she walked over to Phil and pulled his pants down, revealing his still red arse. Nancy followed and chuckled when she saw.

"I'd hope you wouldn't need to be spanked like that. Should we try to see what happens?" Nancy asked, playfully.

"No, Mommy!" Loren replied, shocked that

Nancy would suggest such a thing.

"Oh come on, it'll be fun to have Mommy spanking that pretty little bottom of yours," Nancy said, rubbing Loren's padded pussy, making her involuntarily push against her hand.

"I think you want it," Nancy whispered in Loren's ear. Putting Loren on the floor, Nancy pulled down the cover and undid her diaper. Sitting her up, Steff moved behind her and Nancy pushed Loren back against Steff.

"Let's see how excited you are," Nancy said as she put a finger in Loren's mouth making her suck it before sliding it up and down her pussy slit. Pushing through her lips, Loren bucked her hips, wanting Nancy inside of her.

"Mommy hasn't fucked you in weeks, isn't that right baby?" Nancy asked. Steff stroked Loren's hair and kissed her cheek as a wave of pleasure rolled over Loren making her breathless.

"Yes, Mommy," Loren said as she closed her eyes and bit her lip. Nancy played with Loren's clit and slid one finger into her tight wet pussy, making her moan loudly, waking Phil up. He looked around and was shocked to find Steff holding Loren in place while Nancy slowly fucked her.

"Stay," Steff commanded, clicking her fingers when she saw Phil wake up. She smiled as she saw his cock becoming harder as he watched Loren.

"You can play little boy," Steff said, making Phil smile as he reached into his pants and began stroking his cock. Nancy took her finger out of Loren, scooped her up with one arm and flung her over her knee in a smooth motion. Spank, spank, spank. Nancy rubbed Loren's arse after each spanking just enough to keep her on the edge of her pain threshold.

"You'll be a good girl and take this baby. Mommy wants to see your arse go red," Nancy said as she pushed down on Loren's back while her other hand spanked Loren over and over.

"Mommy," Loren begged as she stopped squirming and took the spanking.

"That's right. Mommy is going to spank you a little longer tonight. You've been such a good girl. I'm spanking you because I want to, not because you've been bad," Nancy explained, picking up that Loren thought she was in trouble.

"Oh, baby, you're turning Mommy on. Let me spank you a few more times," Nancy said, enjoying letting her more sadistic side out. She had been waiting to be able to slightly brutalize Loren. As the sting of each spanking began to be too much for Loren, Nancy spat on her hand and rubbed Loren's pussy, circling her clit and continued to spank her. Nancy could feel Loren's heartbeat on her thigh and felt her pussy begin to drip cum; Nancy shoved two fingers into Loren's pussy, making her scream. As Loren was roughly fucked, Nancy continued to spank her, moving down to the tops of her thighs and squeezing her tightly after each hit. Loren came hard as her pussy gushed cum over Nancy's hand and fell limb over Nancy's leg, beginning to whimper. Nancy forced herself to stop just as her juices began to flow and cuddled

Loren. Aware Loren had been pushed past her limit.

"It's over baby. Mommy has stopped. You did so well, sweetheart," Nancy said as she kissed Loren's tears away. Loren pushed Nancy back against the couch defiantly and pinned her there, pouting, frowning and panting.

"You're OK, sweetie. We just pushed to a new level. Mommy wouldn't hurt you, we just went further than we have before, but you're OK," Nancy said reassuringly, letting Loren have some control. Loren turned around to see Phil being pegged by Steff who was reaching around and jerking him off at the same time. Nancy pulled Loren back to her and held her hands behind her back, making Loren squirm with fear. Nancy let her hands go and smiled in relief as Loren wrapped them around her neck and snuggled into her cleavage. Nancy picked her up and took her to Steff's room to collect her things.

"Mommy, can I please have these," Loren said as she groped Nancy's full breasts. Nancy slowly unbuttoned her blouse and took off her bra, exposing her large nipples for Loren.

"Yes baby," Nancy replied as she positioned Loren for nursing, holding her breast to Loren's mouth and rubbing her nipple over her lips until she opened her mouth and began to nurse while they waited for Steff and Phil to finish.

Chapter 10

Loren's head was a mess. After the night at Steff's, nothing made sense. She had seen a side of Nancy she had never seen in the whole time she had known her. It had been like something had taken over her, and the Nancy she knew had gone for an hour. Loren knew she had been distant towards Nancy since that night, but she didn't know how to go back to the blissful vulnerability she had shown her before. *She just changed*, Loren thought to herself as she watched Nancy make waffles.

It was Saturday, and after their waffles, Loren had gone to the beach. Not particularly enjoying it, but wanting to be alone, moreover, wanting to be away from Nancy. *How can I even trust her? How will I know if she's going to change-up like that?* Loren thought as she enjoyed the warmth of the sun. Nancy had felt Loren's distance as well.

"Seeing her so ready for the taking made me wild," she said to Steff over the phone.

"Yeah, you did take her pretty hard. Was she able to walk after you slammed her pussy like that?" Steff replied as she used Phil as a footstool.

"Barely. Steff, I wanted to hurt her. I was getting off on it. That's only happened a handful of times, and it's never worked out afterward," Nancy explained as she paced back and forth in the living room.

"Maybe you're just crueler than you have allowed yourself to be. Maybe you need someone more masochistic than Loren," Steff replied.

"No, I don't think that's it. It just when I see Loren so sleepy and vulnerable just makes me want to use her until she is broken. I guess that's what everyone else sees in her as well. I'm happy I was able to stop, she's got such pull power," Nancy said before Loren walked through the door.

"I'll call you later, I have to go," she quickly added seeing Loren and hanging up the phone.

"Hi baby," Nancy said, walking over and embracing Loren.

"Hey Mommy," Loren replied absently as

she stood still and let Nancy hold her. Breaking the embrace, Loren walked to the kitchen and made herself a coffee.

"You want?" Loren asked Nancy, who shook her head.

"Can we talk about this?" Nancy asked as Loren sat at the kitchen bench after a week of walking on egg-shells.

"Talk about what?" Loren replied, pretending everything was fine. Nancy lifted her hand to stroke Loren's hair, and Loren flinched defensively.

"Talk about that," Nancy stated, pointing out the distance between them. Loren looked into her coffee cup and wished she knew the words to say.

"You go first," she said. Nancy cracked her neck and sat down next to Loren.

"OK. Since that night, I can see it, I can feel it, you aren't giving your whole self to me, and it sucks," Nancy started. Loren looked at her and continued to listen.

"I guess I just enjoy a rougher side and if you don't then," Nancy said, cutting herself off.

"Then what?" Loren said aggressively, her eyes burning a hole into Nancy.

"You don't get just to walk away from this because I got scared, Mommy," Loren said, adding Mommy in the hope she would be forgiven for speaking so out of turn. Nancy smiled, looking down to the floor.

"Baby," Nancy began to say, stopping herself. Loren looked up at her expectantly.

"No, you know what it might be good for us to have that time apart," Loren said quietly.

"There's a work thing I need to go to, I'll be out of town for four nights next week," Loren said plainly.

"Why," Nancy replied, hurt that Loren wanted to be away from her.

"Because," Loren stated getting up and going to the living room.

"No," Nancy commanded as she followed Loren, "We have to speak about this," she added, sitting down next to Loren.

"Speak about what?!" Loren spat back at her.

"That I'm just your fucktoy like I was for everyone else?" Loren added with tears in her eyes. Shocked, Nancy reached her for, but Loren pushed her hand away.

"Don't touch me," Loren aggressively stated. Nancy could feel her heart being to break as she saw the girl she so dearly loved pulling away from her.

"You are not my fucktoy Loren!" Nancy exclaimed hurt that Loren thought so.

"Then why would you use me like that?" Loren said as she began to weep. Nancy looked at Loren who had brought her knees to her chest and cried into herself.

"I never said it was OK to have Steff hold me down; I never said it was OK to spank me while Phil jerked off watching. You were the one who said there wouldn't be anything sexual that night and it was bloody fucking sexual Nancy!" Loren practically yelled as she got up and stood over Nancy who remained on the couch. Nancy raised an eyebrow hearing Loren say her name with such venom.

"I don't give a fuck!" Loren stated reading Nancy's face, being very aware she was breaking multiple rules by talking in such a manner.

"I didn't realize I'd hurt you so much," Nancy said, deciding to hear what Loren was telling her instead of focusing on the rules she was breaking. Loren stopped pacing around the living room and looked at Nancy.

"You did," Loren replied, forgetting she was meant to be angry.

"How can I even trust you now? She added, misery escaping her voice. Loren sat down next to Nancy in silence.

"I don't trust you anymore," Loren quietly said after some time. She got up and walked to Nancy's bedroom and slammed the door shut. Nancy remained on the couch as tears began to well in her eyes.

Loren had packed her bags the night of the fight and had gone to stay at Jen's. The following morning she had boarded the plane and gone to the conference, without saying another word to Nancy. At the meeting, Loren heard from artist after artist talk about their works and their inspiration. In the evenings, she had stayed in alone. The people she was at the conference with had invited her out two nights in a row, but she had declined both times making excuses for her lack of partying interest. On the third day of the conference, an artist she had listened to an hour earlier spotted Loren during the lunch break.

"Mind if I sit?" the artist said, standing over the top of Loren who ate her lunch alone as an eight seater table.

"Oh, this table is full sorry," Loren replied, making a joke for the first time in four days. The artist laughed and sat next to her.

"Vanessa, right?" Loren asked inquisitively.

"Yeah, Loren?" Vanessa replied. Loren

nodded her head.

"Where are you from?" Vanessa asked. Loren looked at her for the first time. She had crimson color hair and looked like a cover girl from a 90's magazine. She wore flowing, whimsical clothing, and Loren wondered why she had wanted to sit next to her when they were so very different.

"Look, you seem lovely, but I'm not into small talk. I'm not into any small talk right now," Loren replied apologetically.

"That's OK; we don't need to talk, I can feel you're hurting," Vanessa replied. Loren looked at her disbelievingly.

"You can feel I'm hurting?" She stated, almost mockingly. Vanessa just nodded to which Loren rolled her eyes, making Vanessa laugh out loud.

"You don't believe me?" Vanessa asked.

"I don't know what to believe," Loren muttered. Vanessa held out her hand to Loren, who looked at her puzzlingly.

"Give me your hand," Vanessa insisted. Loren sighed and placed her hand on top of Vanessa's, who held it gently.

"Well, someone broke your heart," Vanessa said knowingly.

"You could have just looked at my face and reached the same conclusion," Loren stated bluntly pulling her hand away.

"But at least this time you aren't using sex as a coping method," Vanessa retorted, piquing Loren's curiosity.

"See, not so dumb after all," Vanessa said in a matter of fact manner that made Loren laugh and relax.

"Fair enough," Loren submitted.

"What now?" She added, looking at Vanessa.

"Tell me what happened," Vanessa suggested.

"Nope," Loren replied quickly as she finished her lunch.

"Loren, other people can't see what I can,

you can't-fool me, I know you aren't always a big girl," Vanessa whispered making Loren sit back and looked at her in shock and horror.

"Are you Nancy's friend?" Loren asked as fear escaped her voice.

"No, but as I said, I can feel things, and seeing things. What happened? Let me help you," Vanessa kindly replied.

"You can't help me," Loren stated sadly.

"Not if you don't let me," Vanessa replied. Loren looked around; they were the only people in the lunch room.

"There was a miss-interpretation of a contract, and now it all just feels too scary," Loren honestly explained.

"Maybe I'm just too dumb to understand what I'm doing, or maybe she just found a loophole, but I can't imagine she would knowingly hurt me. She stopped when she was mid-orgasm when I couldn't take anymore. I don't know how to place any of this," she added as she began to tear up. Vanessa closed her eyes and breathed in deeply.

"She didn't mean to hurt you. She thought you would enjoy it and when she realized she was hurting you, it stopped being enjoyable for her. She couldn't bring herself to keep going when she learned you were not enjoying it. She thought that because you had had sex like that with each other in the past that it was still a green zone," Vanessa said in a way which made Loren wonder if it was her or Nancy talking. Vanessa opened her eyes to see Loren running from the lunch room.

Chapter 11

Am I stupid, believing in what some stranger has said, Loren thought as she packed her belongings in the Hotel room. She reached into her pocket and pulled out her phone. Nancy had messaged her every day, only to be left on read. Dialing her number, Loren waited impatiently for her to pick up.

"Hello Nancy's phone," Steff said, answering. Loren knew Steff would have seen her photo come up and knew very well who was ringing Nancy.

"Hi Steff, it's Loren, is...Mommy there?" Loren said, feeling her heart pound in her chest.

"No, she's not Loren. She's gone out with some friends and left her phone here. She's been staying with me since you left," Steff replied, clearly mad a Loren. Loren felt her stomach lurch. *Steff is such a cunt;* she thought to herself. As Loren was about to speak, she heard Nancy's voice asking who it was on the phone.

"Oh wrong number Nance," Steff said down the phone. Before Loren realized what she was saying she was yelling Mommy down the phone as loudly as she could, hoping Nancy would hear and hoping Steff's eardrum would be hurt.

"Baby?" Nancy said, taking the phone away from Steff.

"Mommy, I'm so sorry I ran away," Loren replied quickly, wanting Nancy to know it was her.

"Sweetheart, I've been so worried, you didn't even tell me where you were going," Nancy stated. Hearing the concern in her voice, Loren dropped to the floor and began to cry.

"I'm so sorry, I'm just so sorry," Loren said as she wept.

"No darling, I'm sorry. I made a huge mistake just assuming you would be OK with what I wanted to do to you just because we have done it before. I shouldn't have exhibited you like that. I didn't realize you wouldn't like it. Are you coming home to me baby girl?" Nancy said making Loren cry even more.

"You should be able to do whatever you want with me; I'm yours. I'm sorry I didn't let you do whatever," Loren said between sobs.

"That's not how I want our relationship to be baby. You're mine, but I don't want to hurt you, and I'm so sorry I did," Nancy said lovingly.

"My flight home is tomorrow, but I want to go to the airport and catch the first flight back. Will you pick me up, Mommy?" Loren asked, hoping Nancy would let her back into the house.

"Of course, tell me when your flight lands and I'll be there baby girl. Loren?" Nancy said seriously making Loren's eyes go wide.

"Yes, Mommy?" She replied curiously.

"Mommy will always be here for you baby girl. Mommy might make you mad, but you never need to run away from me, you can always come to me and say I've done something to upset you and we will talk about it until it's better," Nancy said making Loren's heart glow.

Nancy picked Loren up from the airport, and they

held hands the whole car ride home. When Loren walked into the living room and put her bags down next to Nancy's couch, she smiled as she saw her bunny and blankie waiting for her. Loren turned around on the spot and Nancy pushed a pacifier into her mouth before she could say a word making her giggle.

"Has Mommy's baby girl missed this?" Nancy said, picking Loren up and carrying her into the nursery. Nancy took Loren's clothes off, grabbed a vibrator, butt plug and diaper, and walked into the bathroom and ran a bath for Loren who stayed in the nursery.

"Baby?" Nancy asked from the bathroom. When Loren entered, she was holding the paddle in one hand and her bunny by the ear in the other. Nancy raised an eyebrow and smirked.

"I guess you'll need this to Mommy," Loren said, handing the paddle to Nancy who took it and ran her fingers over it.

"You are very right baby, but Mommy is going to wait until tomorrow to punish you. Let's get you settled back in before I remind you who is boss. You aren't going to be doing another disappearing act on me, young lady," Nancy said playfully patting Loren's bottom and helping her into the bath.

After Loren's bath Nancy lubed the toys and filled Loren's holes. Watching as she squirmed uncomfortably, Nancy laughed and picked Loren up for a hug.

"Mommy filled you up with the big toys today baby," Nancy said, pushing the butt plug in further making Loren limb with submission. Nancy fitted Loren into her diaper and turned the vibrator up, causing Loren to gasp and rub herself.

"No little one. You aren't allowed to touch," Nancy explained putting the remote into her back pocket and taking Loren's hands away. She took Loren's hand and led her back into the nursery and chose a white onesie, and pink socks, dressing Loren quickly while Loren squirmed and moaned as the vibrator kept her on the edge of orgasm. Nancy picked Loren up and cuffed her wrists and ankles to the cot. She took a pacifier gag from the draw and secured it around Loren's head and stroked Loren's forehead. Nancy then took a pink leather chastity belt from the cupboard fitted it tight over her onesie, making her diaper push firmly into her pussy.

"You better get used to that sweetheart. Mommy is going to keep you like that all night. I want you to fill that diaper with your sweet cum by morning. Welcome home little one," Nancy said as she turned off the light and closed the door behind her.

Mommy Loves You

An MDLG ABDL dynamic for littles. Mommy will lovingly diaper you, find your favorite pacifier and make sure you have all your stuffies

By Tina Moore

Sunday

I wake up before you and watch you sleep. Gosh, you look so cute in your jammies all wrapped up in blankie. You stir, frowning slightly as the sun hits your forehead and I move my body to shield you from the light. You smile in your sleep. I like to think it's because you know Mommy is here. I begin to stroke your forehead, and I smile as you stick your thumb in your mouth and begin to suck. I gently take your hand away and hold my breast to your lips. Running my hard nipple over your lips until you open your pretty mouth. I whisper to you, "Open wide baby," and fill your mouth with my milky breast. Milk dribbles from your lips as you suckle from Mommy wetting your cheek. You wake up as the wetness tickles you and blink your eyes sleepily.

"Shh little one, Mommy has you," I say making you smile behind my breast. I take it out of your mouth and kiss the tip of your nose.

"Good morning, my little sweetness, did you have a good sleep?" You nod your head and reach for me.

"Does the baby want cuddle time with Mommy?" You clap your hands excitedly, and I sit up and pull you onto my lap. I reach across and grab your pink bunny and jump it up your legs till you clutch it in your sweet little hands.

"Does that feel good baby?" I'm stroking your thigh while you wrap your arms around my neck, pressing your body against mine. I can feel your heartbeat and quicken my breathing to match your rhythm.

"Do you know what day it is today, sweetheart?" You shake your head, tickling Mommy with your hair.

"It's Sunday. Do you remember what Mommy does on a Sunday?" You pull away from me and look at me with a twinkle in your eye.

"Mommy makes you pancakes." I watch as you look excited, happy to be getting a treat. You're always such a good baby for Mommy, and I love giving you tasty treats. You push on my soft tummy, and I groan as you push yourself off me and crawl to the end of the bed.

"Oh, someone is eager." I watch as you drop bunny to the floor and reach down to get her. I like that you can't reach. When I got the bed custom-made, I made sure it was high enough to make it difficult for you to get down. I wanted you to be Mommy's little prisoner when you were in bed with me.

"Alright, alright, I'm coming." You look back at me and whine a little bit wanting bunny back.

"What did I say about that, sweetheart?" I say giving you a warning. You look down sad that I had to correct you. I let you be sad because I know it won't be for long as I slide off the bed and pick up bunny. I hold her up to you and watch as you reach out to grab her. I hold her just out of your reach. I like watching you bounce on Mommy's bed, desperate to have her back.

"It looks like you love bunny more than Mommy," I say looking at bunny. You gasp and shake your head, your hair flying about.

"Yes look, you wanted her more than me. Baby is it true?" I ask. Now you're bouncing and reaching for me. I smile. I like watching you bounce. Your thighs jiggle slightly, and your diaper makes crinkly sounds. You're pouting now, not taking my joke as a joke at all and I climb back up onto bed, and you tackle me in a cuddle.

"Oh, baby, I thought you wanted bunny, not Mommy," I tease. You look at me and take bunny in your hand. You look at her and suddenly threw her off the bed again. I am shocked, you haven't done something naughty like that in a long time, but my eyes soften as I hear your sweet words.

"I love you more Mommy. I want you." I fawn over you and put a paci in your mouth, and you suck as I help you off the bed. You crawl to bunny, and I bend down you feel between your legs.

"Your diaper feels heavy baby. Mommy is going to change you before I make breakfast." You instinctively crawl to your changing area in my bedroom. When I had the house built, I had an area in my room designed just for you so I could change you here instead of always having to go to your nursery. You love the spot in my bedroom that is just for you. It's a long narrow room that has a thick furry rug covering most of the carpet. It has a painted pink feature wall and an elaborate mobile that spans almost the length of the ceiling which has kept you entertained for hours. There's a toy box full of your stuffies and a free-standing cupboard which I keep stocked with your diapers, bibs, paci's, powder, and lotion. I keep the door to your little room in my bedroom open most days, but today it is shut. As I open it, you crawl in and lay on your back as you look up at the mobile. I take out a diaper, some wipes, and powder and decide I'll dress you now. I was going to wait until after breakfast, but you are such a clean little thing. I never have to worry about you getting sticky syrup on yourself.

"Lift your bottom baby." You lift and I take your wet diaper away and place a fresh dry one under you. You've gotten so good at wetting your diapers for Mommy. You use to be so nervous too, embarrassed because you were trying to be a big girl. But we both know you aren't a big girl, you're Mommy's little darling, and I like that you know that now. I wipe you down, making you clean and fresh again as I sprinkle powder over your bottom and pussy. You are giggling to yourself as I tickle you slightly before fastening your diaper and watching as you make a beeline to your toy box.

"Just one baby girl." I know you love to set your stuffies up in a row at breakfast time, but I don't want a teddy bear picnic today. I come up behind you and pull up your diaper cover. You love the one I've picked it's the pink one with the big silver bow at the back. I walk out of your room happy I can hear you crawling behind me and point to the corner of my room which as cushions and blankies sprawled out over the floor. There is an adult sized teddy bear leaning upright in the corner, and I watch as you snuggle into it and begin playing in your little nest. I smile and walk into the shower. I turn on the warm water, and from here I can watch you play. You are making your stuffies talk to each other, and I feel between my legs watching you. I rub myself as the warm water flows over my breasts and steaming up the room. You don't see me slip a finger into my pussy and begin pushing it in and out as I watch you. You're so perfect in your diaper; you're pretty hair loose and free as the teddy bear arms fall over you. It looks like it could just scoop you up and take you away. Not that I'd let it. I wouldn't let anyone else have you, my precious little girl.

I turn the shower off and dry myself with the large fluffy white towels we bought last week and make my way back to you. I'm naked as I walk into my cupboard and sit down on the ottoman in the middle of the room. My cupboard is more like second bedroom if I am really honest and I watch as you sneak your head around the corner.

"I was wondering when you'd appear my cheeky girl." You giggle and look bashful as you take in my womanly figure. I am still in good shape even though my stomach is becoming soft; my breasts are still large and full. Probably from years of letting your sweet lips suckle, but how can I refuse my darling girl? I let you rest your head on my thigh, and you watch as I select my next outfit.

"Something comfortable, I think." I stand up and snap my fingers behind me, knowing all too well you will try and sit on my ottoman. I choose a navy silk wrap around dress and matching lace bra and panty set and change in front of you. I know you think I'm beautiful. I can see it in your eyes. My thick chestnut waves fall loosely just under my shoulders, and I cup your chin as I pass you giving you a little tickle.

"Come on; you don't want to miss out on pancakes, do you?" I say as I watch you crawl quickly after me. Of course, I make it to the kitchen before you. Your little leggies can't keep up with Mommy. I watch as you sit at your little table along the far side of the living room. You're lining up your crayons in their color tones. You do this more than actually coloring with them, but I don't mind.

It gets you out of the kitchen. You're too little to be in the kitchen when the stove is on. I start mixing the ingredients as you take your orange crayon and begin drawing a picture for Mommy. I love your pictures, and I put them up on the fridge and always let you decide which magnet will be used. At the moment you love the shiny magnets we got at the markets. It was your special treat to go after you had been such a good girl for Mommy when I had been sick a month ago.

"It's almost ready little girl." I see you spin around and giggle happily as you tidy your crayons away and crawl over to the kitchen table. I help you up and put your sparkly unicorn plate down. I put a pink bib with matches your diaper cover around your neck gently and take out your paci.

"Be careful; they are hot." You hold your hands back as I serve you two pancakes. You wait for me to join you before you start trying to cut them yourself. You were such a good girl from the beginning with your manners. I hardly had to teach you anything. I remember when I had served you dinner one time and had to take a work call for over two hours and when I came back you were still waiting for me to join you before you touched your food. It had turned stone cold, and I had to make you some more, but I loved that you were so submissive for Mommy.

"Do you want syrup baby girl?" I love hearing your, "Yes please Mommy," as I pour warm sticky syrup all over your pancakes. I help you cut up the rest of them, and stab a piece of pancake with your fork before giving it to you. You like to feed yourself, but you are still too little to do everything. I love that you still need Mommy's help. A little bit of syrup drips onto your fingers, and you put your fork down and try to wipe it off quickly. You hate getting dirt, and I smile as I get a wipe from the kitchen bench. I keep them there for a reason. I wipe your fingys clean, and you happily go back to eating, humming a little song and doing a little dance as you eat. I love watching you when you're feeling playful like this you're just such a cute little girl. You give Mommy big smiles as you finish your pancakes, and I take your plate away to the kitchen. You reach for your sippy cup, and I take you down off the chair before I give it to you.

"Mommy is going to clean up breakfast baby girl. What are you going to do?" I ask watching you point back to your colorings.

"Alright, little one." You bite down on your sippy cup as you crawl back to your picture and I watch as you carefully put your cup down next to your crayons.

"Such a big girl." I am busy cleaning up when I turn around and get a fright. You have snuck up on Mommy, and I almost stepped on your pretty little feet.

"Baby girl! I didn't hear you there. What a pretty picture you've drawn Mommy. Why are you shaking your head at me? Is it not for Mommy?" I love teasing you. You shake your head left and right for longer than necessary. I think that while answering you began having fun swaying your hair around and have forgotten what we were talking about. Bending down, I gently place my heads on either side of your head and look into your dizzy eyes.

"Who is it for then little one?" You point to bunny, and I stand you up so you can put the picture on the fridge.

"What magnet does bunny get baby?" I see you looking very hard between the sparkly red magnet and the sparkly gold magnet. I'm almost about to choose for you when you reach for the gold one and stick it on the fridge.

"There," you say with satisfaction. I've finished cleaning up and straightening the living room. You're a good girl and don't spread your toys everywhere. You like everything to be in neat little piles.

"We have to do some cleaning today, baby. How about this Mommy is going to do the washing, and you are going to go into your room and sort out your toys. I want your blocks back in the toy box, and your stuffies in the bookshelf understand?" I say. You can get very distracted in your room, so I put my hand on my hip and give you a little bit of a stern look so you know I mean business.

"Yes Mommy," comes the words which make my heart sing, and you scurry off to your room. I wait and listen because I know that in about two minutes I'll need to go into your room and remind you of what you are doing in there. Sure enough, I hear a block tower crashing to the floor and make my way to your room.

"Little lady, this is your last warning. Don't make Mommy sad." You look as guilty as anything as I raise an eyebrow at you and rub over my heavy milk filled breast with my hands.

"Bad girls don't get milkys baby girl. You decide," I say watching you snap into gear. I leave you to your chores and go to do our washing. I strip the beds and wash the sheets and towels before putting out new ones for the week. I took your blankies and put them in next making sure you don't see. You hate it when I wash your blankies; you say it makes them feel funny, I say it gets rid of germs, and you know what Mommy says goes. The cleaning lady will do the rest, but I like to do the linen myself. I want to make sure my little girl's things are nice and clean and don't trust another person to look after your blankies the way Mommy does. I go back into your room and see you've been a good girl and put all your toys away.

"Milkys," you say, reaching for me. I would usually make you wait until I had made myself lunch, but they are hurting my back today, and I make my way over to the rocking chair I had made for us. I sit down and watch as you patiently wait to be let on. You know you're not allowed on without Mommy's permission. I pat my lap, and you eagerly climb up and get comfy on Mommy. I adjust you slightly and begin to rock as you suckle. You close your eyes, and I can feel your tongue lapping at my nipples. I squeeze my milk into your mouth, enjoying watching your cheeks go full. You swallow and pull on my nipple. I love how sweet you look there in my arms as I give you everything you need my precious baby girl. I begin to pat your bottom and feel you push onto me wanting all my lovies. I lift you and put you onto my other breast, and you settle quickly as I hold you close while I rock and nurse you. It's funny to think that when I first brought you home, you were nervous to suckle from Mommy. Now you ask for it when you know you shouldn't get it on the off chance I let you have milkys early. Your persistence has paid off today as you empty my breasts you're just lucky you only ever ask once. You know that I don't like to be harassed when I've given you my answer to something. I hear the washing machine go off and feel you getting sleepy in my arms. I love how you fall asleep as soon as your tummy is filled. I gently pull you up and help you into your cot, pulling up the side and securing you in. I know it's a little early for your nap, but I draw the curtains shut and give you your bunny and blankie before kissing your cheeks and closing the door behind me. I go to the laundry and put the washing into the dryer before going into the kitchen and making myself lunch. I make you a sandwich as well; I know you'll be hungry when you wake up from your nap. I give you a ham and cheese sandwich on dense rye and cut it up into eight small pieces. I put it in a container in the fridge and take my salad and spicy mince into the living room and turn on a show.

Just over an hour has past when I hear you through the baby monitor. You're playing with bunny and calling out to me. I have long folded our washing and put away my dishes, but I don't go into your room straight away. I listen to you to giggle as you talk to yourself.

"I know you are there, Mommy. I know you can hear me," you giggle sweetly. I get up and walk to your room, opening your door and see you throw your blankie up like a parachute. I take you out and set you up in the living room with your sandwich as I finish my show. It scares you, and you hide behind your blankie during the scary parts. I let you sit up on the couch with me, and I wrap my loving arm around you and let you lay on my lap.

"Why do you watch such scary things, Mommy?" You ask before quickly hiding under your blankie. I lift the corner of it and hide under it to making you laugh.

"Because Mommy doesn't find it scary," I reply tickling you. The show ends, and I take your sandwich container and put it in the dishwasher.

"What shall we do now, baby?" I ask. The house is in its usual perfect state. You are all relaxed and happy, and I have had a lovely morning doing almost nothing.

"We could go to the park?" You say clapping your hands. You love kicking the football around in the park, but I don't feel like doing so much sport. You have so much energy, and I was seriously thinking of just sending you out on a run by yourself.

"What about we go to the mall and try on pretty dresses?" I suggest. You think about it, and I see your cheeky little mind thinking of a plan as your eyes light up.

"Can we buy frozen yogurt too? It's

healthy." I look at you and laugh.

"In what universe is frozen yogurt healthy?" You look down at your toes, and I can tell you're trying to think of a rebuttal.

"Let's go and if you are a good girl for Mommy then maybe we can get frozen yogurt," I say deciding that I wasn't interested in your cheeky remark. I help you up, and you come to my room to get dressed in your big girl clothes. Sometimes I don't know why I bother changing you out of your clothes; even when we go out together, you look like my little girl. You sound and look bigger, but you're still Mommy's little one. It has everything to do with the fact that I look like the elegant, wealthy woman I am and you look like a little urchin I've picked up off the street. With your skinny black jeans and tight shirts, your particularly cool sneakers and general urban grunge vibe people commonly assume you're my little girl going through her rebellious phase. The diamond bracelet I claimed you with is the only indicator that you belong to me. But that's how I like it. I never wanted you to become a mini version of me; it's far more exciting having people to view me as your Mommy, which to every other degree bar biological, I am.

I take your diaper off, and you run to the bathroom. Cheeky girl, you still get nervous about wetting your diaper and only do when you are desperate. I make a mental note to get you to that desperation tomorrow as I lay out your underwear and give you a choice between two pairs of sneakers. You come back, and I give you a look which reads, you got away with that but you won't tomorrow, and you giggle and come up to kiss me. I run my hands up and down your back and hold your naked body close to mine. I love feeling your grown up body, you're as soft as ever, but you're more open to me, and I love that. You get dressed, and I pat your bottom and squeeze it gently as I take out your jacket. It's just starting to get cold, and the last thing I want is for you to get sick. You put it on, and I take your hand. We go to the car, and I give you your phone as I drive us to the mall.

You get your phone for a couple of hours each day on the weekend and while you're at work during the week and you press around madly catching up on the news you've missed over the evening. I turn the radio on, and you hum along to a song while you text people and tell me about the funny things your friends have said or done on social media.

We arrive at the store, and I hold out my hand expectantly. You give me your phone, and I put it in my handbag, and we get out. I let you get out by yourself today by nodding to the door. I like that you waited to see what mood I was in. You get out, and you quickly make it to my side as I walk us into the store, your little hand in mine. I love that you grip my hand tightly or loosely depending on who we pass. When we pass someone you find scary you grip it tight, and when we pass them, you relax again. We run into someone I met at the last party we went to, and you grip my hand. I look at you, and you say nothing but look back at me with you big pretty wide eyes. I make a note of your fear, but we have already seen them, and they are walking our way. I let your hand go and let you wander off on your own while I talk. I don't want you to have to stand near someone you don't like. I know the sassy mouth you have when someone pushes you too hard, and I don't want either of us to have to be in that position. I finish talking and come to find you, but I don't have to look far, you run up behind me, take my hand, and smile up at me.

"What was that about baby?" I ask.

"I don't like how they play it's rough," you reply. I tilt my head in agreement, and we walk to find you a new dress. You look for the bodycon section first, and I laugh as you dramatically hold up two options: a red one and a black one. I hold up an emerald-green one, and you take it from my hands and put it back on the rack.

"That one is gross Mommy," you say. I raise my eyebrow and look at your selection up and down.

"And these look like you're going to work," I say taking them out of your hands. We finally agree on a navy blue dress with a plunging neckline and a hem that stops mid thigh, and I go to pay. Taking your hand and gripping it firmly as we pass the frozen yogurt shop, you try to suppress your disappointment as I buckle you in the car.

"Good job on trying not to be a pouty baby little girl." You kiss my cheek and a rub your thighs before going to the driver's side and pulling out of the parking lot. I can feel you burning with sadness you don't have any yogurt, but I'm happy you haven't brought it up.

"I did say maybe little one," I say lovingly to you. You just nod, I know you're sad, but you won't be for long. Tonight I'm taking you to your favorite Mexican restaurant and as we pull up you almost give yourself whiplash looking at me.

"Really?" You ask. I smile, and nod and you giggle and clap your hands excitedly.

"You wouldn't have gotten it if you'd complained about the yogurt." You look at me and laugh.

"Stuff the yogurt; this is way better!" You jump out of the car, and I lean forward to grab your hand and pull you back to me as you race for the door. I look at you, and you check yourself and calmly walk beside me. I don't bother asking you want or taking a menu and order straight away. I know what you want, and I order double so that I can take it home, and that'll be lunch sorted for tomorrow. We eat our meal, and you take extra long telling me you're trying to savor the taste. I threaten to start eating your food if you don't hurry up and when you are finally finished, I go to pay. I can see your eyes flutter shut on the way home. The rocking of the car and soft music is playing like a lullaby for my pretty baby. I open the door and take you inside, snapping my fingers to the bathroom.

"Bath and bed, little lady." You go obediently to the bathroom, and I hear you start to take off your clothes.

"Cute little tummy. Are you all full baby? Did Mommy treat you extra special today?" You nod, and I help you into the bath. You play in the warm water as I bathe you, getting you nice and clean and ready for bed. The bath salts that I put in relax you and I hold you in my arms as I dry you. You are almost asleep as I take you into the nursery. You'll sleep here tonight. I put you straight into your cot and pull out an extra thick diaper. You try to push it away, but I take both your wrists in my hand and powder you nicely. You always get fussy when you're over sleepy, and you are wriggling around your cot like a little critter.

"Stay still for Mommy baby, so I can get you ready for bed. Don't fight Mommy." You stop for long enough for me to pull a fuzzy diaper cover over your bottom and tuck you into your cot. You've got your stuffies around you, and you roll around grumpy you're not asleep already. I smile down at you.

"Shh, now baby girl. It's alright; Mommy is here." I kiss you and turn off your light, coming back to rub your back as you fall asleep. I'm sitting in the rocking chair, and you hold one of my fingers as my other hand pats you making you calm and happy as you fall asleep. I wait until your little fist goes limb around my finger and quietly stand up, shutting the door behind me, and within minutes, I can hear the slow breathing of my good little girl fast asleep.

Monday

Mondays are always hard after spending the weekend with you. It's like we have been in our beautiful little bubble and Monday always comes and bursts it. I know it makes you sad when we have to go back to work. I try to make the week nice for you, but we both know you need to be a grown-up sometimes.

I look over to the nightstand and see the clock. 6:58 am. It'll sound the alarm soon and the work week will start. You stir and wake up to find me looking down on you. I love looking into your sleepy eyes. You blink trying to wake yourself up, and I pull you close to me as the alarm goes off. I hear your groan vibrate on my breast and you try to hold onto me as I pull you off my body.

"Come on, baby; it's not so bad." I pull the bed sheets off us and hop out of bed, leaving you there to get yourself out. I look over my shoulder to you as I go to my shoe cupboard and take out the pink pumps I'll be wearing today. I see you're still in bed and I have to suppress a smile as I sternly hint that you need to be out of that bed very quickly. I go to the shower as you begin to take your clothes off. I let you dress on Mondays because after the weekend it's always hard for you to be a big girl again. I feel you coming into the shower as you wrap your arms around my waist and hold me tight. I kiss you tenderly and pass you the shower gel.

"I can't be late today sweetie." I can't begin to count the times I've been late because you distract me with your beauty or the cute things you do. You nod and begin showering as I step out and make a beeline to my cupboard. I have a business meeting today and have already prepared my outfit: a fitted navy suit, white silk blouse, and bright pink pumps. I'm dressed and in the kitchen before you are out of the shower. I hear the water is turned off as I made you toast and put on some cartoons for you. When you come out into the kitchen, you're wearing your uniform.

You've worked in the same company for years, but you still can't get your tie done right, and I feel you up playfully before I get to your tie making you giggle and squirm. You sit down and butter your toast as you watch your cartoons, and I make myself an espresso.

"Time to go darling. Go clean your teeth and meet me in the car." You put your plate in the dishwasher and head to the bathroom. I put a sticky note saying how much I love you onto your lunch and take both our bags to the car. The mornings are so rushed; I hate that I can't keep you as my sweet girl any longer. You jump in the car, and I hand you your phone and smile as you put it straight in your bag and reach for my hand.

"Does someone miss Mommy already baby girl?" You lean over and cuddle my arm as you tell me about what you think your day will be like. I pull up at your train station and kiss you goodbye, watching as you run to catch the train you've almost missed. I pull away and notice you've left something on your seat. My stomach tightens for a moment thinking you've left something behind, but as I look closer, I see that you weren't the only one to get a note today. It's the picture you drew last night. You were so proud of it as you showed me. You have started doing collages for Mommy, and this one was a jungle theme. You had taken so much care in cutting out the green paper to make vines and grasses, and you used the stencils I bought you to make the animals. You even cut out some blue paper to make the watering hole you glued all the animals around. You make Mommy's heart skip a beat as I read the very grown-up poem you have written in pink gel pen on the back about how much you love me. I smile and fold it up, placing it carefully in my bag before leaving the train station and heading off to work.

During the day you send me photos of the different things you do. You always know how to make a boring work meeting exciting. I look at the most recent photo you've sent me. Your boss has told you to clean the back office, and you're there with your work friends posing in ridiculous poses rather than working. I laugh out loud and am grateful that other people are talking too loudly to notice. I love how naughty you are for everyone else except for me. I check my clock and see that in less than 2 hours, you'll be back by my side in the car going home and I can hardly wait.

I close a deal I've been working on for a month and decide to pick up something to celebrate. I go to the jewelry store and try on a diamond necklace. Some may say that it's an extravagant gift, but I am certainly worth it. I buy you some diamond studs and leave the store in time to pick you up from the train station.

As I pull up, I see you're waiting there with another person. I pause I don't want you to have to explain me to someone new or someone who you are unsure of how they will take it. But you wave, and I smile, and you call me over. It makes me laugh to myself that now it is me who is following your request, but as far as relationships go, I do enjoy giving while I take.

"This is Amy. Amy, this is my Mommy." I almost drop dead as you call me that in front of this very lovely looking stranger. I've missed part of the conversation where you two have shared your life stories.

"It's nice to meet you, Ma'am. Oh, that's my Daddy, I have to go. Bye," Amy replies.

I raise an eyebrow at you, and you begin telling me how you two met at a party we went to a while back. I think it's so cute how easily you make friends and you talk about Amy the whole ride home. I think about how she called me Ma'am, that hasn't happened in a long time, and I make a mental note to go to someplace fancy and new to hear it again. I liked it.

I take you inside, and you collapse on the couch dramatically. I go over to you, take your hand and pull you up. I turn you around and push you towards the shower.

"Bath. Now," I say as you flop your head back and shuffle to the bathroom.

It doesn't take you long to regress into the baby

girl of my dreams, and you happily splash around in the bathtub as you play with your toys. I leave you to continue to try and drown your toy duck and head back into the kitchen to start preparing dinner. By prepare, I mean to take out the food my assistant had made and delivered for us and heat it. I place yours on your special plate and put the earring box next to it. I take out my necklace and place it around my neck once more. This time, I won't have to take it off. I love the weight of the diamond strand. The beautifully cut flower design is resting elegantly against my skin. I go back into the bathroom, and you notice immediately.

"Mommy!" You exclaim in your pretty little voice. You clap your hands, you know I've wanted this deal closed. I take you out and dry you off, laying you down and diapering you. You fuss, and I gently slap your thighs, making you stop.

"I want you to be good for me tonight, and I won't put up with any of your nonsense." You look so sweet as I dress you in a fluffy white, legless onesie and I roll up pink thigh high socks on your little feeties. You reach for me, and I give you a big cuddle as I lift you and take you to the kitchen for dinner.

"Mommy are these for me!" You exclaim seeing the pretty blue box. I nod and pour myself a wine and watch as you open your gift. You love them like I knew you would and I come around to help you put them in.

"Very pretty, my baby." I sit down next to you and cut up your food. You don't like dinner tonight, and you refuse to eat until I begin to feed you. I had my assistant organize something healthy and vegan, and my baby doesn't like to eat her vegetables at all. It doesn't bother me to feed you though so I scoop up a big mouthful and push it into your mouth. You've learned better than to refuse me, and I'm happy you don't fight me in eating all your dinner. You pull a face after each mouthful and look so sad as I keep making you eat the ridiculously expensive, completely delicious food. Happy when you've only got one mouthful left I stop and get more for you, almost bring you to tears.

"I'm full, Mommy," you desperately try to tell me. I know you're lying. I keep you hungry in the afternoon for a reason, it's the only way to get you to eat your dinner, and I know you need more. I go to the freezer and put two scoops of ice cream in your bowl and bring it back to the table. I feed you a mouthful of healthy goodness then a mouthful of your dessert until you are finished.

"I'm so good to you baby, do you know that? Do you know that Mommy is the nicest Mommy in the world?" I ask you who right now probably doesn't think I'm the nicest in the world. You nod your head, and I can tell you've had enough to eat by the sleepiness in your pretty eyes and I let you go to the couch and lay down. I clean the plates away and pour myself another glass of wine before I join you. I turn on a show and lazily play with your hair as you drift in and out of sleep. You eventually roll off the couch and head over to your toys. Your little nap has revived you, my darling girl. You play as I shower and put on my pajamas and I come out and sit on the floor with you making you giggle.

"What are we playing baby?" You pass me a toy.

"Am I playing with kitty?" You shake your head and look at me, waiting for me to try again.

"Am I playing with mouse?" You giggle.

"No, Mommy!" You say, and I look at the toy you've given me.

"Am I playing with bunny?" You look at me like I'm silly and I tickle you making you squirm in my arms.

"It's duck Mommy," you said matter of factly making me laugh.

"How could I have not known. I'm a silly Mommy!" I say, and you look like I've just ran over a puppy.

"You're not silly, Mommy. You are the best Mommy!" You are so cute when you defend me against myself. I lean against the wall and sip my glass of wine as you play. I love watching you; it makes me so happy to know that I give you all of this. That without Mommy here to love you, you would be sad and lonely and without me. I need you as much as you need me. I don't tell you that often enough but I hope I show it loud and clear.

By the time bedtime comes around, you have made each one of your toys do a drawing, and you have cut them out and put them on a piece of sparkly silver cardboard. I have tried to take it from you multiple times, but each time you are adamant you aren't finished. I know it's just because you don't want to go to bed, but I play along. You'll be tired soon enough, and that's when I'll strike. You have run out of toys to get to do drawings and try to tell me that now each block has to do a drawing. I give you a look that makes you laugh hysterically, and you giggle as you try to convince me.

"I think someone is trying to lie to Mommy." You shake your head as you giggle, not exactly convincing. I take your hands and pull you up, letting you grab bunny before I take you to bed. You're such a good girl how to go straight into your nursery, assuming you'll be in your cot tonight. You know that on Mondays, Tuesdays, and Wednesdays you're in your cot but tonight I want you with me. As I begin to tell you-you'll be sleeping with Mommy, you jump up and down and hold me tightly.

"I love you, Mommy," you say as you grip my waist. I kiss your forehead and take you to the bathroom for teethies. You love to brush your teeth, but I help you finish off before I'm satisfied you're clean. I put on some night cream, you're youthful beauty doesn't need any yet, and I pat your bottom indicating for you to go into bed. You're still struggling to get up, and I bring you your stool which you have forgotten about as I come out of the bathroom. You climb up, and I lay down, happy to be relaxing in bed. You come over to me, and before you can say a word, my nipple is in your mouth. This is why I wanted you here with me tonight. You suckle, and I hum you a tune as you are rocked in Mommy's arms. Gosh, you are beautiful little baby girl. Such a sweet princess and so wonderful Mommy would be lost without you. I cut your time short on my left breast, wanting you to suckle from both and watch as you fall asleep. Jiggling you awake I hold my breast in my hand and stroke my nipple over your lips, making you open your mouth for Mommy again.

"Just a little more baby. I know you've got a full tummy, but Mommy needs you to drink just a little more." I loving say as you begin suckling again. After I feel the tension release, I take you off and roll your sleeping body onto your side of the bed. I could have done that in your room, I suppose, but I am selfish and want you with me tonight. I place your blankie over your body and press bunny into your side as I begin to listen to a podcast.

I'm almost finished listening as I feel you startle. I take out my earphones and pat your back, thinking you are just having a nightmare. But you roll over, and I smile at you kindly.

"Come on, sweetie." I take your hand and lead you to your changing room. You are so cute how you hate having a wet diaper. I knew that milk would be too much, but I don't mind changing you. I'm secretly happy you woke up now and not in the middle of the night. I lay you down and take off your wet diaper, and you point to the star diaper, and I take it down for you.

"Is this the one you want baby?" You nod your head and begin to suck your thumb. I take your thumb away and put in your paci, and you coo sweetly behind it. I hadn't realized you'd taken bunny and I accidentally kneel on her giving you have a mini heart attack.

"Oh I'm sorry baby girl did Mommy hurt bunny?" I pass you your toy, and you cuddle her on your chest as I wipe your clean and freshly powder you. I put you in your new diaper and put you back in your fluffy white onesie.

"All clean now, baby girl." You clap your little hands, and I put you back in bed, letting you snuggle into me as I wrap my arm around you. You place your hand on my stomach and begin to rub my body.

"Are you feeling Mommy, baby?" You nod. I secretly hope you like how I feel. I would never tell you that you make me insecure sometimes. There are so many younger Mommies, and I sometimes wonder if you would prefer to have one of them instead of me. You give me little kisses along my neck and onto my cheek, and all my insecurities are washed away.

"I love you baby girl, do you know that?" You giggle, and I melt as you tell me how much you love me back.

"Mommy loves you," is the last thing you hear before you fall asleep in my arms.

Tuesday

I wake to the sound of birds chirping outside my window. I feel around in my bed and remember that I put you in your cot in the middle of the night. You had woken to a bad dream, and I took you to your room and lay with you until you fell asleep. Not because I didn't want you with me for the whole night, but because Mommy wanted to do naughty things that babies shouldn't be around for. I had assumed you were still in your cot until I hear you turn up a song in our gym as you slam down some weights. I like that you keep yourself in shape. It makes playtime more fun when I know I can put you into a whole lot of different positions. You come back into my room quietly thinking I am still asleep.

"Hi, there, sweetheart." You look up, surprised to see me staring at you and smile.

"Oh, I'm sorry, Mommy, I didn't mean to wake you," you reply, looking as though I've caught you doing something naughty. I'd usually want you to come and cuddle with me, but you're all hot and sweaty from your workout. Your exercise clothes look like something from a porn movie. You wear tiny shorts that barely cover your ass and a tight singlet without a bra. You weren't running today. You've taken off your gym shoes and are just wearing your knee high sports socks, and your hair is in its usual messy ponytail. I love it; you look so beautiful standing there. My face must have given me away because I see a mischievous gleam in your eye begin to sparkle.

"Do you think I'm pretty Mommy," you say as you turn for me. I nod, enjoying the show you are putting on and sit up to get a better view. You slowly take off your singlet, and I smile, seeing your pierced nipples. I remember when you got them done. It wasn't because I told you to, you'd done it because you wanted to be sluty for Mommy. You're always sluty for Mommy. You turn around and roll your socks down next and walk over to me and take my hands in yours.

"Do you want to take them off, Mommy?" You ask in your sluty grown-up voice. I shake my head no, and you break out of your seduction, confused at my response. I can't help myself and laugh at your confused look, clearly unable to believe I'd refuse you.

"I want you to show me, baby," I say, giving you clarification. Your eyes light up as you go back to teasing me as you take your shorts off showing me your ass. I lean over and grab one of your cheeks firmly, my desire coming out in the intensity of my grab making you gasp.

"Don't tease Mommy if you can't handle the consequence baby," I say in a husky aroused voice. You know that voice well and lie down on the floor and begin masturbating in front of me. You know I love to watch you, I always have. I even love the way other people stare at you, how they want you as you flutter around a room. What I love most is the way you always land right back on my lap, like the good girl you are. I watch you and nod as you look to me wanting to cum and you arch your back and shudder as it races through you. I watch as you go back for more but stop in a breathless whine as I shake my head no.

"Have a shower then make Mommy a coffee baby girl. I want to stay in bed a little longer today," I instruct you as you pick up the trail of clothes and head into my shower. I roll over and must have fallen back asleep because I'm woken by the smell of coffee and realize you have gone from the room. Getting up, I take off my pajama's and get dressed for work. I have an event tonight and will be working late so you'll be home alone for most of the evening. I go into your room and put notes with instructions and cute little messages around and head to the kitchen.

"Fancy Mommy," you say as you see my outfit. I have a cream-colored skirt and my new purple designer blouse I couldn't walk past last time we went into the city together. I left one button, extra undone, and the material gapes elegantly around my diamond necklace. I have opted for matching cream heels and a sophisticated gray coat with cream fur around the collar and base of the arms. I look in the mirror and smirk at myself. *Yes, very fancy,* I think as I take the coffee, you have made me. You bought me this coat with the first paycheck you got when you started your new job. It was your first two paychecks if memory serves me and you had it delivered to my work with a big bunch of roses and a card. You made me feel so special having all the partners of the firm question who my mysterious lover was. I enjoyed watching them try to guess who it could be. I don't take you too many work events, mostly because I am a shark in that world and I don't want my baby to see how vicious Mommy can be or how much I enjoy being.

You've made yourself some toast, and I cut it up for you as I make you an egg.

"Mommy is going to be home very late today sweetie. I've laid out everything I want you to do here," I say, sliding a sheet of paper across the kitchen bench. You read it a few times and get excited each time you read that you can have take out for dinner.

"Nothing over $20 though baby, I'm not trying to have you hyper when I get back," I always give you a limit to how much you can spend. I learned that after I mistakenly said you could ice-cream, and you bought $40 worth of it. I've learned with you that if there's a loophole, you'll find it. You smile at me cheekily and roll your eyes playfully.

"Now I'm serious baby. There'll be trouble if those things aren't done how I want them." I've given you time frames when everything needs to be done and demanded a photo of the completed task. The one I think you'll struggle with the most is getting off your phone by 9 pm. You've tried all sorts of excuses as to why you needed to be online past 9, all of which I have happily punished you for. One time you even tried to tell me that your boss called you and you were so shocked when I rung your boss to ask. You were punished particularly hard for that one; I hate lying.

I pack your lunch in your backpack and fix your tie

for you almost ritualistically and push you out the door. I hold your hand as we walk along the garden path to the car. I open your door and buckle you in pulling the seat belt extra tight and looking at you like you're my prey.

"Mommy don't," you say blushing and pushing me away. I laugh and kiss you, and you almost pull me into the car with you as you wrap your arms around my body. You are so strong; I love it. I break the kiss and turn the car on, backing out of the driveway and onto the road.

I drive in silence, I've got so much on my mind, and I am mildly aware you are looking at me. I can feel your eyes on me; I could almost swear they are undressing me, and I like that I make you want all of me.

"What are you thinking about Mommy?" You ask as you lift your legs and pull them to your chest. I quickly slap them back down and squeeze your thigh firmly. As if I want your shoes on the cream leather. I look at you warningly until you look away I'm not letting you win this power battle baby.

"Don't," is all I need to say for you to curb your attention seeking behavior. You look out the window in annoyance that I don't let you be a brat. You've started that lately, I think it's the influence of another baby you met at a party a while back, that same one you were so excited to introduce me to yesterday, what was her name? Amy, I think. You turn back towards me; maybe you remember what happened the last time you tried that shit on me.

"Sorry, Mommy, I'm going to miss you tonight," you say submissively. I smile at you with a raised eyebrow.

"I know sweetie. You don't need to be a naughty girl, though. I've left you little notes around the house that I want you to find, and I'll be home to tuck you in tonight. Mommy won't be gone for long." I forget how clingy you are sometimes. When you are a big girl, you are so independent and in control, but the minute you're my baby girl, you want to be attached to me constantly. I don't hate it; I hate how it makes you feel when you can't have me constantly. I know it makes your little heart hurt and I know that I try to overcompensate on treats on these nights to make it easier for you.

"You can watch whatever movie you want to watch tonight, baby," I say making you give a faint smile. We arrive at the train station, and I get out of the car and come around to your side. You are trying to act tough, but I catch the little tear which escapes your eye.

"There there come to Mommy princess it's going to be alright. You will have a good time, and I'll be home before you know it," I say as I hold your face to my cleavage and hold you close, stroking your hair and feeing your fast heartbeat.

"I know. See you later, Mommy," you say as you hear your train pull up. I quickly kiss you savoring the taste of your strawberry chapstick and let you run over the road and jump on the train just as the doors shut. I wait and wave as you go and hope you make it through the day. You are so little sometimes I wish we could stop the world and stay in our space.

The first message I receive from you is a topless selfie I requested at 5 pm. I'm in a taxi on the way to the event, and I feel my phone vibrate, and I knowingly smile in satisfaction at what I'm about to see. I open it and am not disappointed. Your beautiful body on display for me your pierced nipples hard and ready to be played with. I put my phone back in my pocket and settle back into the taxi seat. *This will be a lovely evening;* I tell myself as I arrive at the venue. My assistant is waiting out the front with a change of outfits, and I follow her as she leads me to a private suite I have arranged. It would be so wonderful if you could be here. I'd let you play with your stuffies while Mommy worked knowing that my cute little princess was close by. Unfortunately, it is just my work slave and I here, and she is boring me with the details of the evening. I dismiss her and send you a message seeing you online. *Hi baby, Mommy can't wait to come home to you. Have you been a good girl and picked up your dinner? Tell Mommy what you got*, I write. You reply in no time at all telling me about your day and what you've bought for yourself. I enjoy reading how proud you are that you managed to buy three cheeseburgers and an extra large chocolate shake with change to give Mommy when I get back. I laugh out loud at your message knowing full well you're going to have a stomach ache in about half an hour. I put my phone down and go to freshen up before dressing in my evening dress and make my way downstairs.

It's 10 pm by the time I look at my phone again, and I am impressed with the array of messages I have received. You've done everything I have asked you to. The toys are away, you did give yourself a tummy ache like I knew you would, but you've had a bath and are all tucked up in bed ready for me to kiss you goodnight. I have half a mind to leave the event early to come home to you, but I stay an hour longer and mingle some more.

I arrive home and find you already asleep in your

cot. You have dressed in your pink thigh high socks and fuzzy grey bear onesie. You're sucking on the aqua glitter paci I was saving for a special occasion, but I guess you found it. Your hair is untied, and I like how to falls down your back along your onesie. You look so cute with your diaper sticking out a little bit from under your onesie and I tuck it in neatly making you wake up.

"Mommy," you say excitedly although half asleep. I smile down at you, and you sit up, holding your arms out to me.

"You smell like aircon and man perfume," you say as my hair falls onto your face.

"Really? I thought I smelt like money and Mommy's perfume," I reply. Working in a male-dominated industry, it's not surprising that you thought I smelt like them. Their cologne is almost laced into the walls at work.

"I better shower then so you don't get confused about who I am baby," I tease and take you out of the cot. You sit on the bathroom floor as I shower and I put on a little show for you making you giggle. It's so nice to come home to you after having such an aggressive day. I don't mind you staying up late tonight; you don't have work tomorrow so you can sleep in with me. I've taken the morning off as well, and I can't wait to play with you in the morning.

"Mommy, can I please sleep with you tonight?" You ask. Your hair has fallen either side of the onesie bear hood you have put on your head, and I honestly can't think of seeing anything cuter than you right now. I nod, and you excitedly clap your hands and hand me my towel as I turn off the shower water. I don't bother with pajamas tonight; I know you'll be suckling on me before too long anyway.

I lift you onto the bed and hear my phone ring. It's my bloody assistant. I answer it and hold my finger to your lips so you'll be quiet. I lay down and take your wrist, pulling you towards me and hold your mouth to my nipple. I'm answering her multiple questions while enjoying nursing you quietly as she talks my ear off. You giggle, and I look down at you excitedly, I love how cheeky you are, and I know you love this. I know it makes you feel like Mommy has put you first. I'll always put you, first baby; Mommy still needs to work though. I move you to my other breast and pat you as you nurse. You are more interested in playing with my nipples tonight than filling your tummy, which is understandable, you gorged yourself on takeout a few hours earlier. I hang up the phone and take you off me instead of wrapping you in my arms. I put on a bra, so I don't leak milk all over your pretty onesie and lay you on top me as I stroke you.

"You were such a good girl for me today, doing everything I asked you to on your list. Did you have a good night? Tell Mommy what you did," I say as I gently grope your little body. I love the feel of your soft full skin under my hands. I could massage you forever. You tell me how you went to three take out places before deciding to get a burger from each one and how you went somewhere else to get your shake. You explain to me how not all chocolate shakes taste the same and how some places don't make them chocolaty enough. You're the expert, I haven't had that shit for years, but that's what you always order any chance you get. You tell me how bunny didn't want to do any drawings tonight and that you watched one of Mommy's movies until it scared you and you went back to watching your movies. You tell me how you used the new bath crayons to draw because you wanted to even though bunny didn't. I listen and hold you close as you explain to me all your little girl dramas.

"My little teddy bear had such a big evening. She worked so hard and did all the big girl things didn't she bunny," I say holding bunny up and talking to her instead of you. You giggle and reach for her, and I put her in your arms as you nestle your head into me. You ask me how my night was, and I roll my eyes and tickle you.

"Mommy had a nice night, but I'm happy to be home with my sweet little teddy," I say, pulling up your blankie and tucking you in. You roll off me and almost cocoon yourself in your blankie, but I pull you back into my arms, brushing your hair out of your face. You feel better than ever, and I rock you gently as you drift off to sleep. I stay up a little longer and reply to some emails but kiss you goodnight as I put my phone down before I close my eyes.

Wednesday

"Oh baby, it's alright, Mommy is here, you're just having a bad dream," I say as you toss and turn in your sleep. I rub your back and gently shake you awake. You open your pretty eyes and look around fearfully.

"Mommy!" You say finding me and snuggle in close.

"Did someone have a bad dream little girl?" You nod your head and search around for bunny. I feel her under my pillow and hand her to you.

"Mommy is here. It's OK baby, I've got you." You roll back onto your tummy, and I pat your bottom until you are back asleep.

The next time you wake up, it's to me rushing around the bedroom.

"I'm late. Why am I always late?" I say as I hurry to put on my heels. It's your day off today, and you jump out of bed to make me breakfast. I love that you're such a good helper for Mommy, especially on days like today.

When I come into the kitchen, you are looking very impressed with yourself. You've made our breakfast smoothies, and you're lucky you've already tidied everything away.

"Here Mommy," you say as you pass me my smoothie in a travel cup.

"So thoughtful little girl," I say taking it and kissing you over and over until you are giggling for me to stop. Gosh, you look cute in your teddy bear onesie I'm going to be buying you more of those. I notice you haven't started your smoothie yet and I take out your paci and lift your cup to your lips. You try to fuss, but I hold your chin in my other hand and look at you until you begin to drink.

"I need my baby girl to be strong and healthy little one. Mommy doesn't want her sweet girl to get sick because she isn't getting her vitamins." You playfully roll your eyes at me, and I make myself a coffee. I wait for the machine to start and finish writing you your job list for the day.

"You're going to need to get out of the house for most of the day today, baby. Mommy has a lot of things she needs you to do, and I want photos of each of the jobs being completed," I say as you read over your list. You jump off the kitchen stool and go to your coloring in table and bring back your pink crayon.

"For ticking," you say. I try to suppress a sideward smirk as I turn back to put sugar in my coffee. You are so cute.

"You'll need to pick up the dry cleaning and a few more groceries, the list is attached, but you'll have to go to a few different places to get everything on there. Also, I need you to return the books to the library; you can pick out some more if you'd like." You love the library. I think it's funny you like to borrow the books when I could buy them for you. I think you like the whole, scanning it yourself, element. It makes you feel very clever. You go to your bookshelf next to your coloring in table and bring all your books back to the kitchen bench. I'm secretly delighted you'll be taking these books back, I've read them almost a hundred times to you, and I swear I know them by heart now.

You finish your smoothie and pass me your cup, and I give you your paci back, popping it in your mouth.

"Stay here, sweetie; Mommy will be back in a minute. I want to dress you in something cute today," I say. I know if you had your way you'd stay in your jammies all day my cheeky little one. You nod while looking me up and down and I go back into my room and take out what I want you to wear. I select your denim ¾ overalls, a white t-shirt for underneath and your pink chucks. I grab your olive-green backpack to match and look inside. You've left a stuffie at the bottom of your bag you cute little thing.

"Here sweetie, come to Mommy," I say coming back into the room. I walk to the living room, and you follow. I lay you down as I change you out of your diaper and into big girl panties and hold your hand as you step into your overalls. You look so cute as I roll up the hems and you hold onto my shoulder as you balance putting on your socks.

"Mommy, can you please tie my shoelaces?" You ask slipping on your shoes. I rest against the couch and look at you. I hold out my hand to you, and you take it as I pull you onto my thigh, making you straddle it. You smile at me bashfully, you love the feeling of my thigh between your legs, and I see you begin to blush as I move it under you making your panties rub on your clit.

"Mommy stop it," you playfully say trying to grab my hands to get me to stop. I love playing with you; you're so cute how you try to stop me. You should have learned by now that I'll do whatever I want with you my sweet little girl. You're giggling stops, and you move closer to me, letting me hold you, and you rest your head on the nape of my neck.

"I love you, baby," I whisper in your ear. You snuggle further into me and I stroke your back never wanting to let you go. Eventually, I sit you up and bend down to tie your shoelaces. You look so sweet, and I stand you up as you put your hair up. I make a note to take you to the hairdressers next week to get your hair trimmed. It's getting ever so slightly ratty at the ends, and you know I like my princess to look perfect at all times. You go back into the kitchen and put a packet of crackers and your water bottle into your bag as well as your sketch pad and pencils.

"When do you think you'll have time to draw baby?" I ask, curious about what you'll do today. You say on the train, and I remind you not to lose track of time. Last time you drew on the train, you missed your stop, and I had to come and get you. You laugh, and I pack you a muesli bar worried you hadn't packed enough food.

"Ready?" I say as you head to the door. I know you've forgotten something, I can see it on the bench, but you nod your head confidently.

"Then why is the list of jobs you need to do still on the bench?" I ask making you laugh and run back into the kitchen. I hold the door open for you and slap your bottom as you pass me on the way to the car. You turn around and give me one of your cheeky smiles as you ponytail sways in the breeze. I drive you to the station, and you kiss me goodbye. I take my time letting you go and slip my hands down the top of your overalls and play with your perfect tits.

"Be a good girl for Mommy and don't forget anything on that list, sweetheart," I say warningly. You kiss me and say adamantly that you won't forget and walk to the train. I sit back in the driver's seat and have to take a call from my assistant but make sure to wave goodbye to you as your train pulls away.

Throughout the day you send me texts with photos of the different things you have ticked off from your list. I know you'd much rather stay at home and wait for Mommy to get back, but I like you out and about. It's good for you to move around the world and not just stay in your little bubble all the time. I give you enough of that as it is you, lucky girl.

As the day winds down and I begin to drive home, I think back to the time when we went on our first road trip. You had insisted that we listen to the latest 100 pop songs, and by the end of your playlist, I was ready to through your phone out the window. I love letting you drive me crazy like that. It was so much fun hearing you sing your little heart out to all the songs. You make my heart so full and happy to have you as my baby girl.

I slam the brakes on suddenly as I see your ball bouncing onto the street as I pull into the driveway. You run out onto the street and smile at me apologetically. Picking your ball up you bounce it back off the road and up to the garage door. I hope you've cleaned your toys away before you decided to play outside or you'll be in so much trouble.

"Sweetie, are you trying to get yourself run over?" I say, grabbing my bag and shutting the car door. I walk over to you, and you look so sweet. You've clearly been shooting hoops for hours by the redness of your cheeks, and I kiss the top of your head and lead you inside. You bounce your basketball up the path, and I count to ten before I ask you to stop. I don't want to be angry with you, but it's so very annoying. You put the ball down by the front door and follow me inside, taking your shoes off and leaving them in the mudroom.

"How was your day? What did you do today?" You ask going to the fridge and taking out two bottles of water. You shake a water bottle in your hand, offering it to me, and I decline instead tilting my head to the whiskey cabinet, and you smirk knowingly.

"Are you doing your whiskey on Wednesday thing again?" You ask playfully as you inhale deeply. You love it as much as I do, but you won't be getting any tonight. Tonight this is just for Mommy. I ignore your tease and wait for you to serve me my drink before playfully pulling you on top of me and letting you rest in my arms. You're so dirty from playing outside, but tonight I don't care I want you cuddling me now. You wrap your arms around me and watch as I take a sip of my drink. I can see you are still hoping you'll get a sip. I shake my head no and smile as you look down disappointedly.

"My day was productive, but it was long, and Mommy had to keep telling people what do you, and you know how I hate to repeat myself," I honestly reply. You open your bottle of water and drink half in one go.

"Thirsty girl," I say as you shrug your shoulders. I love it when you start to enter your little space. Your big doe eyes following me around the room curiously, the way you become so sweet and dependent on me for everything, how you stop talking and use body language to communicate. It's great when I've got a headache. You are easier to look after as a baby than you are when you're a big girl.

"My pretty baby girl so easily pleased and so happy to be a good girl for Mommy," I say taking the water bottle away from you and leading you into the bathroom. I strip you down, and you pick out your favorite bubble bath scent. I honestly don't know why we have anything other than strawberry and vanilla which you insist on putting together because that's all you ever use. And yet, every time we go to the store you assure me that we need wild berry or watermelon or some other variety I know you won't ever use. Some other Mommies have told me I spoil you but what's the point of having such a sweet baby girl if I can't spoil you? Of course, when you are naughty for Mommy, you've seen how mean I can be, so it's always a good idea to be good for me.

I test the water before throwing in your duckies and help you in. I wash your hair, and you spend the better part of an hour trying to drown your duckies. I don't know why you want to keep them under the water you're like a kitty who wants to catch the mouse popping up in a box. When one duck reaches the surface, you push it back down just as another one comes to the surface and repeat. It's cute watching you, though. I giggle at how into your game you get.

"Did you do everything Mommy needed you

to baby?" I ask as I take your towel off the rack. It's nice and warm from being heated all day. You look at me and nod your head as you point to my room.

"Is my dry cleaning hanging up in there sweetie?" I ask, and you smile and nod your head.

"Such a good girl getting everything Mommy needed princess," I say pulling the plug on your bath. You look at me and pout but don't say a word as I hold your towel open for you. I wrap you in your warm fluffy white towel and dry you off. You are a bit fussy tonight and want to cuddle me, making it difficult for me to dry you off.

"Come on; baby girl don't be silly for Mommy. We can cuddle as soon as you are in your jammies, but I can't let you stay in the bathroom forever." I lead you to your nursery, and you go to sit in your reading corner with your big teddy and pillows. I take out your cute little fox onesie and black pacifier. I walk over to the changing mat, and you crawl to me. I love that you are Mommy's little magnet when I am home. You lay down, and I rub lotion over your body, massaging you gently and almost putting you to sleep. By the time I am finished with you, and you open your little eyes again you are diapered and in your onesie, your white ankle sockies are on, and I'm lying next to you stroking the bridge of your nose.

"Come on darling Mommy is going to get you some dinner and then you can fall asleep in my arms, alright?" I say as I pull you to your feet. You stand for about two seconds and then fall back down on the floor and slowly crawl to the kitchen. I look down at you in your cute little tired state and decide I'll carry you, so you feel loved. I don't usually carry you, but tonight I can see you need it and Mommy always wants to give you what you need. You start to cry as I pick you up, and I stroke your hair as I hold you.

"It's alright baby; Mommy is here. Let's fill that little tummy of yours and then we can cuddle together on the couch or in Mommy's bed alright?" I had planned to put you in your cot this evening, but that plan has gone straight out the window. I can see you need me tonight and putting you in your cot would only make your little heart hurt. You nod and try to wipe your tears away, but I come with some tissues when I bring your plate over. I sit by your side and feed you little mouthfuls. I know why you are so emotional tonight. You've had a big day outside with heaps of new situations that have scared you, new parts of town you had to find your way around, and I know that you are completely overstimulated from the day to the point where you are just breaking down from finding it all so stressful.

"I am so proud of you, sweetheart. I know you found today hard, I know it was new, but you did such a great job, and Mommy is so grateful you did those jobs for me," I say wiping your tears away. I give you my finger to hold while I feed you with my other hand until you are finished. I didn't even have to seduce you to eat your vegetables with ice-cream tonight, which shows how overwhelmed you are. You finish up, and I put your plate in the dishwasher and set you up on the couch. I bring you bunny and blankie and put on one of your favorite movies. I make a little bowl of popcorn for you and turn all the lights off, so your eyes don't hurt. You smile at Mommy as I tuck blankie around you before I walk down the hall and into my bedroom.

I take my clothes off and feel the warm water on my body, happy you are content watching your movie. I'll put on my most cuddly pajamas for you tonight, the soft ones you like to rub your face on when we cuddle. I accidentally shrunk the top, so my full chest pushes out against the buttons, and I think you like that.

When I come back to the couch, you haven't touched your popcorn, but you reach for my breasts as a little gleam sparkles in your eye.

"Oh, feeling better are you miss?" I playfully say taking your bowl away and putting it on the bench. I don't know why I even bothered to do up my top I'm already unbuttoning it again. I sit next to you and pull you onto me. You've lost all interest in the movie as you latch onto my nipple and begin nursing.

"My sweet girl just needs her Mommy, isn't that right baby?" I ask as you close your eyes and get lost in milky happiness.

I hear you playing before I see you this morning. I love that you constantly surprise me with what you are up to. I hear you giggling and talking to your stuffies. I think you're in the living room. I don't bother staying in bed late today and get up, showering and getting dressed before I come to find you. You hear my heels on the floorboards and you go quiet.

"Are you trying to hide from Mommy sweetie?" I playfully ask looking around the living room not being able to see you. You giggle, and I look behind the couch to see you two little feeties sticking out. I smile and turn around to make you breakfast.

"Oh well, who will eat this yummy yogurt if my baby isn't here. I guess Mommy gets both. Maybe I'll even sprinkle muesli on top to make it extra yummy and crunchy. But baby won't be having any coz she isn't here," I tease making you pop your little head up from behind the couch.

"I'm here, Mommy!" You exclaim jumping up, and I act surprised like I hadn't seen you 3 minutes before. You are just so sweet like that; I love it.

You crawl over to the kitchen table, and I lift you onto your stool and feed you as you set up your row of stuffies.

"Look, Mommy, I drew a picture of everyone," you say, showing me a very accurate representation of the number of toys you have.

"Wow baby, you have so many. Maybe Mommy should stop buying you stuffies. I don't think you need any more," I playfully tease laughing at your shocked face.

"Baby, you're going to have to get dressed after breakfast," I say making it clear you will not fight me on going to work today. You nod and open your mouth for more yogurt, but I hold the spoon away from you.

"Use your words, sweetie," I instruct and try not to smile as you pout and look annoyed.

"Yes, Mommy, I'll get ready after yogi's," you say as I feed you another spoon.

"When can I wear click clack shoes like Mommy?" You suddenly ask, taking me by surprise. I look you up and down and laugh.

"Baby, you can't wear heels yet, you're too little. But how about after work, you come home and get dressed in big girl clothes, maybe that dress sexy green dress and come to Mommy's favorite bar for a drink? You can wear click clack shoes then?" I ask, hoping you'll say yes. I love taking you out and watching as people fall over themselves to get close to you; it only pushes you further into my arms. I love how you turn into Mommy's sweet angel when you wear your big girl clothes. You clap your hands and almost run into my bedroom to get changed into your uniform as you finish your last mouthful.

I pack your lunch and wait in the car for you, turning on the heating and listening to the news. It's raining and cold today, and you come out of the house without a jacket or an umbrella. I feel your cold little arms as you get in the car and send you back into the house to get your warm jacket and a big umbrella. You complain, and I can tell you forgot on purpose by your giggling.

"Don't be silly for Mommy baby girl, you'll catch a cold, and then Mommy will be very cross," I say as you shut the car door. I see you a few minutes later in your warm black leather, faux fur lined bomber jacket and a bright pink umbrella. Gosh, you look stunning. Your hair is out today, and the way it bounces when you walk is so beautiful. You smile your wide toothy grin at me, and I turn on the windscreen wipers to catch a better glimpse of you.

"Good job sweetie," I say, pulling out of the driveway turning the news off. I pass you your phone, and you cross your legs as you tap it with a feverishness that makes me wonder if everything is ok.

"Mommy look," you say, holding up the screen to my face. I obviously can't read it now.

"Baby tell Mommy what is says, I can't look

while I'm driving." You begin reading out a message your friend Amy has written to you about how there's a party next weekend. You want to go.

"Forward me the message, and I'll see if we are free, I think we are though baby," I say getting you excited. I wish you'd found a different friend, I think Amy is a brat, and I don't like brats. The minute you try any of that shit on me, you'll feel the sting of my hand on your pretty little bottom. But I don't tell you that because I don't want to shatter your excitement. I just let you talk about all the things you guys can do at the party, and I listen and smile at you.

"I'm happy you've found a friend sweetie, just remember that you're Mommy's good girl and don't let her lead you into any trouble alright?" I ask lovingly. I look at you and can see you remember the last time you were punished. You've got your little serious face on, and you nod knowingly.

"I won't Mommy," you say seriously. I'm glad you remember your punishment. I worked very hard, making sure you would.

I pull up at the station and give you $5 to buy yourself a treat making you gasp excitedly. You stash it in your pocket and come around to my side of the car and open the door. You lean in and kiss me on my cheek, making my heart flutter.

"Bye, Mommy," you half-whisper in my ear. Gosh, you are just divine darling.

"I love you baby girl, see you later," I reply, pulling you forward for a hug. You hear your train and do your usual cute dash over the road as to not miss it, and I drive to work.

You're a good girl as usual and send me photos of the sneaky things you do at work. Today you and your work friends finish the rubber band ball you've been working on, and it's as big as your basketball. I constantly wonder how you all get away with such naughtiness but I'm happy you have so far. I don't like it when other people punish you, that's Mommy's job. You show me the drawing you did of a fairy and prove that you've eaten all your lunch and had your medicine. I can tell you're excited about tonight because you're sending me makeup ideas you have. I love them all and cannot wait to take you out and talk to you about whatever grown-up thing crosses your little mind.

It feels like no time at all before I am sitting in a dark bar drinking a cocktail waiting for you. You're ten minutes late by the time you walk through the doors, and I smirk as I see a man double take you. I know you are purposely standing in the entrance, letting the sunset of the city illuminate your silhouette against the darkness of the bar. You eventually walk in and go to the bar, leaning against it and sticking out your bottom. A bunch of suits approaches the bar, and you giggle as you take your drink, making them excited. I stand and come up behind you, making them wonder if we are together or if I am just as predatory as they are. *Oh, little boys, I am both,* I think to myself as I push against your bottom and place my arms on either side of you on the bar. You turn in my arms and kiss me deeply.

"Mommy," you whisper into my mouth, and I pay for your drink and take your hand, leading you to the dark corner table I was previously sitting at.

"You look, beautiful baby," I say taking you all in. You've freshly blow-dried your hair and let it fall elegantly around your shoulders. You've chosen a fantastic natural look with your makeup, and your bodycon dark green dress looks like it was made for your body. You blush at my compliment and look down to your new pedicure. You're wearing the open toe dark cream heels I bought you last summer, and I'm happy you chose them they were too expensive to be kept locked up.

"So, how was work? Where are you stashing your rubber band ball?" I ask, mildly aware that people continue to steal glances of us. You laugh and take out your phone, flicking through your photos. I do find it bizarre that your generation insists on having visuals for one on one conversations, but I allow it, noting how proud you are when you find what you are looking for.

"Well, we are going to take it in turns, so everyone gets to have it for a week, and we played straws to figure out who would get it first, and I kinda won," you say before showing me your phone. I smile and look down at the photo you're showing me and laugh at out loud. I look back up at you and see that you've been mesmerized by my raspy laugh and I love that I have such power over you.

"So we get to have it in the house this week, huh?" I ask raising an eyebrow to your happily nodding head. You have this whole grown-up thing going on while letting your sweet little self escape more and more, and I can hardly take it.

"Baby you are such a darling," I say full of love looking at you. We talk for a few more hours, and I turn down the people who come over to us. I love that you let me handle things like this you don't even bother registering that they are there and I think that makes them even more interested in you.

"I remember when you tried that on me, it didn't work on Mommy though did it, sweetie?" I say, referring to the man you just stared right through. You shake your head, your hair catching the dim lighting of the bar.

"You didn't let me, Mommy," you say in a hushed tone smiling at me.

"Do you think I should have?" I ask, already knowing the answer. You look horrified.

"No, Mommy!" You say placing your hand dramatically over your heart as I've just broken it. I stand and walk over to your side of the table and wrap an arm around you, instantly feeling you turn into me.

"Just checking baby girl, ready to go home with Mommy?" I ask kissing your neck and enjoying hearing your soft moans. You let your hands fall on my lap, and I have to remind myself that we are in public. I'd happily lay you down and take you right here in full view for everyone to see.

But then I'd be arrested, and jail isn't a good look. I take your hand and lead you out of the bar and can feel the people sad to see you go, making me blissfully happy.

It's late as we drive home and I let you take your heels off in the car.

"Is that enough of being a big girl for today?" I ask you as I take out your paci from my handbag and pop it in your mouth. You rest your head on the seat while looking at me.

"Yes, Mommy," you say softly as you bite down on your paci. You reach into your backpack you keep in the backseat of my car and take out bunny.

"I didn't know you took her today sweetie." You haven't taken bunny out for ages, and I'm surprised, but you giggle.

"I thought I might need her today Mommy," you reply cuddling her and showing her the stars. I reach over and rub my hand under your dress, and you close your eyes until we get home.

"Come on sleepy girl," I say taking you out of the car holding your hand. I push my tailored suit pant pocket into your hip, waiting you to reach in and take out the keys, which you do and open the door for us.

"Thank you for helping Mommy sweet girl," I say, putting everything down and taking your dress off. You take off your panties and bra and pass them to me.

"Bath time baby," I say, and you instinctively head towards the bathroom. I put your clothes in the wash basket and hear that you've already turned the water on.

"Careful little one," I say making sure the water isn't too hot. I decide to bathe with you tonight, and you go into full organization mode to make sure we have enough bath toys.

"That's enough," I say calling it quits on five duckies, your bath crayons, and two water pistols. You pout and put down your bubble, making octopus and climb into the bathtub with Mommy. You love bathing with Mommy and are busy passing me toy after another, but I put them to the side and tickle you under the water.

"Mommy no!" You squeal, and I disappear under the water, laying flat and being impressed with the huge tub I bought. You reach under the water for me, not wanting to get your hair wet and grab onto my breasts and squeeze them, making me come back up for air. I'm wiping the water from my eyes when you squirt me with your water pistol, resulting in me splashing you.

"Hey," you giggle coping a mouthful of water and choking on it a little bit. I laugh and pull you into my arms.

"Oh did Mommy play too rough baby?" I tease patting your back and taking a cloth to wash you clean. You shake your head no as you splash me but stop when I look down at you in the playful but very serious manner I've mastered.

Thankful that we ate while we were out, I take you out of the bath and dry you off. You escape into your nursery as I turn around to pull the bath plug out and I walk in after you.

"This one please Mommy," you confidently say holding a princess printed diaper up to me.

"Do you feel like Mommy's little princess baby girl?" I ask, pushing you down on your changing mat and begin to diaper you. You try to help me tonight, and I laugh as I swat your hands away, which makes you giggle.

"This isn't a game baby," I say making you stop. I go to your cupboard and take out a pink long sleeve onesie, and you fuss as I try to dress you.

"Baby," I say warningly and spank your thigh to show I mean business. My silk robe tie is tickling your tummy, and you pull on it opening it up. I sit back and look at you, trying to figure out what is going on with you and where your head is at. You sit up and cuddle me. *Playful,* I decide and turn you on your tummy and playfully spank you to remind you who's the boss. You giggle and roll around.

"Someone is very playful tonight. Are you all excited, baby?" I ask, doing up my robe again.

You reach for it, but I tilt my head at you, and you know better than to persist.

"I am so happy, Mommy," you say, reaching up for me again. I pull you into my lap and force you to nurse. I do enjoy it when you are slightly forced to suckle from Mommy, it makes you suck harder, and Mommy loves the feeling of your little mouth pulling on my nipples. You settle down and hold my hand while you nurse, looking up at me lovingly.

"There's my good girl," I say as I pat your tummy gently. You have your fill, and I let you play in your nursery while I watch from the rocking chair. You got a race car track for your birthday, and you are busy constructing new paths for your cars to race on for the next hour. I get up to go to the kitchen for a snack, and when I come back, you have moved onto creating what you've called a dinosaur jungle museum. You are showing your stuffies through the museum by the time I tell you that it's bedtime and you look at me like I've just said the meanest thing to you.

"Come on, darling, in your cot, which stuffies do you want tonight?" I say as you point to what turns out to be all of them. Your cot looks like a toy store shelf, and I turn off your light and rub your back until you fall asleep.

You're fast asleep as the clock alarm goes off. I leave you in bed and get ready. I place my necklace against my skin and feel your hands clasp it in place for me.

"Good morning, Mommy," you whisper in my ear, kissing my cheek. I take your hand and sit you on my lap.

"I didn't hear you get up, darling," I say holding you close.

"I know you're tired today, baby, but I'm so proud of you for going to work. You are such a good girl and Mommy is so happy to call you my baby," I say kissing you on the tip of your nose. You make soft happy noises, and I hold you for as long as you need before you get up by yourself and go to get dressed.

"Last day of the week baby," I say following you into my cupboard as you take out your uniform. I help you with your tie as usual and I you reach up for extra cuddles.

"It won't be long until you're back with Mommy and bunny baby," I say trying to give you all my lovies to get you through the day. You're such a good girl going to work when you don't want to, and I'm so impressed with how you can be a big girl when you don't want to be.

I make you a smoothie and put it in your sippy cup, and you come to the table like a good girl. I put your coloring book in front of you and you color while you have breakfast and I see the little sparkle in your eye returning.

"I don't wanna go, Mommy," you say, and I nod my head understandingly.

"I know my baby, but we all must do things we don't want to, and it's only for a few hours. I know you can be a big girl for a few hours and then you can come home and stay Mommy's sweet princess for two whole days. You're so lucky, baby! I haven't told you the great things we are doing this weekend, but you've got to get through one more work day before you can have them. The fun things start on Saturday, and it is still Friday. So even if you didn't go to work you still wouldn't get them yet, so you might as well go baby," I say hoping to give you something to hold onto today. You nod your little head while you color, understanding what Mommy is saying and I write you a special note and stick it on your sandwich container you'll take for lunch.

"Will there be stickers involved, Mommy?" You ask. I smile and come around to sit next to you.

"There will be baby. There might also be a new stuffie for you. Does that sound good?" I ask and see you clap your hands excited about the weekend.

"But I have to go to work first, but then it'll be fun time," you say nodding your head, and I think you're talking more to yourself than to me.

"That's right darling," I say replying to you anyway. You push your coloring book to the side and sit up with determination.

"Then can we leave now, I'm finished

breakfast," you say making me smile.

You go to brush your teeth and finish getting ready, and I do the same. I'm waiting at the door ready to go as you race around the house packing your toys away. I honestly don't know how they can always need packing and rearranging; it's not as though you have even made a mess of them this morning. I think it's more like you want to cuddle them all before you go more than actually packing anything away. I tap my heel on the slate floor entrance of our house, impatiently.

"Come on, let's go," I say looking at my watch. You race into the living room, grab your backpack, and are at my side in a moment. I take your hand and lead you down the path for the last time this week.

"You won't have to do this tomorrow little one; you'll have the whole day with Mommy," I say to you as you happily skip by my side.

"And stickers!" You exclaim as I buckle you into your seat.

I drive to the station and say goodbye to you,

sending you a voice message after you get on the train.

"Good girl for going to work today, sweetheart, Mommy loves you so much, and I'll see you very soon. We can do all sorts of fun things tonight because you've been such a good girl for me today," I record. I get an emoji reply of unicorns and rainbows and ghosts, and I know you're going to be ok today.

I send you a message in the afternoon, sending you the times to the cinema and asking if you'd like to go. You reply almost instantly sending me a selfie, of your excited little face all lit up. As I am looking at your cute little face, I see you are calling me. Surprised, I answer the phone. I'm in my office and get up to shut the door; these animals don't need to hear how lovely I am to my little princess.

"Hi baby, this is a lovely surprise," I say, sitting down in my office chair and turning around to look out the window.

"Hey Mommy, I hope you don't mind that I

called I know you're at work, but I just wanted to say that yes I'd love to go to the movies and that I'll be finished a little later today because someone called in sick." I'm happy that someone wasn't you and I smile as I gently swing side to side in my chair. I wish you were here in my arms and I could show you the view from my lap. We decide what to see, and I tell you that I'll buy our snacks before you get there. Excitedly you hang up the phone, and I stay sitting by the window a little longer. *I'm such a great Mommy; I love that I can you what you need and more,* I think to myself before turning back around to yell at some interns.

Happily, I leave work and walk to the cinema. You aren't there yet, so I go inside and collect our tickets and snacks. You love gummy bears, so I buy you those, and I buy myself a chocolate bar and a small popcorn for us to share. I don't have to wait for very long until you are walking down the street towards me. You are so cute, you've loosened your tie and taken your hair out, and it catches the last rays of sunlight beautifully.

"Hi, Mommy," you say out loud, and I love that people don't take any notice. I hand you your gummy bears, and you rip the packet open and begin searching for all the red ones. I laugh and take you inside. We watch the movie, and I put my arm around you, enjoying how you feel leaning against me. I give you a bite of my chocolate bar and hold it to your mouth, letting you bite it yourself. You happily share the popcorn, we've been working on sharing, and I am pleased with how well you're behaving. The movie ends, and we walk back to my office building, where I left my car and began to drive home. You tell me all about your day and how you had hotel guests who tipped you $100 because you found their lost wedding ring. I say you can keep that money and use some of it this weekend to buy things that I won't buy you like extra stickers or something else that takes your fancy.

"Imagine if you didn't go to work today, how sad that you would have missed out on such a great tip for helping those people," I say as you look at your bill. You look up at me and smile, completely content with the world.

We run the car through the car wash on the way home, so it's all nice for the weekend, and pull in at 9 pm.

"If you're hungry little one Mommy can make our grilled cheeses, and we can play a little bit longer, but you are going to bed at 11 do you understand?" I ask flicking the lights on and going to the kitchen.

"Yes, Mommy, can I have a grilled cheese please?" You ask, taking off your shoes and placing them neatly at the door.

"May I please have a shower tonight, Mommy?" You ask coming up to me and hugging me. I look down at your pretty little face and kiss you.

"Sure, but be careful alright, darling," I say as you skip down the hall.

I make my grilled cheese first still hearing you in the shower. You are happily singing, moreover, performing, and I tap on the bathroom door asking you to hurry up.

"Yes, Mommy!" You sing out, and I like that I hear that water is turned off immediately. I stay standing outside the door, I don't mind that you want to be a little bit bigger tonight, I'll give you your grilled cheese and milky's, and you'll be right back to my sweet baby.

True to form, you finish your grilled cheese just for me to unbutton my blouse and hold my breast to your mouth. You try to push me away.

"Oh don't be naughty little miss," I say swatting your hands away and making you suckle. You stop fighting me after your first mouthful and nurse like the good little girl you are.

"That's it, baby," I say enjoying this. You drink Mommy's milk until I have none left and I let you play in your nursery while I shower.

As I put on my pajamas, I hear you crawling out of your nursery and into my room. You stop when you see me and look up shocked to see me almost waiting for you.

"I was wondering when you'd show up miss," I say. You give me a cheeky smile trying to get away with whatever trouble you were about to get into.

"Come on, if you stay naked you'll get sick," I say, taking you back to your nursery.
You go to your cupboard and shake your head to everything I take out for you to wear. Deciding you've lost your right to choose; I take out what I want you in, you try to fight me as I dress you. I take down the wrist cuffs and put them next to you.

"Do you want to fight Mommy baby? I have no trouble punishing you and then dressing you if that's what you want?" I say sternly. You pout but let me dress you. I make your diaper particularly thick tonight to drive home the message that I'm in charge. I tie your hair up and finish it off with a pink bow and turn down your light. I let you play for a little while longer. Your playing tonight it just lazily rolling around on your teddy bear but you calm down, and I come to sit next to you. You sit in between my thighs, and I wrap my legs around you while you lean against my breasts, and I read you a story. You love this one and touch all the characters and repeat what they say, so it takes twice as long to get through it, but I don't mind. It's nice reading to you and seeing your little face look up at me all excited and awestruck by the story you've heard a hundred times before.

"That's it little one," I say as I close the book. You look at me sad it's over. I shake my head no already knowing what will come next.

"We aren't reading it again, it's bedtime now," I say before you can ask. You sigh and crawl over to your cot and look back at me.

"You're wrong about that too baby," I begin to explain. You look at me, confused.

"You'll sleep with Mommy tonight," I instruct. Clapping your hands, you crawl back over to me and give me a big cuddle.

"Come on," I say, taking your hand. I push you up onto my bed and join you from the other side. You have forgotten bunny and blankie, so I go back to find them in the living room. Coming back you have snuck onto my side of the bed, and I tickle you until you move back over to your spot.

"Here," I say covering you in your blankie.

"Look, Mommy, I'm a ghost," you say, hiding under your blankie. I pull you into me and turn off the light.

"Are you Mommy's ghost?" I ask in a sleepy voice. I can feel you nodding yes, and I take your paci from the nightstand and push it into your mouth.

"Night night baby girl," I say kissing you goodnight.

"Goodnight Mommy," you reply taking out your paci to answer before I push it back in.

The sun was pouring through the windows when I woke you up this morning. After such a big day yesterday, I am not surprised that you are still asleep. I stroke your forehead making you stir. I love that when you wake up, I'm the first thing you'll see this morning. You open your eyes and see Mommy staring down at you and you.

"Good morning, sweet girl," I say, leaning down to kiss you. You giggle and reach up to play with my hair as it falls on your face.

"Is Mommy's hair tickling you, baby," I say making you nod your sleepy head. Your paci has tangled up in your blankies, and you've kicked your sockies off during the night. You jump off the bed, and I see you going to your little room in Mommy's room.

"Go lie on your changing mat baby girl, Mommy needs to get you all nice and clean," I say as you head for your toy box. You turn mid crawl and head over to your changing mat.

"Sweet little girl," I say as I come behind you and turn you on your back. I unclip the bottom of your blue and white cloud onesie and wriggle it off your body.

"Not that one please Mommy," you say to the diaper I was going to change you into. I look at it.

"What's wrong with the princess one's baby?" I ask, yesterday you chose these above all the other ones.

"Can I please have animals instead?" You ask. You're such a good girl for Mommy I don't see why you couldn't have the one you want so I lean over to the shelf and take down an animal print diaper. There are not many of these left, and I make a note to buy more for you tonight.
I wipe you down and sprinkle the fresh powder over your making sure to rub it all in so you don't get any hurties and then fasten your diaper. It's raining today, so we won't be able to go into the garden like I had planned for this morning so

instead I put you in a white bunny onesie and give you your purple glitter paci.

"There, little one all done and ready for the day. Mommy is going to make your yogurt and muesli for breakfast, how does that sound?" I ask taking your hand and leading you out into the open kitchen and living space. You nod your head and run back into your nursery. I wait for you, and you come out with bunny, and I look at you shocked.

"I can't believe you were going to leave bunny behind!" I say making you giggle.

"I didn't leave her behind Mommy; she was sleeping," you explain to me. I let you play with the train set you have set up under your coloring in table and watch as you play.

"Such a sweet girl," I say to myself as I make our breakfast.

I come over to you and sit at your coloring in table making you laugh.

"You're silly, Mommy," you say as I feed you. I take a spoonful of muesli and yogurt and get it in your mouth as you push a train past me. You are not making it easy for Mommy today, but I don't mind. I drink my coffee and feed you when I get the chance and am grateful neither of us has to go to work today because we'd already be very late.

"So what can we do today baby girl?" I ask. You swing your head around, remembering that I told you we would go to the store to buy stickers.

"Stickers," you say like a sticker demon has overtaken your soul. I laugh at you; you're very serious about stickers. You have a sticker folder which you are constantly trying to add to and have been working on the sparkle sticker section for some time now.

"Well, how about this, we finish breakfast, and Mommy has to work for about an hour, and after that, we go to the store? You could even see if there's something you want to spend your $100 tip on?" I suggest watching as your eyes light up. You take a piece of paper and your blue crayon and begin writing down a list of things you want to get. I put on a movie for you and kiss your forehead as I go into my study.

When I come back just over an hour later you have, much to my surprise, dressed and are sitting on the couch watching the movie with bunny. I look at you and raise an eyebrow.

"I'm all ready to go, Mommy," you say proudly. I look at what you've chosen. You have your grey fluffy knit sweater, and a pair of skinny black jeans rolled up at the ankles and your maroon sneakers.

"Very cute little girl. But you forgot one thing," I say making you pull a face trying to think about what it is. I go to your nursery and take out a maroon bow and attach it to your ponytail.

"There, now you are ready. I hope you're still wearing your diaper, you know how Mommy likes you to have a diaper on when you are wearing your jeans little girl," I say knowing full well you won't have a diaper on. You look down nervously and then look back up at me.

"I forgot Mommy, can you do it for me?"

You ask in your little voice, back to being my baby. I take your hand, and this time, I chose which diaper you'll have. I chose a thick one that will rub on your pussy the whole time you're in your jeans because they are so tight. You know this and begin to squirm, but I hold you down long enough to get it on you and your jeans zipped back up.

"There," I say in satisfaction as I rub your bottom through your jeans. I know you can feel your diaper being pushed into you and it makes me happy knowing you'll feel it all day. I let you play in your nursery as I go and get changed out of my pajamas and into something a little more, Mommy. I like to dress from the heel up, and I've selected a pair of deep red heels, the pair that makes the sound of pure authority with each confident stride. It's the pair of heels I wore when we first met, and I'll never forget the look of absolute submission you gave, winning me over. Next, I select the black lace panty and bra set you bought me last Christmas. You had my assistant ring ten places before you found the one you knew

I'd want and I did enjoy how you bent her over backward until you knew I'd be satisfied. I see your little head peeping around the door, so I decide to do my makeup and hair next to let you enjoy the view.

"Are you spying on Mommy little girl?" I ask, making you blush red.

"Come in then; I'd hate for you to be denied any of me," I say more seductively than I had planned. You crawl in, and I look at how cute you are, my little teddy bear.

"How should Mommy have her hair, today, baby? What do you think will look prettiest," I ask teasing you. I know you would take me right now if I let you, but this is payback for your cute little strip tease earlier in the week. You'll get nothing today but horny denial.

"Maybe have it down, Mommy," you say coming closer. I point a finger at you, making you stop.

"That's far enough my good girl," I say, you look so disappointed. I hold my hair up and then let it fall out of my hands and cascade down my back making your mouth gaped open with desire. I smile to myself. I finish doing my makeup and strut over to my cupboard, gently pushing you to the floor with my heel and pinning you there as I pass you. You let me, hardly resisting and I love that your eyes are full of so much love and lust and raw sexual desire.

"You know, Mommy never saw what you had on under your perfect little sweater. Show me," I instruct making you lift your sweater slowly. You know how I like you to undress for me. I see you've got on a soft lemon t-shirt and I almost jump on you right there and then.

"Could you be more adorable?" I ask, making you blush. I let you pull your sweater back down as I take out the wrap around white dress and my black trench coat and do the tie at the back. I look at myself in the mirror and am impressed with what I see.

"Do you think Mommy looks, pretty baby?" I say snapping my fingers at you making you involuntarily stand.

"Yes, Mommy," you say almost as if you were in a dream. I laugh and take your hand and lead you out the door.

You are squirming around in your seat in the car as I drive us to the store, and I put my hand on your thigh to make you stop.

"You're only going to make it rub more if you keep moving," I say, lowering my voice. You whimper, disappointed you have no release and wait patiently as I park. I take your hand and lead you into the different shops. Despite your adult age, our difference in height and dress style makes you look much younger, and I like it that people don't pay any attention to you when you call me Mommy. I take you into your favorite sticker shop, and you chose three packs of stickers, and the cashier pays no mind as I hold your hand on the way out, and you thank Mommy for your stickers.

"Do you think we could go to the toy store next Mommy?" You question. I look at you and see that this is where you're tip will be spent and nod my head as I take you in.

There are toys everywhere, and after 30 minutes, I wish there was a place for me to sit while you gush over the toys. This will be the last time you'll be in here for about a month, so I let you have your fun. You eventually have narrowed your choice down to a box of building blocks, two trains, a pink dinosaur stuffie and what looks like a cat/raccoon stuffie with sparkly paws.

"Have you got anything left after this?" I ask, referring to any possible change you might get. You nod your head impressed with yourself, and I take you to pay. The cashier gives you a $20 back, and I take it for you, putting it into my purse.

"It will not be spent today," I say to you playfully, and you smile knowing that you can trust Mommy with your money but that I have just laid down the law.

Your bags are heavy, so I take them for you as we head back to the car.

"Mommy, we didn't get you anything!" You

say as if you've just realized something terrible. I smile and shake my head.

"Mommy doesn't want anything today baby girl," I reply honestly. Today was all about you and rewarding you for being such a big girl on Friday. We drive back home, and you spend the next few hours pottering around the house, organizing your new toys and planning out where you are going to put your stickers. You are very serious about this, so serious that you don't even mind that you are still in your big girl clothes. As night falls, I pull you out of your play to bathe and change you into your jammies.

"It's been such a big day Mommy," you say before explaining to me stuffie drama because kitty is now jealous of the new kitty. I love the stories you tell me, and I listen and respond appropriately. You're talking doesn't stop until you are nursing in my arms as I rock you in the rocking chair and it's as though all of the day's excitement comes crashing around you and you're asleep almost instantly. You keep lazily sucking, and I hold you to me for hours just rocking you and giving you all my love. I eventually guide you into your cot and kiss your goodnight, saying, "Mommy loves you."

Clare's Naughty Girl

An MDLG and ABDL story of a lesbian Mistress who trains a brat to be Mommy's good girl

By Tina Moore

Chapter 1

Clare had been focused, driven, and very alone for as long as she could remember, so it was not uncommon for her to be early to work. In fact, for as long as she could remember, she had been early for everything. Her attentive nature prevented her from ever being late, even when she had accidentally overslept one morning before work. Today would be no different as she picked up a bagel on her way into the office. Clare had worked for a large accounting firm in the heart of the city for the past six years. During that time, she had quietly gone about her business, happily avoiding the office bullies who always had a new piece of gossip to share and popularity contests that reminded her of high school.

"I can't believe Stacey is wearing his ex-wife's necklace," Clare heard Holly gossip on the way down the corridor.

Holly was one of those women who stopped men in their tracks and who made wives jealous. She had the typical vogue look of full, bouncy blonde waves of hair which tumbled down her back. Her blue eyes looked like sapphires, and her soft pink lips were contrasted against her creamy white skin. She had a slender figure, one which often made Clare wonder why she was an accountant instead of a model. Clare, on the other hand, could be described as naturally beautiful, however, was not painted with the same elixir as Holly. Clare maintained short manicured nails in a light shade of beige; her hair was a mahogany brown falling straight down her back, and her green eyes were nothing out of the ordinary.

"I know, the divorce isn't even settled yet, and he is already giving her stuff away to the next. What a jerk, and what a mole for actually accepting it. It's bad enough that they all work on the same floor, they don't need to rub it in her face," said one of Holly's minions.

Holly turned around to see Clare behind her and

her friend Tracey.

"What do you think about it, then?" Holly asked Clare. Clare wishing she hadn't, turned and looked out the wall-length window which gave a 180' view of the city.

"I don't think it's any of our business," Clare replied, being less than amused. Holly, unsatisfied with her answer, waved her hand dismissively.

"I knew you would say that," Holly stated turning left at the end of the corridor making Clare relieved she was going in the opposite direction.

Grateful that Friday night had finally arrived, Clare jumped out of the shower and looked at herself in the mirror. Her full double D breasts were going to look amazing in the leather bra and top she was planning on giving a whirl tonight. She pulled on her black leather pants and zipped up her matching boots as she put her hair up in a high, slicked-back ponytail and put her whip in her bag. She walked around her house topless as she made herself a drink and did her makeup. Dark smoky unforgiving eyes stared back at her as she applied a dark shade of red to her lips. Highlighting her cheekbones, she sipped her drink and began thinking of the fun the night would bring. She walked back into her bedroom and put on her new bra, and top enjoying the tight feeling of it against her toned body. Flicking through social media and chatting with a few girls online, Clare finished her drink but stayed chatting until the conversation became boring. Closing her laptop lid, and taking one last look in the mirror as she grabbed her wallet, and keys, she headed out the door.

She arrived at the party 3 hours after it had started. She didn't consider this late she considered this making sure the party was in full swing by the time she got there. As she walked up to the warehouse, a sudden flash of blonde hair from the entrance caught her attention. Clare smiled, knowing that tonight would be fun. She had been looking forward to this party for weeks.

The host was a close friend of hers, and she had explained that there would be different rooms for different types of kink. Clare was excited. Usually, she had to choose between attending to a Mommy Domme party or something more aligned with her strict, merciless Mistress side. Tonight she was hoping she could combine both.

Clare followed the blonde haired woman into the party and was not disappointed. She made her way through the crowds of people. There was a large circular bar in the middle of the warehouse with topless slave girls and boys which you could write a message on while you ordered. Although the warehouse was only one level, the way Clare's friend Sophie had sent up the rooms made it look unusually large. Clare ordered two shots of whiskey followed by a vodka lemonade chaser, grabbing her waitresses jaw and writing something obscene along her throat. Clare shot the whiskey and got up to mingle, running into a few people she knew along the way. As the music echoed through the warehouse, Clare found herself going from room to room. She had no interest in half of them, but she was thorough and didn't want to miss a thing. Leaving the puppy playpen behind, she made her way to the flogging stations and finished her drink as she watched a pretty girl be whipped by three people. Going into the next room, Clare smiled wickedly at what she saw. The feel of this room was unlike the others as Mommies and Daddies played with babies, sat around watching babies play or were punishing their naughty little ones. But what made Clare's blood burn with desire was the baby playing by herself in the corner. Clare sat down and watched her. She was playing with a set of blocks, making a tower and then knocking it over, giggling to herself. Clare got up and walked over to her, kneeling and enjoying the woman's surprised face.

"Hey Baby," Clare said sweetly, taking a block and putting it onto the blonde's tower. The baby was lost for words as she stared at Clare.

"What are you playing?" Clare asked.

"Blocks," the pink diapered baby replied

blushing slightly and looking down at the ground.

"Can I play too?" Clare said, smiling as the baby nodded her head.

"You're good at that Holly," Clare said as Holly pushed over the tower she and Clare had just built. Holly giggled and reached for Clare who pulled her onto her lap.

"Does the baby like cuddles?" Clare said cuddling Holly tight. Holly nodded and turned her head; a nervous look came across her face.

"Clare, you won't tell anyone about this, will you?" Holly asked fearfully. Clare liked seeing the most popular woman at work almost shake in fear in her arms. She took her time to reply, looking down and rubbing the front of Holly's thick diaper.

"Mm, I don't know," Clare said when she finally replied making Holly hold her breath.

"Of course I'll keep it to myself, little baby. I wouldn't want to see those pretty eyes cry!" Clare said feeling Holly's body settle into her arms.

"Thanks," Holly said, looking down,

suddenly embarrassed to be seen like this by Clare. Holly had heard the stories about how Clare was weird and into all sorts of dark magic and stuff. Seeing her tonight Holly knew that none of that was right she was as weird as she was.

The night carried on with Clare and Holly playing together before Clare kissed her on her forehead and went back into the flogging room and went to work on a slaves back. She was almost satisfied when the lights of the warehouse were turned on, and the music stopped suddenly.

"Oh I hate how she does that," Clare said, referring to Sophie's method of ending a party. She rolled her eyes and began to walk out of the room and bumped into Holly, who had changed back into adult clothes. Clare took in her short schoolgirl skirt and white buttoned top, grabbing hold of her tie and pulling Holly towards her. Holly giggled and looked to the floor.

"The party is over Clare," Holly said nervously as she looked down and kicked at the ground.

"For some," Clare replied seductively reaching out and lifting Holly's head so her eyes met hers. She leaned forward and whispered in Holly's ear as she ran her hand up and down her back. When Clare had finished talking, Holly nodded and followed her to her car, reaching for her hand, which made Clare excited. She liked to have girls need her, to want her to love them and Holly's, take me now, attitude had always excited her.

"I'm interested to see your place," Holly said as Clare drove them to her house. Clare looked at Holly and placed her hand on Holly's thigh, caressing it gently.

"Show me," Clare said in a low voice, taking Holly's hand and pulling it towards the top of her skirt. Holly giggled as she began to play with herself. Clare bit her bottom lip as Holly's giggles turned to moans and she watched as Holly came in her passenger seat.

"Did I say you could come?" Clare asked as she pulled into her driveway. Holly looked at Clare apologetically.

"That won't work on me pretty baby," Clare stated bluntly. She unlocked her front door and pulled Holly inside by her schoolgirl tie.

"Strip," Clare ordered over her shoulder as she made her way into her bedroom. Holly was unsure of where exactly Clare wanted her, so she took her clothes off and waited for Clare to return. When Clare came back, she was topless and holding a baby blanket. Holly's eyes were wide, and her heart was racing.

"Come and cuddle Mommy Holly," Clare instructed sitting on the couch and waiting for Holly to join her. Holly's naked body felt cold as Clare wrapped her in the blanket.

"Now, tell Mommy what kind of things you like sweetie. Let me know all your dirty little secrets," Clare said, beginning to stroke Holly's arm up and down. Clare had whispered in Holly's ear the things she had wanted to do to her, but she always wanted to know what her playmates wanted as well. Mostly, Clare just she liked to use it as leverage to push a limit slightly.

"In like sex or with general age play?" Holly replied, seeking clarification. Clare kissed her forehead.

"Both," she bluntly said.

"Well, in sex I like being penetrated, my clit is kinda useless, and I don't feel much. I like anal but not being fisted there. I like being spanked but not whipped or canned, and I like being gagged with anything except for feet." Holly thought for a moment before continuing.

"I like being tied up, but I don't really like being hurt too much. And age play stuff, I am pretty general. I like cuddles and Mommy time and diapers, and I love playing with building blocks," Holly explained. Clare had given Holly her undivided attention and enjoyed watching as Holly lit up when talked about what she liked as a baby. *So, she'll let me fuck her, but it's love she's really after,* Clare thought to herself noticing the animated way Holly spoke.

"What do you like?" Holly asked Clare. She

moved Holly onto her breast and made her suck her nipple while she replied.

"As a general, I like spanking naughty girls firmly. I like dressing them in leather while they are in their diapers and I like to mercilessly use them as pretty little fuck-dolls. I think I might be too rough for you, sweetheart. I love treating my little girl like a princess, but I thoroughly enjoy disciplining her. Clare moved Holly to her other breast and lovingly stroked her hair.

"We could still try though Mommy," Holly said around Clare's breast. Clare looked down at Holly who was happily sucking and licking her nipple.

"Oh yeah, I'm going to let you try," Clare agreed, taking Holly's hand and leading her to the floor. She went back into her room, and when she came out again, she was jerking her leather harnessed strap-on.

"You don't look like a little girl anymore, Holly; you look like a little slut, so I'm going to fuck you like one. Kneel," Clare instructed. Holly knelt before her and Clare slapped her cheek with her cock before pushing it past Holly's lips and down her throat, making her gag instantly.

"Swallow," Clare commanded ramming her cock further down Holly's throat, smiling as tears rolled down her face. Holly's saliva dripped from around Clare's cock and onto her tits which delighted Clare. She bent down slightly and pulled hard on Holly's nipples making her open her mouth wider as she yelped in pain. Clare took the opportunity to force her thick cock deeper into Holly's mouth and would pull on her nipples when she felt like Holly's mouth wasn't full enough. Clare roughly fucked Holly's mouth until Holly couldn't feel her jaw and had given up trying to push Clare away, instead she had taken it like the fuck-doll Clare was using her as.

"Here," Clare said, taking her cock out of Holly's mouth and snapping her fingers towards the floor. Holly lay down on her back on Clare's living room floor, and Clare went to her bedroom once more. This time when she came out Clare carried a big teddy bear, a pacifier and another blanket. She pulled Holly to her feet and held her as she put the teddy bear on the floor, the blanket over the top and pushed Holly back down next. Clare wrapped the blanket around Holly and rubbed the pacifier over her spit covered cock before pushing it gently into Holly's mouth. Clare grabbed her hips and turned her over, so Holly was laying tummy down on top of the adult-sized teddy bear. She lifted Holly's hips and rubbed her cock up and down her wet slit before using the tip of the cock to part them.

"Pretty baby," Clare said slapping Holly's left ass cheek.

"I'm going to spank this slutty little ass until you let me in do you understand?" Clare explained. Holly nodded her head as Clare came down on her right ass cheek, making her bottom jiggle. Clare grabbed two big handfuls of Holly's bubble butt and pushed herself into her pussy, spanking her left cheek again when she was still not inside of Holly. Holly moaned and wriggled under Clare's touch getting wetter and wetter as Clare spanked her. Clare grabbed Holly's reddening ass after a series of spanks and pushed against her pussy again, feeling Holly's submission. Just as an hour passed, Holly gave in, falling limp on the teddy which was now covered in her cum and Clare finally filled her with her cock making Holly cry out but not refuse her.

"Did you think I'd give up little girl?" Clare asked as she powerfully thrust into Holly's pussy, making her gasp each time Clare filled her. Holly just nodded.

"I thought I could outlast you," she said breathlessly through moans and gasps. Clare laughed as she pounded Holly's pussy.

"Outlast Mommy? I don't think so," Clare replied, feeling Holly close to cumming. Holly felt it too as she clenched her pussy and released feeling the warm liquid of her squirting cunt drip out from around Clare's cock. Impressed with herself, Clare kept her cock inside of Holly who wriggled uncomfortably underneath her.

"What's the magic word, baby?" Clare prompted knowing that Holly had had enough.

"Please," Holly said breathlessly.

"Please Mommy," Clare said, ramming her again making her squeal.

"Please Mommy," Holly half begged and sighed with relief, happy to feel Clare gently pull out of her. Holly shuddered as the aftershock of her intense orgasm hit her, and her pussy leaked cum onto the teddy bears thigh. Clare smiled and took off her cock. She laid down next to Holly, who weakly smiled at her, completely spent and laying in her cum.

"Shower and bed little one?" Clare asked nodding Holly. She took Holly's hand and gently lifted her, holding her lovingly as Holly adjusted to standing. Clare led her to the bathroom, where she ran a warm shower and took off her pants. She pushed Holly under the water and watched as Holly began to wash. Clare enjoyed the surprised look on Holly's face when she turned around, and Holly saw her back piece.

"I didn't know your whole back was tattooed," she said in amazement. Clare just raised an eyebrow and got into the shower with Holly.

"I want you gone by morning little one," Clare said, pulling Holly in for a cuddle. Although she was kicking her out, she still wanted Holly to be alright with it.

"Yeah, sure. Clare?" Holly asked Clare, who was shaking her head.

"Mommy," Clare corrected to a nodding Holly who looked down at her feet. The water felt nice on her spanked red ass, and Clare noticed a bratty smile come across her face.

"Mommy. My bottom doesn't even feel sore anymore. Guess you're not as tough as you think you are," Holly teased. Clare smirked, and before Holly could say another word, Clare had Holly's neck firmly in her grip and had taken off the shower head from its mounted position. She flicked the cold water down and held the shower head right onto Holly's freshly fucked cunt. Holly squirmed and squealed as Clare remained plain-faced as she let the warmer water run onto Holly's sensitive skin.

"Do you still want to play stupid little games with me baby girl?" Clare said after two minutes. Holly shook her head.

"I can't hear you, baby," Clare replied to Holly's response.

"No, Mommy!" Holly half yelled, desperate to have the high pressured warm water off her aching pussy. Clare kept the shower head on Holly for another minute before taking it away and pushing her down onto the shower floor. Clare got out of the shower and went to the cupboard. She took out a jar of expensive lotion and threw it into the shower at Holly.

"Don't fuck with Mommy Holly; it'll never end well for you," Clare instructed bluntly as she left the bathroom and turned the light off behind her.

Chapter 2

Clare was on a high all weekend as she replayed her evening with Holly. It had felt good to blow off some steam from the work week. She was all smiles as she dressed in her high-end business attire. A section of her cupboard that felt more like drag. In these clothes, Clare felt the collar and leash of her bosses. In her leather pants and whip, she felt like herself. *Everyone's someone's bitch*, Clare thought as she entered her office. Clare had made her way up to the sixth floor of the ten-story building but was more than interested in making it to the top. If her progress on her ten-year plan was anything to go by, she was right on track. Looking out her office window into the building, she saw Holly walk up the corridor. Holly turned her head and smiled meekly at Clare as she passed, causing Clare to sigh in contented bliss as she got back to the pile of paperwork which had made its way to her desk. But true to form, Holly had converted back to her bratty, self-righteous ways come lunchtime and was swaying her hips as she walked back down the corridor.

"Good afternoon Mr. Haze," she said as she passed one of the partners in her high pitched. I'm ready to be bent over and used as a cum dumpster type of manner. Clare watched as she looked into her office and gave a small victorious huff and walked away.

"And then, you'll never guess who I saw. I was coming out of Barry's Bar, and there she was, full leather, a dominatrix with this dude with a pink collar standing next to her. She must have been to some fancy dress party or something I had thought, but then he knelt on the dirty sidewalk and sat at her feet while she halted a taxi. It was so weird," Holly said, telling her friends a story over lunch. Clare had been sitting on the other side of the large potted plants and had heard the whole conversation. How when Holly's friends had asked her what she did on the weekend she had made up a complete lie. Clare would have been fine with Holly lying about what she did. But it was that she had lied about what Clare had done that had made her blood boil. *As if I would be caught dead with a gimp boy at my feet,* Clare thought as she angrily ate her salad as Holly and her friends laughed at the lies Holly was telling them. The last thing Clare wanted was this little bitch ruining her chance of a final promotion. She knew this would spread around the office like wild-fire, so she took the rest of the day off.

Hurt, Clare took the long way home. She walked past her favorite shops but didn't feel like going it. *Why would she feel like she needed to lie about anything? Why not tell them what she did on the weekend?* Clare thought to herself as she kicked a stone onto the road. Her sadness turned to anger by the time she got home, and she slammed the door shut to her apartment. *If she's there tonight I am going to fucking break her,* Clare thought to herself as she got ready to go to a kinksters meet and greet evening at one of her favorite bars. She wore her hair down tonight; it was not the scene where dress protocol was enforced. So she pulled on a smart pair of fitted black pants and an elegant red chiffon blouse matched with cream pumps. She wore a black fitted leather jacket over the top and a stare that could cut glass. Clare was still fuming from hearing Holly spread lies about her through the workplace and she was grateful none of her colleagues had her phone number. The last thing she wanted to do was get into a who did what and who said what over Holly's little games. Parking, Clare got out of her car and walked into the bar. She mingled with the usual people, slightly disappointed but slightly relieved that Holly wasn't there. As the night passed, Clare met several women she would have usually been happy to spend time with, and yet, tonight they seemed dull. She excused herself from the girl she had been talking to for the better part of an hour and decided to go home. She exited the bar and turned the corner to see Holly walking in the opposite direction. Smiling widely, Holly sped up to catch Clare who stopped walking and waited for Holly to reach her.

"Hi!" Holly exclaimed excitedly as she approached Clare. Clare just grabbed her by the wrist and firmly pulled her to the car.

"Hey, I wanted to go to the bar," Holly said as Clare unlocked her car. Clare looked at Holly with fire in her eyes.

"Get in," she roughly ordered. Holly made a pouty face and got into the car without a word. Clare went around to the driver's side and pulled out onto the street.

"Take off your panties," Clare ordered. Holly lifted her skirt almost without thinking and pulled them off.

"Play with your pussy, it'll be the only action it gets tonight," Clare explained. Holly reached down and began to stroke her clit.

"Keep your skirt up baby," Clare said in the kindest tone she had used with Holly knowing that she wanted to fuck with her mind tonight.

Mommy, can I please cum?" Holly begged.

Clare pulled into her driveway and pushed Holly's hand out-of-the-way and pulled her skirt down.

"No that's Enough. Come, baby," Clare said unbuckling Holly's seat belt. Holly got out and followed Clare into her house. This time Holly made it further than the living room as Clare took her into the bathroom straight away. She brought Holly to the bathroom counter and took a cake of soap out of her bathroom drawer and pushed it into Holly's mouth.

"Who the fuck do you think you are little one, making up lies about me," Clare angrily yelled as Holly struggled under her grip.

"I didn't," Holly tried to say, but the soap taste just intensified with her attempt to lie, so she shut up very quickly but continued to struggle.

"Don't even fucking try to tell me you didn't because I heard you, you little bitch," Clare added before taking out the cake of soap from her mouth. She ran the water for Holly who lapped it up eager to get the taste of soap out of her mouth.

"I'm sorry," Holly begged as she looked up

at Clare who was still furious. Clare didn't believe her, but there were still ways she could make sure Holly never lied about her again, and that was about to begin.

Clare took her out of the bathroom and into her bedroom. Holly looked around and took it all in. Clare's bedroom looked like a room from some vampire movie. It had high ceilings and a gothic style bed in the middle of the room. The candles illuminated dark linen Clare was lighting which sat on marble shelves that wrapped around the room. On the floor was a thick fur rug and there was a flogging cross in the corner facing the bed. Holly felt nervous.

"We are just still playing kinda safe right, Mommy?" She asked as Clare took one of the candles and brought it over to the bed where Holly was sitting. Clare nodded, and Holly felt her energy shift. She knew Clare was going to give her a wonderful time; she just hoped she could handle it. Clare affectionately pushed Holly down and kissed her lovingly enjoying feeling Holly's arms wrap around her, but Holly's shocked gasp broke their kiss as Clare poured candle wax onto her thigh.

"Shh, let Mommy show you some new things baby," Clare said in a low, slightly depraved voice. Holly, who was still fully clothed, reached down to pull her skirt up, not wanting to get wax on it. Clare noticed and smiled.

"Oh, does the baby want her pretty clothes to stay nice and clean?" She said as she deliberately poured wax over Holly's skirt before lifting it and pouring the leftover wax onto her panties. Holly gasped and moaned as the warm wax stimulated her clit. Clare put the candle down on the concrete floor and looked down at her plaything.

"Don't worry, Mommy will get you some new clothes baby girl," she said, slowly taking off Holly's ruined garments. Clare stood and took Holly's wrist firmly in her hand and pulled her over to the flogging cross. Clare's fingers were on Holly's pulse, and she felt her blood pump faster in her veins and laughed.

"I'm not going to hurt you, little girl," Clare reassured her as she tied both wrists high above her head. Clare stood back and saw Holly's elongated body. She pulled up her shirt and ran her fingernails over Holly's toned stomach, making her tense her muscles nervously.

"I guess you're going to stay there for Mommy until I'm done with you. Isn't that right baby?" Clare asked as she left the room. Ten minutes later, Holly was nervously sweating with the heat from the candles, and her nervousness and a trickle traced down her stomach delighting Clare who had returned.

"Don't you look divine and ready for the taking my pretty little doll," Clare said as she slapped Holly's thighs making her part them. Clare never broke eye contact with Holly as she began to rub her gently. Holly broke and looked behind Clare to see what she had bought back into the room. A bondage rope lay sprawled across the bed next to shiny gold and white pacifier gag, and a vibrating butt plug.

"Are you going to tie me up?" Holly said breathlessly. It was hot in the room now, and Clare ran both her hands through Holly's hair, slicking it back as she kissed her neck.

"Yes, baby girl," Clare replied lovingly. Tonight, she was going to use Holly until she was nothing more than her good girl knowing that she could stop at any time but refusing to. Clare took the gag, gently buckled it in place and rubbed Holly's pussy feeling how wet and eager she was. Clare was somewhat relieved Holly was still so willing to play and untied her from the cross. She smiled in amusement as Holly came in for a cuddle, needing to feel Clare's love and Clare filed away that Holly needed aftercare throughout playing not just after playing. Clare sat down on the bed with Holly and held her close, looking into Holly's sweet, vulnerable eyes after each kiss of her cheek and forehead.

"Do you want to keep going?" Clare asked and patted Holly to spread her thighs when she nodded yes. Clare placed one hand on Holly's chest, letting her weight drop and pinning Holly to the bed, making her gasp for each breath as she slowly snaked her fingers down to Holly's cunt.

"You'll feel this," Clare said as she spanked Holly's pussy with her full hand making Holly yelp from behind the gag. Clare rubbed her after each spank and enjoyed feeling Holly get wetter with each hit.

"You like this don't you baby," Clare asked coming down hard on Holly's wet pussy. Holly nodded, and Clare could see her trying to push past a limit. Clare spent longer rubbing Holly, made her spanks less painful, and loving smiled down at Holly as she pushed two fingers into her. Clare enjoyed at how open Holly's pussy was, how desperate she was to be fucked.

"I'm going to fist you, darling," Clare said and pushed her fist into Holly without further warning. Holly clenched her muscles but was too horny to be able to keep Clare out, and Clare began fisting Holly ever so gently. Holly moaned and tried to escape Clare's reach only resulting in Clare pumping her harder.

"It looks like you can take it baby girl, Mommy is going to use you tonight. Your pretty body is made for fucking, isn't it Holly?" Clare asked rhetorically, putting some muscle behind each thrust of her fist. Holly just lay there, moaning and panting as cum covered Clare's wrist time after time. She took her hand off Holly's chest and the sudden fullness of her lungs combined with the heat of the room and the fucking she was taking almost made her pass out. Clare saw her eyes begin to roll back and felt her body go limp and pulled out of her. Clare decided the rope would have to wait and took out the gag and blew out the candles, opened her long wall length window, and held Holly as she came back down.

"I have never felt something so intense before," Holly said in a slurred haze of exhaustion. Clare kissed her and ran her fingers through her wet hair as the sheer white curtains flew out the window and into the small green space outside her bedroom. Holly asked for water, and Clare took her to the bathroom, holding her as they walked. Clare liked having Holly so dependent on her, and she sat her in the bath as she got her a drink. Clare bathed Holly and watched as Holly worked through her space.

"I'll be gone by morning," Holly said to Clare wanting to keep Clare's rules. She smiled down at Holly and finished washing her hair as she decided on what she wanted to do with her.

"I'd like you to stay if you'd like that?" Clare asked, and Holly smiled weakly obviously happy with Clare's response.

Chapter 3

Clare called in sick to work the next day. She wasn't interested in working when she had a perfect baby girl to play with. Holly needed no convincing at all to also call in sick, and the two of them stayed in bed for the better part of the morning. They talked about the night they had had and about themselves in general. Deciding that they would need to eat something before they both starved, Clare took Holly's hand and only let go once she was at her kitchen table.

"How do you like your eggs baby?" Clare asked Holly who was sitting naked for Clare's viewing pleasure.

"However really, but I like fried," Holly replied, not fussed on what she was eating, all she knew was that she was starving. After the workout Clare had given her the previous night and having not eaten since lunch the previous day, she was famished. Clare finished making breakfast and put a plate in front of Holly.

"Don't touch it," she instructed as she went out of sight. Holly pouted and waited for Clare to return, being very happy when she did. Clare lifted Holly's arms and pulled down a white t-shirt with small cupcake prints on it. She snapped her fingers to the floor, and Holly jumped off her seat quickly to lie down and enjoyed the softness of Clare's touch as she was diapered. Clare stood Holly up and buckled thin pink leather ankle, and wrist cuffs to her perfect skin, leaving her ankles uncuffed but restricting her wrists.

"I don't want you accidentally stabbing your pretty little mouth with a fork baby girl, Mommy will feed you when you are here," Clare said cutting up Holly's food and feeding her until she was finished.

After breakfast, Holly was taken to Clare's living room floor where she was kept in her cuffs but allowed to roll around and relax into her little space. Clare did the dishes and washed the sheets before she came out to join Holly.

"Well well, look what I found little one," Clare said unclipping Holly's wrist cuffs and letting her reach up to grab the block Clare was holding. Holly giggled, and Clare sat next to her as she opened the bag of blocks she had especially bought for Holly and watched as she played. Clare turned on the TV and sat on the sofa while Holly made tower after tower and giggled every time Clare kicked them down with her foot. As Clare grew tired of playing with Holly, she picked her up and put her on the sofa as well. Clare felt Holly through her diaper, and Holly giggled and playfully pushed Clare's hands away.

"I told you not to mess with Mommy baby girl," Clare said, holding both Holly's hand in hers as she gently slapped Holly's face. Pouting and looking down, Holly let Clare feel her and excitedly cuddled into Clare when she opened her arms and let Holly in. Holly began to suck her thumb as Clare played with her hair as she watched her show and was soon asleep in Clare's arms. Clare noticed how Holly smiled in her sleep and gently stroked her cheek, happy she had taken the day off.

Clare had waited for her to wake up and had then taken Holly into her sewing room and let her pick out which material she would like for a diaper cover. Holly had happily selected a light pink, poly viscose that was thick, very soft and extremely fluffy.

"Mommy, this feels nice," Holly said as Clare measured her.

"I bet it does," Clare replied, taking the material and cutting it out along the pattern. Holly played with a jar of buttons Clare had given her and watched as Clare transformed the material into a custom made diaper cover making Holly feel very special.

"I didn't know you could sew Mommy," Holly said, sitting at Clare's feet. Clare looked down at her and smiled.

"How did you think Mommy could have such lovely clothes that no one could ever find in the stores baby girl?" Clare replied. It was not as though her figure was hard to find clothes for, but Clare always wanted to make sure that the clothes she had fit her body to perfection and that was too hard to find in stores. She enjoyed altering them herself, adding something, or taking something away. She didn't ever want to run into someone with the same outfit she had on, and she never did. Clare finished sewing the material together and held up her creation.

"Gosh you are going to look so excitingly vulnerable in this baby," she said eyeing Holly like prey. Holly giggled and reached up to touch the soft material just as Clare had an idea.

"Do you want to be Mommy's cute little bunny baby girl?" Clare asked, taking out a large white pompom and tickling Holly's cheek with it. Holly nodded and rested her head on Clare's thigh as she attached the fluffy white tail.

"There, come here and let me see you," Clare said, taking Holly's hand and standing her up. Holly wiggled into the diaper cover, and Clare buried her hands in the fluffy material as she rubbed all over Holly's bottom.

"Wow," Clare said, genuinely impressed with herself and wildly aroused by the sweet girl she had at her disposal.

"Do you like it, Mommy?" Holly asked, turning around in circles to try and see what she looked like.

"Yeah I do little girl, I like it very much," Clare replied still in her daze. She sat back down at her sewing machine and got to work, creating another diaper cover for Holly as well as a light purple onesie in the same material. She made sure to give the onesie a little hole at the back so Holly's bunny tail on her diaper cover could show through.

Clare spent the better part of the afternoon making Holly's new garments and loved watching Holly potter around the room. She grew tired of playing with the buttons and moved onto the collection of ribbons Clare had been collecting for years.

"You are going to be Mommy's pretty little

girl aren't you Holly," Clare said finishing off the onesie two hours later.

"Yes Mommy," Holly said obediently making Clare's clit throb. *I want to do unspeakable things to you,* Clare thought to herself as she watched Holly.

"Mommy, can I wear it now please?" Holly asked Clare who was already nodding. Holly beamed and stroked the front of her new diaper cover loving how soft and thick it was. She dressed her in her new onesie and turned up the aircon to make sure Holly wasn't too warm.

"You look so cute for Mommy baby girl," Clare said as she took out her phone and began to take photos of Holly.

"No Mommy," Holly gasped reaching for the phone and making Clare laugh cruelly.

"Your face isn't in it, I'm not stupid baby," Clare said as she continued to capture Holly in her fluffy purple onesie. Holly pouted and began to suck her thumb and Clare put her phone away.

"Has the baby had enough? Do you want

to go home sweet girl?" Clare asked Holly who shook her head and held up a ribbon.

"I want to play Mommy," Holly said, smiling when Clare took it and tied it in a bow around her wrist.

"Oh look, who is a pretty baby for Mommy?" Clare said as she began to play with Holly.

Chapter 4

Clare and Holly played for the rest of the night, and at 2 in the morning Clare drove Holly back home.

"See you at work in a few hours, Mommy?" Holly asked, holding Clare's hand as she pulled up to her apartment. Clare had changed Holly back into her original clothes, but her skirt and panties were beyond ruined. Clare had told Holly that on the weekend she would take her shopping to buy her replacements much to Holly's delight.

"See you then baby girl," Clare said stroking Holly's hair and kissing her goodbye.

It wasn't long before they saw each other again and Clare shifted in the elevator to get closer to Holly. There were only three other people in the elevator with them, and Holly and Clare were at the back. Clare came behind Holly and reached under the mid-thigh hem of her skirt and toyed with her ass cheeks, predatorily groping her as

Holly tried to remain straight-faced.

"Cute satin panties," Clare whispered in Holly's ear almost making her moan out loud. Clare knew that more people would be on the elevator at the next stop and took her hands away, flattening Holly's skirt. Turning around, Holly quickly and almost silently kissed Clare on the lips before turning around again and acting as though she hadn't been her diapered baby girl for the last 24 hours. Clare looked up and smiled to herself; *I want her*, she thought to herself surprised the office slut turned out to be such a sweet baby girl.

As Clare ate her lunch in her usual spot by herself, she saw Holly and her friends sitting on the far side of the abundant water feature in the middle of the green office space. Clare watched as Holly made jokes and ate her lunch, the way she laughed and the way she flicked her hair had Clare mesmerized. Holly got up and made her way over to Clare, who was shocked that she would risk her popularity to sit next to her.

"Hi," Holly said, sitting down and continuing to eat her lunch. Clare looked at her expectantly.

"Hi, Mommy," Holly said, trying again. Clare smiled at her and made a face, wondering what Holly was doing there.

"Oh, I saw you sitting alone and thought you might want company," Holly said replying to the look Clare had just given her.

"If I wanted company, don't you think I could get it, baby?" Clare asked, making Holly blush.

"I just thought," Holly began to say, stopping as Clare put her hand on her thigh making her look down.

"It's OK, sorry that was mean. Are you having a nice day?" Clare said stroking Holly who giggled back at her and nodded her head.

"Yes Mommy," Holly said, hushing the word Mommy and making Clare smirk. She liked having this power over Holly.

"Holly, I have something I want to ask

you," Clare began to say, stopping to see Holly's reaction. Holly looked back at her, waiting for her to finish.

"I want you to be mine. I have loved the time we've spent together, and I don't mind not whipping your sweet little body, there are other things I've enjoyed doing far more, and I think you'd love to be my sweet little girl," Clare said. She hadn't been nervous until now. Holly thought about it for what seemed like ages and Clare watched as she finished her lunch before speaking again.

"I think you are too rough for me, I think I need a softer Mommy, Clare," Holly replied, as tears began to form in her eyes.

"Don't get me wrong, I have loved how we've played, but I need more of the soft stuff and less of the hardcore psychological stuff. I'm not a slave; I'm a," Holly said, stopping before she had finished her sentence. Clare smiled and took her hand and stroked it lovingly.

"I know what you are, baby, and I'm sorry

I've scared you. I can be soft as well darling, but I understand what you mean. Would you still be interested in playing together if we are at the same event?" Clare asked a little disappointed. Holly nodded and leaned over to hug Clare, who embraced her body fully, almost forgetting where they were.

"You can keep the things I made you, you looked adorable in them," Clare said, kissing Holly's cheek.

"Thank you, Clare," Holly replied, getting up and making her way back to her friends. Clare stayed stilling in her favorite place for the next hour, disregarding the work she knew she had piled up on her desk. As she thought back on their time together, she slowly began to feel herself letting Holly go and decided that working through that process was more important than working through her inbox.

Clare and Holly smiled to each other knowingly every time they passed each other in the corridors, and Holly had defended Clare when her friend had said she was quiet and weird. It was a civil and courteous work relationship they had developed but had not spoken a word to each other since that day two months ago when Holly had called it quits. Clare had gone back to her usual professional manner but was happy to see Holly had handed over the title of office slut to one of her friends. As the night of a new party was drawing near, Clare spent her evenings making a new outfit to wear and was hoping Holly would be there.

"You will not believe how cute she is!" Sophie, Clare's friend, said talking about a girl who she had just seen walk into the house party. Clare loved these types of parties the most, where everyone was there because they knew someone. It was nice to catch up with friends and not have idiots causing a scene.

"Who?" Clare replied as Sophie looked around the room, but Clare saw her first. The whitetail of her diaper cover sent a shiver down

Clare's spine as she tried to bury the feelings she had for Holly.

"There," Sophie said excitedly pointing Holly out to Clare.

"She must have made that herself, clever baby, I haven't seen those online," Sophie said, making Clare smirk.

"Yeah, she must have," Clare replied, not interested in ruining the excitement of her friend. Clare watched as Holly played and spoke with other babies and Mommies how she giggled when they said something funny or how she showed them her toys. Clare wished she hadn't of seen Sophie go over and talk to her, Holly lighting up when Sophie gave her candy.

"Forget it," Clare said as she made her way through the house and out into the back yard. A couple of puppies and their owners were playing and talking as Clare looked down to see a cute puppy with a black collar kneeling in front of her.

"Do you want me to throw this?" She asked the puppy who had dropped a toy at her feet. The puppy yipped, and Clare had half a mind to throw it over the fence to see what the little thing would do but just tossed it down the yard and into the darkness.

"She likes you; she always likes the sad ones," came a voice behind her. Clare turned around to see a woman standing close behind her. She was wearing a leather corset which looked a lot like Clare's, making her irritated instantly.

"I'm not sad," Clare said, making the woman laugh and come to sit down next to her.

"Right, that's why you're sitting out here all alone with that depressive look on your face," the woman replied.

"Fuck off," was all Clare could be bothered to say, making the woman smile.

"Or you could just tell me what happened?" The woman asked. Clare turned to her about to give her a lecture as she saw Holly being viciously backhanded across the face by someone Clare didn't recognize. Getting up, Clare rushed back inside and stood in the crowd of people watching what was happening. Holly was crying, and her hair had been pulled out, a woman was standing over the top of her with a whip she had used on Holly's arms and legs. Holly had rolled up into the fetal position, and the woman was resting her foot on Holly's head.

"Did you think I'd just let you go you, little filthy whore," the stranger was yelling. Clare caught Holly's gaze, but Holly looked back down to the ground, broken.

"I'm the one that took you in when you were fucking nothing, and look at you; you're still fucking nothing. You're pathetic, do you know that?" The woman yelled, kicking Holly. Clare stepped forward and bent down next to her as the stranger started to push Clare away.

"Do you want to come with me little one?" Clare asked in a voice that she didn't recognize as her own. Holly nodded and reached out her hand slightly as the woman stepped on it making her scream in pain. Clare stood up and punched the woman square in the face taking her by surprise, making her stagger backward. Clare bent down to pick up Holly's bag and took her sore hand gently in hers.

"Come on sweetie," Clare said as she helped Holly up and held her close as she walked Holly out of the house. The woman followed them to Clare's car yelling and swearing, no doubt informing the entire neighborhood what kind of person she thought Holly was, doing her best to humiliate her. It worked, and Holly began to cry uncontrollably, and as Clare shut the door on Holly's side, she ducked a punch the stranger threw.

"You'll have to do better than that," Clare said, hitting back and landing the woman on her ass on the sidewalk.

"Who was that?" Clare asked a very shaken Holly who was still in her baby clothes as she was driven out of the suburbs and back into the city.

"My ex," was all Holly said through her tears. Clare held her hand the entire drive back to her house and understood why Holly had broken it off with her. She didn't want that kind of rough play; she was traumatized by it.

"You can stay at mine tonight, and over the weekend if you'd like, I won't try anything I promise, you can trust me," Clare said, making Holly laugh through her tears.

"You must think I'm pathetic Clare; I don't want you to have to worry about me, I called it off, remember?" Holly replied.

"Yeah I do baby girl, but I kinda want to make sure you're OK and have what you need to get over the shit that just happened so, will you let me look after you?" Clare asked hoping Holly wouldn't fight her. Holly sighed and rested her head on the seat and looked at Clare.

"I'm really lucky to have you, Clare," Holly replied, bringing Clare's hand up and kissing it. Holly nervously looked around, and Clare could feel her mind ticking over, knowing what she wanted before she even asked.

"Can I call you Mommy again please?" She

added, her voice giving her away as she entered her little space again.

"Of course baby girl," Clare replied, feeling her heart swell for the first time in years. It was a different kind of domination she was about to have over Holly, and she was surprised at just how excited she was about it.

Clare slowed the car down as they reached her street and looked down at Holly who was nervous about what she was wearing. Clare got out and took her long coat to Holly's door and unbuckled her seat.

"Here," Clare said softly to Holly as she wrapped her long coat around her tying it up tight around her waist.

"Everyone will just think you've got a thick booty," she added, making Holly laugh as she got out of the car and they made their way to Clare's front door. Clare opened the door, and as she shut the door behind them, Holly took off her coat and hung it on the coat hook. Feeling lost, Holly stood still and waited to be told what she could do. Seeing this, Clare took her hand and led her to the bathroom. She gently took off Holly's shirt, diaper cover, and diaper as the bath filled up with water and tipped in some bath salts before helping Holly into the bath.

"This will help baby girl, but I think you're still going to bruise," Clare said, taking a washcloth and gently began to wash Holly. Holly just nodded, and she brought her knees to her chin and began to cry again.

"I'm not all those things she said I was, am I?" She asked Clare, who shook her head no.

"She just didn't handle the end very well, actually, how did it end between you two?" Clare asked, pulling Holly's legs down. Holly leaned back and let Clare rub her pussy with the washcloth and Clare liked how trusting Holly was of her.

"Kinda the same way it did with us, except we had been together for five years. But she just got too rough. I didn't want it anymore, and she wasn't prepared to go back to being soft like it was in the beginning, so I just packed my stuff one day when she was at work and left," Holly explained as Clare washed her hair.

"5 years, wow," Clare stated impressed with the time frame. She had never had anything last more than three years. Holly nodded and wiped the water from her eyes.

"I'm so embarrassed, I'll never be able to show my face in the scene again," Holly said sadly.

"Oh yes you will, as if those people there tonight have never had some awful ex do something awful to them, I think they were all anxious about you," Clare replied making Holly smile slightly.

"Come on baby girl, let's get you diapered and ready for bed," Clare said, making Holly laugh and touch her phone to see the time.

"But it's only 9 o'clock Mommy," she replied. Clare thought about what she would have done 3 months ago in response to the same remark and was happy she had changed her response to, "I didn't say anything about going to bed did I, sweetie, just that we would be ready so when you fall asleep in Mommy's arms, you are already in your jammies."

Holly lay down and followed Clare's instructions as she was diapered.

"Lift for Mommy baby girl," Clare said patting Holly's bottom up. Holly sucked her thumb and Clare was excited to replace her thumb with a warm bottle. She dressed Holly in a new onesie she had made her three weeks ago when she was missing her dearly and warmed up some milk in a bottle. Bring it over to the sofa, Clare pulled Holly onto her lap and enjoyed the feeling of the snuggly blankets she had set up on the couch.

"Drink it all up baby girl, Mommy doesn't want your little tummy to be hungry," Clare said, taking Holly's thumb out of her mouth and replacing it with the bottle. Clare fed Holly and just as she had predicted, Holly eventually fell asleep in her arms.

"What a good sweet little girl," Clare said, taking the bottle from Holly's mouth. She knew Holly was asleep but found herself liking their current dynamic and didn't feel like breaking it. As she held Holly, she gently touched her face where the bruising was ever so slightly coming through and frowned, angry that someone had dared hurt her baby.

"I'm sorry Mommy wasn't there to protect you little one," Clare said to Holly who she had assumed was asleep. Holly opened her eyes slowly taking Clare by surprise.

"You are now Mommy," Holly replied, making Clare kiss her on the sensitive parts of her face.

"I'm not going to let anything like that happen to you again sweetie, do you understand?" Clare asked.

"But I don't want to play rough as we did before, I like this, I like Mommy as Mommy," Holly replied to a nodding Clare.

"I know, and that's what I want to be for you. I'm going to take care of everything little girl," Clare said, making Holly beam up at her. Clare reached for her bag and took out her pacifier.

"Binky," Holly said as Clare put it in her mouth before continuing to watch a show.

The new work week was fast approaching, and Clare took Holly back to her apartment, going inside for the first time. It was modest and small with just enough space to fit two people comfortably, which surprised Clare. By the way, Holly dressed Clare was sure she would have lived in a luxury apartment or at least had luxury furnishings. But she kept that to herself as she looked around Holly's apartment and smiled at the down to earth family photos on the wall.

"Cute baby," Clare said, holding Holly in front of her while she looked at the photos of graduations and family beach holidays.

"Thanks, I use to live with them, but they don't live around here. I moved," Holly replied. Clare could tell by the sadness in her voice that there was a story there but didn't press. Holly broke the embrace and turned around to face Clare.

"Do you think it'll go down by tomorrow?" She asked, referring to her face. She had done a good job of covering it up with Clare's help, but the slight tinge of blue was still visible under some lights.

"I think you'll be fine in a week sweetie. Mommy can touch it up every day at work though if you'd like?" Clare replied, making Holly gasp. She hadn't thought that Clare would want to continue the dynamic past the weekend. She had just assumed Clare had done the nice thing and that would be that.

"So does that mean?" Holly said excitedly but not wanting to jump the gun.

"Yeah baby, it means you can call me Mommy all the time again. It also means that we'll have to sort out some agreements and such, but yes, I would happily be your Mommy," Clare replied, almost getting knocked down by Holly who pounced on her for a hug making Clare laugh as she held her baby.

"Do you like being in my arms?" Clare

asked Holly who nodded and snuggled into her neck. Clare knew that there were things she needed to get done that night, but held Holly for as long as she needed. Feeling her heartbeat on her chest and stroking her hair until Holly pulled away, smiling.

"Yeah, I love it, Mommy," Holly replied.

"Holly, meet me at our spot at the park baby girl, Mommy has some exciting news," Clare said, leaving Holly a voice message. It had been six weeks since the party incident, and Clare and Holly spent every spare moment they had with each other. They had even begun looking at colors to redo Clare's bedroom because it scared Holly with its dark and sordid vibe.

Holly got the message and was waiting for Clare when she arrived at the park bench by the pond. It was late afternoon, and Clare had been in meetings all day, and she cracked her neck as she approached the bench, happy to be outside and feeling the warm sunshine on her face.

"Darling," Clare said, addressing Holly. Holly waited for Clare to sit down and hugged her affectionately.

"Mommy," Holly whispered in Clare's ear, making her pussy instantly wet. Clare moved Holly onto her so that she was leaning against Clare as they looked out over the pond. Ducks had begun to come back to the pond after the winter, and they swam about happily. The breeze picked up the leaves, and it looked like a postcard picture with the water lilies and blue sky, happy walkers and dogs running to catch balls.

"Mommy has some exciting news to tell you baby girl. So exciting that we are going to be celebrating," Clare whispered in Holly's ear as she wrapped her arms around the slightly older woman. Looking at them together, it would seem like they were the same age, but that was only because Holly had such youthfulness to her, she was 5 years older than Clare.

"What is it, Mommy?" Holly replied, turning her head back as far as it would go.

"I've been promoted baby, Mommy has made partner," Clare said getting flicked in the face by Holly's hair as she spun around in her arms. Clare watched as Holly thought through what that meant. Clare was now not only her Mommy but her boss.

"My gosh, congratulations!" Holly exclaimed a happy smile spread across her face.

"Thank you, baby," Clare said, turning Holly back around and repositioning her again. They watched the ducks, Holly resting her head on Clare's shoulder as the sunset and Clare wondered about how they would celebrate.

"Come on baby girl, Mommy thinks you need a few new things," Clare said as they saw the first star come out. Holly took Clare's hand, and they walked out of the park and towards one of Holly's favorite toy stores.

"I've never been in there wearing this before," Holly said nervously. She looked down at her clothes and then looked back up to Clare, who was amused at her discomfort.

"If anyone asks, I'll say I'm buying something for my little girl and your helping. It's not as though I'd be lying," Clare said, enjoying herself. She stroked Holly's hand as they walked through the store and Holly picked out three stuffies she loved.

"Just pick two, baby," Clare whispered in her ear and watched as Holly spent the next ten minutes figuring out which one to leave behind. Finally deciding a purple kitty with a white tail and a big soft duck with orange feet, Clare took them to the counter and paid.

"Do you want to hold the bag baby girl?" Clare whispered as they walked back out onto the street. Holly nodded, and Clare knew she was in her little space.

"Little space with very grown-up clothes, I need to get you home little one, you look like you've played dress ups for long enough," Clare said, making Holly blush. On the way home Clare stopped into a store and bought herself a new fragrance and paid of heels she had been eyeing off for weeks.

"They are pretty Mommy," Holly said when the assistant had been dismissed. Clare looked in the mirror, and a life she had dreamed of was reflected. There she was, a successful partner of a top accounting firm, a beautiful baby girl by her side and more money than she knew what to do with.

Clare held Holly's hand all the way home, both delighted with their purchases as they planned a holiday to the Alps together.

"Will you be Mommy's little snow bunny baby girl?" Clare asked Holly who was already nodding. Clare made a mental note to make Holly some warmer onesies so she wouldn't be cold as she turned the key and opened the door to her house.

"Dinner, bath, and bed Mommy?" Holly asked, repeating the routine Clare had set her on as Clare took off her heels and unzipped her dress.

"Take those off first baby girl," Clare instructed, pointing to Holly's black and gold bra and panties. Holly giggled and took them off before passing them to Clare who had her hand out expectantly.

"Tonight we are going to do bathies first baby," Clare said walking to the bathroom followed closely by Holly who had taken her stuffies out of the bag and was cuddling into them.

"Not for in here, baby. Go put them on Mommy's bed and come back; I'll count to ten," Clare said as Holly turned on the spot and walked very quickly to the bedroom. Clare heard her running to get back in time and enjoyed seeing the rise and fall of her chest as she pretended that she hadn't been running in the house. Clare decided to let her feel the tension of her body gasping for air but being denied it and didn't bother punishing her further for running in the house. Leaving Holly in the bath to play after she was clean, Clare went to put away her things that she had left at the doorway. Walking into the bedroom, she smiled when she saw that Holly had tucked her new toys in bed on her side.

"Cheeky minx," Clare said loud enough for Holly to hear who just giggled in response. She undressed and went back into the bathroom for a shower. Clare watched Holly play in the bath as she showered and enjoyed how the room quickly got steamy. Getting out Clare dried herself before pulling the plug on Holly's bath, making her pout.

"Don't pull that face at Mommy, you know very well you've had enough time in there," Clare said patting Holly down and making her giggle and squirm when she dried in between her legs. Clare took Holly to her room and put her in a thick diaper before fitting her into her snuggly fluffy legless onesie.

"I don't want this one Mommy," Holly said, trying to pull it off. Clare looked at Holly who cheekily smiled back at her.

"Baby, Mommy isn't in the mood for naughty girls," Clare said, taking Holly's chin in her hand holding it firmly. Holly couldn't help the wicked gleam of mischief escaping her eyes, and Clare held her gaze which just made Holly giggle more.

"But Mommy I don't wanna," Holly said again.

"Why are you fussy for Mommy? Do you want to be spanked? Is that it? Has Mommy not spanked you in a while and now you want to test me?" Clare asked, pulling Holly to her and turning her around to face the wall. Clare moved her hands over the front of Holly's body, squeezing and pulling on her curves, making her wriggle but unable to escape.

"Does the baby want Mommy's attention sweetie?" Clare asked rubbing Holly over the front of her diaper making Holly moan and push back against Clare.

"Not tonight sweetheart," Clare whispered in her ear making Holly pout again and try to turn around. Clare spanked her and pushed her back against the wall.

"Did Mommy say you could move baby?" Clare asked making sure not to hurt Holly too badly. She had thought about fucking her on the teddy again; she had learned that Holly could take much more when she was cuddling the teddy but decided against it. Instead, she went to her cupboard and took out a vibrator and gently put it into Holly's mouth.

"Suck it, little girl, Mommy is going to stick it inside of you, and it'll hurt if it's not wet," Clare said as Holly cautiously licked the toy. Clare watched as Holly licked and kissed it to the top and back down again and smiled as she saw Holly try to deep throat it.

"Good girl baby," Clare said as Holly forced it down her own throat. Clare had steered away from throat fucking her baby but was impressed to see Holly try it another time as tears ran down her cheeks.

"Don't hurt yourself, little girl, Mommy doesn't want that pretty little throat to be sore," Clare said, making Holly smile and go back to licking it. Taking it out of Holly's reach, Clare reached in between Holly's thighs and unclipping the onesie and rubbed over her diaper.

"Do you where this is going to go?" Clare asked Holly who was biting her bottom lip nervously. Clare raised an eyebrow and slapped Holly's bottom, making her jump.

"Yes, Mommy, in my pussy," she replied

quietly, blushing, and looking down.

"Good girl, are you going to let Mommy put it in?" Clare asked rubbing Holly's diaper covered pussy.

"Yes, Mommy," Holly replied, trying to suppress a smile. Clare could see the excitement in her eyes.

"Mommy's naughty girl," Clare whispered as she pushed Holly onto her back. Holly spread her legs for Clare as she pulled her diaper to the side.

"Take it, baby," Clare said as she felt Holly tighten her pussy around the thick vibrator. Holly took a breath and relaxed as Clare pushed it in until it reached her hilt.

"There, my naughty little girl is going to cum in her diaper over and over again baby, and only if you're good will Mommy take it out before bed," Clare said turning it on and watching as Holly let out a frustrated moan.

"Mommy likes it when you're forced to cum baby girl," Clare said clipping up the clips on

Holly's onesie, dressing her again.

"Be a good girl for me, or I'll make you have it in for work tomorrow," Clare whispered as she played with Holly's nipples. She moved Holly up onto her and reached under her arms to play. Holly just moaned as she rolled her head back and came again. She had lost count and felt her body become exhausted by the orgasms Clare was forcing on her.

"Now that Mommy is your boss at home and work, I can punish you everywhere, can't I?" Clare said reaching down and pressing on Holly's diaper, making the vibrator buzz hard inside of her.

"Yes Mommy," Holly breathlessly replied, wondering how much she could keep taking. Clare wrapped her arms around her and held her tight as she was forced to orgasm again and ran her fingers through her hair.

"Good girl. Mommy doesn't like having to punish you sweetie, but you can't be cheeky with me," Clare said, but Holly didn't hear as she bucked her hips and ground down on her diaper as another orgasm built inside of her.

Chapter 6

"Mommy, I'm wet," Holly said quietly leaving Clare a voice message. Clare had taken to making Holly wear pull-ups at work, mostly to make sure she wouldn't become too sassy but also because she liked being able to keep her in her little space all the time.
Clare listened to the voice message just as a meeting began and smiled to herself, knowing Holly would have to stay like that until the meeting was over.

"Come to my office baby," Clare replied to a waiting Holly an hour later. It took Holly no time at all to knock on Clare's office door, and Clare very formally invited Holly inside, locking the door behind her.

"Is Mommy's pretty baby all dirty," Clare asked as she put Holly up on her desk and lifted her dress over her pull up. Holly just nodded and began to suck her thumb as Clare changed her. She had often wondered what would happen if one of them forgot to lock the door, not being able to decide if she would like to be found out or not. Clare stopped when Holly had a fresh pull up on and admired her baby girl. Red heels on her black desk, her pretty pink love heart pull up showing, and her borderline slutty black business dress pulled tight across her breasts. Holly knew Clare liked what she saw and was grateful; the last thing she wanted was for Clare to stop being hers.

"Do you want me to rub it, Mommy?" Holly asked, wanting to please Clare. Clare smiled at her sweet girl's request and shook her head before helping Holly down and adjusting her dress over her pull up.

"No sweetie, if I let you start, I might never let you stop," Clare said as she kissed Holly and held her close. Holly melted into the kiss and was relaxed in Clare's arms before a knock came on the door. Breaking the embrace and beginning to blush, Holly forced herself quickly back into her adult space and cleared her throat.

"Thank you for passing on that feedback, I'll be making those improvements in my next close," Holly said, making Clare almost laugh as she walked to the door. Opening it, to see one of the interns almost shaking in fear of Clare who eyed them in a way Holly never wanted directed at her.

"For you, Ms Jones," the intern said almost bowing as he passed her a note and hurried away.

"Why are they so scared of you, Mommy," Holly teased, whispering Mommy and smiling cheekily.

"Because they knew just how mean Mommy can be," Clare replied quietly before going back inside and shutting the door behind her. Clare opened the note. It was a playful message from one of the other partners. *You can take your baby girl on that trip next week, just had it cleared,* Clare read sitting back in her chair and smiling up at the ceiling. Not only could she make the intern's life a living hell, but she had real dirt on one of the other partners who had become very accommodating to her desires and requests. She had discovered that he had been stealing from the company for years to pay for his secret stash of illegal's he had set up out of town. His career and political aspirations would be ruined, not to mention his legitimate family publicly shamed if word of his harem were to be made public knowledge. Clare had known for years, but knowledge is power, and she had kept this little gem until she could cash it in, and that was now.

Clare arrived home before Holly, she had gone out with some friends to a bar and would be back later that night. She had tried to get Clare to go with her, but those women pissed her off at work, she wasn't about to spend her free time with them as well. Opening a bottle of wine, Clare poured herself a glass and went out to the courtyard, admiring the blooming flowers she had planted as she sipped her wine.

She was still relaxing outside when she heard Holly come in. It was earlier than Holly had said she'd be home and Clare smiled when she saw what Holly was holding.

"Mind if I join?" Holly slightly slurred and Clare pushed a garden seat out for her to sit in. Holly placed the cupcakes she had bought on the table and gazed lovingly at Clare who just laughed.

"If I had known you'd be so cute drunk, I'd have had you drinking vodka instead of milk from the bottle," Clare teased as she bit into the cake before indicating to Holly she could have hers.

"I am going to need you to take the next week off work Holly," Clare began to say, using Holly's name it get her attention. It worked, and Holly flicked her head around to see why she was being called by her name and not baby.

"I'm taking you on a trip. You won't have much work to do on it; you're purely there for my benefit," Clare explained, making Holly excited.

"Where are we going? Will we catch a flight? Will there be Champaign?" Holly questioned, her eyes growing wide, happy to be getting treats. Clare just looked at her until she settled back down again and continued to eat her cupcake, slightly put out that her questions weren't answered straight away.

"We are going to Sydney, Australia so yes, of course, we are flying. Mommy is going business class, but you are going economy," Clare began to say, enjoying her white lie of Holly having to go economy and watching her face try not to give away she was extremely disappointed with the plan. Satisfied that Holly didn't complain, Clare continued.

"I'm joking as if I'd make you do that, of course, you're coming with me on business class, how else will I make sure you're a good girl and not being a brat to the hostesses?" Clare said as Holly sat back up, feeling at peace with the world again.

"Mommy has to work during the day, but after work, we can play, and you can show me the places you visited in the day time. We are staying a day longer because I want to see some things and you can go shopping with my card as well," Clare said, making Holly jump up and dance around the courtyard.

"I love you, Mommy," Holly said happily.

"You love Mommy's money you little brat," Clare replied, making Holly stop and look at her puzzlingly.

"I love that too, but Mommy, don't you know I love you?" Holly said in her serious little voice. Clare shook her head, and it almost brought Holly to tears.

"Haven't I showed you how much I love you, Mommy?" Holly said, coming over to her and sitting on Clare's lap. Clare bounced her off and pointed to the floor. Holly looked on the concrete floor and knew it would be cold, it had been dark for hours now, and she shivered as she sat feeling the coldness in her bones instantly.

"Show me how much you love me. I want you to make me dinner, run me a bath and be a big girl tonight. Mommy doesn't want to have to do a thing baby," Clare said, pointing her shoe at Holly who began to take it off.

"Good, and the other one," Clare said as Holly obediently followed her instructions. Clare took Holly back inside and pointed to the bathroom.

"What did I just say?" Clare said as Holly remembered and quickly walked to the bathroom, making Clare smile when she heard the water being turned on. Clare walked into the kitchen and poured herself another wine before walking into the bathroom to see Holly standing proudly beside the bath she had just ran. She had turned on candles and put rose bath salts in the water, making the room smell divine.

"Undress me, baby," Clare said as she sipped wine while Holly slowly pulled off Clare's work trousers and panties. She reached up and gently unbuttoned Clare's blouse buttons, and the silk material slipped off her shoulders and landed on the floor behind her. Holly smiled, seeing Clare's full breasts curve at the top of her bra and forced herself not to kiss her as she unclasped it. Meeting Clare's sharp gaze, Holly giggled and tilted her head down, excited to be serving this powerful woman.

"Pick that all up and put it in the wash. Then come back here with my pajamas baby," Clare instructed as she sank into the steamy water. She let Holly wait at the door for her and made her watch as she enjoyed her bath, the hot water relaxing her muscles, the bath salts adding to the sensuality of it all.

"You may come in now, Holly," Clare said and pointed to her towel. Holly took it and passed it to Clare who shook her head and raised an eyebrow.

"Dry me, baby," Clare lovingly said as Holly realized what she wanted. Holly made sure not to spend too much time rubbing Clare's breasts or ass and was sure not to rub her too hard against her pussy being very aware this was not the time to tease Clare.

"Good girl," Clare said as Holly handed her her pajamas and dressed her without having to be told. Holly wondered when she would be allowed to get clean after the work day, but her thoughts were cut short by Clare's hand slapping her ass.

"Not right now, obviously," Clare said as though reading her mind.

Holly went to the kitchen and began making dinner. Clare knew it would be nothing fancy, Holly was a terrible cook, but it was the intent behind her cooking that Clare wanted tonight. Holly had settled on an Italian shrimp dish and the house smelt alive with flavor by the time it was finished making Clare very impressed.

"You've been holding out on me," Clare said, wrapping her arms around Holly's waist, not being able to resist pushing into her spank-able ass.

"I just googled," Holly replied, not wanting Clare to think she was only so clever because she wanted a reward. Clare settled at the kitchen table and made Holly watch as she ate, very aware Holly's dinner was going cold. Usually, Clare would let Holly eat with her, but not tonight, tonight Clare wanted to make sure Holly knew who was in charge. Finishing her meal, Clare nodded to Holly, who began to eat, and Clare watched as she tried not to complain that her dinner was cold. Deciding she had had enough of that, Clare got up and took Holly's plate away. Holly, who would have usually complained one way or another just sat there and excepted her fate, but was delighted when she saw Clare come back with a plate of hot dinner for her.

"I'm not that mean baby girl," Clare said kissing Holly's forehead and accepting a hug from Holly who gave it almost involuntarily.

"Thank you, Mommy," Holly replied as she ate happily. After dinner, Holly tidied and washed up while Clare listened to music and flicked through social media. She looked at pictures of Australia and was surprised she had never been. Holly came to kneel in front of her making Clare particularly delighted, and she let Holly stay there as she ran her fingers through her hair lovingly.

"I want you to make a list of all the things you want to see baby girl," Clare said to Holly who got up and went to find her phone. Clare let Holly on the sofa, and they cuddled while they planned their trip.

"Let's go to see all the big things on a bus tour, so we don't get lost. We can see the Opera house and the bridge; they have some amazing looking cafes. I wish we had places that looked like this," Holly said excitedly showing Clare the photos she had found. Clare took note and began to write down all the ideas Holly had knowing that this would go late into the night.

Clare could see that Holly would be a brat the next day the minute she laid eyes on her. It wasn't that Holly was doing anything particularly bratty, it was that she wasn't doing anything in particular at all. Clare listened as Holly quite effectively cleared her morning schedule being delegating almost everything to the interns she had taken from another floor and was happily swirling around on her chair as Clare left her office and walked by.

"Are you right there, miss?" Clare asked her stopping her chair with her thigh.

"Yes thank you, Ms Jones, can I do something for you," Holly replied as Clare walked away, making her turn her head back and look over her shoulder in playful disbelief on her way to a new meeting.

My Mommy's the boss, and I can do whatever the fuck I want, she thought to herself as she strutted through the office. Clare noticed her continued air of superiority as she waltzed up and down the corridor.

"Holly," Clare said coming out of her office to catch her on one of her model like corridor catwalks.

"Yes Ms. Jones," Holly innocently replied, making Clare roll her eyes and keep her door open as she walked back into the office.

"Will you settle down Holly," Clare said, sitting in her chair as Holly closed the door behind them and slunk down in one of Clare's chairs.

"What am I doing, Mommy?" Holly replied, looking at Clare like she was ready to challenge her.

"Get over here," Clare said patting her lap, delighting Holly who eagerly jumped up. Clare bent her over her lap and turned her chair to face the window behind her desk. She was hoping someone could see as she spanked her naughty girl's ass, her heels kicking up as she tried to escape.

"Do you need a little reminder, Holly,"

Clare asked. Holly was sure that Clare couldn't possibly mean what Holly thought she meant but was grounded hard and fast as she felt the tip of a butt plug pressing into her pull up.

"Mommy is going to remind you what slutty little office dolls get when they are too cheeky," Clare said, pulling the pull up to the side and forcing the butt plug into Holly's mouth.

"Get it wet darling, or it'll hurt like a bitch," Clare said fucking Holly's mouth until she was satisfied. Slowly pushing it past her ass cheeks, Clare forced it into a resisting Holly, enjoying the struggle she put up.

"Fighting Mommy just makes me wet baby are you trying to turn Mommy on so you get to fuck me?" Clare whispered in her ear as she stood her up, smiling as Holly winced as the plug adjusted inside of her.

"I'll enjoy watching you sway those little slutty hips of yours now you've got that big toy filling you up," Clare said pressing her fingers into Holly's ass over her work dress before dismissing her.

For the rest of the day, Holly was reminded that she was Clare's and Clare was happy to see her humility return by the afternoon. Taking a break, they strolled through their favorite park and talked about their soon to be taken trip.

"You know, I've never been happier with anyone else," Holly said as she linked her arm in Clare's.

"I don't doubt that I am the best," Clare playfully replied, making Holly laugh.

"No, I'm serious. You always seem to know what I need, and I love that," Holly said stopping and looking Clare dead in the eye.

"I love you, Mommy," Holly said, making herself blush. Clare pulled her in and held her tight as a warm breeze blew around them.

"I could stay here forever baby girl," Clare said as she began to stroke her hair, mildly aware that people could very well be watching. *It must look so out of place, two women dressed in power outfits holding each other so tenderly*, Clare thought quickly disregarding her care of anyone else but Holly.

"You can take that out when we get back baby girl," Clare whispered in Holly's ear kissing her on her cheek.

"Thank you, Mommy," Holly replied happily.

Clare waited for Holly to finish the work she was doing at the end of the day. She had already worked two hours after everyone else had gone home and Clare wondered what on earth was taking so long.

"Holly, get an intern to do it tomorrow, it really shouldn't be taking you so long," Clare said, annoyed she was still at work. Holly typed furiously as Clare rushed her and happily swung around on her chair as she finished.

"Done!" Holly said triumphantly as she hit enter and sent the work to Clare for proofing.

"Good, let's go," Clare said impatiently as she began to walk down the corridor to the marble lobby. Holly quickly walked behind her but stopped when she reached the lobby; she knew that the cleaners would be polishing the floors and they were always slippery when they did that. Clare turned around to see where Holly was just as she made her way across the floor to take hold of Clare's extended hand. Reaching out to take her hand, Holly felt her heel give way and slip from underneath her making her fall. Clare heard the crunch of Holly's ankle as she hit the floor and Holly yelled in pain and gripped her ankle with both hands as she began to cry. Clare dropped to her knees and held Holly trying to soothe her, and the cleaning staff stopped to come and see what had happened.

"Can you ring an ambulance please," Clare said through her teeth trying not to rip the cleaner's heads off. They scurried away, and Clare whispered to Holly, who she could tell was in a great deal of pain.

"Mommy's got you, little girl, you're going to be alright, I'm here, we will get you all better soon baby," Clare said lovingly, wanting Holly to stop crying. After what felt like hours, the ambulance pulled up, and Holly reached for Clare as she was stretched away.

"I'll be right behind you alright," Clare said as she saw Holly try to be brave as she nodded her head and began to cry again.

Clare ran into the hospital just in time to see Holly being taken to get her ankle X-rayed and held Holly's hand.

"Hi sweets," Clare said stroking Holly's forehead.

"It's OK Ma'am, she'll be fine, she's a big girl," the nurse said as she pushed Holly through the doors, stopping Clare.

"No, she's not," Clare whispered to herself as she longingly looked through the windows of the door watching Holly be taken into one of the rooms.

Clare waited for an hour before she saw Holly coming down the hallway on crunches. Clare was relieved to see her giggling and smiling with a nurse who carried her heel in a bag.

"Well, don't you look interesting," Clare said, seeing Holly in her business dress and heel on crutches with one foot plastered up.

"It feels so funny," Holly giggled back making Clare pull a face and look at the nurse before she took Holly's shoe.

"Pain killers," the nurse replied.

"She'll come off them in a few hours and then just over the counter pain killers should do the trick. She's broken part of her ankle bone if you see here," the nurse explained, showing Clare the X-ray. Clare listened to the care instructions and made an appointment to come back and get the cast taken off as well as the ankle rehab methods before they left the hospital.

"Mommy, I was so scared. I asked for the pink cast; I hope you don't mind," Holly asked as Clare helped her into the car.

"I don't mind at all; you look so cute!" Clare said before shutting Holly's door and beginning to drive away.

"It hurts Mommy. It hurts so much I think I want to start crying and never stop," Holly said dramatically touching her cast. Clare looked at her with an expression that made Holly laugh and was happy they were able to deal with her broken ankle so quickly and efficiently.

"I bet it does baby; I think it'll hurt for a little while yet. But Mommy will take you home and take real good care of you. I won't even make you do the dishes tonight little one," Clare replied.

"Take the next few days of work, I'll stay home and look after you baby," Clare said, reaching out to hold Holly's hand.

Chapter 8

"This is awesome, I never want to go back to work," Holly said as Clare handed her a bowl of popcorn as they started to watch the second movie of the day. Clare looked at Holly, who just giggled.

"But then, we wouldn't have this great life baby," Clare replied.

"You can go to work Mommy, but I could stay home and do this all day every day," Holly explained, making Clare laugh and throw a stuffie at her. This was Holly's second day out of four that she was going to be staying at home for and Clare was already ready to go back to work.

"That sounds like a very boring life little one," Clare said, pulling Holly between her thighs and cuddling her. Clare loved feeling Holly in her lap like this, pressing her tits into her back, reaching around to play with her.

"But I could color all day!" Holly said, trying to sound convincing. Clare looked at her and

Holly leaned back into Clare and rested her head on Clare's chest.

"I love you, Holly," Clare said, holding her tight. It was the first time Clare had said it, and the words came out like butter. Holly smiled.

"I know Mommy," she replied contentedly, taking Clare's hand to her lips and kissing it. After the movie, Clare took Holly to her room, and she laid her down on the bed.

"Are we going to play naughty games, Mommy?" Holly asked, disappointed when Clare laughed and shook her head.

"No baby, we are not. We are going to go shopping," Clare replied, taking her tablet out and connecting it to the TV that was mounted on the wall.

"What?!" Holly exclaimed when what she thought was a mirror turned out to be a TV.

"Pretty cool huh," Clare replied happily she could still impress Holly.

"Yeah, really," Holly said, unable to form a proper sentence.

"So, come here and cuddle with Mommy while we go shopping," Clare said. Holly hurried over to her and pushed her face into Clare's soft breast.

"I like this Mommy," Holly said before Clare put a pacifier in her mouth.

"Shh baby have binky," Clare said, typing in her and Holly's favorite stores.

"I like that I don't have to talk to anyone," Holly said. Clare looked down.

"Holly all you've done is talk baby," Clare said, amused at her joke. Holly pouted playfully and went back to sucking her binky.

Clare bought Holly two new sets of dinnerware. One was a lion theme and the other an owl theme with pinks and purples that made Holly clap her hands excitedly. Holly picked out which socks she would like, selecting pink and white striped thigh highs and a pair which had bunny ears at the tops. Clare passed the tablet to Holly who went to town selecting an array of new crayons, felt tips and three coloring books which came with stickers.

"Can I take these to Australia Mommy?" Holly asked as she selected her fifth stuffie. Clare took the tablet and removed one of the stuffies and clicked on a new tab for Holly to search through before handing it back to her.

"I don't see why not, hopefully, everything comes on time," Clare replied watching as Holly added almost everything pink to the cart.

"Are you paying for this Mommy?" Holly asked, suddenly aware that she would scale her selection right back if she had to pay for everything. Clare playfully thought making Holly bounce on the bed to hurry her up sweetly before Clare took the tablet and had a look at what she had chosen for herself.

"Well, you don't need these. And I don't want you having that just yet. But I'll pay for these things baby girl as if Mommy was going to make you buy your things. Your money is for important things, like candy," Clare replied, causing Holly to clap her hands happily.

"I should break my ankle all the time!"

Holly exclaimed as Clare settled her down for a nap.

"No, don't you dare try to hurt yourself," Clare said seriously making Holly look down at her feet.

"I did you know," she quietly said to Clare who was putting the tablet down after paying just over a thousand dollars for Holly's ten-minute shopping spree.

"You did what baby?" Clare replied, not quite knowing what Holly was talking about.

"I did hurt myself," Holly explained. Clare looked at her ankle.

"Yeah, I know, I was there baby," Clare said, beginning to feel like she had missed something.

"No, Mommy. I hurt myself before you. That's why my side is all inked up, I use to cut there," Holly said hoping that Clare would still love her. To her surprise, Clare got to her knees and pulled Holly's princess t-shirt off, exposing Holly's beautiful side torso piece.

"Show Mommy baby girl," Clare said lovingly. Holly took Clare's fingers and traced them lightly over the scars she had slashed into her little body, ashamed of who she was and what she had been through. Clare stopped at each new scar and kissed it gently, giving Holly all her love.

"I'm sorry you felt like you had to do that baby girl. Was that when you were with your ex, the one from the party?" Clare asked, pulling her in and holding her. Clare took the blanket that was at the end of the bed and wrapped it around both of them, feeling Holly snuggle under with her.

"No, it was even before her. I got busted having diapers when I use to live at home. They didn't understand; they thought I was weird and sick and dangerous. I guess I believe that too for a while. Like, I was so ashamed to be who I am, to need what I need and to want who I want and I didn't think anyone would love me when they found out my real truth. I didn't know how to process it, so I punished myself because that was what everyone around me was doing as well. I got kicked out of home and lived on the streets for a while. I didn't have anywhere to go, so when Sharon, my ex, took me in; I let her do whatever she wanted with me because at least I could be in diapers and stuff. It took so long to figure out that she was not a Mommy, just an abusive, power-hungry person, and it took even longer to leave her. I felt like I would never find another person who would want me. She would say things like, I'm the only one who knows you, and I'm the only one who will ever love you, it made me stay with her longer than I really should have. I didn't know where I was meant to go if I was to leave her. But when I did, when I found out that there's this massive scene with huge numbers of people who do get this and don't find it weird it was like breathing for the first time. That's when I go this job and got the tat over my scars to show where I'd been and where I was going, that I survived the hard times," Holly explained. Clare was dumbfounded so she stayed holding Holly for the longest time before speaking.

"I'm so proud of you baby girl," Clare said when she finally spoke which made Holly burst into tears with relief.

"You're safe with Mommy now, and there's nothing you could do that would make me think you are weird. You are my little girl and Mommy is so happy to have you," Clare added, making Holly look up at her with tear filled eyes.

"So you don't want to leave me?" Holly said through her tears. Clare pulled her into her and wrapped the blanket around them tighter.

"Not darling, my little warrior baby," Clare said as she rocked Holly in her arms until she stopped crying.

Chapter 9

Clare had decided it was time for Holly to move in and was relieved when Holly had agreed so readily. However, moving weekend turned into, renovate Clare's house weekend as Holly came with a list of things she wanted either changed or rearranged.

"Mommy, it won't take that long I promise," Holly said as Clare drove them to the hardware store.

"Read that list out to me again," Clare instructed. She was mildly amused she was going along with this.

"Mommy, I'm too little to read," Holly said as Clare looked at her.

"Well if you're too little to read, you're too little to have an opinion about what Mommy's house should look like," Clare replied.

"The shower taps in the bathroom and sink, they need to be more modern and easier to use," Holly began without batting an eyelid making Clare smirk and laugh to herself.

"The kitchen cupboards need to be more modern and so does the paint; I'm thinking of ceiling white. I'd really like new rugs for the floors, in like, pink and maybe we could even get new linen for the bed, yours is scary," Holly said as Clare made a mental list.

"And we should get some duct tape for the baby, so I can tape her mouth shut when she talks too much," Clare teased making Holly gasp.

"We can get everything ordered today, but I want a man to come out and fix everything up for us, I'm not about to play builders with you," Clare said taking Holly's hand and leading her around the store.

"Maybe it's a lady, not a man," Holly said adamantly.

"I don't care who it is, all I'm saying is that I'm not doing any of it, so it won't get done today Holly," Clare said not as amused as Holly was by her political correctness.

"We could get hard hats," Holly said, walking over to the protective gear section and trying one on. Clare was about to dismiss it but looking at how cute Holly looked, she went over and tied a tool belt to her waist.

"Take it off, you're turning Mommy on," Clare whispered in Holly's ear.

"I said take it off, not put it back," Clare said, grabbing the tool belt and hard hat Holly was about to put back and placing it in the trolley. Holly clapped her hands in delight.

"Do you need one?" She asked Clare who just scoffed at her.

"No, because you're going to be my little worker, and I'm going to bend you over my workbench and fuck you until the cupboards aren't the only thing that's broken," Clare replied confidently, excited to get Holly home.

"Well, we can't because today's the day I get my cast off my ankle, and the doctor said I couldn't put any serious weight on it," Holly replied, trying to have all the control. Clare just rolled her eyes.

"Then you can be on your back my little slut," she said as she spanked Holly with an offcut piece of wood as they made their way around the store.

After the store they did, go to get Holly's cast off and were told not to do any strenuous exercise. Clare bit her lip to try and stop herself from getting turned oh as the doctor lifted Holly on the table.

"Lollipop?" She asked, offering Clare and Holly the jar. They looked at each other, making the doctor laugh.

"Everyone is a kid at the doctor's," she said, making Clare raise an eyebrow as she took a red one. Holly chose a yellow and happily sucked as her cast was taken off.

"Will I be able to wear heels soon," Holly asked, she had not enjoyed being off balance with only wearing one heel. The doctor looked at her like she had lost her mind.

"You broke your ankle Holly," she said plainly.

"Yes," Holly replied bluntly, and Clare enjoyed the show sucking on her lollipop. She liked watching Holly be inspected by another woman who was clearly in charge of the situation. She liked it, even more, seeing Holly disciplined by her.

"No, you are not allowed to wear heels for a good two months to make sure that everything heels properly. Don't even think about it, Holly," the doctor replied. Something in the doctor's voice gave her away, and Clare knew where she had seen her before. She thought that she must have had seen her last time they were here, but it was before that.

"Puppy owner," Clare said making the woman turn around in surprise.

"I saw you at a party Sophie was hosting, you have a sweet puppy, a girl, you asked me why I was so depressive looking," Clare explained, making the woman laugh.

"Wow, yes OK, and this is the girl you bailed on our conversation for?" The doctor replied. Holly looked at Clare and looked at the doctor, realizing it was better to stay quiet.

"Yeah, this would be her," Clare said, running her fingers through Holly's hair, comfortable to show her affection.

"Well, she looks worth it," the doctor replied gently slapping Holly's left cheek a few times before turning back to Clare.

"There's a party tonight, if you and yours want to come, we'd love to have you," the doctor said inviting Clare who just smiled and laughed.

"Oh no, she's my baby girl, not my pup, but thanks," Clare said as the doctor shrugged her shoulder.

"If you ever get one, hit me up," the doctor said as Clare and Holly left the hospital.

"Mommy, I don' like her, she would be so mean I can tell," Holly said the minute they were both in the car.

"Yeah she might be, but we will never

know so don't stress about it baby," Clare said, wanting Holly back in her little space.

They finished making their rounds to the different stores for linen and rugs before eating lunch at a restaurant. When they got home, they moved Clare's flogging cross to the spare room and redecorated Clare's bedroom with the lighter linen and rug.

"It looks like my room is for a five-year-old with these pink sheets and rug," Clare said as Holly set up her stuffies against her pillow.

"Um, yeah," Holly replied, stating the obvious. Clare laughed and went out to the living room where she had begun to set up a play space for Holly.

"Do you think I need a playpen Mommy?" Holly asked as Clare set up the 2x5 meter wooden pen in the nook of the living room. Clare had it custom made and painted in Holly's favorite colors, candy pink and purple.

"Yes, I do little one because Mommy

doesn't want your toys spread all over the house and this is the place you're going to play with them in. Look, there's a spot to do reading and coloring in and all the pillows and toys you could ever want," Clare replied as she started to strip Holly.

"Hey Mommy," Holly said, beginning to fuss.

"Don't baby girl, Mommy is tired, and you're going to be good and have bathies for me while I make dinner. You're going in your fluffy onesie tonight, and when I cuddle you, you'll feel like a little bunny all sweet and soft," Clare said picking up Holly's clothes and throwing them in the washing basket as she led her to the bathroom.

"And duckie, and giraffe, and a bucket," Holly said telling Clare what three toys she would like to play with in her bath.

"OH, please Mommy, baby girl where are your manners?" Clare replied, withholding the toys from Holly.

"Please Mommy," Holly replied.

"Because I had to tell you, you aren't

getting giraffe tonight, maybe tomorrow night you'll be a good girl, and I won't have to remind you," Clare said splashing Holly with water.

Clare dried Holly and was happy Holly didn't fight her to put on a diaper like she did most nights. Clare clipped up Holly's onesie and rubbed her all over, loving how the material felt on Holly's body. Holly hadn't crawled much in Clare's house but began to as she followed Clare back into the living room was put in her playpen.

"Are you a sleepy baby tonight little miss?" Clare asked Holly who was watching her in the kitchen from the bed of stuffies she had made for herself. Holly just nodded her head slowly and rubbed her eyes as she rolled over and began to drift off to sleep.

"Not yet darling," Clare said as she came over with a bowl of pasta and began feeding Holly.

"Mommy, I just want milkies," Holly said, pushing the pasta away.

"You can have milkies after dinner baby girl, but Mommy needs you to eat this now," Clare said as she spoon fed Holly another mouthful.

"But it's yuck," Holly said, kicking her foot in a tantrum.

"That's OK, eat it anyway," Clare replied motherly, knowing full well that the dinner was not yuck at all. She knew this was one of Holly's favorite dishes and forced another mouthful into her when she went to speak again.

"I think you're just fussy because you're so sleepy little one, is that it? Did Mommy work you too hard today, baby?" Clare said giving Holly one more mouthful before she was satisfied she was finished. Holly pouted and nodded her head, not sure if she wanted to be angry or sleep as Clare stepped out of the playpen and went to get her a bottle.

"Here my sooky baby," Clare said coming back with Holly's blankie and bottle. Holly reached up, and Clare lay down next to her as she drank and snuggled her blankie.

"There's my good little girl," Clare lovingly said stroking Holly's hair as her eyes grew sleepy.

"Mommy, I'm done," Holly said, passing the bottle back to Clare and rolling over. Clare leaned forward and saw Holly's eyes were already closed.

"Are you falling asleep here tonight, baby girl?" Clare asked Holly, who just nodded and yawned.

"Alright little one, sweet dreams," Clare said, kissing Holly on her head and going to have a shower herself.

Chapter 10

The day had arrived where they would be flying to Sydney, and Holly was in fine form. Clare had already spanked her ass red and made her put back one stuffie she had packed.

"Do not keep testing me baby girl, Mommy will have no trouble diapering you on the plane if you keep this up," Clare said. She wasn't joking either, the thought of Holly having a diaper on in public made her excited, and she had been waiting for the opportunity to arise. Clare wondered why Holly was acting up today. *Is she nervous about flying? Is she over excited because it's a new experience? Or is she just being a little brat because she wants all my attention?* Clare asked herself as she grabbed Holly by the arm and forced a pacifier into her mouth.

"You'll keep it in young lady," Clare ordered making Holly's demeanor change instantly as a soft moan escaped her throat as she felt the words hit her clit. Sucking her paci, she reached for Clare who reluctantly held her.

"Are you excited or nervous little one?" Clare said patting Holly's bottom gently. She was aware that her ass would be sore for a few hours after the almost flogging she had dished out this morning. Holly nodded to excited and Clare rolled her eyes.

"Then don't mess it up be being so naughty for Mommy," Clare replied, taking their bags and heading out the door to the waiting taxi.

They made their way through the airport and checked in their luggage. Holly constantly asked for candy from the vending machines which Clare continuously refused before boarding the plane and finding their seats.

"This is nice," Holly said as she sat down and began fiddling with everything she could get her hands on. Clare looked over to her and knew that Holly couldn't calm herself down, so she took her hand and held it tight as the plane took off.

Grateful when it was finally time to sleep, Clare put Holly's seat down and tucked her in. The flight attendant who was to take care of them for the duration of their flight noticed the very clear power distinction and came up next to Clare.

"Please forgive me if I am overstepping, but would your baby like a coloring in set?" She asked Clare in a hushed tone. There was only one other person sitting in business class, and they were at the front, Clare and Holly had been sat at the back, and Clare was sure he wouldn't be able to hear anything. Clare looked at the flight attendant and smiled as they exchanged knowing looks.

"That would be wonderful thank you," Clare replied, happy to have their dynamic so open. Holly sat up and looked from Clare to the flight attendant and back to Clare when, the flight attendant, who introduced herself as Jenny, came up to Holly and gave her the coloring in set.

"Aren't you going to thank the nice lady baby girl?" Clare said making Holly blush.

"Thank you," she said, looking down, and Jenny smiled at her kindly before disappearing behind a curtain.

"Mommy," Holly said alarmed at what had just happened. Dismissing her, Clare took out the colors.

"Draw Mommy a picture baby," she said as Holly got to work almost immediately.
Soon time passed before Clare saw Jenny again, this time she passed Clare a wine and Holly a juice box and told Holly what a great picture she had drawn. Holly beamed, and Jenny helped her open her juice box.

"I've got a little one too," Jenny explained, talking to Clare. Clare enjoyed listening to Jenny's Australian accent and noted that it wasn't like those bush accents she had heard on the TV.

"Oh, I'm from the city, where, the more British you sound, the higher class you are and the more respect you get. But that's more of an Australian secret, I'm happy I don't have the typical come to mind accent that is portrayed over the world, it's hideous," Jenny said making Clare laugh as Holly finished her juice and handed it to Clare.

"Oh I can take that for you," Jenny said, holding her hand out to Holly.

"No," Holly said, making Clare instantly mad.

"Holly, that's not what we say too nice people," Clare said as Holly passed her juice box to Clare. Clare passed the container to Jenny and decided it was time for Holly to be humiliated.

"I'm just going to teach her a lesson, would you like to watch?" Clare asked Jenny, who smiled eagerly.

"Very much so," Jenny replied as she crossed her arms and bit her bottom lip as Clare buckled a pacifier gag over a silently struggling Holly. Clare took the blanket off of Holly, which made her cold and reached into her bag for a diaper. Holly's heart skipped a beat as she saw the diaper Clare was holding and began to blush as Jenny moved to stand behind her.

"You can take off her panties if you like," Clare offered Jenny who gladly moved to stand over Holly. Clare had laid her down in her seat and Jenny, with Clare's approval, grabbed at Holly's thighs to lift her taking her panties off.

"You have a sweet one, but you're right, she is naughty," Jenny said, handing Holly's panties to Clare. Clare threw them forcefully onto Holly who pouted and looked annoyed as she was diapered in front of Jenny. Clare parted her pussy lips and teased her before powdering her and fastening the diaper on tight, its thick pad forcing Holly's thighs apart.

"This is what naughty girls get," Clare said, pulling Holly's pajamas pants back up and rubbing her hands over her diaper. Jenny joined in, and Holly wriggled as she was teased and toyed with.

"Does she have a pacifier? In Australia, we called them dummy's," Jenny explained as Clare passed her Holly's paci.

"Is that because they are for cute little dumb babies who aren't good for their Mommy?"

Clare said playing with Holly. Jenny laughed.

"I don't know why, we just do," she replied giggling at the face Holly was pulling. Clare had notice Jenny's large breasts the moment she had seen her and wondered if they were full of milk. Holly had wondered too because she reached for them as Jenny bent over to put her dummy in her mouth, making Jenny laugh.

"I don't think you're Mommy would like that very much baby," Jenny said, taking Holly's hands away. Clare thought for a moment. Ordinarily no, she wouldn't have liked it, but she didn't feel threatened by Jenny, in fact, she was enjoying babying Holly with her.

"You can if you'd like, they do look particularly full against your uniform," Clare said to Jenny. She sat down in Clare's chair and pulled Holly onto her lap as she slowly unbuttoned her uniform and let it fall to her waist. Holly nervously touched Jenny as Jenny took out Holly's dummy and Clare came behind her and took off her bra, exposing her two heavy milk filled breasts. Jenny held one in one hand and pulled Holly's mouth to it with the other, gasping when Holly began to suckle.

"Oh I needed this, thank you baby girl," Jenny said.

"I bet, the pressure must be painful at times," Clare said as she stroked Holly. Holly reached for Clare as she suckled from Jenny, loving the feeling of the two Mommies pressing against her.

"This has turned into a reward rather than a punishment hasn't it baby," Clare whispered in Holly's ear. Holly looked up at her with her usual cheeky grin but shook her head not wanting it to stop.

"This one now baby," Jenny said, moving Holly onto her other breast. She could tell Holly was getting full by lazily she began to suckle and she smiled and stroked Holly's cheek.

"They are all the same, my little boy always attacks one tit but takes his time on the other too," Jenny said to Clare who was rubbing over Holly's diapered pussy.

"Do you have to spend much time away from him? Is the distance hard?" Clare asked.

"Well, he is the pilot, and we fly together. The other stewardesses don't know, and I let him fuck whoever he wants, I have him as my baby. I have a husband at home, and it's hard leaving him, but it's easier on him knowing that I'm not going to fuck my little prince," Jenny explained. Clare loved how open she was with was and was surprised by her story. Holly drank Jenny's milk as the sun began to come up and Jenny took her off, wiping her mouth clean and pulling her uniform back up.

"We will land in about two hours. I've enjoyed meeting you," Jenny said to Clare as they exchanged social media accounts. Jenny kissed the top of Holly's head and went back to being the perfect stewardess bring them hot buns, and bacon and eggs for breakfast.

"Mommy, can I take this off now please?" Holly asked as she finished her breakfast. Clare reached over and patted her as she smiled.

"No baby, you'll keep it on until we reach the hotel, then I'll change you, and you'll keep that one on until you're wet," Clare replied making Holly's mouth gape.

"But Mommy," Holly started to say stopping when she copped a look Clare usually saved for the interns.

Clare dressed Holly in a baby doll dress and sandals to hide the fact she was wearing a diaper and thanked Jenny again as they left and made their way to the hotel.

"Stay still for Mommy baby, you look so cute in your diapy I want to put it online," Clare said as she took her phone and lifted Holly's skirt.

"Jenny might even like it, this is the one she saw you in today," Clare said taking photos of Holly as she lay on the hotel bed, making sure to leave her face out.

"Mommy," Holly said embarrassed to be on display, but Clare just kept clicking.

"I told you not to fuck with Mommy didn't I Holly," Clare said as she posted the photos online for the world to see Clare's naughty girl.

Victoria's Baby Girl

An MDLG and ABDL lesbian tale of an MTF transgender Police Officer who saves her baby girl in more ways than one

By Tina Moore

Chapter 1

I come from the side of town that good parents warn their kids about, and the stories are all true. We fight for fun and money; your Mum could also be your sister because you're Dad's a fucking rapist and we drop out of school before we have learned anything that's going to help us go out of this shit hole. But the one thing they don't tell you is just how important loyalty is to us. Maybe it's because it's all we've got and when that's given, and blood is shed to prove it, it's the strongest bond you could imagine. So there we were a bunch of street kids who joined together for one reason or another. I intended to escape the violent outbursts of my Uncle, who had taken to using me as a punching bag for boxing practice. He'd come home drunk and throw some fists, usually passing out before any real damage could be done. I considered myself pretty lucky. Another girl called Hope hung around with us for a while so she wouldn't be fucked by her sister's boyfriend, but he had already forced himself on her a couple of times.

We spent our time throwing stones at each other, standing around on corners glaring at the people who walked by, drinking in parks and running from cops. We'd break into stores and steal candy and condoms, and knew all the best hideouts where we'd wait while the cops ran around looking for us. I couldn't even count the times Victoria caught me. We all just called her Vicki for short, she was our favorite cop, and I'd grown up running from her. She would chase the gang and me over fences and under bridges. She'd always catch one of us, throw us into the backseat of the car, hands cuffed behind our backs. She'd try all the tricks to get us to rat out the other people involved. Saying things like, "We already have it all on CCTV so you might as well do yourself a favor and try for a lesser sentence," or "I won't be able to help you if this gets pushed further up the chain, you know what happens next." But I would always laugh or respond with, "No comment," and she would have no choice but to let me go after 24 hours. She was the only cop who had ever caught any of us and sometimes, we'd even wait for her to be on duty before we robbed a store so that she'd chase us. She wasn't like the other cops. They were pretty dumb, and we could easily give them the slip. But not Vicki. She would hunt us down for hours, making us run until we thought our lungs would give out. But when she caught one of us, which she always did, she was nice and kind and made us feel kinda like shit for ripping off the store manager. She'd make us go around there and apologize, hitting us over the head if she didn't think we were sincere enough. She knew we'd never call her out on 'Police Brutality,' despite her strength and size, she wasn't brutal at all. Her arms were full sleeves of ink, and her shoulders were broader than any woman's I had ever seen. She stood tall, taller than most of the men in town and when she walked down the sidewalk, people had to move out of her way, or they'd be knocked to the ground by accident. I thought she was gorgeous but I never admitted that to the guys. I just found myself letting her catch me as I got older, just excited to be near her.

But I had stepped away from the gang a little bit now that I wasn't a minor anymore. Now if I got caught doing the shit we use to do, I'd be given a much bigger sentence maybe even jail time, and the thought of that didn't thrill me. I did miss those days, though. Now I work at a local store in town selling furniture during the week and getting drunk on the weekends. It a pretty basic and boring life, but at least I wasn't a Mum or in jail. My 21st was fast approaching, and I had invited a couple of the old gang over for some drinks on the weekend. I'd gone to buy some party supplies and was on my way out of the store, looking into the bag of candy and glitter I had just bought when I felt a familiar arm almost knock me over.

"Oi Vicki," I said looking up at the muscled arms she used to use to pin me to the ground. She had done that so many times I had a scar under my chin from the repeated gravel rash I sported during my late teens.

"Where're your mates. I haven't seen you around them in a while," Vicki said, looking over my head and into the store.

"Show me the receipt," she added, grabbing the bag.

"Hey," I said, trying to pull away from her. Vicki just raised an eyebrow, but I hardly saw because I didn't want to meet her eyes. I was embarrassed about what I had just bought. I reached into the bag and took out the receipt before passing it to her and looking down at the ground.

"Are you having a party?" Vicki asked, suddenly sounding kinder. I nodded and reached for the receipt.

"I'm turning 21 tomorrow," I whispered and tried to sidestep Vicki, but she moved before I could and blocked my way.

"Hey, happy birthday for tomorrow Ava,

it'll be nice not to have to kick you out of bars anymore," Vicki said kindly. I looked up at her and gave her a sideward smile and walked out of the store. *Damn why does she have to smell so good,* I thought to myself stepping past her quickly as I felt my face begin to turn red. That was the last thing I needed, her seeing what she could do to me.

Chapter 2

"Happy birthday bitch," Hope said, handing me a drink and a slice of pizza. I laughed, and we danced around my kitchen while the guys played beer pong in the living room. It was almost midnight when we heard a knock at the front door, and we all looked at each other. Everyone that was supposed to be here was. It wasn't uncommon for people to crash parties and steal a whole lot of stuff, so I grabbed a kitchen knife, and the others followed suit. I approached the door and felt myself square up, ready to attack any intruder. Opening the door aggressively, I held the knife up in front of my face.

"What!" I yelled angrily but bringing the knife down when I saw her standing in front of me. She had some dude standing behind her, and I liked that she silenced him when he started to have a go at me for threatening Police.

"How could I be threatening you when I

didn't even know you where there fuckwit," I said back as Vicki pushed her way in and rolled her eyes. She looked around the room before she turned back to me.

"Any minors?" She asked as the other cop circled behind me, making me feel uncomfortable.

"No, do you think I'm stupid?" I replied, taking a step forward to get away from the cop at my back.

"We've had noise complaints, Ava, I need you to turn the music down," Vicki said sitting on the couch.

"Comfy," she said, bouncing slightly. One of my mates, Connor, laughed.

"Ava? Vicki, I didn't know we are all on a first name basis," he said making the other cop angry.

"We're not, it'll be Constable to you," he said shoving his baton in Connor's chest. Connor scoffed, pushing it away and took a step back.

"Just keep it down, yeah?" Vicki said, standing up and coming over to me. I could feel everyone's eyes on me as she paused in front of me and put her hand on the small of my back. She eyed me up and down, taking in my short dress and heels. Her eyes twinkled, and I had to catch my breath as she smiled at me in a way that no one ever had before. She winked at me before walking out, closing the door behind her.

"What in all of hell was that about?" Hope squealed.

"Are you fucking her?" Connor said, and I shook my head and went back to the kitchen, grabbed a bottle of whiskey and jumped out the kitchen window. I made my way down the fire escape and onto the street, but my legs took over, and I was running before I knew it. I didn't know where I was running too, but I just had to get out of there. *Fuck, fuck, fuck,* was all I could think as I made my way to the park and found a spot under the bridge. I opened the bottle and drank as much as my body could hold in one go before swallowing and almost throwing it all backup.

"What's a pretty girl like you doing here all alone?" A man's voice said, waking me up. It was early dawn, and the water by the river was beginning to glisten. I got up wanting to leave, but he pulled me back down and onto his lap. I could feel him easily under my short dress, and he reached around to try and rub me through my panties. I elbowed him in the face and scrambled up the river bank back to where the morning runners were doing their routine exercises. I knew he wouldn't chase me up here, which meant I was safe, so I walked along the path, realizing that I had left my shoes down by the river. *Great, now I look like I'm coming home from a wild night and all I did was pass out under a bridge*, I thought to myself, pulling a face when I saw Vicki walking towards me.

"Good morning," Vicki said, clearly amused.

"Did you have fun last night?" She added.

"I was having a great time until you showed up," I spat back at her making her stop walking. I wish I hadn't, but I turned around to look at her.

"Look I'm sorry, just stop being so bloody nice to me alright, it's got people talking," I tried to explain. Vicki wasn't wearing her uniform, and I hated myself for thinking that her running shorts and singlet looked hot on her. Her shiny black hair was in a loose ponytail, and her short shorts showed off thigh tats I hadn't realized she had. Catching me staring Vicki crossed her arms which just made her forearm muscles bulge and made me blush.

"This isn't me being nice, your friends would have something to talk about if I was nice," Vicki said as she placed her hands on her hips. I don't know what came over me but seeing her like this, hearing her non-Police voice made my head spin. *What is her game? Does she really want me or am I reading way too much into this*, I thought to myself as I bit my bottom lip and tried to decide on what to do next. I ran forward, kissed her quickly on the mouth, and turned before I could see her reaction and sprinted towards home. I knew she could catch me if she wanted to, she had always managed to catch me before, but when I didn't hear footsteps coming behind me, I turned to see her standing where I had left her. She extended a finger and motioned for me to come back to her. I stayed looking at her for the longest time, and seeing her reassuring smile, I slowly made my way back to her.

"You want to explain that to me?" Vicki said, sitting down on a park bench. I shook my head and looked at her.

"Well, let me explain it to you. When you kiss someone do it like this," Vicki said, wrapping her arms around my body and pressing the back of my head into her mouth. She ran her fingers through my hair and pressed my mouth harder on her as her tongue parted my lips and explored my mouth. I could hardly breathe, my heart was beating hard against my chest, and I gingerly placed my hands on her thighs as I melted into her. Breaking the kiss, Vicki looked down into my eyes and held my head in both her hands, stroking my cheeks with her thumbs.

"That's how you kiss someone Ava," Vicki said, kissing the tip of my nose before getting up and walking away.

Chapter 3

My mind had been racing since that kiss. I had gone back to my apartment in a daze, unable to explain what had happened or where I had been. Hope and I had cleaned up after the party, and I had told her I had a headache and needed a nap. In truth, I just wanted some time alone. I had not only kissed Vicki, but she had kissed me. Her touch had been soft but firm, almost protective, and I still had her perfume on my dress. She had whispered in my ear that she'd see me around and I couldn't wait until the next time she saw me. Things would be different; I would be different. I had to become the sort of person she wouldn't be embarrassed to be with. I went to my cupboard and started going through my clothes, throwing out things that looked trashy or cheap. I booked an appointment at the hairdressers to get a fresh color and cut, and I pulled on some activewear and went for a jog around the block.

It had been three months since that first kiss with Vicki when I saw her again, and at first, she didn't recognize me. I had swapped my usual grunge look for something more clean-cut. A pair of dark denim high waist jeans and a white fitted t-shirt tucked in, some tan heeled sandals and my hair was a Scandi white blonde. I had learned how to apply makeup that wasn't solely black eyeliner and I had taken to getting a shade of baby pink on my nails at the nail salon. Tonight I had decided to try a new bar that had just opened up on the other side of town but hadn't invited any of my old gang. It wasn't my choice to go alone, but ever since that first kiss, I had lost one friend after another. They didn't like the new me, though that I thought I was better than them or something stupid like that. It hurt me at first, but I had been used to being alone, so I just adapted and had even put in for a promotion at work.

"Mind if I sit?" A voice smoothly said as I sipped my cocktail. I turned my head and saw

Vicki standing in front of me. Her eyes grew wide when she realized it was me sitting there.

"Oh my god, Ava?" Vicki asked, still not believing it was me. I giggled and nodded, and Vicki pulled a face I knew meant she was impressed.

"Wow, look at you all grown up," Vicki said, sitting down next to me. I looked around her and saw that some of the other cops were here tonight, probably with her.

"Don't worry, as long as you don't get up to any mischief they'll stay away, I always told you that, but you never listened, did you?" Vicki teased. She got the bar tender's attention and ordered a beer and another cocktail for me making me blush.

"I had no idea you could be so adorable Ava," Vicki said as she began drinking with me.

"What else has changed?" She added, placing her hand on my thigh and squeezing it sensually. I liked knowing that she wanted me, but I took her hand off my thigh, making her face look confused.

"For one thing, now I make people ask permission before they just take what they want," I said hoping that Vicki wouldn't be annoyed. She just laughed and nodded in agreement.

"Well, may I?" She asked, holding out her hand as the music in the bar changed to a slow song. I kept her waiting as I finished my drink before accepting her hand, and she led me to the dance floor, twirling me before bring me in and slow dancing with me. Even with my heels on I was still a head and shoulder shorted than Vicki which meant my eyes were in line with her breasts and I held my breath as a fire began to grow inside of me. Wanting to distract myself from my thoughts, I looked up at her to find that she was already looking down at me.

"You're lovely Ava," Vicki said lovingly making me wet as she pulled me in closer.

"You've always been lovely," I quietly said, making her smile.

"I knew you thought so, you went from being the hardest to catch to being the easiest overnight, I knew something had to give," Vicki teased twirling me around again, but I let her hand go and walked back over to the safety of the bar.

"Are you alright?" Vicki asked coming over to join me, sounding concerned. I shook my head.

"We are from two completely different worlds, don't you understand everyone will think I'm fucking the enemy Vicki," I said. I felt more emotional than I wish I had as a tear escaped my eye. Vicki took my hand in hers and held it softly before speaking.

"Are you worried about what people will think, baby?" Vicki said. I looked up at her, shocked. No one had ever called me baby before; I had always just been a tease, something to fuck. I was about to speak when that cop that Vicki had brought to mine came over.

"Causing any trouble over here," he said, making me roll my eyes.

"Oh please fuck off," I replied, making Vicki laugh, and she placed her hand on his chest, making him stop talking and go back to the group of cops sitting in the back.

"Come on, let's get out of here, baby," Vicki said, taking my hand. I felt my arms tingle as I took her hand and followed her out of the bar, shivering in the cold night air.

"Here," Vicki said, taking off her tan leather jacket and draping it over my shoulders.

"You've done that before," I said, enjoying the weight of her jacket on my shoulders, the arms coming down to my mid-thigh.

"Maybe just once or twice," Vicki said, laughing. We walked until we found a café that was still opened and she held the door as I walked inside. It was fun being here. These were the types of places I use to rob now I was here with the one cop who would have been able to catch me.

"What would like darling?" Vicki said, running her fingers through my hair. I forced myself to read the menu.

"Just a caramel latte please," I replied being surprised when Vicki paid, following her as she found a booth away from the other people who were in the café.

"I'll get the next one," I said, not wanting her to think I couldn't pay my way.

"Alright, are you asking me out on a date then?" Vicki teased. I just nodded, and she happily wrapped her arm around me.

"I think this is the start of something very exciting baby," Vicki said, and we drank our coffees in silence as we watched the world go by outside.

"I've had a wonderful night," I said as Vicki walked me back home. I liked having her by my side. She had held my hand the whole way, and I was seriously considering fucking her tonight. It would have been too easy to let her come up to my apartment and let her have her way with me. But I wanted her to think I was special and not just another slut she could easily have so I kissed her again at my front door and handed her back her jacket.

"You're going to make me wait?" Vicki said,

placing her hand on the front door and pushing her body against mine, making me stumble back and I had to suppress a moan as she ground into me against the door. I just nodded and bit my bottom lip. She brushed my cheek with the back of her hand, and I suddenly was hugging her, feeling her heart beat against my face.

"I'm going to try," I softly said, resulting in her kissing the top of my head and giggling.

"Well, I have waited this long, I guess I can wait a little longer," Vicki said before she winked at me and began to walk back out onto the street. I put the key in my door and turned the handle, almost falling inside in a haze of happiness and dizzy excitement.

Chapter 4

"Hi Vicki, it's Ava," I said, trying not to sound as desperate as I felt. I had waited until the next morning before ringing Vicki, and I was excited she had picked up almost instantly.

"Hey sweetie, how are you?" Vicki replied, making me smile immediately.

"Yeah good, whad bout ya?" I said kind of annoyed my backwater accent came through. Vicki didn't seem to mind as she began to tell me about a drug bust she had just come from.

"Oh sorry I didn't realize you were working," I said, kicking myself for being so stupid.

"It's not a problem, baby. What's up?" Vicki said. I could tell she had moved out of the noisy room she had previously been in and wondered what room of the station she was in; I knew almost all of them.

"I was just wondering if you'd want to meet up again?" I said, holding my breath and only exhaling when Vicki replied.

"Yes. When are you free?" Vicki said. We arranged a time to meet, in three days at the museum in town and I hung up the phone, practically dancing on air.

"Hello sweetness," I heard Vicki say before she came up behind me and hugged my waist. I loved how small she made me feel. It wasn't just her size; she made me feel so protected and safe when she was around like I could cuddle into her whenever I felt scared or nervous.

"Hi," I said taken by surprise, and I turned in her arms to feel her mouth on mine before I could say another word. Breaking the kiss, I giggled and held out my hand, which she took in hers as we walked inside.

"I can't believe you've never been to a museum before," Vicki said as we passed a bunch of old looking stuff. I looked to surprise, making her laugh her deep raspy laugh.

"Shall I explain all these things you've

missed?" I said to her stopping to look at something to prove I was into looking at old things, which I most certainly was not. But I liked listening to how educated Vicki was about the things we were looking at. She told me stories about how she had gone to Rome and saw the ruins and to Egypt to see the Pyramids. It made me smile in wonder.

"Where to now?" Vicki asked as we exited the Museum. I looked around the green space that rolled down the hill to the river that wound through the city. I turned to look at Vicki with nothing but pure mischief in my eyes.

"Race ya," I said, tearing off down the hill followed by Vicki who overtook me, grabbing me and picking me up. She whirled me around in her arms and slowly put me back down, and the whole world faded. All I saw was her as her long black hair was blown by the wind in the late summer afternoon breeze.

"I want you," I said before I kissed her and grazed my fingertips over her breasts. I was surprised, it was the first time she had seemed unsure of herself, and it made me feel nervous.

"Or not, like if you're not into it, that's cool," I said trying to backpedal so she didn't have to turn me down. Vicki sat down and looked up at the white clouds that floated by.

"It's not that I don't want to, it's that I am not sure you'll want to," Vicki said softly. I looked at her with a confused expression.

"Um, wasn't I the one who just tried to instigate it?" I said, using a word I had learned only last week, I was quite impressed with myself. Vicki took my hand and pulled me close to her. She put it on her thigh and watched my face as she moved my hand up her thigh and pushed it down onto her crotch. I gasped and pulled away involuntarily and looked up at her in confusion. She just looked plain faced at me as I put my hand back down on her and felt her over her trousers.

"But," I said before stopping. Vicki cleared her throat before she spoke.

"I'm trans sweetie, I just never had the

surgery. I kinda like my dick, so I kept it, having it doesn't make me feel any less female. Everyone is different; this is how I feel," Vicki said. I took my hand away and looked at her.

"Is this a bad time to tell you that I've never," I said.

"Never had sex with a trans woman? That's a pretty common thing never to have done baby," Vicki said, but I shook my head.

"No, I've never had um, I don't know how to say this without sounding offensive. But I've never fucked a dick before," I said trying not to hurt Vicki's feelings. I was glad when she smiled.

"Little gold star hey?" Vicki said.

"I want to, though. With you," I replied, not wanting her to think it was off the table and over between us. Vicki raised an eyebrow.

"Really?" She said, kissing me deeply when I nodded my head.

"Come on, baby girl, let me get you home then," Vicki said, standing to hail a taxi.

"Lay down," Vicki said when we were back in my apartment. It was close, so I had suggested we go there. I lay down on my bed and watched as Vicki slowly took off her clothes. Her pink button-down falling to the floor made my mouth gaped open as she began rubbing her large breasts over her pink bra.

"Do you like what you see?" Vicki said smirking at my lustful stare. I swallowed hard and nodded.

"Use your words, baby," Vicki said, making me blush.

"Yes, Vicki," I replied softly, watching as she unzipped her pants. She let them drop to the floor as well and took off her bra before climbing onto the bed with me.

"Come here," Vicki said in a commanding voice. I moved to her, and she picked me up and placed me on her lap facing her. She held me tight as she lifted my t-shirt over my head and groped my smaller tits excitedly. I closed my eyes and melted into her embrace as she pulled off my shorts and panties in one go. Feeling slightly exposed, Vicki noticed and pulled the bed sheets back down and I climbed into bed followed by Vicki.

"If you want to stop, baby girl, you must tell me, alright?" Vicki said lovingly as I began to feel more confident.

"Yes Vicki," I said as I began to kiss her and climbed on top of her. She let me place my hands around her neck as my body dropped between her thighs and began to grind on her making her pant in my ear. I could feel she was getting hard, and I liked that I had this power over her.

"Do you like that Vicki?" I said sweetly, knowing that she was letting me be in control.

"Yes, baby," Vicki moaned before grabbing my body and rolling on top of me.

"Come to Mommy," Vicki moaned, making me freeze.

"Mommy?" I questioned, making Vicki open her eyes widely realizing what she had just moaned.

"Um, I," Vicki stammered before I reached down and placed my hand firmly on her dick.

"Mommy, teach me," I said, enjoying the new dynamic she had just slipped us into. Relaxing, Vicki went back to feeling my body and sucked on my nipples, making me giggle.

"God, you're a cute baby girl. You've always been such a cute girl," Vicki said, reaching down and feeling between my thighs.

"Do you like it when Mommy talks to you baby girl?" Vicki moaned in my ear as I grabbed her firmly and began to push her panties down.

"Oh baby girl, rub it for Mommy," Vicki said as I began to jerk her off.

"Just like that, good girl, tell Mommy you want it," Vicki said making me moan as she flicked my clit over and over.

"Mommy, I want it," I moaned feeling Vicki fill my tight pussy with her finger.

"Louder," Vicki commanded, forcing my pussy open with another finger.

"Mommy, please fuck me, I want it," I

squealed as Vicki pumped my pussy making me cum. She suddenly jumped up and pinned my two wrists above my head with one hand as she guided her dick into my virgin pussy.

"Mommy," I breathed, feeling her fill me. She stayed inside of me until my muscles relaxed around her before she slowly pulled out of me to push back in with a little more force.

"There you go baby girl; you're going to get fucked by Mommy sweetheart. Hold onto Mommy baby," Vicki said, lowering herself on me and letting my wrists go. I wrapped my arms around her as she gently fucked me. I loved having such a powerful woman be so gentle with me, and I began to suck my thumb, which delighted Vicki.

"Such a cute little girl getting taken by Mommy, you're going to cum for Mommy baby," Vicki said beginning to fuck me harder. She reached down and cupped herself as she pushed her dick hard against my hilt taking her other hand and pressing down on my pelvis, making me feel her deeper inside of me.

"Mommy, please," I moaned feeling my cum around her dick, getting long strokes from her as she edged herself.

"Oh good girl," Vicki said, pulling out of me and cumming on my tummy. She surged through her hand and covered me until she was finished, stroking my hair with her other hand, her strong thighs keeping her over me.

"Baby girl, oh that was the best Mommy has had in a long time, thank you," Vicki said as I began to tear up.

"Oh, sweetie did I hurt you?" Vicki said, suddenly worried. I just shook my head no, and she held me as I hyperventilated and tears rolled down my cheeks.

"Talk to me baby girl," Vicki said lovingly when I began to calm down.

"It was just a lot, Mommy," I replied, hoping Vicki was happy to be called Mommy even after sex. She smiled down at me and patted my bottom gently.

"Sorry, I should have told you I cum hard,"

Vicki said, missing my meaning.

"No Mommy, it was like, better than I have ever had. You've blown my mind," I replied, kissing her arm softly. Vicki took me to the bathroom and washed me clean before she carried me back out into the living room and sat me down on the couch with her. It was the first time that I had seen her dick, and I was surprised she had fit it all inside of me, she was big and still hard, which made me surprised.

"I can put my clothes back on if it's a problem," Vicki said, catching me looking intensely at her.

"Oh no Mommy, I just like, it's all so new and big," I replied, making her laugh and look down.

"Yeah, I suppose it is, but I'm kinda big too so anything smaller would look weird I guess," Vicki replied, making a tea and bringing it over to me.

"Here little girl," Vicki said. I sipped the tea and let the stream of thoughts run through my mind as we drank in silence. I imagined her bending me over the kitchen table and ramming into me, pulling my hair back as she came, forcing herself in my ass and filling it with her cum. Breaking my thoughts, I shook my head and looked at Vicki who had begun flicking through her phone.

"So, does this make me your girlfriend?" I said grimacing at how stupid I sounded. Vicki just laughed.

"Do you want to be my girlfriend?" Vicki asked, putting her phone down and repositioning herself. I looked at her like she just asked the dumbest thing in the world.

"Yeah, of course, are you lost? I've always wanted to be your girlfriend!" I said, putting my tea down before crawling into Vicki's lap.

"Oh baby careful, now you're asking for it," Vicki said as I felt her hardening against my ass.

Chapter 5

Vicki stayed the night, but we had agreed to meet up in a few days, she was going to cook me dinner. I felt the work week drag on and was happy to be coming home Friday afternoon. I stopped in on the way home and picked up a bottle of wine to have with dinner and smiled as I saw a group of teens standing outside the bottle shop asking people if they would buy them alcohol. I remembered doing that with my mates just four years ago, but it felt like yesterday. I passed the kids but stopped when they started talking to me.

"Can you buy just anything, Miss?" One of the older looking girls said. I looked at her, and she looked familiar.

"No sorry, you know I can't. Hey, you're Hope's sister, aren't you?" I asked. Now I knew where I had seen her before. She was about to reply when I saw her friends scurry off behind her, and a shadow fell across her face. Confused, I turned around to see Vicki in full uniform standing behind us.

"Hello there, haven't you got somewhere to be, like somewhere doing homework?" Vicki said to the girl who just scoffed and walked back slowly before turning on her heel and bolting after her friends. I laughed.

"Same old Vicki," I said, reaching up to cuddle her but she pushed me away, making my heart ache instantly.

"Not now sweetie," Vicki said. She had started to say something else, but I didn't hear it. I was walking away from her, having her rejection was too painful to stand around and hear her reasons why.

I was almost back at my car when I heard her footsteps coming behind me.

"Hey, come here," Vicki said, opening her arms just for me to push her away.

"No, not now sweetie," I mocked trying to hold back my tears.

"Baby, Mommy has to be a certain way

when I'm at work. I'm sorry you felt unloved, it's not that at all baby girl," Vicki said softly so no one but us could hear. She looked around before reaching down and cupping my chin in her hand she forced me to look at her.

"Ava, you know you're my good girl, I should have told you the rules for when Mommy is working baby, I'm sorry," Vicki said making me annoyed I could feel soothed by her so easily. I nodded, and she wiped the last of my tears away before opening my door for me.

"You really should be more careful about locking your car baby," Vicki said frowning.

"Who is going to try and rob me? I may not get into any trouble now, but they all know I can beat a bitch down," I replied, making Vicki smirk and grab my upper arm.

"My tough little princess," she teased, making me laugh as I got into my car and before to drive away.

Walking up to my apartment, I knew something

was wrong straight away. The opened door was a pretty big give away since I knew I had locked it this morning.

"Hello?" I said, slowly opening the door and peering inside. The house had been ripped apart, looking like the typical robbery scene. Couch cushions were all over the floor and candles, photo frames and appliances where all broken and scattering around the living room. One of the walls had a spray painted 'Cop fucker' written in black paint and the other wall had 'Five-O Homo' in red and blue. My TV had been stolen, as well as my laptop and camera equipment. I had been relatively calm until I walked into the bedroom and found them. The group of kids that had been outside the bottle shop, but this time they had traded in their bikes for baseball bats. There was four of them; I was happy. Hope's sister wasn't one of them. But there was only one of me, and I knew this was about to get ugly. The thing about growing up here was that this wasn't my first break in and it certainly wasn't my first fight. The rules of a fight around here are pretty simple if someone tries to beat you down, make sure you don't lose. These kids were about 18 years old but out here that didn't matter, I wasn't about to go easy on them, and I slowly put my bag down.

"So you like to fuck cops hey?" The first person to speak in a gang is always the leader, so now I knew who to hit first. I looked around at them and felt the old me come through my eyes. They use to call me wild cat because of the way furry burned in my eyes when I fought, and I could see by the fear growing in one of the other guys that I hadn't lost my touch.

"Yeah, what of it cunt?" I replied, spitting at them. The leader laughed and swung the bat, but I blocked him before he could hit me and punched my fist into his mouth, knocking a tooth out and sending him backward. I stopped and looked around to see the other three who had stepped back when I stepped to them.

"I thought you bitches wanted a fight?" I yelled, grabbing a bat off one of them and swinging into another's knee cap. I wasn't about to see if they were going to back up their threats; they should have known not to fuck with me. I heard a baby cry as their leader got up and tried to swing at me again, but this time I used the bat as a ramming stick and made him double over as his dick was hit.

"Get the fuck out," I yelled, making the two uninjured boys bolt for my door. I grabbed the boy I had hit over his knee cap by the ear and enjoyed feeling him wince in pain as I threw him out before going back to get their leader.

"Come around here again, next time I'll be packing so we can play target practice you useless mother fucker," I viciously whispered in his ear before kicking his ass as I pushed him out the door, slamming it behind him. I fell to the floor and began shaking and crying. I pulled my legs to my chest and muffled my screams as I felt my body shake with fear and sadness. I stayed there, my back to the door until Vicki was calling my phone. I had completely forgotten that I was meant to be having dinner with her tonight.

"Hey baby, just wondering if you are on your way?" Vicki said lovingly. I hadn't stopped crying for hours, and I knew my voice would give me away.

"I'm sorry, I lost track of time, I," I replied before getting cut off.

"What's wrong baby?" Vicki said. I didn't know how to reply. I looked around my apartment and felt embarrassed. Embarrassed that I thought I could have a life with her, embarrassed that I had to go back to old ways to stay safe, but mostly I was embarrassed, I was ruining my chances with her.

"Sweetie?" Vicki said, breaking my thoughts.

"I can't do this," I said softly making her go quiet on the phone.

"Alright," Vicki said which just made me cry again.

"I'm coming over baby, will you let me come over," Vicki said making me surprised she wasn't giving up on me. I looked around my apartment, and I couldn't care, she would see it if she wanted too.

"Yep, OK," I said before hanging up the phone.

It wasn't more than 20minutes later when a knock came from the door, and I pulled myself up to open the door for Vicki.

"Baby come here," she said as soon as she saw me. She pulled me in tight and held me, making me cry all over again. I was getting sick of all this crying; it had started to give me a headache.

"What the fuck?" Vicki said she had seen the apartment. She looked down at me.

"Are you alright? Did you get hurt?" Vicki said, starting to look me over making me laugh.

"No, I won, Vicki, you know I always win," I replied. Vicki picked me up, and I wrapped my legs around her waist.

"Mommy," Vicki said correcting me and I snuggled into her before repeating,

"Mommy," into her neck. She smelt like her usual sweet perfume, and I breathed
her in deeply, wanting all of her.

"Tell me what happened baby girl," Vicki said, clearing a spot on the couch and sitting me on her lap while looking around the room.

"I came home, and the door was open," I said before getting cut off.

"So you thought you'd go inside and not call Mommy?!" Vicki said shocked I wouldn't think to call her.

"Well, yeah," I replied honestly.

"Mommy, you know how things like this go," I replied, putting my fingers to her lips playfully before continuing.

"Then I saw all of this, and when I went into my bedroom, four guys were standing there with bats, but I took one of them and kicked them out. Nothing bad happened, but my place is trashed," I said cuddling into her. She wrapped an arm around me and patted my back as I snuggled.

"Cop fucker, original," Vicki said, but I could

tell she was angry, I could feel it in her pulse, her blood was pumping quicker, and her face was stern.

"I understand why you wanted to call it off baby. But I don't want you too," Vicki said, looking at me with a seriousness I knew all too well.

"I don't want to either, it was just a lot, I went kinda feral on those guys, and I hate to admit it, but I was a little shook," I said putting my hands down into her lap. Vicki raised an eyebrow at me as I began to pat and rub over her jeans.

"Now, you want to play now? After everything that has happened?" Vicki said, repositioning herself and biting her bottom lip.

"Yeah, why not?" I said a little disappointed when Vicki shook her head no.

"You don't owe me, baby," Vicki said, making me annoyed she could read me so easily.

"But I don't know how else to thank you for being so lovely," I said softly looking at her getting hard, wondering how she could have so much self-control.

"How about, you pack a bag and come and stay at mine over the weekend instead of staying here? We can come back tomorrow and clean it up. I doubt you'll get your gear back but do you have insurance?" Vicki said. I got up, and Vicki followed me into my bedroom and sat on my bed.

"Yeah I do, I'll probs get something back from them right?" I asked. I had never filled out an insurance claim before. I'd only got insurance because the employers at my job made everyone have some. I had thought it was a waste of money until right now.

"I'll help you with it, it can be tricky," Vicki said, helping me pack.

"You won't need these," Vicki said, taking out my panties. I looked at her, confused.

"I don't like wearing no panties, even when I'm at home," I said to a laughing Vicki.

"Oh you'll be covered don't worry, but it won't be with panties," Vicki said smirking and playfully spanking my ass. I shook it for her, and she grabbed my hips and roughly pulled me down on her making me sit on her lap.

"Don't tease Mommy baby girl, there's only so much control I have," Vicki whispered in my ear as she flicked my nipples, making me squirm and moan on her lap.

"Yes, shake that little ass for Mommy," Vicki said, slapping my ass firmly making me jump.

"Oh Mommy's sensitive little girl," Vicki said slowly as she pushed a finger into my mouth and grabbed the crotch of my shorts, pulling it to the side. I could feel her getting hard under me, and I bounced on her lap, wet with excitement. Vicki took her finger out of me and slide it up and down my wet slit, teasing me and holding me in place with her legs wrapped around mine, forcing them open.

"Do you like it when I hold you like this baby?" Vicki said, grabbing my tit and shaking it in her hand.

"Does Mommy make you feel safe?" She continued, smiling as I moaned in response. She did make me feel safe, she made me feel like nothing could ever hurt me again, and she knew it. I bucked against her hand, she had made me cum more times than I could count, and I needed her to stop.

"You can't get away from Mommy baby I'm too strong for you to escape me," Vicki said as she bit down on my neck. I felt her lift me and when she put me back down, she slid me onto her big dick and filled my used pussy, holding me in the air as she fucked me. She pounded into me as I tried to escape her, enjoying how her grip only tightened on my thighs.

"Don't you fucking dare move little girl, you'll take Mommy as long as I want you too," Vicki growled, as she dropped me on her lap and pushed me forward. She pushed my body down on the bed. She pinned me there, grabbed my shorts by the crotch again, and rammed back into me, slapping my ass when I tried to fight her.

"What did Mommy say about that princess?" Vicki moaned as she pulled out and turned me over before pushing her cumming dick into my mouth.

"Suck it baby girl, let Mommy use you," Vicki said as I swallowed her, gagging as she poured down my throat. She smiled as she saw her cum spilling from my mouth and pulled out slightly when my eyes started to water and stroked my cheek while pushing her dick along the side of my mouth.

"Cute baby," Vicki said as she took it out of my mouth and pulled me in for a cuddle.

"I love you, Mommy," I said as she held me against her breast and let me fall asleep in her arms.

When we finally got to hers, it was late, and I was tired. We had fucked for hours at mine, and I had happily let Vicki use me as I lay exhausted and limp on my bed. Her stamina was incredible. She had practically carried me to her car and buckled me in, putting a blankie over the top of me and let me drift in and out of sleep as she drove us to her home.

"We're here, darling," Vicki said, gently shaking me awake. I opened my eyes and looked around. We lived in different suburbs. The streets here were like something from a movie. The street was lined with tall leafy trees and the houses where big colonial style homes with perfect gardens and sidewalks. Vicki came around to the passenger side and opened the door for me and helped me down from her big SUV. I liked her car, it had cream leather and wood trim, and the navy blue paint was always clean. She grabbed my backpack and took me inside. Her home was modern, and I was surprised that a cop could afford something like this. She must have seen my face because she laughed as she shut the door behind me.

"I wasn't always a cop baby," Vicki said, leading me through the house. Her bedroom was as big as my entire apartment and looked out over the manicured back yard.

"Why are you even messing with me?" I said to her, feeling stupid and out of place her in her luxury home. Vicki frowned and came over to me, making me feel even smaller.

"Baby, I'm not *messing* with you. I loving on you," Vicki said, grabbing me and holding me tight.

"But like, what can I even offer you, like, I can't match this!" I said, pulling away from her and letting the house overwhelm me. Vicki laughed and walked into the kitchen. Worried that I would get lost, I quickly followed her.

"Let me explain something to you baby girl because you have a few things mixed up. I don't need you to match this, I need you to be your cute, baby self and let Mommy take care of you," Vicki said, passing me a drink in a sippy cup. I looked at it and looked at her, rolling my eyes.

"If you're going to be a brat, Mommy can spank you if you'd like?" Vicki said, making me giggle as she pushed the drink into my hands.

"No, Mommy," I said, drinking obediently. Vicki got herself a wine and went into the bathroom.

"Bathies baby girl," she said, reaching down to pick me up.

"Hey, I can walk," I said, wriggling out of her grasp.

"You'll let Mommy carry you, or you'll crawl my darling," Vicki said, smiling victoriously when I reluctantly lifted my arms accepting her embrace.

"Good girl," Vicki said, taking me into the bathroom. She ran a bath and undressed me before helping me into the bath.

"Mommy, are you coming?" I asked making

Vicki smile.

"Would you like me to baby?" She asked, taking off her shoes. I nodded and watched as she undressed and sat down on the opposite end of the bath.

"So Mommy, is that for me?" I asked, pointing to the diaper and clothes Vicki had placed on the counter. She turned to see what I was pointing at, turning back and moved over to where I was sitting. I moved into her arms and loved how she kissed me softly, smiling when I moaned between kisses.

"Yes, baby," Vicki said before washing me clean. I enjoyed that she was so gentle on my cunt, I could still feel her in me and flinched thinking she would be rough.

"You don't need to be scared of me sweetie, Mommy isn't going to hurt you," she said before getting out and drying herself.

"You are going to look so cute in these baby," Vicki said, taking my hand and pulling me out of the bath. She put a duck hooded towel over my head before she playfully dried me off, making she giggle and squirm under her touch.

"Stay still for me little one," Vicki said, putting a pacifier in my mouth. I froze, I don't think anyone had ever given me one before. Vicki must have sensed my shock and pulled me to the floor, she had placed a clean, dry towel down, and I followed her instruction and spread my legs and lifted my bottom.

"It's OK baby, Mommy is here now, and I'm going to give you all the loving you could ever need," Vicki said placing a hand on my tummy and gently pressing down.

"Come on, let's fill this little tummy of yours," she said, picking me up and carrying me back to the kitchen.

"Mommy," I whispered in her ear from behind my new pink paci. Vicki patted my bottom and just pushed my face into her neck as she moved around the kitchen getting everything she needed for dinner. She eventually put me down on her couch and put a movie on, wrapping me in a fluffy blankie before she went back to finish making dinner.

"Here little one, do you want to feed yourself," Vicki asked as she handed me my plate. I looked down and was impressed with what I saw.

"How did you know how to make something like this, Mommy?" I said, smelling the Asian dish she had made us.

"I told you I wasn't always a cop. I worked as a chef for a few years in Bali before I came back home and settled down here," Vicki said as I began to eat.

"This is delicious," I said. Vicki fed me the last few mouthfuls and patted my tummy.

"Full baby girl?" Vicki asked as I climbed into her arms and snuggled up on her with my blankie.

Chapter 7

The sun woke me before it did Vicki and I looked down and touched the front of my diaper over the pink diaper cover Vicki had dressed me in. I was surprised I was so chill about playing along with this game she had going on. It felt nice to have someone care about me so much, to want to take away all the mean things that the world threw at me. I liked that I didn't have to do any of this grown-up stuff alone anymore. I thought back to yesterday, how she had been so patient and calm about me trying to push her away, instead of just bailing on me she had made me feel more loved than I had ever felt in my life.

I slowly got up and went out into the spacious living room and tried to turn the wall length TV on. Struggling to understand the table looking remote, I gave up and walked into the kitchen where I saw a note saying that there were crackers and coloring ins on the table. I looked over and smiled, seeing the colors and books. Strolling over I sat down and flicked through the pages, seeing that they were empty. I liked that, I didn't want to share Mommy with anyone else, she was mine. I found a page I liked and began to color, humming to myself happily.

I was almost finished my page when I felt Vicki come up behind me and grab my waist in a hug.

"Good morning baby girl," Vicki said, kissing my cheek and looking at my picture.

"Pretty little one, Mommy might have to rip it out and put in on the fridge," Vicki added, looking to see if I had eaten any of the crackers.

"Hi Mommy," I said, still focused on my drawing. I loved this, but it was Saturday, and I knew that Vicki was working tomorrow and didn't know when we would get my apartment cleaned.

"Mommy, maybe I should go and sort out my apartment?" I asked as she began to make breakfast. Vicki turned around and passed me a juice in my sippy cup.

"Baby, Mommy has already taken care of

that. I have people there right now fixing it up," Vicki said making me wonder when she had done all of that, and how she had done that. I looked at her, confused.

"So what, we just live happily ever after?" I said, unsure how to handle all this nice stuff that was happening. Vicki just laughed and nodded her head.

"That's kinda the idea baby girl. Not everything has to be so hard," she said, cutting up my omelet and feeding me a mouthful. I ate silently thinking about what happily ever after was meant to feel like. It was nice, but it was new, it was scary, and it was not something I knew how to live with. I so used to having to struggle, to hustle and be on constant guard that I couldn't understand how to drop that down and be at peace. I also didn't know how to tell Vicki any of this, so I just ate my breakfast and looked away from her.

"It's too good to be true Mommy, what gives?" I asked, feeling vulnerable for the first time. Vicki sat back and looked at me.

"You just got lucky baby girl, I didn't think that you'd hate this so much," Vicki said laughing and cleaning up our plates.

"I don't hate it; I don't know how to do this. Pretty suburban easy life with no drama, like what do you even do for fun?" I asked, shifting uncomfortably wanting the diaper off.

"Come on, baby, let Mommy help you. Mommy's feisty little wild cat," Vicki said winking at me making me laugh.

"I heard them call you that once and I thought how fitting it was for you," Vicki explained as she took off my diaper and passed me some big girl clothes.

"Can I still call you Mommy when I look like this?" I asked, feeling more comfortable and coming up to kiss Vicki full on her mouth.

"Yeah baby girl, let's try for just nights in diapies OK?" Vicki said, and I thought about it for a moment before nodding my head in agreement.

"I think I'd like that," I said, pulling on my

tight pink tracksuit pants. I could tell Vicki liked how they looked, she wasn't even trying to hide her hardening dick and rubbed it opening in front of me.

"Mommy, do you like it?" I said, teasing her. I dropped to my knees and was surprised how excited I was to suck her. It was only the second time I'd had her in my mouth, but I swallowed her deeper than I had before.

"Oh Jesus baby girl, you're Mommy's little slut now aren't you," Vicki said, arching her back and shooting down my throat. She got up and ripped at my pants but stopped when I told her I was still too sensitive to have her there. She just smiled.

"We can work with that, let me play with you like this then," Vicki said as she rubbed her dick along my slit hitting my clit and teasing me.

Chapter 8

I stayed over at hers Saturday night but come Sunday; I could tell she had work on her mind. She was less playful, and her energy was very controlling.

"What are you going to do today? I'll drop you home before work Ava," Vicki said. I frowned when I had heard her say my name, and she noticed, coming over and grabbing hold of me.

"I have to be serious now baby, going out onto those streets is not a joke, I can't be feeling all lovely and Mommy right now. Do you understand?" Vicki explained, trying to sound like she had all weekend. I smiled and nodded, knowing that she was right; those streets were no joke.

We finished breakfast, and I packed my things away, explaining that I was going to look for a new apartment when I got home.

"Why don't you move in here?" Vicki said,

taking me by surprise. She picked up my bag and walked to the door before I grabbed my wallet and keys and joined her.

"I don't know, do you think it's too soon?" I asked her nervously. She just shrugged.

"It's not like you won't be at mine every minute I'm not working anyway baby girl, Mommy owns you now, remember?" Vicki said. I didn't like how controlling she was being. I had learned from a young age to take care of myself, and here she thought she was gods gift to the world.

"I still don't know," I said softly before suddenly feeling her hand on my thigh prying my thighs apart and rubbing me roughly.

"It's not really up for discussion. You'll move in with me after my shift today baby girl," Vicki said. I squirmed in my seat, which just made her laugh cruelly as she pulled my shorts to the side and forced a finger into my pussy.

"See how wet you are baby girl, don't try and tell Mommy you don't like this," Vicki said, pulling over to the side of the road and rubbing her dick wantonly. She pushed another finger into me and moved them inside of me. She reached into her pants and pulled her hard dick out, grabbing the back of my head and forcing herself into my mouth.

"Be Mommy's little fuck doll baby girl," Vicki moaned as she tilted her head back and closed her eyes as she used me. She worked her thumb over my clit and used her little finger to tease my ass, only stopping when I bit her. I couldn't think of anything else I could do to make her stop, and I was happy when it worked.

"Ouch you little bitch," Vicki said, pulling my head up and slapping me hard across my face. I looked at her, broken-hearted and she changed back into my loving Mommy in an instant.

"I'm sorry baby, I," was all I heard her say as I jumped out of her car, grabbed my backpack and ran down the street.

I knew she couldn't follow me as I jumped a fence down an alley and felt the familiar gravel tracks under my feet. I could feel the tears pouring down my face, but I didn't bother to stop them, I just kept running.

"Ava!" I heard her angrily yell, and I could tell she wasn't following me. I ran until I thought my lungs would give out and found myself in one of the old warehouses that I use to hide in when she would chase me for stealing something. I looked around the dirty place and was surprised I could have ever felt safe here. There were a couple of crack whores shooting up in the corner, and I decided that this wasn't going to be where I would stay. Leaving, I felt my legs take over, and I was running again, but this time, I knew where I was going, home.

I hadn't seen my apartment since the night of the attack, and I was surprised just how well together it looked. After opening the door, I put my backpack down and looked around the space. Vicki hadn't lied when she said she'd take care of it. Looking down to see her ringing for the fifth time, I switched my phone off and went back to staring at my apartment. She had organized to have new furniture brought in, and it looked expensive and modern, like something from a luxury home magazine. She had artwork on the walls and had even put new appliances in the kitchen. There was a colorful rug in the living room, and she had even set up a new laptop and TV for me. She had bought me a new bed and had it dressed in pretty pink linen with two bunny's tucked into the middle of the bed. I went into the bathroom and was happy nothing had changed in there. She had bought me expensive shower gel and lotion, put sweet berry scented candles on the counter and new hand towels. *Did she think I owed her? I never asked her for any of this,* I thought to myself going back into the living room and sitting in front of my new laptop. It was the kind I could never afford, and I felt embarrassed and out of place in an apartment which I knew was mine, but that didn't feel like mine at all.

I got up and went to have a shower. After showering and enjoying the feel of the shower products on my skin, I looked in my cupboard to see that she had also bought me a selection of new clothes and shoes. Looking through the rack I was happy she had left me with clothes I had bought but had to admit, she knew my style. I pulled on a pair of light denim, ripped jeans, and a light bubble gum pink t-shirt and went to make myself a cup of tea.

Turning my phone back on, I saw that she had called 12 times and sent three texts before I nervously read the messages. 'I am so sorry baby girl, please forgive me, it won't happen again, I don't know what came over me.' 'You are the most precious thing to me, please ring me back baby girl.' 'I hope you aren't scared of me now Ava; I truly am so sorry, baby girl.' I was happy her messages weren't as angry as she was when I had left her. Deciding that I needed some time before I spoke to her again, I replied with, 'I am just going to need some time, I don't trust you anymore. Talk soon.' I didn't know how I was supposed to feel about this. I had been felt up heaps before, a couple of times it had even gone further than what she had done, but this was different. Maybe I was different. It hurt more, and I couldn't seem to brush it off. Maybe it was because I had let her in and she had been the only person ever to make me feel safe, then for her to shatter that feeling of security was just too much. Or maybe it was because I had liked her and she wasn't just some punk with wandering hands. Deciding that it was all just too much, I lay down on my new couch, pulled my new blanket over me and fell asleep on my new cushions.

Chapter 9

I woke up to police sirens whirling down the street and blinked around my living room, wondering why it was so light. I didn't remember turning any lights on before I fell asleep, and I also didn't remember making any food, but the smell of Asian cooking made me instantly nervous. I quietly looked over the back of the couch to see Vicki standing in my kitchen, drinking a glass of red wine, and making dinner. She had on soft gray sweat shorts and a pink singlet, her hair down and knee-high black socks.

"Vicki," I quietly said, making her turn around. I was scared of her, and she knew it. Her face going from happy to sad upon seeing the fear in my eyes.

"Baby girl, Mommy is so sorry," Vicki said, coming over and reaching of me. I flinched and pushed her hand away, pushing myself back to the edge of the couch. I was happy she looked hurt;

she should be.

"How did you get in?" I asked sleepily. I could tell that I'd been asleep for hours by the hoarseness of my throat.

"I had a key cut when they fixed your apartment up," Vicki said, crossing her legs on the couch.

"I want you to leave," I said, looking down at my feet, they were cold. I stayed looking at them, I didn't want to look at her, she looked good, and I hated myself for finding her so wildly attractive when I was feeling so nervous about being around her. She took the blanket and put it over my toes and held them gently in her hands.

"Ava, I am sorry. You have to know that was an innocent mistake?" Vicki said lovingly. I looked at her as tears filled my eyes once more and she moved closer to me, kicking my foot that I held up to try and stop her out of the way and pulled me into her arms.

"Just because you're stronger than me doesn't mean you can do that," I said, crying into her neck. I felt her arms tighten around me as she began to rock me.

"I trusted you," I added, looking up at her heart broken. I was happy; she just nodded her head and didn't try to say anything. I could smell the dinner slightly burning, and I wriggled out of her embrace, happy she let me and went to the kitchen. I turned the wok off and stayed there looking at it as I felt her move behind me and drape her arms over my shoulders.

"I know you did, you still can. I didn't think your no was a no and I'm sorry," Vicki said. For the first time, I saw how vulnerable she really was, and I liked that I felt like I was talking to the real her.

"I still want you to go, I need some time Vicki," I said. I could see she was hurt by me calling her by her name, but I was glad she just nodded her head and started to collect her things.

"Just add the noodles if you want, everything is ready," Vicki said as she put her shoes on, left her key by the door, and walked out.

I hadn't heard from her for a week before I felt like I could breathe easy again. I had stopped feeling like she was watching me, and I even started going for jogs again around the park. I had worked the usual 9-5 at the furniture store and had got myself into a routine of cooking every night instead of just ordering out. Things were going well. I missed her though, but I knew that that would pass soon enough as well. I had even set up a couple of dates with some girls online to try and shake her out of my system. One of those dates was tonight.

I had tried the usual dating sites, mostly because I'm lazy and didn't want to get off my couch and also because it's just hard to find girls in the hood who don't have kids, a convict record or some kind of addiction. But I had narrowed my search down to this one girl who seemed really nice. Her name was Melanie, and she lived in the same area as me. She had shoulder length blonde hair and a sweet smile so when she asked me out for dinner at a local restaurant I figured it would be a nice time. I got dressed in a short red dress and pulled on cream heels, touching up my makeup before I left my building.

Walking down the block, I saw the usual working girls, a few pimps looking out the window of the diners that were scattered up the street and our local homeless man who always told me how pretty I was. I liked him and would buy him cream buns or coffee most afternoons after work, and he had chased away more than one guy who had mistaken me for one of the streetwalkers. I couldn't blame them. These guys weren't from around here, and every girl in a dress looked the same to them. But to us, we were worlds apart. For one, I looked fed, I didn't have that hungry, will fuck for food or pills kind of vibe, and I looked like I had somewhere to be. As I passed one girl who was clearly new, she bumped shoulders with me accidentally.

"Oh I'm so sorry, are you OK?" She asked. She had dropped her wallet, and I reached down to pick it up for her. She had sad runaway eyes and a painted smile, and I wondered what they'd get her addicted to so they could keep her, she looked like a runner.

"Yeah, I'm fine, stay safe," I said as I handed her wallet back just as her pimp came out of a diner. I could tell she was hers by the way she quickly walked to us.

"I'm going, I just bumped her making her drop her stuff," I said, putting my hands up in defense. I had learned not to mess with these guys.

"Yo Ava, we're all good," she said. Growing up here, you ended up knowing everyone.

"Still fucking that cop?" She added. I didn't know who she was, but she certainly knew me. Playing it cool, I spat on the ground.

"Fuck the police," I said, making her laugh, and we pounded fists as I walked off, happy to be out of there. *You did fuck the police;* I thought to myself in amusement as I entered the restaurant I was meeting Melanie at. I looked around and saw her sitting at the bar waiting for me. *Cute,* I thought, seeing her black dress and pink heels. I made my way over to her and sat down next to her.

"Hi," she said, looking over to me.

"Hi, wow, your photos don't really do you justice," I said to her making her laugh. We paid for our drinks and made our way to the table by the window. I was aware that there were a number of cops walking the street tonight. They were in plain clothes, but growing up here, we learned to see a cop before we learned how to count to ten.

"I'm really glad you took me up on this date Ava, not many people I've spoken to have been as interesting as you," Melanie said. I laughed, she was trying so hard, and I liked having someone practically beg for me.

"I wouldn't be here if you hadn't told me about how you captured those aerial shots over the river. They were so beautiful, you're right, drones are the future of photography," I said. The waiter came over, and we ordered our dinner as we continued to talk. She told me about the other photo series she had taken and how she sold them online. I told her about how I had to start again after my gear got stolen and she offered to lend me her equipment over the weekend. I had just finished my dinner when an angry police officer walked in and stood by our table. At first, I didn't pay any attention to her. I had assumed that she was looking at someone else, not us.

"Ma'am I'm going to need you to step outside with me," she said, stopping our conversation. We both looked at each other before Melanie quickly jumped up and sprinted past the cop who reached for her taser but stopped when I got up, grabbing me firmly and pulling me to her before turning me around and walking me out the door.

"What the fuck, let me go you fat fuck," I said, struggling against her grip. I could tell she was going to leave bruises on my arms.

"Had to wait until I wasn't running to get me, huh," I said. The cop was obviously not in the mood for my sass as she flung me against her car, winding me, making me cough and moan in pain.

"Well well haven't you grown up little Ava Meadows," the cop said reaching around and patting me down over my tits. I hated that she knew me. I hated that she had the 'right' to touch me. I also hated that I knew even if I stopped resisting her, she would still be as rough and grabby as she was now. I had tried that, just doing what they wanted without a fight, but the result was always the same around here. They'd cop a feel and force it on you regardless of how well mannered you were, so you might as well try to get them off if you could.

Chapter 10

"Get off of me," I yelled, struggling against the cops weight. She pulled me back just to push me against the car again and kicked my feet out, making me spread my legs. Pinning me down, I could feel my lungs being crushed, and I gasped for air. I could feel her hands on me, reaching around and patting me down just as my eyes closed and my head went dizzy. Just before I passed out, I felt her reaching up my thighs before being pulled away, and the sudden fullness of my lungs made my legs buckle. Strong hands held me up, and I knew whose touch was on me now instantly.

"Vicki," I said softly, feeling my head spin and her hands take over the search. She was gentle; there wasn't the hate in her touch like there was in the first cops, and I moved my body to her instructions.

"Turn around for me," Vicki said affectionately. I slowly brought my feet together before I turned very slowly to face her. It was the first time I had seen her in a month, and she frowned as she saw the gash across my cheek.

"Be more careful next time," Vicki aggressively said to her partner who just huffed and kicked the dirt. Vicki placed her hand under my chin and moved my neck as she ran her fingers through my hair. She placed both her hands on my stomach as she felt down my front and whispered that it was OK when she felt me whimper as she ran her hands down my thighs. I could feel the blood from my cheek run down my face, and Vicki took out a tissue and offered it to me kindly. I gladly accepted and pressed against my face, grimacing with the pain.

"We are still going to need you to come down to the station Ava; we need to ask you a few questions," Vicki said. I could see in her eyes she wasn't in cop mode, and I liked how she was talking to me. It was soft and kind and didn't make me feel worried.

"Hands behind your back," the other cop

said, grabbing my upper arm and spinning me around and pressing me hard against the car again. Vicki grabbed her shoulder and pulled her back, spinning me around and half holding me to her side.

"She doesn't need them," she said glaring down the other cop and subtly patted me on the back. It took all my strength not to snuggle into her. I could feel her hot breath on me and her protective stance, and it made me realize how much I had missed her. I liked that I could tell she had missed me too and I smiled at her weakly as she opened the car door for me.

At the station, it looked as though nothing had changed in years. The rooms were just as cold, and the cops were just as noisy. Vicki walked me to a room at the end of a corridor and got me a cup of coffee while I waited. I looked around the room; it felt funny being back in here. At least this time I knew I wasn't in any actual trouble. The cop who had interrupted my date came in first and slammed some folders down on the table. *Why did they always do that?* I thought to myself watching her try and be assertive. *I shall name you, Constable fuckface,* I thought adamantly, smirking to myself.

"So you know Ms. Hunter?" She said. I looked at her and wondered if she was this angry because she never got laid.

"Not really, I met her online, and we went out for dinner tonight before you guys jumped us," I replied. I didn't mind being honest with her, I was definitely not about to see Melanie again, and I didn't owe her anything.

"Where did you meet?" Constable fuckface asked. Flicking through the files, she placed multiple pictures of dead girls in front of me.

"Online," I replied, looking down at the photos she was showing me.

"This is who you really met. A drug mule who is known for recruiting over dating apps. Do you do drugs, Ms Meadows?" She asked as Vicki walked into the room. I could tell she had heard what I had said about meeting Melanie online by her sad expression.

"No, I don't do drugs," I said, looking at Vicki.

"Try to focus on Ms. Meadows. She can't help you now, you've made a right mess for yourself," the cop said, sounding impressed with herself. Vicki sat down and leaned back in the chair, crossing her arms over her chest.

"How long where you talking with her?" Vicki asked. I could tell she was not asking for any reason connected to this case.

"Only two weeks," I replied, enjoying ignoring the other cop who was obviously mad that Vicki had taken over.

"Did she ever say anything about her work?" The other cop said, trying to gain control again. I death stared her before reaching into my clutch and pulling out my phone. I slid it across the table towards Vicki, who grabbed it without looking away from me.

"You can read the messages; I was hardly in love with the girl. We talked about photography and growing up around here. She invited me to dinner, it's not like I was doing anything anyway," I said as Vicki held the phone. Silence fell between the three of us before the other cop broke it.

"That'll be all for tonight, Ms. Meadows. Lovely to see you again, I'll let Constable Smith show you out, although I'm sure you remember the way," the cop said leaving the room. Vicki and I just stayed sitting there. She spun my phone on the cold metal table, and I watched as the clock ticked by.

"I'm not mad," Vicki finally spoke.

"Not here," I said, standing up wanting to leave. Vicki nodded and got up, handing me my phone back. We walked in silence out of the station, constable fuckface was right, I did remember my way out. It was near midnight, and the air was cold as I kicked my foot along the sidewalk, I was hoping Vicki would be finished her shift soon.

"You'll need this," I said, turning to her and placing her spare key in her hand. Vicki looked down, and I could see her heart, almost jump out of her chest, and she inhaled deeply. She looked at me with a surprised look, and I smiled.

"Don't make a fool out of me, I can forgive once, but never twice Vicki," I said, feeling in control of my life for the first time. Vicki went to hug me but stopped herself, looking around to see if there was someone else out here with us. Nodding her head at another cop who walked past she gave me a sideward smile before speaking.

"I'll never hurt you again, Ava," Vicki quietly whispered. I could tell she meant it too, which made me happy.

"Come home to me tonight? I've missed you," I asked Vicki who nodded her head.

"Let me drive you home, or call you a cab, whatever you want," Vicki said. She was right, it was probably too late to be walking the streets, and it was far too cold. I hadn't brought a jacket, and my arms were stone cold.

I waited inside to wait for the cab Vicki had called me, and she walked me down to tell the driver where to take me.

"Make sure she gets home safely," she said in her angry cop voice before placing her hand gently on my cheek and stroking me with her thumb.

"See you soon," Vicki said affectionately before paying the driver and closing the door. The cab driver looked at me in the backseat, but I was happy he didn't say a word the whole drive home. I also knew he'd done jail time by his crude tattoos and wondered how he felt about taking the girl of a cop home. People knew not to mess with Vicki, and it felt good knowing I had her reputation to protect me again. When we got to my building, the driver got out of the car and walked me to the building door.

"You'll be alright miss?" He asked, accepting my tip.

"Yeah, thanks," I said, going inside. The truth was, I was a little scared, but I really didn't want him knowing where I lived. I'd had enough dramas in this apartment for a while.

It was early morning when I heard Vicki unlock the door and creep into the house. She dropped her gear, and I could tell she had showered at work. Her hair was a little bit damp but smelt like sweet strawberry hair products as she climbed into bed with me. I could tell she wasn't sure how close she was allowed next to me, so I rolled over and put her mind at ease. I climbed on top of her and rested my head on her chest, happy when she wrapped her arms around me and relaxed.

"I've missed you baby girl," Vicki whispered in my ear as she stroked my hair and patted my ass. I loved feeling her again and snuggled into her body, falling back asleep safe again in her arms.

Chapter 11

"This is weird. Does it feel weird to you?" I asked Vicki the minute her eyes opened the next morning. I had been watching her sleep and playing with her hair, and she smiled, kissing me before she opened her eyes.

"Why does it feel weird?" Vicki said, sitting up and stretching as she yawned. I curled up into her and waited for her arm to find its way back around me before I spoke.

"Because, like, last night and the last months and now you're laying in my bed and I feel so happy I could just punch you," I replied.

"You could punch me?" Vicki questioned.

"Yeah, you're the only woman I've ever wanted, and I hated you so much for making me so sad and now I feel like I was in hell before right now," I explained. Vicki jumped up and kneeled on the bed, spreading her arms out wide.

"Then punch me," she said. I looked at her

questioningly.

"If that's what it will take for you to be happy with me again, punch me," Vicki said smirking.

"Don't laugh just because you know my punch won't hurt you," I said, looking down at her dick.

"No, this doesn't turn me on, it's just what happens in the morning," Vicki said as if reading my mind.

"Punching you won't hurt you, but this will," I said as I kneed her dick. Grabbing herself and looking like she was about to vomit, Vicki fell down on the bed and breathed in labored breaths.

"Even?" Vicki asked she tears rolled down her face. I felt bad for about half a second.

"Even," I said, kissing her cheek and holding her until she could move again.

"So how are we going to do this?" Vicki asked over breakfast. She had made buttermilk pancakes, and I had eaten more than my stomach could hold and lay in a food coma on the couch.

"I think we just lay here until breathing doesn't hurt anymore," I replied, closing my eyes. Vicki laughed as she came over with a cup of coffee and sat by my side.

"I meant us little one," Vicki said, bending down to kiss my tummy. I opened my eyes and reached up to cuddle her, getting tickled by her hair.

"I don't know, I don't want to move in together straight away though," I replied. Vicki smiled and began stroking my hair, and I could feel the little space beginning to take hold. Vicki must have noticed too because she lay down next to me and began cuddling my body.

"I figured that much baby girl," she said, wrapping her arm around my head as she pushed her tits into my face. I loved the feel of them, the heaviness, and her thick nipples. I could tell she was fighting herself; I could tell what she wanted by the look in her eyes and smirking back at her cheekily, I pulled on her nipple through her shirt.

"Want to play little one?" Vicki said as I nodded my head. She pulled out her full breast, and I sucked her nipple immediately, enjoyed the throaty moan that involuntarily escaped Vicki as she pushed her nipple into my mouth.

"Mommy has missed this little mouth baby girl," Vicki said, making me smile around her nipple.

"I think we should sit down and come up with some rules and lay a foundation for what our limits are baby girl, what do you think?" Vicki asked, taking her nipple from my reach. I knew that we should do this, but I didn't want to do it now, I wanted to have her now. I reluctantly watched as she put her breast back into her shirt before I went to get a notepad and pen.

"Ok, so, ground rules, give the baby everything she wants, all the time," I said cheekily as Vicki came to sit at the kitchen table with me. She rolled her eyes and took the pen and pad away from me.

"I don't think so," she said, crossing out my

first rule.

"Let's start with the important one, safe words," Vicki said, eyeing me. I nodded and thought before I spoke.

"Let's just do traffic lights, green for go, yellow for slow down and red for stop; they are easy to remember," I said as Vicki wrote it down agreeing.

"I only want to tell you an instruction once," Vicki said writing that down too.

"I don't want to be used as a fuck doll," I said looking Vicki dead in the eye.

"You have to ask permission before you fuck me, I'm yours, but I'm not just open for business," I added. I like that Vicki agreed to that one, I had been worried she wouldn't. We kept going, creating rules and frameworks, punishments, and expectations well into the afternoon.

"Come on, baby girl, let's go outside before the whole day is over," Vicki said, picking me up and carrying me into the bedroom. She placed me down on the bed before she grabbed my jeans and a diaper. We had agreed she could diaper me if I was wearing jeans and I smiled at how she let me decide which one I wanted.

"I haven't worn these since last time Mommy," I said, referring to the last time she had diapered me. Vicki smiled happily.

"Good," she said, pulling my jeans up over my diaper. She passed me a pink bra and almost see-through pink blouse, and Vicki took my hands away to do up the buttons herself.

"Let Mommy baby girl," she said, groping my tits when she was finished.

"You are so beautiful baby," Vicki whispered in my ear, and I knew she wanted to fuck me. I liked that she actually always wanted to fuck me and I kissed her deeply while she rubbed my diaper and jeans covered ass. It felt so good that I moved on top of her thigh and straddled it, rocking back and forth on her as she let me dry hump her leg.

"Baby girl, Mommy needs to get ready,"

Vicki said playfully throwing me down on the bed and grabbing my tits one last time before she went to freshen up. I lay on the bed and watched her as she brushed her teeth and ran her fingers through her hair. I liked that she had taken her top off and walked around the room with just her pants on. She saw me staring at her, and she winked at me before finding the shirt she wanted and putting it on.

"Ready?" Vicki said, taking my hand and pulling me to her. She kissed down my neck and picked me up, turning me around and pinning me against a wall. I kissed her, feeling her hands on my sides and making me hold my breath as she enveloped me.

"Ready," I breathlessly said, slightly annoyed when she put me back down again.
We walked out of my building and to her car.

"Get in," she said, making me wonder where we were going. I opened the door and waited for her to buckle me in like we had discussed, kissing her on the mouth when she did so.

"Where are we going Mommy," I said feeling Vicki move her hand to cup the front of my pussy. I wriggled and pushed it out, making her smile as she patted me like her pet.

"To a place, I think you'll like baby girl," Vicki replied, turning into my favorite fast food restaurant and buying me a shake and small fries. Vicki ordered three hamburgers, and I laughed at how much she could eat. I liked that she took her time eating them. I was worried she'd get a tummy ache.

"I'm starving, I only had 6 pancakes for breakfast," Vicki said, catching me looking at her.

"I only had 2!" I giggled. Vicki played with my hair as she turned the corner, her forearm flexing.

"These muscles don't grow by themselves baby girl," Vicki added making me curious.

"Don't you just go to the gym and bam, muscles?" I asked. Vicki looked at me like she couldn't figure out if I was serious or not.

"No...we can get into my gym schedule later, we are here," Vicki said parking the car. I looked around, she had taken us to a spot out of town, and I smiled, noticing that there were no other cars in the parking lot.

"Out you come," Vicki said, unbuckling me and lifting me out of her SUV. I went to grab my backpack, but she slung it over her shoulder and held my hand as we began walking along a hiking path.

"It's so lovely Mommy," I said, enjoying being outside and alone with Vicki. She smiled and looked down at me.

"I use to come here for runs when I didn't want anyone around. Look," she said, pointing to a bird's nest with a mama bird feeding her baby birds.

"Pretty Mommy," I said, standing on my tippy toes to get a closer look. Vicki smiled and walked ahead of me, turning around when I didn't follow her and held out her hand to me.

"Come on sweetie," she said, smiling as I

ran to catch up to her. We continued walking for an hour until we reached the edge of a cliff and the view took my breath away. Looking out over a cliff, there was a waterfall to the right of us, and in front of us, there was nothing but the silhouette of the city we had left behind. The sun was about an hour from setting, and Vicki laid out a blanket and began unpacking the picnic she had made.

"You know, I could get used to this," I said, laying down and resting my head on her thigh. Vicki took my hands in hers as she poured anti-bacteria gel over them and washed them clean before passing me a sandwich.

"Good baby girl, this is the life Mommy wants to have with you," Vicki replied, putting me in my little space. Her hair was being swept up gently by the breeze and every now, and then the water from the waterfall would sprinkle on us, making me giggle. Vicki kept me laying down and put a paci in my mouth after we had finished our picnic, laughing when I looked at her with wide eyes.

"Don't worry about girl, I'll hear if someone is coming and you can give it back to Mommy, but right now, it's either your paci or Mommy, which one?" Vicki said, raising an eyebrow at me. I touched my paci and Vicki brought me into her lap and wrapped her arms around me as I enjoyed the warm sun on my face, watching rainbows form in the waterfall.

Chapter 12

Vicki and I had picnics at our special spot for the next three weeks. We had spent most of the time at my apartment, but I had slept over at hers for a few nights at a time before I wanted to go back home. I was happy that she had been true to her word and not broken our contract, and I had totally forgotten that anything wrong could ever happen in the world. That was until I got a phone call from an old friend.

"Hey, where you at?" Came a familiar voice down the phone.

"Rory?" I asked, surprised she would have my number.

"Yeah who else. Look I'm out, can I meet you somewhere?" She said. I had met Rory when we had been kids. She lived on the same block as me and had taken the wrap for me the first time I got caught by Vicki. She was a quiet kid, the kind who came up with ideas but had lost almost every fight she had ever been in. I had heard she had been away, got caught stealing a car from a wealthy lawyer the day after she turned 18 and had been tried as an adult. She'd gotten 10years, but I guess she was out early for good behavior or something.

"Yo, you there?" Rory said, breaking my train of thought.

"Yeah, sorry. Where are you?" I replied. She gave me the address, and I knew that I could probably get there and back before Vicki got home. She was coming to mine tonight to stay over, but I still had a few hours before she'd be here so I told Rory to meet me at a diner around the corner from mine and said I'd meet her there.

I had only been waiting for five minutes before I saw her come in, but without the scar on her face, I wouldn't have even recognized her. She was bigger, and her head was shaved. She walked with a limp and had really aggressive energy. *I guess she did just get out of prison;* I thought to myself watching her walk over to me. People were looking at her fearfully, and she just looked back them, not seeming to mind.

"Hey there wild cat," Rory said, looking me up and down. I got up to hug her, but she just sat down. I guess those sort of things were lost on her now.

"You some sort of office broad now?" She said accepting the free coffee from the waitress.

"You hungry?" I said, ignoring her tease, she just shrugged her shoulders, and I ordered two big all day breakfasts before the waitress left.

"So?" Rory said, looking around. I looked around to thinking that something was going on. However, there was nothing out of the ordinary.

"So," I repeated, sipping my coffee.

"You got a man?" Rory said. I could see she was trying to make conversation, but it didn't feel like the old times. She had tattoos down the side of her face and on her knuckles. I don't think anyone would even enter into a fight with her these days.

"I'm gay," I said, shaking my head, making Rory instantly excited.

"Alright, I always knew there was a reason I liked ya. Not many of us around here back then. What's it like now, get a bitch easy hey," Rory said as the waitress placed our meals in front of us. I wasn't really sure how I could reply to her without getting a punch in my face. I wasn't about to say I was in love with a cop.

"Yeah look last time I went on a date with a girl she turned out to be a drug mule, so," I chose instead making Rory laugh.

"You still rolling with Hope and them?" Rory said, hunching over her food and making me wonder how many times she had her food taken away in there. She was almost annalistic.

"No, actually. I stepped away from all of that. Got myself a steady job and all of it," I decide to say, not wanting her to think I was about that kind of living anymore.

"Good girl," Rory said, making me surprised my body reacted the way it did. Instantly I got a usual throbbing between my thighs, and I looked at her in shock. She was a far cry from anything I found attractive and yet my cunt was immediately on fire. Swallowing hard, I pushed my plate away, knowing that I wouldn't be able to stomach anymore.

"You done?" Rory said, pointing to my plate. I nodded, and she switched plates and began finishing off my half-finished food. Looking at my watch, I knew that Vicki would be home in an hour.

"Where are you staying?" I asked Rory hoping that she wouldn't try and bunk down with me. I had long stopped taking in strays.

"Here and there. I'm good though, I don't need your help, I just wanted to see ya, pretty little thing," Rory said making me bite my lip which just made her laugh.

"You got me through you know," Rory said, sitting back in the booth and signaling to the waitress she wanted more coffee. I knew what she meant, but I really wished I didn't so playing dumb I gave her an opportunity to change her story.

"What do you mean?" I said, shaking my

head at the waitress who offered me coffee.

"Yeah, she will actually," Rory said, calling her back and ordering for me.

"But I don't want it," I said to Rory, annoyed that I could feel my little voice coming out which just seemed to excite her.

"I know you don't, but you'll take it and give it to me instead, see," Rory said, drinking from my cup. I watched her drink, her eyes never breaking from mine.

"I have to go," I said, standing up, but being blocked by her. She stood in my way and grabbed my hips.

"Always such a pretty girl, I meant it what I said, you got me through. Thinking about you, the way you laughed as you ran, your tanned legs dodging the cops. You should be with me since you ain't got no one. You're too little to protect yourself, always have been. It was always me who looked after you," Rory said. I hated how she was making me feel. Her eyes had become soft, but I wondered how mean she would turn when I turned her down.

"Rory," I said, taking her hands away, happy when she let me. I looked at her and tried to stay calm, but my heart was pounding, and I had to fight myself to not run away from her.

"I'm glad you're out, but I really do need to go," I repeated. She smiled and nodded to the floor, letting me pass.

"I'll be seeing ya," Rory said as I left the diner making me turn my head and look plainly at her. *Am I just some fucking slut that'll let any Mommy fuck her?* I thought to myself as I quickly made my way back to my apartment.

"Baby girl?" Vicki said as I entered the apartment. I dropped my bag and jumped into her arms; happy her reflexes were so acute. She held me as I wrapped my arms around her neck, pushing myself into her and kissing her deeply. She moaned in my mouth as she grabbed the top of my jeans and broke the kiss looking for my consent.

"Yeah, fuck me, Mommy," I said nodding

and kissing her neck and along her shoulder. Vicki didn't need to be told twice, walking to the couch and throwing me down, dropping to her knees as I bounced on the couch. She grabbed my shirt and pulled it off, moaning when she saw I wasn't wearing a bra and kissing my tits, and down my tummy making me wriggle under her. She unbuttoned the multiple buttons of my jeans in one go and ripped them off, smiling in primal satisfaction when she saw my diaper.

"Oh good girl baby," she moaned, seeing that I kept her rules even when she wasn't there to enforce them. She reached under my arms and picked me up and took me to the bedroom, carrying me with one arm while her other one pulled her belt off her trousers. She placed me gently down on the bed and turned me over, before placing one hand on the middle of my back and belting my ass with her belt. She knew that I needed my diaper on when I was belted, she was just too strong, and it just hurt way too much. I liked that I could trust her again. She belted my ass until I was just about to call it off before ripping off my diaper and undoing her trousers. Her dick was hard, and when she ran it between my ass cheeks, I enjoyed her moaning as she came instantly, slipping the tip of her dick into my ass, squirting down inside of me.

"Holy shit baby girl, you get Mommy excited," Vicki said, drying her dick off with her trousers before spitting on her hand and rubbing it over my aching cunt. I knew I was wet; I'd been wet since I was with Rory. I pushed the image of Rory out of my mind as I felt Vicki spread my pussy wide and enter me forcefully. I loved that she never fucked around when it came to fucking. She grabbed my hips and buried her dick inside of me, holding it in me as she squirted into me before she began thrusting against my red ass.

"Tell Mommy you need it baby girl," Vicki said as she pounded me from behind. She reached around and rubbed my clit as she sat back and bounced me on her lap, making me take her dick hard.

"Mommy, I need you, please fuck me, Mommy," I said, closing my eyes and opening them suddenly as the image of Rory standing in front me playing with herself entered my mind as Vicki fucked me until she was coming for the third time.

"I'm not done with you yet," Vicki said in a tone I had heard multiple times. She pulled out of me and slapped my face with her dick before going to my cupboard and taking out a bondage rope and nipple clamps. I looked at her warningly making her laugh.

"I know the rules baby girl, Mommy isn't going to hurt you, you're going to love this," Vicki said as she grabbed my wrists and tied them to my ankles. I was happy she did, in fact, know the rules and left my throat untied. She rolled me over and flicked my nipples until they were hard and clamped them before going back into the cupboard and taking out my black bunny butt plug.

"Mommy no," I said, smiling. Vicki raised an eyebrow seeing that I wasn't really asking her to stop and stuck the plug into my pussy, making it wet before pushing it into my resisting ass.

"You've always got to fight Mommy on something don't you baby girl?" Vicki teased as she guided herself back into me, making me scream in pleasure.

"I told you you'd like it. Mommy's pretty little slut," Vicki said as she held my shoulders and rammed into me until my eyes rolled back and I shut my eyes.

"Tell Mommy where I can finish baby girl," Vicki moaned edging herself. My pussy juices were squirting out onto her pelvis, and Vicki pulled out of me, jerking herself, waiting for my answer.

"You can put it in my mouth, Mommy," I said as Vicki quickly filled my mouth. I hadn't had her down my throat at this angle before, and she slid down deeper than I had ever taken her. She moaned as she came in my mouth, rubbing my throat and smiling as she felt her dick deep inside of it.

"Baby girl," she said, cupping my chin and gently pulling out of me. I swallowed one more time and Vicki reached over, passing me a water bottle, laughing when she realized I was tied.

"Let me, sweetie," she said, bringing the bottle to my lips and letting me drink. She untied me, and I lay spent on the bed sheets that were now covered in cum and sweat.

"That was the best sex we've ever had," Vicki said, picking me up and taking me into the bathroom. I just nodded and relaxed in her arms as she bathed me.

"I love you, Vicki," I said sleepily. I closed my eyes and heard her smile as she replied.

"I love you too, Ava; you're my whole world."

Chapter 13

"I didn't think it could be true when I heard, but I guess you are a sell out after all," I heard Rory say, as I walked up the street. I knew this wasn't going to end well, and I slowly turned around to see her angry face. I had been right; it was terrifying.

"Fucking a cop, low bitch, real low," Rory said. I looked around, hoping that she didn't have anyone with her.

"I can't help who I fall in love with Rory," I said softly. Clearly pissed off, Rory started shaking her head and looking around moving from one foot to another.

"Na see I don't believe that. You had a choice; you chose them over us. I had even defended you bitch, told them they were talking wack but I seen you too, holding hands, kissing," Rory said as if she was talking about the most disgusting thing on the planet. I stood there, looking at her weighing up my options. I could run, but I had a sneaky feeling she could catch me despite her size. I knew I couldn't fight her, and I knew that no one was going to help me if she threw a punch.

"Rory, I'm sorry it's upset you but," I started to say, getting cut off by her shaking her hand in my face.

"She's got a cock you know, didn't know you was into that, fucking a freak she's not even a real woman," Rory said making the biggest mistake she could have. I burned with rage and swung at her, surprising her and myself as I slammed into her face making her stumble. She looked at me before spitting a mouthful of blood out onto the sidewalk.

"Oh, you asked for this bitch," she said, swinging back and slugging me in the guts. I doubled over stepping back, trying to escape her.

"Learnt a couple of things while I was away," Rory said, punching me again, this time coming down on my back.

"First thing is you either ride or die and guess what baby girl, you just tapped out," Rory said, pulling my hair back and punching me in my eye socket. I fell to the ground just as she stamped on my leg and getting up; I tried to run from her. I got about ten paces until she had me with my arm locked behind my back and pushing me into an alley. I knew what was going to come next and thought of Vicki, trying to get wet to make it hurt less.

"I'm going to enjoy this," Rory said, reaching up my skirt and pulling my panties down. I screamed before she had done anything only resulting in getting turned around and punched in my stomach, but it was too late.

"You're fucked bitch, you couldn't have me then, you couldn't even have me now," I said as I spat a mouthful of blood at her hearing Vicki's unmistakable footsteps racing down the alley.

"Oi, come here," Vicki yelled in her angry cop voice as she chased Rory and slammed her to the ground, pinning her head down as she cuffed her wrists behind her.

"Ava, can you hear me," Constable fuckface gently said, shining a torch in my face.

"Yeah," I replied softly.

"I'll put her in the back, you stay with Ava," I heard Vicki say as I passed out in Constable fuckface's arms.

When I woke up again, I was in the hospital. I knew it was hospital by that distinctive hospital smell. A nurse was looking at something on the monitor when I made a soft sound that I was happy she heard.

"Welcome back," she said before leaving the room again.

"Baby girl," Vicki said, rushing in obviously the nurse had told her I was awake. Vicki stroked my hair and kissed my forehead, making me smile and cough.

"Shh it's OK sweetie, you don't have to talk. Mommy's here," Vicki said. I tried to touch my eye, but there was something covering it.

"You'll have to have that on for a little while baby girl, you're eye socket is a little broken. The woman who did this to you, you knew her?" Vicki said. I nodded and heard a person clear their throat behind Vicki.

"You know I have to ask the questions Victoria," Constable fuckface said making Vicki roll her eyes.

"But I hate you," I said softly making Vicki laugh.

"Yes well, I'd hate me too if I was you wild cat," she said, making me laugh.

"Tell me what happened. Why are you always getting into trouble?" She added as I got up, helped by Vicki.

"I knew her from way back. She got done for stealing a car and got out recently. I went to see her," I said, looking at Vicki.

"I'm sorry I didn't tell you, I just kinda didn't want to bring you into that world, it's shit," I said apologetically. Vicki just laughed.

"Baby, I'm in this world every day," she said

frowning when I shook my head.

"Na is different when you come from it, Victoria," I said enjoying calling her by her real name. She raised an eyebrow at me, making it very clear that would the only tease I would be getting away with.

"And then what happened, you met up with her and then what?" The other cop pressed.

"She was keen on me, said it was me who got her through her time, but I said I wasn't in that world anymore. I saw her again today, she started talking shit and then," I said, stopping to look at Vicki. I was pretty sure people would know at her work, but I still wasn't sure, and I didn't want to out her if no one knew.

"She started saying some shit about you, and that's when I punched her," I said.

"What did she say?" The other cop said making me look nervously at Vicki who just smiled lovingly.

"It's OK baby girl," she said, bending down and kissing me.

"She said you were a freak and not a real woman, so I slugged her," I said, my little voice coming out and resulting in Vicki bending down cuddle me.

"You're a cute little girl for defending Mommy baby girl," Vicki whispered in my ear, making me feel proud.

"You sure took a beating for that baby," she said louder standing back up and going over to Constable fuckface who was busy jotting down my story.

"Charge her for attempted rape Jane," Vicki said.

"Jane?" I said questioningly. Jane nodded her head before she bopped me on the nose with her notepad.

"But what's it to you?" She said, making me laugh.

"I may call you constable, only constable," I replied, repeating what she had made me say countless times before. Vicki smiled, almost enjoying watching me be controlled by someone else and sat on the bed when Jane had gone.

"Really to go home little baby?" She asked. I nodded my head and let her help me up.

"Cops are such control freaks," I said making Vicki laugh.

"Um, yeah, that's kinda the point," she added, wrapping an arm around me and helping me walk out of the hospital.

"Mommy!" I said 4 months later as Vicki placed the big painting I had just finished on the wall. I had moved into her house a couple of months ago and had happily gotten used to my new suburb in the nice part of town. It hadn't been as hard as I had thought it would be hanging out in Vicki's world and I had enjoyed starting to meet her friends, and she had even started to meet mine from the furniture store. I had been given the promotion I put in for which meant I could move to a store closer to our home and had bought a drone to take photos over the waterfall Vicki and I seemed to spend most of our spare time at.

"Looks good doesn't it baby girl," Vicki said. I sat in front of it and was happy with how I had designed it. The pinks and gold leaf had been constructed to represent a heart that had been broken and put back together; the broken pieces merging to create an even bigger heart than the original was.

"Snackies baby girl?" Vicki said, picking me up and covering me in kisses as she bought me into the kitchen and took out the pizza we had made together. She had two, I finally understood her food and gym schedule, and she had let me use cookie cutters to cut mine into different shapes.

"This is nice Mommy," I said using the tongs to put my dino pizzas on one side of my plate and the teddy pizzas on the other side. I held my plate in two hands and beamed up at her deeply impressed with myself.

"I love you baby girl," Vicki said, beaming back down at me.

Kira's Little Princess

An MDLG and ABDL lesbian story of a backpacker hostel event manager and how she convinced her baby girl to stay

By Tina Moore

Chapter 1

"Thank you for flying with us, enjoy your trip and if you are coming home welcome home," the pilot said over the speaker. I was happy to be landing; it had been a terrible flight. I had thought that getting the window seat would be great, and it had been until I needed to use the bathroom in the middle of the night. I had to carefully climb over the two people sitting next to me to get to the aisle; I was happy I hadn't stepped on them. I had tried to get some sleep, but the plane had flown through turbulence most of the way and the smell of the plane food had made me feel sick. I looked out the window and was surprised how big the airport was, I hadn't traveled very much and had just assumed everywhere expect my home town as well, less than. But the size of the terminals here rivaled any at home, and I followed the signs sleepily until I reached the one I was looking for.

"Hi, I'm Sasha, do you guys go to Waker's

Beach hostel?" I asked a tanned blonde. The woman was more excited than I was ready for and almost blew me away with her enthusiasm.

"We sure do! I'm Kira, I'm the events co-coordinator at the hostel and today, the taxi, how long are you going to stay with us, we have some great things planned this week," Kira said ticking my name off the clipboard and writing something down. I looked at her with tired eyes. I smiled at Kira and went to find a spot to sit while I waited for the other people to be ticked off Kira's clipboard list. Watching Kira, I wondered how long she had been at the hostel to be given the job. I liked how friendly she was. Her big smile and brown eyes had been so welcoming and warm; it made me feel less alone. I had initially planned the trip with my best friend Georgia, but she had bailed last minute. We had even made it the airport before Georgia had started having a panic attack just as we were going through customs. She had to be escorted out; it was pretty embarrassing. I had already gone through and was waiting for her on the other side when I heard them say they would have to take her away. Georgia had yelled that I could still go, and if it hadn't been for Georgia's repeat offending with this type of stuff, maybe I wouldn't be here at all. It wasn't the first time Georgia had let me down like this and I had felt so fed up with her on and off again way of being, I had decided to go on without her.

"Alright everyone, on the bus," Kira called, breaking me out of the sleep I hadn't realized I was in. Laughing, Kira came up to me.

"It's OK sleepy head; once we get to the hostel you can sleep all day, I know the flight is rough!" Kira said, taking one of my bags and walking with me to the bus. Kira started talking to me about how she had planned to take everyone dune tobogganing and to watch the turtles hatch on the beach over next week, but I hardly heard a word.

When I was finally on the shuttle bus, I put in my earphones and listened to the songs Georgia and I had put into a playlist and wondered how she was.

No, fuck her, I thought, being angry that Georgia had let me down once again. The bus seemed to drive for forever, and Kira would stand up and talk on the microphone when we were passing something important or exciting. I liked her voice; it was full of excitement and playfulness. I imaged that Kira would be the first person on the dance floor at a party twirling and giggling as she let the music take over her. Going through the city, I looked out the window on the other side to see people walking down the street wearing fancy business suits and dresses and smiled to myself thinking about the life I had left behind.

I had worked for a photography company, and while I never wore such high-end fashion, I took the pictures of the types of people who did. I would go into their homes, take their photo with their picture-perfect families and purebred dogs. Trying to capture something other than the fake happiness, they were all trying so desperately to portray. Once or twice, I had ended up fucking the maid or the au pair in the main bedroom or outside on the balcony. I had wondered why I could never refuse them but knew deep in my heart; it was because I just wanted the thrill. My job was easy, almost too easy, and I liked the idea of getting fired and having to find something else to do with my time.

The bus came to a screeching halt, pushing me forward and then back against my seat, making me wondered if the driver had done that on purpose or not.

"Alright everyone, welcome to your new home!" Kira said, opening the door as people started to leave the bus. For the first time, I noticed that I was slightly older than most of the people who had been on the bus, watching them as they dismounted. At only 25, I hadn't felt very old, but listening to the conversations of the kids, on the bus, I felt like I had my life together way more than they did. I saw the typical 18-year-olds excitedly drinking cheap wine as they walked past me, offering me some.

"No, I'm good," I just replied. It's 10 in the

morning, you bloody moron; I thought as I looked behind me to realize I was the last on the bus.

"Come on sleepy head," Kira said kindly doing one last sweep of the bus. She waited for me to get up and follow her out of the bus.

"Hey you forgot this," Kira said, holding up a photo of a girl that had fallen out of my pocket. Kira looked at me, questioningly.

"Girlfriend?" She asked, her sparkling eyes making me look down, feeling stupid for what I was about to say.

"You'll think I'm dumb. She's my ex, this trip, was to get over her," I said, getting embarrassed. Kira thought for a minute before grabbing the photo from my hands.

"Well, you won't get over her by having her around. I'll hold onto it, and if you're still hooked by the time you leave, I'll give it back to you," Kira said. Usually, I would have grabbed the photo back, but I liked how sweet Kira was and could tell she wasn't trying to be mean, so I just nodded and looked to the floor as I got off the bus.

"You'll be alright. Good girl for listening to me," Kira said as she passed me my bags from under the bus. I held my breath, making Kira laugh as I registered the words Kira had just said. Giving me a mischievous smile, Kira tapped the side of the bus, and it drove off in a plume of smoke. Waiting for the dust to settle, I turned and looked at the hostel.

"Come on, princess, let's get you settled in. You'll love the room I'm going to put you in," Kira said, linking her arm in mine and walking me through the hostel. I smiled to myself and felt the sun on my face. Maybe this isn't going to be as bad as I thought it would be, I thought to myself.

Chapter 2

I was given my room key and shown which bunk was mine before I unpacked a few things, had a shower and crashed in my bed. I had the bottom bunk and liked that I had a window behind my bed. I was also happy that I had been given a room where no other backpackers were in and thought that it was strange they would have so much space in the hostel that I could have my room.

When I woke, it was night time and raining. Great, cold, just what I was trying to avoid, I thought as I pulled a jumper over my singlet and slid on my flip flops. Opening the door, I was happy to see Kira's familiar face.

"Hey princess, I was just coming to look for you, how are you feeling after your nap?" Kira said, handing me a wrist band and laughing when I didn't put it on.

"Here," she said, taking my wrist in her hands and sticking the wrist band down.

"You are just the sweetest. Come on, there's a movie night tonight, and it might be good for you to meet someone else. Do you like popcorn? It's backpacker style, homemade using 55cent popcorn kernels, but it tastes just as good," Kira said, taking my hand and walking me to the common room. I liked how soft her touch was, she made me smile, and I needed that right now. The heartbreak I was running away from feeling like a black dog at my back. My ex and I had broken up because she was just so depressive and harmful for my general wellbeing, and I hated having to leave her when I felt like she needed me. But I had learned that I wasn't in charge of how she felt, she was, and if she weren't going to do the things that would help her, nothing I could do would help her either.

Walking into the common room, I took a deep breath, smelling the buttery homemade popcorn and was handed a beer by an angry looking girl with piercings up her ears.

"Here, I'm Danni," the girl said, opening the

beer for me.

"Hey, I'm Sasha," I replied, drinking happily, tasting a type of beer I had never had before. It felt nice to be here. Danni walked past me, giving Kira a knowing look, and I laughed, thinking that Kira must be the fuckgirl or something around here. I couldn't blame her; she had the perfect hunting ground for it. I grabbed a bowl of popcorn and sat down next to some German's who just smiled at me, and I nodded my head at them as they passed me a blanket as we all settled in and watched the movie. It was some stupid chick flick that I would never pay to watch, but it felt nice throwing popcorn at the TV when the two main characters kissed and laughing along with people I had never met before. I was aware that Kira had been watching me as she walked in and out of the common room. After the movie, I got into a game of hostel monopoly as I drank with Danni. I liked that Kira had continued to steal looks, I didn't mind in fact it excited me.

"Are you teaching her all my tricks?" Kira

said coming and sitting behind me. She had her legs on either side of me and wrapped her arms around my waist as she cuddled me, and I was taken by surprise with how touchy-feely she was. She must have felt my body tense up because she turned me around slightly so I could look at her when she spoke.

"I'm super handsy, if you hate it, just say so OK?" Kira explained. Making Danni smirk and roll her eyes.

"She does this with everyone, don't worry. If someone comes up to you and slaps your ass randomly, it'll be Kira," Danni said making Kira gasp in playful shock.

"But you're just so cute; I hope you don't mind," Kira quickly added, making me relax and lean into her as she held me. It felt nice to have someone showing me affection again, even if she did do it to everyone. Danni and I played the game well into the night, only getting up to get drinks and packets of chocolates from the vending machine. I bit my lip at one stage, excited when

Kira patted her lap and pulled me down as I continued to play. It was just after midnight when the common room was closed, and Kira walked me back to my room.

"Goodnight princess," Kira said, wrapping her arms around me. I held her firmly, almost desperately not wanting to let her go.

"Oh sweetie, are you OK?" Kira said, taking my key from my hands and opening the door, taking my hand and pulling me into my room and shutting the door behind us. The room was dark, only the moonlight coming through my window shining on the white wall as Kira sat down on one of the empty beds with me.

"Tell me what's going on princess," Kira said, sitting opposite me but leaning forward to brush my hair out of my face. She looked serious, almost as though she was genuinely concerned, and I laughed at how stupid I felt getting sucked into her.

"I'm just exhausted, I'm OK," I tried to say to her as she shook her head.

"No, tell me the truth princess, don't try and lie to me," Kira said, making me curl my toes.

"You have to stop that," I whispered, biting my lip. I looked at Kira, who just smiled knowingly.

"But aren't you a little princess Sasha?" She teased. I rolled my eyes and got up, surprised when Kira grabbed my wrist and pulled me back down. Holding my face in her hands, she kissed me, making me gasp as she stood up and pushed me against the wall as she kissed down my neck.

"Is this what you want princess?" Kira said as she reached into my pants and gently rubbed my pussy over my panties. I pushed her away; I hadn't been touched like that in years.

"Get out," I quietly said, going to the door. Kira rolled her eyes and kissed my forehead on the way out.

"You know where to find me if you get scared princess," Kira said as she left my room and made her way back to hers. I shut the door and climbed into my bed, shutting my eyes and tried to get some sleep.

I tossed and turned all night. Every time I got close to falling asleep, a new sound would wake me up, or the memory of Kira would come back to my mind. Why did I refuse her? It felt great, I thought to myself, confused as to why I kicked her out. At 3 in the morning, I decided to go for a walk to the beach. Getting up, I put on some warm pants, and a pullover found my glasses and tied my hair in a messy bun. I opened the door to my room and used my phone as a torch as I made my way down the clearing to the beach. I was not disappointed. The air was cool and salty, and the light breeze had a thin layer of sand lifting as I took each step. The waves looked blue and black as they crashed and for the first in what felt like forever, I felt totally at peace. Walking along the beach, I was aware that someone was walking in the opposite direction. I walked down to the water's edge, hoping to avoid them.

"Sasha?" I heard her voice before I saw her. I was nervous; why would she be out here this late.

"Kira?" I asked back.

"Princess, I thought you'd be all tucked up in bed, what are you doing?" Kira asked hugging me. It was more me hugging her, and I liked that I took her by surprise as I held her tightly, like she was the answer to questions I didn't know I had. She smiled and kissed my forehead as she stroked my hand and let me hold her.

"I could ask you the same thing," I finally said, sitting down on the sand. I dug into the cold sand with my toes and shivered as the air whipped around us. Kira opened her oversize zip-up jacket, and I snuggled into her. I didn't care if she did this with everyone; I needed her to do this with me.

"I like going for walks at night. I feel the night calling to me sometimes, so I go with it," Kira said. I was impressed with how open she was about who she was; she didn't seem to hide anything. Looking at me, I could tell Kira wanted an answer from me now.

"My reason is lame, I just couldn't sleep," I

said, shrugging my shoulders. Kira laughed and pulled me in closer.

"That's not lame princess," she said, pressing my head down until it was resting on her shoulder. As we looked out over the ocean, a liked that I could almost hear her heartbeat and feel her breath on me as silence came between us.

"How long have you been here?" I asked her, breaking the silence that had come between us.

"4 years. I came out as a backpacker but fell in love with it and stayed after I was sponsored," Kira explained.

"Was it easy?" I asked, interested in the process. Kira shook her head.

"Nothing good is ever easy princess," she said, laughing.

"It took three years of back and forth paperwork, but I'm here now, and I'm happy I can stay," Kira said in a serious voice I hadn't heard her use.

"Why, are you thinking of staying?" Kira

asked, suddenly excited again. I looked at her before I kissed her deeply, surprised with myself but happy when I heard her moan in my mouth.

"Maybe," I whispered as I pushed her back on the sand. I moved my body on top of her and kissed her until I had run out of ways to kiss her as dawn broke behind us over the ocean and lit up the beach. Kira rolled me over, obviously not wanting to be on her back anymore and lay down by my side as she kissed me while we watched the sun move up into the sky.

"This is going to be an amazing day princess; I can just tell," Kira said softly into my neck as she played with my hair.

Chapter 3

She wasn't joking. The day had been awesome. She had organized that everyone would go the jetty and jump off the end of it at lunchtime, followed by a big BBQ in the park. There was food and drinks and music, and I loved watching how she floated around the different groups of people. I had learned that she spoke five languages, and she was always making someone laugh or telling them a story. I liked that she kissed me openly in front of people. I had learned that things moved very fast around here and slight attraction turned into a full-blown relationship after a few hours of staring at each other.

"It's just the way when everyone is living together," Danni explained to me as I asked her how long another couple had been together, laughing when 3 hours came her response. I had hoped that Kira wouldn't use me for a few hours and then get rid of me when a new girl turned up being relieved when Danni shook her head.

"You guys are as good as married now; she won't leave you. She never leaves; it's the other girls who go. When is your flight out?" Danni said raising an eyebrow at me as the reality that I would be leaving too settled in.

"In two months," I said quietly as Danni nodded her head as she drank.

"See?" She added as I got up and walked over to where Kira was playing in the playground.

"Hey princess, having fun?" She asked, making me feel like the only person in the world all over again. She laughed as she grabbed my hand and pulled me to the swings.

"Sit, let me swing you," Kira said, pulling my hips down onto the swing. I closed my eyes as she started to pull me back, forcing my mind not to go there. I knew what was just behind my eyes, and as I opened them again, I felt it hit. It was like a drug, her motherly nature, the way she called me princess and the way she made me feel as she swung me high into the air, catching me every time

I came back. I wondered if she knew what she was doing to me, what headspace she had me in constantly. I wondered if she would still like me if she knew.

The BBQ finished and walking back to the hostel. Kira grabbed my hand as I was about to walk out onto the road.

"Hold Mama's hand princess," Kira laughed as a car sped past. The people around us didn't seem to care, but I almost died hearing those words. A guy grabbed a girl's hand and told her to hold Daddy's hand, and everyone laughed. Oh, it was just a joke, everyone is joking, I said to myself trying to calm down. Kira looked at me with a gleam of mischief in her eye, and I looked at her quickly before looking down at the ground as she led me back to the hostel. Stopping outside my room, I could tell she wanted to come in, but I turned to look at her.

"I'm just really tired, probs still the jetlag, I think I'm just going to have a nap and maybe see you later?" I said as she held my hips and swayed me gently.

"Or maybe you're tired because you're a little princess and need Mama to let you have a nap?" Kira said, smiling, before kissing my cheek and walking away.

I took my clothes off and put them in the wash bag I had set up on the end of my bunk and walked into the shower, turning the water on and letting it pour over me. I was happy I had brought my shampoo and conditioner and washed my hair for the first time since arriving. I lathed shower gel over my body, enjoying how it felt rubbing over my tits before I exfoliated and got out. I dried myself and hung my towel up before walking back into the room, surprised to see Kira sitting on my bed.

"Kira what the fuck!" I screamed as I tried to cover up. I reached behind me to try and get my towel and Kira jumped off my bed and grabbed my wrist, pulling my naked body to my bed.

"I can't let my little princess go to for naps without a diaper, what kind of Mama would that make me?" Kira said, making me freeze.

"What did you just say?" I asked, making her laugh.

"I knew you were a baby the minute I saw you, princess, why do you think Mama spent all that special time with you?" Kira said, moving my body as she sprinkled the powder over me. My mind was lost for words, so I just lay there and let her diaper me, trying to fight the headspace she was forcing me back into.

"But," was all I could say as she pulled up my pajama pants over my fresh diaper and tickled me before putting on my long sleeve pajama shirt.

"Gosh what a cute little princess for Mama," Kira said, looking at me laying on my back, my thighs pushed apart by the thick diaper she had just put me in.

"Come on, time for pretty little princess naps," Kira said. She lay beside me, making me snuggle into her chest as her arms wrapped around me.

"No wonder you couldn't sleep last night

little princess, Mama wasn't here then, but I'm here now," Kira said, stroking my hair as I fell asleep in her arms.

When I woke up, Kira was still cuddling me but was on her phone, scrolling through social media.

"Hi princess," she said, kissing my cheeks. I blinked sleepily at her which just made her squeeze me tighter, and I tilted my head back to see what time of day it was. The first stars had just come out, but the sky was still a light blue, so I knew it wasn't too late. Kira placed her hand on my diaper and frowned.

"Princess, you are still dry," she said, making me silently beg her not to make me wet my diaper. Kira reached into her bag and pulled out a baby bottle filled with water and rubbed the nipple over my lips, getting cross when I didn't open.

"Don't be a silly girl for Mama, drink up my little princess," Kira said, spanking my thigh until I opened my mouth as she held the bottle as I drunk.

"Good little princess for Mama," Kira said slowly, enjoying how I looked looking up at her. She placed her hand on my bladder and pushed down, making my eyes go wide as I drank.

"Don't try and fight Mama princess, you can wet your diaper here, or I'll take you out there and you can keep it on until you wet it in front of everybody, which do you want," Kira said, smiling when I began to wet my diaper, getting embarrassed and looking away slowly.

"Oh does Mama's little princess not like wetting herself," Kira said, taking the empty bottle out of my mouth. I shook my head and brought my arms up to my face, covering my eyes from her. Kira ran her hands up and down my body before gently taking my hands away.

"Alright sweetie, Mama likes it though. Come on, let's get you all cleaned up so you can go play all night," Kira said, taking my hand and leading me into the bathroom. She took my pajama's off, followed by my diaper, and I stood in the shower as she washed me.

"All clean now little princess," Kira said, passing me a new dry towel.

"What do you want me to wear Mama," I said, making Kira beam with delight.

"Oh, you are such a good little princess!" She exclaimed going through my clothes and taking out a pair of baggy ripped jeans and a tight singlet.

"This will look so cute on you little princess, and when you get tired, there's enough room in here to put you in a diaper, and no one will even know," Kira said playfully spanking my bottom as she dressed me.

Chapter 4

The days began to have a happy routine to them, and I started to find my place within the crazy hostel. Kira would organize events a week in advance, so there was always something to look forward too. So far we had gone on nature walks, seen wildlife and gone snorkeling along the reef. Next week we were all going skydiving, and I had finally mastered the tricks in winning hostel monopoly. I had gotten used to Kira diapering me during my nap times in the middle of the day, and she had even started to make me wear one in the night. She had moved into my room and would cuddle me as I slept and choose what I would wear during the day.

"This one Mama?" I asked her, holding up a bikini. It was hot today, but we were still going to the beach to have a bonfire that night. Kira had to go early to help set it up, which meant that I was going early too. Kira said I could go for a swim while they set it all up and that if I was good, she wouldn't put a limit on the number of roasted marshmallows I could have.

"No, the other one princess," Kira said coming out of the shower and towel drying her long blonde hair. I picked up the more revealing bikini but was stopped by Kira who wanted to dress me instead.

"Such a slutty little princess for Mama, I'm going to enjoy watching you in this tonight," Kira said, tying my red bikini around my neck. It was a halter style and made my cleavage look like I had porn star tits the way it shaped me. The tiny, Brazilian cut bikini bottoms didn't leave much to be imagined and rubbed my clit when I sat down. When I had told Kira this, she had made me wear them to a picnic in the rainforest. She let me have my small pair of offcut high waisted denim shorts on as we walked through the rainforest, but made me take them off and sit on her lap during the picnic, enjoying my slight moans and begs for her to touch me. She had subtly spread my thighs under the table and reached down, lazily stroking me while she played cards with Danni, enjoying my squirms and soft grinds on her lap wanting more. I hoped she would do something like that tonight as well.

We arrived at the beach, and Kira kissed me before slapping my ass as I walked down the beach to the water. It was nice to cool down after such a hot day, and I dived under waves until I was tired and made my way back up to the beach. Laying down on my towel, I dried in the afternoon sun and fell asleep under the shade of a palm tree as the bonfire was starting to be lit.

"Come on sleepy head, either come and play or let Mama take you to bed," Kira said, coming over and kissing me before whispering in my ear.

"I'll come over Mama," I said, waking up to her touch. She had sat next to me, blocking anyone's view of where her hand was and turned me over, so I was on my back looking up at her.

She grabbed at my body, looking down at me like she would take me right there. She slipped her fingers into my bikini bottoms and parted my pussy lips with her fingers before subtly toying with my cunt.

"Stay nice and quiet for Mama little princess," Kira said as I placed my hands over my mouth. I was happy I had chosen a spot that was away from the bonfire and the partying going on around it, but I could still hear the laughter of my friends as they danced and drank. I moaned, and Kira slapped my tits to silence me.

"I said be quiet princess," she hissed. I hadn't heard her be angry at me before and I whimpered, not wanting to hear that voice again. She teased me, sliding in and out, just enough to make me wet but not enough to cum for what seemed like forever until she bent down and kissed me.

"Tell Mama how badly you need to cum princess," Kira said finger fucking me slightly harder.

"Mama please," I moaned in a breathless whisper. Kira laughed in satisfaction as she began to fuck me harder. Rubbing my clit with her thumb and sucking on my nipples, biting them gently as I bucked my hips against her hand. She was tall and skinny, and I was surprised that she could push me down with such strength. I was curvier that she was and had just assumed that I was stronger, but as she pinned me to the ground and made me take her until my orgasm was over, I knew that she was not someone to mess with.

"Pretty little princess," Kira said, putting her cum covered fingers in my mouth.

"Taste yourself, princess, lick Mama's fingers clean," Kira instructed, making me gag slightly before she took her fingers out of my mouth. I reached up, and Kira cuddled me, letting me nuzzle into her neck and watch the party from the safety of her lap as she cuddled me.

"Ready to go party little princess? Did Mama fuck you enough to make that slutty little pussy of yours not seek out attention from anyone else?" Kira said cupping my cum soaked bikini bottoms, rubbing me predatorily. I just nodded into her neck and felt her kiss my cheek as she moved, motioning for me to get up and follow her to the fire.

We danced and drank, and skinny dipped in the water well into the night, with couple after couple leaving to fuck either back at the hostel or somewhere along the bush lined banks of the beach. I ate my fill of marshmallows and Kira enjoyed showing me off, ripping my bikini top off and grabbing my tits in front of some boys who had only just moved into the hostel a day ago.

"You can look, but you can't touch my precious little princess. She's all Mama's," Kira said, making them laugh even though they didn't know what she was saying. I liked that Kira thought I was so special, and I really liked being shown off by her. We had talked about stuff like that and Kira had said that she'd never do anything that made me overly embarrassed, but that she did like making me a little humiliated and had been excited when I told her that I found it hot to be on display. It felt nice to be with her, but I was aware that my flight back home was fast approaching. I had already been here a month, and I knew that I only had one month to go before I would have to say goodbye. The thought of leaving Kira torn at me. I had never had someone adore me as much as she did and I just didn't know what to do about us.

Chapter 5

I had decided to go on a road trip before I had come to the hostel and had already arranged for a rental car to drive through the country to another big beach town.

"Everyone gets stuck out there, make sure you tell Kira where you are going so that when you get stuck, we can come and bring your broken down ass home," Danni said over breakfast a day before I was meant to be leaving. Kira had said how excited she was for me, but I could feel in her touch that she didn't want me to go. Mostly because all she did was touch me. If she wasn't holding my hand, she was sitting me on her lap or fucking me in my bed, the shower or the secluded areas at the beach. She had even taken me to a nudist beach and fucked me in a cave we found. I hated that I made her feel like she was losing me.

"Has Kira said anything to you about not wanting me to go?" I asked Danni, making myself a coffee and eating some leftover pizza. Danni just shook her head.

"Nothing, the only thing she said, was that if she really loved you like she claims, that she'd have to let you go because she would never deserve you if she couldn't give you what you needed or wanted," Danni replied.

"That's not nothing!" I said in shock. I had no idea how deep her affection for me was. Danni shrugged her shoulders as she got up.

"Try not to worry about it too much, she always knew you'd leave Sasha," she said before going back into the kitchen and washing her dishes. Kira had gone to the airport to pick up the new people who were arriving today, and I knew she'd be gone for another hour as I took my coffee cup and headed for the beach.

I walked up and down the beach, drinking my coffee, wondering how on earth I was meant to go on without her. It's the biggest mistake leaving her, I thought, thinking about how she had given me something that most people couldn't. How rare it was to find someone as attractive as Kira, who wanted me, who also was a Mommy Domme. They don't just appear Sasha; you know that! I yelled at myself, looking out over the ocean. The waves were rough today, almost as rough as my heart was feeling. I sat down and watched as they crashed onto the shore, bringing in rocks and big shells from the depths of the ocean and smashing them down.

"I thought I might find you here," a familiar voice said coming behind me. Kira sat down, her legs on either side of me and pulled me into her, wrapping her arms around me and kissing me gently behind my ear.

"I need to say this selfishly. Don't go, little princess," Kira said, her voice shaky. I dipped my head and hated how this felt. I turned in her arms and put my head to her chest.

"Come with me," I whispered as she held me to her, her hand on the back of my head, making me breathe in her scent of coconut tanning oil and ocean spray. She looked down at me and brought my mouth to hers, kissing me deeply.

"I can't. I have to stay here, princess," she said, breaking the kiss.

"But why?" I asked. I knew I sounded whiney and I knew she hated that, but I didn't care, I didn't want to leave without her. I didn't want to live without her.

"Because I have to work. It might look like I'm having one big holiday, but I get paid by the hour princess, Mama is working, even now. I can't just take a month off and go with you. I could take like a week, max but that would only be if it was approved and they would have to find someone to replace me, and it's way too short notice," Kira said explaining everything to me. I nodded.

"Then I just won't go," I said confidently. Kira laughed and shook her head.

"You have to go princess. You only have a short time left here, and I don't want you to be here just because I don't want to lose you," Kira said, running her hands over my tits.

"You could never lose me, Mama," I said,

feeling my heartbreak. I knew then that I had to go, I knew that this would be the last time I kissed her lips as I felt her tongue in my mouth gently teasing me as tears streamed down both our cheeks.

On the day I left, Kira woke early and took my diaper off me in silence, kissed my forehead, and left the room. I waited for her to come back, but she never did. Packing my things into the back of a taxi, I tried not to cry as I helped the taxi driver put my things in the boot and hugged my friends' goodbye. I looked for Kira, but she wasn't there, and I ground my teeth, trying to stay strong as the taxi driver drove me to the car rental place. Danni had said that she'd say goodbye from me to Kira when she saw her, but I knew that we had already said goodbye.

I got to the car rental place, picked up my car, and began driving through the city and onto the high way. I realized that I had never gotten the photo of my ex back from Kira and I laughed, thinking of how stupid I was forever wasting my time on a girl who thought drinking her problems away would solve anything. I drove along the highway, listening to music, and thinking about Kira. How she had always made sure I had enough snacks and drinks, I looked around to see that I hadn't packed anything to eat or drink and wished she was here to look after me as I pulled into a gas station and bought some snacks. Walking back out to the car, I felt my phone vibrate in my pocket. I looked at the caller, happy it was Kira.

"Hey! I was just thinking about you," I said excitedly.

"I bet you were turn around," Kira said. I smiled, my tummy instantly full of butterflies as I slowly turned. Getting kissed full on the lips, I felt Kira's arms wrap around me, holding me tightly and squishing the snacks into me, making my bag of chips pop and fall out onto the floor.

"I guess Mama owes you some chips now hey princess," Kira said, taking the things out of my hands.

"But how?!" I said excitedly.

"I pulled some strings. I meant it when I said I couldn't let you go," Kira said, taking the car keys from my hand and jingling them in front of me.

"Mind if I drive?" She said as I just nodded silently.

"How did you get here?" I asked as we dropped the snacks into the car. I noticed that she didn't have anything with her. She looked back and pointed to Dann, who just waved and took Kira's bag out of her car.

"Surprise!" Danni said making me run over to her and punch her shoulder.

"I was in tears, you bitch!" I said, making her laugh.

"Yeah I know, I felt really bad actually, but I knew that you'd like this so, yay," Danni said. We said goodbye, this it was a far happier departure, and Kira buckled me in before we drove out of the gas station.

"Were you just going to keep going until I

stopped?" I asked her, pouring the drink I had bought into the bottle Kira had instructed me too.

"Yeah, that was pretty much my plan. I knew you'd be stopping pretty soon; I knew you wouldn't have packed any snacks," she said sighing contentedly as she pushed my bottle into my mouth.

"It feels good to be here alone with you princess, Mama is going to love this," Kira said, pulling my seat down and making me have a nap as she drove.

Chapter 6

We stopped into a motel as the day ended. Kira had driven 6hours, only stopping to change me into a diaper at the side of the road which she enjoyed immensely.

"I'd love it if someone stopped behind us and saw what I was doing to you princess," Kira said, taking longer to redress me, enjoying how I looked on the back seat, diapered and sucking my thumb.

She took my hand and rubbed my ass as we walked into the motel reception, got our keys, and made our way to the room.

"This looks really nice, good call princess," Kira said, opening the door and looking around. I was happy she liked my choice. We had passed a number of motels along the way, and I had said all of them looked gross. This one had a pool, which was the only reason I had picked it, so I was glad when Kira also approved.

"Let's get you all clean and ready for bed princess. You'll have to wet that diaper for Mama first though," Kira said, taking out our shower things and laying out the onesie she had bought for me along with a fresh love heart diaper. I shook my head, not wanting to wet my diaper and Kira laughed in shock that I would refuse her.

"Oh, is that how you want to play it, little princess?" She said, grabbing my neck and bending me over her lap. She didn't give me any warning as she spanked my ass, making me squeal and squirm on her lap.

"Be a quiet little princess, or I'll open the door and let everyone see why you are making so much noise," Kira said making me half believe that she wasn't making empty threats. She kept spanking me until she felt me wet my diaper. My head bowed in defeat, and she patted me gently until I finished.

"Good girl. You can stay like that though until Mama has finished her shower, and maybe if you good for me next time I'll change you straight away princess," Kira said making me sit down on the floor and watch as she showered. I loved watching her slender body turn in the water, and her hands glide over her body as she washed. I wouldn't think that she could be a Mama upon looking at her. She had the typical, straight white girl look going on, with on-trend clothes and a beach babe style, she was certainly not the kind of woman I would have thought would want to be Mommy, let alone my Mama. But she was, and I loved how cool she was. Whenever we went anywhere, boys would always hit on her, but she would just playfully turn them down and cuddle up to me instead. I had asked her what she saw in me that she liked so much and was happy when she could give me a list.

"You are soft and cute, with your little tummy and these big titties and this thick jiggly butt that Mama loves to play with. You are quiet, and when you're slutty, you're slutty just for Mama which I love too. I like that you are clever and that you read books instead of wanting to watch movies and I think your glasses are just so cute. I like that you're a little princess and don't like to get messy or dirty. Sasha, you're so lovable, all I want to do is smother you in Mama's love, wrap you in my arms and never let you go. You make me feel like a Mama; you get me in that headspace the minute I look at you, and I love it!" She had said making me blush and tear up with happiness, which just made her kiss me all over and shake my tits in her hands.

Kira finished in the shower and looked at me frowning back at her.

"Oh is someone pouty with Mama princess?" Kira asked, pulling on her pajama shorts and shirt. I nodded and crossed my arms, looking angrily at the floor.

"Well be a good girl next time and do what Mama says the first time I say it silly girl, and this won't happen to you. Come on, crawl to the bathroom for me," Kira instructed, watching me crawl to her. She reached down and rolled me over, taking off my jeans and diaper, making me happy it was off.

"Get in," she kindly said, turning the water on for me. I loved that she always managed to find the right temperature, and I washed in front of her as she played with her pussy.

"You are making Mama horny little princess," Kira said as she stopped herself just as she was about to cum.

"You can finish me off with that pretty tongue of yours when you get out," she said, turning my shower off and rubbing me down with my towel. She took me to the queen-sized bed and laid me down, before putting my love heart diaper on and clipping my short sleeve onesie up. I loved how it felt and ran my hands over my tits, making her laugh.

"Little princess, take those hands away and put them behind your head for Mama," Kira said, climbing on top of me. I hadn't realized she had taken her pants off until her wet pussy was on my lips as she began to make me kiss and suck her, grinding on my face.

"You'll be a good girl and make Mama cum little princess," Kira moaned as she rode my face. I licked her slit and sucked on her clit, flicking my tongue against it, worshiping her pussy. I reached my tongue into her pussy as far as it would go and liked that I could feel her shudder as her cum covered my tongue. I kept licking and sucking her, making her grind down harder, making me gasp for air.

"I'm sorry little princess," Kira said, lifting off me slightly and reaching back to play with my tits. She shook them, holding them by my nipples as she came again, this time grabbing my tits as she did, making me moan into her pussy. She must have liked the vibration of my moan because she grabbed at my tits, again and again, making me moan into her and against her clit.

"Fuck little princess, you're so good for Mama," Kira moaned, lifting off my mouth and coming to lie down next to me. She kissed my lips and licked them, tasting herself. She smiled at me, wrapping her arms around me and pulling me in close to her.

"Look how cute you are princess," Kira said, rubbing the front of my onesie and kissing me all over my face.

"Stay there," Kira instructed as she went into the bathroom and wet a corner of the towel, coming back other to me and wiping my face clean.

"I can't have my little princess being all dirty can I baby?" Kira said delighting me that I didn't have to stay dirty. She pulled the bed sheets down and tucked me in before turning the lights off and coming back into bed, letting me snuggle into her. I felt her ribs against my tits, and she ran her fingers through my soft hair.

"Sweet dreams princess," Kira said as she began to stroke the side of my breast.

"I'm happy I have you back Mama," I replied, getting gently squeezed as I fell asleep to her gently groping hands.

Chapter 7

We had left in the morning at 9 and had driven for four hours before we noticed that the fuel light was dangerously low.

"Look up where a station is on Mama's phone baby," Kira said, passing me her phone. She had put me in a fresh diaper and told me just to get used to being in them, stating that she would only let me use the bathroom for emergencies. I was happy she knew my limits and didn't try to push them. She had dressed me a summer dress, and sandals, but let me take them off when we were driving, and I could cross my legs on the seat.

"There's one about an hour away Mama," I said, showing her the phone just before we lost reception.

"Ok, well, we will just have to make it," Kira said, putting her foot down. There was nothing but red dirt on either side of us on this long stretch of road, and I wondered what would happen if we broke down. Kira drove ten over the speed limit, and I hoped that she would get us there in time.

"What happens if we don't make it, Mama?" I asked, holding Kira's hand and turning down the stereo. Kira gave me a funny look.

"We will have to walk little girl, and don't think for a second that'll mean I let you put on your big girl panties," she said, looking back at the road. Her phone beeped, reception returning but just as the car began to slow down. Kira looked at me, rolled her eyes, and sighed. I was happy it wasn't an angry sigh, and I looked at her with wide eyes.

"I hope you like walking little princess," Kira said as she pulled over to the side of the road and parked. I looked at her and then looked out into the emptiness of the land.

"But Mama," I said as she unbuckled my seat belt and pushed a paci in my mouth.

"Complain, and I'll make you suck it all the way, so everyone will know you're a naughty little girl for her Mama, is that what you want?" Kira said. I shook my head, and Kira groped at my tits for a while before taking the paci out of my mouth and putting it in her bag. We got out of the car and felt the hot sun on our skin immediately before we put our water and snacks in our bags and started to walk to the gas station we knew was only a few kilometers ahead.

"What if they are closed, Mama?" I asked, holding her hand.

"Well then we figure out a plan B princess," Kira said.

"I'm happy you're here, Mama," I said, kissing her.
We walked for an hour before we stopped to put on more sun cream and had a drink.

"It shouldn't be much further baby girl," Kira said, reaching her hand out to me and waiting for me catch up to her.

"We can get a nice cold ice-cream when we get there, we have definitely deserved it!" She added, wiping the sweat off her forehead. We continued walking for another hour before we saw a truck coming behind us. Usually, I wouldn't have wanted it to stop with nowhere to run, but it was hot so I just hoped that we wouldn't be in any danger. The truck slowed and stopped in front of us, and I squeezed Kira's hand firmly scared of what would happen next.

"It's OK princess, Mama is here, you'll be fine," Kira said. I was relieved to see that it was a woman who got out of the truck, but surprised when I saw what type of woman it was. She was hot! The type of hot that you'd find as a pin-up model in a tattoo artist back room. She wore ripped denim shorts and a baggy muscle singlet. Walking confidently to us she smiled and stuck out her hand at Kira.

"Looking little lost girls?" She said, shaking Kira's hand and then mine.

"I'm Mel, saw what I'm guessing is your car a little while back. Where you headed?" Mel said. I liked that Kira took over, I was pretty sure I had heat stroke and found it hard even to stand up.

"We were going to Paradise Island, but our

car's out of gas. We thought there was a station up here," Kira said. I held Kira's hand, and Mel smiled at me.

"Well, I don't think she'll last much longer in this heat. Let me drive you to the station and then back to your car. It'll be a long walk yet, they've just moved another half hour's drive north which will mean you'd be walking an awful long way and back," Mel explained. Kira gladly accepted, and Mel helped me into the cab of her truck, letting me lie down and have a rest in the cold aircon as she drove us.

"Thanks for this," I heard Kira said. I closed my eyes and was happy that I hadn't done this trip alone, Danni was right, everyone breaks down along this trip.

"It's alright. Your friend is cute," Mel said to Kira, who just turned around to look at me.

"Yeah, she's lovely," Kira said. That was the last thing I heard before I fell asleep. When I woke up, it was dark, and I had rolled onto my tummy, my dress had ridden over my ass, my puffy diaper on full display. I tried to open my eyes, but everything was black. I tried to move, but my arms and legs were tied, making me splay across Mel's bed. I tried to yell, but there was a gag in my mouth. I knew we shouldn't have gotten a lift from her! I thought, hoping that she wasn't hurting Kira. I began to cry; hot tears rolled down my cheeks and onto the bed as I felt hands moved the back of my legs. I tried to scream, but only muffled sounds came out, crying harder.

"Shh it's OK princess Mama has you, you're alright baby," I heard Kira say, I relaxed and whimpered wanting to see her and cuddle her.

"Mama just tied you up because you looked so cute laying there. You will never believe it, Mel is a Mommy too!" Kira said, sounding very excited. She had told me she had tried to find friends in the scene but hadn't had any luck. Clearly, she had been successful here. I heard a door open, and Mel climb inside, closing it behind her.

"Oh, has she woken up?" Mel asked Kira who just patted my ass.

"Yes, she has," Kira replied with a voice I knew meant that I was about to be fucked. I felt Kira loosen the ties around my legs and arm before she turned me around so that I was on my back.

"Do you want to play little princess?" Kira asked. I thought for a minute before nodding yes. I liked that Kira asked. I liked that I knew I could say no. She made me feel so protected and loved. She knew getting bound in my sleep was one of my fantasies, and I loved that she had been so bold to try and make it come true.

"Can Mel touch you, princess? Kira asked, kissing my neck, slowly pulling off the blindfold. I let my eyes adjust until they could see Mel. She smiled down at me, and I blushed as I nodded yes, making her smile.

"Thank you baby girl," Mel said, slowly stroking my thigh. I liked that she let me get used to her touch before she tried anything else and I moaned and wriggled against the gag and the ties.

"No, I think you're going to need to stay like

that baby girl. You're going to make too much noise if we take this out," Kira said, grabbing the strap of the gag and making my head shake. She grabbed the bottom of my dress and wriggled it up to my body until it was over my tits, making Mel raise an eyebrow and smile hungrily at me.

"May I?" Mel said, asking Kira who just smiled.

"She likes it like this," Kira said, pulling the front of my bra down and pulling out my tits by my nipples making me squeal.

"Cute baby," Mel said, slapping my tits and flicking my nipples. She was stronger than Kira, and I felt her touch on my clit as she licked my nipples until I tried to pull away from her. Kira rubbed my pussy over my diaper as Mel held my neck down and continued to lick my nipples, going from left to right, only stopping to bend down and suck them firmly, biting them as she pulled them up before going back to flicking them. I arched my back and moaned loudly, feeling the start of an orgasm building. Kira took off my diaper and tossed it the side before spitting on my pussy and sliding her strap-on against me, pulling it back and letting it hit against my clit.

"I think she likes that," Kira said to Mel who had started slapping my tits and groping them. Kira spat on my pussy again before sliding her cock into me as Mel rubbed my clit, making me cum instantly.

"You have to still ask for permission little princess. I don't care if you're gagged, you won't have such bad manners," Kira said as she began pounding into me. I knew she was mad. I didn't have to ask; I could just tell by the force she was putting behind her thrusts. I started begging her to let me cum, squealing when I felt Mel lift me up and slide our thin dildo into my ass.

"I wouldn't let her if she was my baby girl," Mel said as she matched Kira's thrusts. Mel turned me in her lap so that she and Kira were fucking me from the side. I felt Kira grab my ass and shake it in her hand.

"Oh she won't be cumming, and if she does,

Mama is going to tied her hand behind her back and let strangers finger fuck her until she is crying for them to stop. Isn't that right baby girl," Kira said as I bit down hard on the gag and held off my orgasm.

We had come up with punishments, but she had only ever spanked me and made me stand in the corner, this was a punishment we had come up with for when I was really naughty, so I guessed she was really mad that I had cum without permission. I nodded and moaned, holding off another orgasm. Tightening my abs for so long to hold off cumming began to make my tummy hurt as Kira and Mel used me. I had a sneaky feeling Kira was trying to make me cum as she grabbed my hair and pulled my head back, making me look at her.

"Be Mama's good little princess. Show Mama how good you can be," she said. Usually, these words would have sent me over the edge, but I refused to cum, letting Mel fuck my ass and rub my clit as Kira fucked my pussy. I smiled at

Kira behind my gag and felt her lovingly stroke my face, I knew she knew I was only holding on by a thread and she leaned down, kissing my cheek but fucking me deeper.

"You can cum princess," Kira said, making me explode and squirt all over her as I relaxed my pussy and abs. Mel untied my hand and held my hand to her breast, making me squeeze and toy with her as her other hand refused to stop fucking me. I shuddered as my orgasm lasted longer than it ever had in my life and lay limp, my only movement, the forced groping of my hand on Mel's big breasts.

"What a pretty little used slut," Kira said, pulling out of me, only making my pussy juices drip out of my cunt as the aftershock of my orgasm ravaged through my body. Mel untied me and took the toy out of my ass and pulled my dress and bra off.

"What a good girl," Mel said, putting me in her lap and forcing her nipple in my mouth. She took me by surprise, and I pulled away, not knowing if Kira would be mad or not but settled when I felt her stroke my forehead.

"It's OK princess, you can suck on Mel's juicy titties," Kira said lovingly. Mel was larger than Kira, and I felt small in her arms as she pushed more of her breast in my mouth. I was obedient to Kira because I loved her, but I was good for Mel because I knew I couldn't overpower her. I stayed sucking on her nipples until I began to close my eyes, weary after the fucking I had just been given, and Kira came into Mel's arms and watched as I suckled.

"We'd make a cute little family," Mel laughed, wrapping her arm around Kira. Kira smiled and rubbed my tummy.

"Unfortunately our little princess would be leaving us too soon though, she's going back home in a few weeks," Kira replied. I tried to speak, but Mel held my mouth to her nipple and gently slapped my face. I looked up into her eyes. They were different to Kira's and I could tell she had something else in mind.

"I didn't say you were finished, baby girl," she said, quieting me back down.

Chapter 8

Mel drove us to the gas station, and we filled two cans of petrol before she drove us back to our car. It was dark by the time we got there, and I could feel my pussy still leaking cum into the new diaper Mel had put me in.

"Thanks so much, Mel, we would have been really fucked if it hadn't of been for you," Kira said hugging her goodbye. Mel reached out and stroked my hair as she held Kira.

"Well, somebody was fucked anyway," she said, making Kira laugh. I hugged Mel goodbye, letting her lift up the front of my dress and rub over my diaper one more time before we parted ways.

"Be a good girl for your Mama baby girl," Mel said, smiling at me. I nodded and sucked my thumb, reaching out to hold Kira's hand.

"Take care," Kira said, putting me into the car.

"I liked her Mama," I said as Kira drove us back onto the road. She looked at me and winked.

"That's good. I'm glad you had a good time. I had hoped that you'd like it, princess," Kira said, rubbing my head.

The rest of the trip went like clockwork. We saw all the big tourist sites, figured out where the gas stations where before we ran out of fuel and I took more photos than my camera and phone could hold. Kira and I ate at amazing restaurants, and I loved spending all my time with her. As we drove back to Waker's Beach, I knew that our time was ending and it tore at me as it had done all those weeks ago.

"It's just so unfair Mama," I said as Kira drove through the city. I knew we were only an hour away from the hostel, and in three days I would be on a plane going back home. Kira looked at me with sad eyes.

"You could always come back next year?" She said. I guess I could, but would it be the same?

Would we be the same or would we have found new people? I wasn't sure and decided to just look out the window until we got back to the hostel. The next two days were a blur as I saw the familiar faces, wondering if these people would ever leave. It the last day when Kira and I finally talked about what would happen after I left.

"So what do you want to do? Like realistically, where do you think this can go?" Kira said. I had taken her out to have coffee and cake at a café. This had become one of our favorite spots. The café was situated on the beach front, and we sipped our coffees looking out over the ocean. Surfers were catching the last waves of the day, and some of the backpackers were having a competition who could dig the biggest hole in the sand.

"I'll really miss this. I'll really miss you. We can stay in touch, though, right?" I said, looking at Kira. She had worn my favorite flowy beach dress, and her hair was done up in a half bun. The sun had streaked her hair white blonde in some parts, and she looked down and smiled into her coffee.

"Of course we can princess," she said. I didn't know how to make it better. The ache I felt in my heart was unlike anything I had experienced before. I had weighed up all my options. To stay and try to get sponsored like she had done, to go and come back every year for holidays to see her. To have her fly over to see me in my home town. The wind picked up, and I shivered. None of those options were long lasting, and I could feel her slipping away from me.

"I have been thinking about things though," Kira said, making my stomach turn. We had played the; everything will be the same game for so long, I was really hoping she wasn't about to shatter the façade.

"Maybe I could come and see you in a few months and see if we mesh just like we have here. Maybe some time apart once you have settled back into your daily routine, will make you realize that this was just a holiday thing, that you aren't really into it and I could come over and see if I still fit in your world?" Kira said. It was the first time I had seen her nervous. She had always been in such control of every situation she had been in that seeing her so worried about my response made me realize she was just as nervous how parting ways as I was.

"I don't think this is a holiday thing, Mama," I said, leaning forward to call her Mama and making her smile. She reached for my hand and squeezed it tightly.

"But I'd love that. Maybe you even like my city and can find a job you like or something," I said, stopping myself as I began to race through the possibility of her moving to be with me. She just smiled and looked out at the glimmering ocean. The sun was setting behind us, and I knew that I had seen my last sunset as I looked through the café and out over the mountain range that was to our backs. Turning back around, I saw that Kira had placed a letter on the table.

"Will you read it when you are back home?" She asked, but I could only nod my head. I felt as if

I would burst into tears if I spoke again, so I just looked down and looked at my letter. She had kissed it with red lipstick, and I held it as though it was the most special thing I had ever held. A waitress came to ask us if we wanted our cakes to go as they were closing and I realized that we hadn't even touched them.

"That would be great thanks," Kira said and gave a fake smile to the waitress who walked away to get us containers.

Walking down the beach and back to the hostel, Kira linked her arm in mine as we talked about the last two months.

"I can't believe it's already over," she said, kicking the sand.

"I feel like it was only yesterday that I picked you up. I thought you were so cute how you kept falling asleep," Kira said, making me laugh.

"You have no idea how nervous you made me when you kept calling me princess and talking about yourself in the third person," I replied.

"Yeah, well, I knew you needed Mama to

look after you, what can I say," Kira said, grabbing my tits and bending down to kiss them.

"I still can't believe you let me fuck you as you did. You're such a slutty princess for Mama. It made me really proud watching you let Mel fuck you," Kira added, making me blush.

"Yeah, I'm surprised I did too. I guess you just make me feel really safe like even when I am nervous about something, I look at you and know it'll be alright," I said.

"Like wearing your diaper in public," Kira whispered as we walked through the hostel and back to our room. I giggled and turned around as she slapped my ass, and playfully grabbed my hips, pushing into my ass as I opened the door to our room.

Chapter 9

Even though I knew that Kira couldn't surprise me by being on my flight home like she had surprised me by coming on my road trip, I still had a glimmer of false hope as she drove me to the airport.

"I'm sorry, I can't stay. I tried, but they only let me have the shuttle as a favor, and it has to be back as soon as possible," Kira said as we drove. Usually, the shuttle was only for picking people up, but she had called in a favor so she could drive me.

"I know," I said. I held her hand as we drove, talking about when she would be able to video call and what I would do when I got home.

"I don't expect you to keep the rules I had for you here when you get back princess, I know you have a whole life there," Kira said, turning the radio down. I turned to look at her.

"But I want to Mama," I said more little than I had liked. I was about to go on a flight by myself where I had to make sure I was safe, and at the right terminal, I didn't have time to be little. But holding onto Kira's hand made me feel like her princess, and that was all I wanted in the world. Kira looked at me and smiled.

"Keep my rules then, but let me know if you start to get rid of them, OK?" She asked. I could tell this was as hard for her as it was for me. A friend told me not to fall for anyone while I was away and I had scoffed in their face saying as if I was that stupid, that I was only going for two months and what on earth could happen in two months? Well, I was wrong, very wrong as I ached to stay with Kira for one more minute. We reached the airport, and I got out, forcing back my tears. I looked at her and tried to burn her image into my memory, her long blonde hair, tall, slender body, mischievous brown eyes, and tanned skin. The way she smiled like she had a big secret; she was just about to share and how her long arms wrapped around me as she held me tight. We stayed holding each other as silent tears rolled down our cheeks, being told twice by the security guards that she had to move on before she broke our embrace.

"Have a safe flight princess," Kira said, holding my face in her hands and stroking my tears away with her thumbs.

"I'll talk to you really soon, Mama," I said, not caring who was around to hear. Kira smiled warmly, kissed me one more time before letting my face go and stepping back. She just nodded as she took a deep breath and walked back to the driver's side, honking the horn as she drove away. I stood there, watching her go, new tears forming in my eyes, Kira taking my heart away with her.

I made my way through customs, numbly followed the signs to my terminal and sat, waiting to be let on the plane. *This sucks,* I thought, pouting and wanting her back. I was not looking forward to going home. I thought about my job, the things I did for entertainment, and it just didn't compare to the experiences I had had with Kira or even the beachside life in general. I thought about what I could do for work here and did a few internet searches on the types of visas that I was eligible for. I could study something and come on a student visa; *I'll just study the degree which has the longest duration,* I thought hopefully as I looked into how to apply for that. I heard my flight being called and walked over to the gates and took a deep breath as I made my way down the ramp and to my seat.

The flight was as annoying as the one coming over, and I took a sleeping pill so I could just sleep through the whole thing, waking up just in time to leave the plane. It felt so weird coming back. I had changed so much but looking around, it felt like I was the only thing to have changed. I hailed a taxi, was driven back to my apartment, walked inside, and sat on my couch.

"Well, I wasn't expecting that," I said out loud and looked around my place. I stood up and walked to the window and looked out onto the city street. I heard basketballs bouncing, cars honking their horns and people yelling, ambulance sirens rang down the street, and I turned away from the window, sad that I wasn't back in my laid back seaside home. I went to my suitcase and started unpacking as I found the letter Kira had given me. I ran my fingertips over her red lipstick kiss, remembering how her kiss had tasted and smiled, excited to be hearing from her.

Hi princess,

I guess you'll be home now and wondering what I'm doing. If you're not wondering what I'm doing, why not?! Mama should always be on your mind, cheeky girl! Anyway, I'm looking through our photos; I'll probably print some of them off and stick them around my room. I have claimed our old room as my room, I have to pay a little extra to have the whole room to myself, but I don't care, I couldn't cope if someone else was to sleep in here if it wasn't you. The days are starting to get cooler here so you should be happy you got your pretty little tan while you did! It'll be sweater weather here before long and too cold to go to the beach. The first night here without you sucked liked I thought it would, but I felt better knowing that you had the big puppy I bought you to cuddle and imagine me cuddling with you as we did pretty much your whole trip. Message me when you get home, so I know my little princess is safe.

Mama loves you XX

I put the letter down and grabbed the puppy Kira had bought me and pressed it into my face as tears began to fill my eyes. She had sprayed her perfume all over it, and my heart skipped a beat as I smelt her so close to me. I had decided that I would buy that perfume the minute I could and spray it over my pillows so when I slept, it would be like she was still with me. I took out my phone and messaged her straight away. Having a shower, I put on a fresh diaper and sent her a message of that too and was so happy when she replied. We messaged back and forth all night, and I fell asleep listening to a voice message she sent me, happy to have Mama back, even if it was through a screen.

Chapter 10

I went back to work the following Monday and answered everyone's questions about how my trip was and how they thought the photos I put up of skydiving and the nature that I had seen were so cool. I sat at my desk, looked at the pile of paperwork that had collected there. I opened the letters, was given a new project of photographing a sporting event and had several calls from past clients asking me to photograph this event and that event. By lunchtime, I had to walk out onto the street for some fresh air and wondered how I could have ever been happy living this life. I took my phone out and looked at Kira's social media accounts. She had gone fishing today and had caught a colorful fish, posing with it before writing a big spiel about how it's important to make sure the hook is out of the mouth of the fish before putting it back in the ocean. I smile as I scrolled through, looking at the photos of her organizing a beach clean up after a festival and how they had had a costume movie night. She had dressed up as a belly dancer, and I was pretty sure it was only so she could wear next to nothing. I saw Danni doing her usual angry glare in some photos and missed them terribly as I looked up and around my world. It was gray. Literally, the buildings were gray, the sky was gray, and the people were gray. No one looked happy to be here; no one smiled, no one's eyes shone with excitement. They just looked blankly faced, staring right through me as I looked in front and behind me. I looked at my phone again and knew I had to get back to her. I had to get back to Kira.

I knew I couldn't just get on a plane and head back. I knew that because I had no visa just to go back on and I really didn't want to go back just to have to leave again so soon. I into the student visa again and applied. I choose an arts degree, majoring in photography, I figured I might as well do something I actually loved and who knows, maybe

I would learn something new. The degree was four years, and I knew that I would have to return to this gray mess after I graduated, but I also figured that Kira and I would have a solid understanding of where we wanted to take our relationship by then. I paid for the visa and was happy. I fulfilled all the medical and financial requirements. Now all I had to do was wait to hear if I got it or not.

Kira and I talked daily and fell into a routine really quickly with me messaging in my morning, and her messaging in her morning. That meant that I would message her when I woke up, and by the evening my time, I would get a response. I liked that nothing seemed to change with us. I had been worried that the distance would slowly start to break our relationship down. I had finally heard back about my visa status and was over the moon that I had been granted it and was set to start the degree in a months time. I booked my flight back to her, happy this time I was only booking a one-way ticket. I had decided not to tell her; I thought it would be better to surprise her by just showing up. I handed in my two weeks' notice to leave my job and was happy to be finally rid of this gray city. It had been three months since I had last held Kira, and as I boarded my plane back to her, I could hardly keep a straight face.

It felt like coming home as I left the airport, the warm air hitting my face instantly. I had decided to take a taxi to the hostel; I didn't want Kira to see me until I casually strolled into the common room or something and clapped my hands excitedly as we pulled into Waker's Beach hostel. I had booked a room under a different name so that she wouldn't know it was me and grabbed my bags out of the boot of the taxi, inhaling deeply as my lungs filled with the sea breeze. I had sold all of my furniture before coming back, knowing that I wouldn't need it and looked at all my worldly possessions which had been carefully packed into my three suitcases.

"No fucking way!" I heard, turning around

to see Danni. She hugged me before I even had a chance to lift my arms and laughed, feeling more at home here than I had when I went back to my real home.

"Oh my god, Sasha! What are you doing here?!" She said squealing.

"I actually am studying here now. I'll be here for the next four years!" I replied happily, frowning when I realized that Danni was in fact, still here.

"Um, what about you? Why or how are you still here?!" I asked. She just rolled her eyes.

"I got a shit house job, but they are sponsoring me so meh, I just wanted to stay really," Danni replied, making me laugh. She looked down at my bags before looking up at me.

"Does Kira know you've come back?" She asked cautiously, making me nervous.

"No, I thought that I'd make it a surprise," I said. Danni bit her lip, and I felt my stomach lurch instantly. *Was she with someone else? Had she moved? Had something awful happened to her? I* thought as I watched Danni.

"I think she'll be really happy to see you. But she's not the same girl you left behind," Danni said hesitantly. I just looked at her, waiting for an explanation but when one wasn't given, I looked at the ground nervously.

"Should I have not come back? Danni will you just tell me if she's with someone else?!" I said angrily, feeling my voice become shaky.

"What?! No nothing like that she's completely obsessed with you! She's been in an accident though. She's at the hospital," Danni said, relieving my fears.

"Take me there," I said hoping Danni still had her car. She agreed, and I put my bags in my old room, happy to see Kira still had my photos on the wall and drove with Danni to the hospital.

"What kind of accident?" I asked nervously. I really hadn't wanted to ask, but I figured I needed to know what I was walking into. Kira hadn't posted anything online in a few days, but I hadn't thought that was strange, she had gone days without posting before.

"We went to the jetty to jump off the edge like we've done hundreds of time before. But this time, when she jumped, she jumped right in the way of a shark. It bit her and um," Danni said, stopping and looking at me making me hold my breath. Her face was white; she had clearly seen the whole thing.

"There was a lot of blood, Sasha. And her screams, I'll never stop hearing them. By the time we got her to hospital," Danni said. I could tell she was reliving it.

"Do not fucking tell me she is dead. Do not!" I said as tears began to stream down my face. Danni just shook her head.

"She lost her arm, she lost so much blood she is in a coma, they don't know if she'll wake up," Danni said as we arrived at the hospital. I jumped out of the car and ran inside, asking where her room was, but I didn't have to. There were flowers and balloons around the fourth room I went past and looked through the window, my whole world stopping.

I don't know how long I stayed standing there for, but when I felt Danni's hand on my shoulder, I snapped out my daze.

"What?" I said, looking at Danni angrily.

"You can go in," Danni said. I was happy that she understood that I wasn't angry at her. I walked in slowly, Kira had a tube going down her throat, and the monitor was beeping every couple of seconds. I looked at her body and tried to take it all in. I couldn't seem to register that she had lost her arm, but there she was, laying in the bed, hooked up to a monitor, missing her arm. The shark had gotten the arm Kira had complained about, saying that there was a birthmark on it that she hadn't liked. I didn't think she'd hated it so much that she'd want a shark to bite it off. I sat down by the bed and looked at her. Reaching out slowly, I brushed her hair out of the way as she suddenly popped her eyes open, breathing in deeply like she had been holding her breath for years. Startling me I jumped and screamed, making Kira turn to me and try to scream. Her voice was hoarse, so it was more of a wheeze, and we looked at each other for the longest time before she relaxed again.

"Am I dead princess," Kira said. She sounded like she hadn't had a drink of water for weeks and I looked around but couldn't find a glass.

"Shh, don't try and talk Mama, you're not dead. I'm here now," I said, pressing the buzzer for the nurse. Nurses rushed in, and they asked me to leave before they hurriedly closed the curtains and shut the door behind me.

Chapter 11

The next time I saw Kira was two weeks later because I was not immediate family. But I stayed at the hospital for those two weeks, always sitting outside, looking at her through the window when was awake. She had been able to stay awake for long periods at a time, gradually having built that up and the doctor told me that she should make a full recovery but that he couldn't go into any more detail. I had to start my uni degree in a weeks time, and I was relieved that Kira was allowed to go back home with me at the start of her third week in the hospital.

"It's OK if you don't feel like talking, we don't have to talk," I said, driving her home. I had bought a car since I was going to be staying here a while. She just smiled and put her hand on my thigh.

"I hope you don't mind that I'm here. I'll understand if you want to be alone. And we don't have to worry about our dynamic if it's all just too much," I added, not wanting her to think she had to be something she wasn't ready to be. Kira looked at me with the same amused expression she always had when I began to ramble, and I liked that she hadn't changed that much.

"Princess, everything stays the same. I'm over the moon you are here I actually don't think I could do this without you, but you might have to help me while I get used to this," Kira said moving her shoulder. She frowned. The shark had taken her arm up until her mid-upper arm, and I could tell that she could still feel it as though it was there. The doctors had called it 'Phantom feeling,' where she would feel like it was still there even though it wasn't.

"Also, you'll have to get used to me fucking you with this hand," Kira said, laughing. I loved that she could still find humor in this. The shark had taken her writing hand, and I knew she'd be pretty clumsy until she learned how to use her other hand.

"I'm a really good helper Mama," I said, and I liked that she stroked my hair like she always used to.

"What a bloody awful time for you to come and see me. Did I hear right, you're like staying for school?" Kira asked as we pulled into the hostel. I nodded proudly. I was happy she wanted me here and hadn't pushed me away.

"Clever princess, I expect perfect grades from you baby," Kira said as we got out of the car and were surrounded by happy backpackers.

The months that followed felt like a blur. I had gone to uni and was doing really well. It helped that I knew what I was doing, but Kira had made me a gold star chart and would frequently tell everyone how clever she thought I was. I had moved in with her in her room, and she had moved the other bunks out so that we had a queen size bed, a beach rug, and cupboard in the room. It actually looked like a real bedroom, and not a room in the middle of the backpacker hostel. She had been going to therapy and rehab to get used to not having an arm and had made a lot of progress. So much so in fact that she had started saying that it was a waste of time going.

"I just don't think I need to go anymore like going won't bring my arm back, and in fact, I kinda like my new look. I think I rock this," Kira said, making me toast for breakfast. She had gotten mad when I hadn't let her do all her usual Mama things for me. She had even slammed some people down when they had criticized me for not doing things like making food and carrying things, thinking that I wasn't fair to her. I like that she had defended me. I was already trying to work through letting her do her usual stuff for me. I didn't need them making it any harder.

"I think you should go for like a year, just to give it a really good amount of time before you step away. And maybe don't even step away from all at once, maybe just go less until you don't go at all," I suggested worriedly that going cold turkey on the support front might not be the wisest decision. Kira came out of the kitchen, pushed some empty beer bottles away, and place my eggs and toast in front of me.

"But they are all so whiney! You should hear them," Kira said, stabbing her eggs. I smirked, I hadn't realized she was so independent until the accident.

"Maybe go until the nightmares stop," I said quietly. Kira rolled her eyes.

"That happened for like a week princess," Kira said more sternly that I would have liked signaling that the conversation was over.

"What are you going to do today?" She said, starting a new topic of discussion. I looked at my watch and was happy it was so early.

"I don't have class until this afternoon, I was hoping that I could come with you guys to fly kites on the beach," I said more asking than telling. Kira nodded.

"Yeah, but I want you to do at least 2 hours study today, you've got that exam that I know you aren't prepared for princess," Kira said. I was happy that it had only been the two of us in the outdoor space of the common area this morning. It made me feel like the backpackers weren't really backpackers, but just our home and we were just outside. I nodded, finishing my eggs and watching as Kira lay down on the wooden bench we had been sitting at.

"You know, I think tomorrow we should go into town and pick you up a few things princess," Kira said closing her eyes, oblivious to Danni who had come to sit next to me.

"Oh, what kind of things Kira?!" Danni said, making Kira laugh and sit up.

"Wouldn't you like to know!" She replied. All I did was blush and make Danni laugh at me.

"Well when we all hear sex moans coming from your room, we'll know you have gone shopping," Danni said as she dealt out a hand of cards, starting the day.

"Where's Kira?" I asked, coming home from class and not having found her in our room. We had all gone kite flying, which had turned into, who could fly a kite blindfolded the longest, who could do it while drinking the longest and who could fly the most kites in one go. I liked that the backpackers always kept life exciting. The class had been eas, and I liked that I knew all the answers. Coming home, I noticed that it had started getting dark earlier and quickly walked past the pub, happy to be almost home.

"I don't know actually, haven't seen her for a few hours, maybe she's gone to get food or something?" Danni suggested. Leaving the common room, I went to our room and had a shower. I hadn't realized that I was so tired, but the minute I lay down on our bed, I was fast asleep.

Waking up, the room was dark, and so was outside. I stretched and looked at the time. It was 1:30 in the morning and I was surprised I had slept through the party I could hear going on on the beach. Pulling on some clothes, remembering my jacket, I walked to the beach, thinking that Kira would be there. She loved bonfires and had not missed one since I had known her. I made my way down the beach to the group who were partying and looked for Kira. I walked through the crowd, not catching their excited energy because I felt something else. Something was wrong. I walked to the water's edge, wondering if getting some perspective on the party would make Kira visible. I saw people dancing and drinking, some people sneaking off into the bushes, and people just being generally happy to be alive. I turned back around and looked out into the blue and black waves, jumping when I felt her behind me.

"Hey," Kira said, smiling at me. She had wrapped her cardigan around her, and she had looked like she had been crying.

"Hey, what's wrong?" I said, worried that something had happened. Kira just shrugged her shoulders.

"I don't know, wanna walk? I'm not really in the mood to party," Kira said, moving to my other side and taking my hand in hers. I just nodded as she led me away from the warmth of the fire and the loudness of the party. We walked in silence, just feeling the cold night sand under our feet and tasting the salt on our lips. Kira walked slowly, in an easy rhythm, and I hoped that she was OK.

"I want to show you," she said quietly as she led me to the jetty. I stopped and pulled on her arm.

"You don't have too if you don't want to Mama," I said, making Kira turn around and smile lovingly at me. She brushed my hair away from my face and kissed me.

"I love that you didn't want to stop being Mama's princess Sasha," Kira said, making me proud to have her love.

"But I want to show you; I need to show you. I think I need to show myself, but I want you here, please, princess?" Kira said. It felt strange to have her asking me for permission. I nodded and continued to walk with her to the edge of the jetty.

"This is where it happened," Kira said,

looking down into the blackness. I wasn't really sure what I could say so I just held her hand and moved into her lap when she sat down and pulled me to her. She buried her face into my neck, and hair nuzzling me while she played with my tits.

"I hope you are OK with how much I've needed you lately princess, I just really don't think I could do this without you," Kira said running her fingers over my crossed thighs.

"I'm happy you've still wanted me, I was kinda worried you'd push me away or something," I said as Kira shook her head no.

"No, I could never push you away, you are too precious to me, princess," Kira said as I leaned back and melted into her.

"Tell me what happened Mama," I said softly. Kira patted me tenderly and exhaled like she was trying to rid the memory from her body.

"We were jumping off the end here. I'd gone a couple of times; we were all going to do one last jump. I jumped, but I didn't bother looking down this time. The next thing I know, there's blood everywhere, people are screaming. I didn't feel it at. First, the pain, I just looked around, wondering what had happened. Then I felt it come back; it hit me on my side and pushed me into the water. I held my breath and shut my eyes," Kira said before becoming silent again. I didn't really know what to say, so we stayed sitting in silence, listening to the party going on down the beach watching the ocean glimmer like stars.

Chapter 12

"I've decided I'm going to get it tattooed," Kira said the minute I opened my eyes the next morning. She had obviously been watching me sleep because she was sitting up in bed, looking at me with wide eyes. I blinked a few times and adjusted my ears, getting used to her loud voice so early in the morning.

"What?" I asked, unsure of what she was talking about. Kira rolled her eyes and got up, running to the shelf on the other side of the room.

"Here, this is what I want," she said, handing me a drawing. One of the backpackers had drawn her a mock-up of what her tattoo could look like, and Kira beamed with excitement. It was an image of a big blue-gray shark, surrounded by water but jumping out to bite into the air. It looked cool I had to admit.

"When do you want to get it done?" I asked. Kira took the drawing from my hands and smiled down at it.

"Soon princess, right now, let Mama see if you've been a good girl," Kira said, feeling the front of my diaper. She frowned and cupped my face making me look at her when I tried to look down.

"You know I don't change you out of your diapy until you've wet it princess. Mama is going to make breakfast, and when I come back, you'd better have been a good girl for me," Kira said, jumping off the bed and walking out the door. I laid in bed for a minute, thinking of how I could get away with not wetting it but deciding that was a hopeless case, I began as Kira walked back into the room with buttery toast she had just made. She placed the plate down on the table we had set up for eating and came over to feel me.

"Good girl," she said, kissing my forehead.

"I'm pretty sad that I had to ask you to wet your diaper when you know that it's something you have to do. Just because Mama has been a little out of it, doesn't mean you can stop being my good little princess Sasha," Kira said, taking my hand

and making me sit at our table. I hated this. I pouted while I ate my toast, which just made Kira laugh.

"Oh, has the baby forgot who is in charge little princess?" She said, grabbing my cheek and pulling it firmly. I tried to look less pouty, but I was failing. Kira finished her toast before grabbing me by my hair and bending me over her knee.

"I'm not going to spank your ass; I'm going to spank these lovely exposed thighs of yours. Then you can explain to everyone why you are wearing jeans on a hot day like this because, by the time that I am done with you, you'll be red for hours," Kira said taking a gag and buckling it in place. She had become really good at only using one hand, and I found it so sexy that she could still powerfully dominate me.

"Be quiet, or people might come in here princess, and you know Mama would have no trouble with that," Kira said, making me stop squealing behind my gag. She spanked my thighs, running her nails over the red skin over and over again, making me squirm on her lap.

"Hold still, princess I'm not done with you yet," Kira said spanking me until I felt my legs burn deep in my muscles. I lay there wondering when it would stop when I felt cool balm over my burning skin.

"Pretty, princess," Kira said as she made sure my legs would be alright. She turned me over, and I looked at her big brown eyes and found that I was smiling a smile, I couldn't wipe from my face.

"Thank you, Mama," I said softly making her match my smile.

"I won't be bad again," I added, making her laugh.

"Oh, you probably will princess, little girls always say they'll be good but then are naughty," Kira replied, standing me up and taking off my diaper. It was late morning, and she let me have a shower and get clean as she picked out what clothes she wanted me in.

"I think you'll be in these and your new singlet princess," Kira said. The water muffled the sound of her voice, but I knew what she was talking about. I got out of the shower and dried off before walking naked into the room.

"Pretty princess," Kira said, seeing my body and her red handprints on the tops of my thighs.

"Here," Kira plainly said, pointing to the bed. I frowned we hadn't done this before. She held a pull up, and I wondered what she would do with it.

"You are going to be in this today, to remind you of who your Mama is and that you are mine. Lay down," Kira said, sliding up my thighs. She slapped my sides, and I lifted my bottom for her as she pulled it on.

"Cute," Kira said, rubbing the front before pulling my jeans up. She bit my nipples making me giggle and squirm on the bed as she pulled down my singlet, rubbing my nipples under it before putting my paci in my mouth.

"I know you don't have school today, so you'll stay here a while with Mama before we go out this afternoon princess. Go get your colors and draw Mama a pretty picture," Kira said as I made my way over to my special box of things. Kira had bought me a wooden chest where I could keep my stuffies, coloring in books, pacis, and all my princess things. I liked that it doubled as a table so I could sit on the floor and color until my hands hurt. Kira lay down on the bed and watched me. At first, it always made me so nervous, but as I showed her the bunny I had just drawn and colored and the duck I was working on next, I relaxed as she told me what a clever girl I was.

I felt like Kira knew almost everyone in tow, so I wasn't surprised when she had been able to get a tattoo appointment that very afternoon. She had kept me in my little space all day, making me her princess when I tried to be a big girl again. She even held my hand while we walked to the shop even though it was only ten minutes away.

"Hold Mama's hand little princess," Kira said as we crossed the road. I liked that no one was around us and that we could have our dynamic so open. Kira had told me that we might be there for a few hours and made me pack a juice box and some crackers in my reversible sequin backpack. Kira had bought it for me when she saw how excited I was over my reversible sequin pencil case. I had played for hours with it, making the color change from pink to silver and back again. My backpack was green on one side of the sequins and black on the other, and I loved it.

We walked to the shop, but it looked like it was closed and I pulled on Kira's arm worried that she wouldn't be able to get it done.

"It's OK princess, we aren't going in that way, come on," Kira said, going around the back of the shop. It had graffiti on the brick walls and looked scary, making me hold her hand tight and snuggle into her.

"Oh little princess, you're alright with Mama," Kira said as the back door was opened for her.

"Hey babe," a burly looking woman said. She was covered from neck too; I could only imagine, toes in ink. She towered over Kira and made me feel like she was not someone to mess with.

"Hey Star, this is Sasha, my little one I was telling you about," Kira said making me gasp. *She had told someone about me?!* My head screamed. Star looked at me and smiled sweetly.

"I know someone who is very excited to meet you little one," Star said, leading us into the shop. It was indeed shut, but in the corner, I saw something that blew my mind — another baby playing with connecting blocks, the small kind. I wondered how 'old' she was. Kira walked me over to her, and I nervously sat down.

"This is Sasha, Evie, she is really excited to play with you," Kira said before kissing me on my cheek and patting my bottom. Kira turned and walked over to where Star was waiting, ready to begin the tattoo. I sat down on the edge of the blanket Evie was sitting on and watched her play for a while before she passed me some blocks.

"You can build the princess tower," Evie

said. She was really emo with black hair in high pigtails, a frilly goth style skirt and I could see she had a thick black diaper on. Her top was a white t-shirt with a big pink skull on the front, and she had suspenders over the top. She had knee high white socks on, and she giggled when she saw me staring at her.

"Do you think I'm pretty?" Evie asked, making me just shrug my shoulders and nod my head. She had her lip pierced on both sides of her bottom lip and big blue eyes that were lined in heavy eyeliner. She was pretty, but in a kind of way, I never wanted to be.

"You are so quiet," Evie said, taking the tower I offered her after I was finished.

"Oh yeah Evie, my little princess is shy sweetie," I heard Kira say. I moved to the corner and watched what was going on. Kira not even grimacing as Star began coloring in her upper arm. Evie was playing mostly by herself and me bringing my knees to my chest and placing my chin on them as I watched. I reached for my backpack and stroked it up and down as I watched. I really just wanted to be by Mama's side but knew that I would just be getting in the way, so I stayed with Evie and took out my crackers and juice.

"Do you want some?" I softly asked Evie, passing her a cracker. She nodded and clapped her hands, eating the cracker in one go and holding out her hand for more. I smiled, and we made a little table out of the blocks and had a picnic. I wasn't sure how much time had passed when Kira came over to where Evie and I were playing and said that we had to go home now. I looked up at her with a slight pouty frown making Star laugh.

"She can stay with us for the night if you'd be happy with that?" She asked Kira. My eyes went wide, and I quickly picked up my backpack and came to cuddle Kira's legs. I liked playing with Evie, but I didn't want to be away for Kira. Kira looked down and stroked my hair.

"I think my little princess is a bit too little for sleepovers just yet. But thanks," she replied. I liked that she always seemed to know how to get out of a situation. Star nodded and reached down to pick up Evie. I was surprised at how strong Star was, and it made me nervous to think of how painful her punishments would be. I could still feel the sting of Kira's hand on me, and she was significantly slimmer and less muscly than Star. After saying goodbye, Kira took my hand and led me back out onto the main street.

"Did you have an OK time princess," Kira asked. Her arm was covered with plastic wrap, and I looked at it curiously when we stopped at the traffic lights.

"You'll see it soon enough, princess, it looks great though. I'm really happy with it," Kira said.

"Well that's good Mama because it's permanent," I replied, making her laugh.

"Not really, if I don't like it, I'll just get a shark to bite it off or something," Kira said. She held my hand, and for the first time in a long time, I knew that she'd be OK.

"Mama," I said, wondering how I could bring up the topic I was about to bring up. Kira could tell I was nervous instantly and stopped walking just as we reached the hostel.

"Yeah, princess?" She said, getting comfy on a park bench. The air was still warm even though it was evening and the crickets chirped in the darkness.

"Tell Mama what's wrong princess," Kira said lovingly. I looked at her and held her hand.

"I want to move out of there. I want us to get our own place so that we have more room to be like this," I said, making Kira just nod her head slowly.

"But the rent is so cheap, as in, no rent here princess. Mama can give you so many things because I get the room as part of the job," Kira replied. I just nodded and looked down. I understood why she wanted to stay there, we saved so much money only having to pay my very small amount of rent for water, electricity, and Wi-Fi included but I wanted to be her baby in more spaces than just a room.

"I think I could arrange something though

princess," Kira said, lighting up. She had that wicked gleam in her eye, the same one she had the day I met her and I held my breath as I waited for her to tell me what her plan was. But Kira just laughed and told me to get ready to have some fun if she pulled it off.

"I've got to run it past a few people first, so I don't want you to get your hopes up, but if I pull this off, I think you'll have a great time!" Kira said, leaning forward to kiss me and rub me over my pull up.

Chapter 13

Kira had gone out early the next morning, saying something about needing to use a printer in the backpacker office. I tried to reply, but I was still so asleep I just smiled as she kissed me and rolled back over, never even hearing her close the door behind her.

Getting up a few hours later, Kira had obviously been in and out of the room several times. There were balloons everywhere and colorful bunting, glitter, adult-sized pacifiers and things to decorate them with.

"Mama?" I said sleepily looking over at Kira who was busy tying ribbons onto the balloons. I was excited to see pretty ribbons dangling down from the ceiling.

"Hi sleepy head, did you have a good rest princess?" Kira said, blowing me a kiss.

"Mama, what are you doing?" I asked, rubbing my eyes and smiled when I saw the big bag of candy Kira had bought.

"Well, you know how you said that you wanted more space to be Mama's little princess in? Well, we are going to have a fundraising party and all the proceeds are going to go to a charity that looks after sick kids, and everyone has to dress up as a baby, and the winner gets two weeks free rent and a 12 pack of beer," Kira said excitedly without taking a breath. I looked at her in amazement. Seeing my bewilderment, Kira continued.

"There's also going to be competitions for the best coloring in, and the best sandcastle and the best-decorated paci. Here, I made posters," Kira added, handing me a flyer. I had to give it to her; she sure was a clever Mama. I giggled, and she jumped up and cuddled into me on the bed.

"Is Mama the best princess?" Kira asked tickling me.

"Yes, Mama!" I squealed in happiness that in a few days time, I would have my chance to be little in public.

The hostel was a hive of excitement in the afternoon before the party. I was actually surprised at how into it everyone seemed. Most of the boys had been walking around in just diapers all day, pacifiers strung around their necks and they looked funny getting day drunk dressed as babies. The girls had taken to it all really well as well, but Danni had decided that she'd rather be a Mommy than a baby and had bought a shirt saying 'Mama bear,' on the front. I was busy putting on my skirt and tucking my shirt into it when Kira came in.

"Princess, let Mama," she said, coming over and helping me.

"Someone looks cute," she said, taking my pacifier and clipping it to my shirt.

"What if they all see that I like it more than just doing it for fun, Mama," I softly whispered.

"Oh baby girl, I think you'll find there are a couple of little babies out there that feel the same way. Which is surprising I thought you were the only one here!" Kira said undressing and pulling on a tight black cotton dress. She took her hair out, and waves of long blonde hair fell down her back making her look even more beautiful than she already did.

"You don't like them though do you, Mama?" I said nervously, not wanting her to fall for someone else. Kira spun around as though I had just used a bad word with a horrified look on her face.

"How could you even think that princess?! You are the only little girl I have ever, and will ever want!" Kira said, making my fears instantly disappear. She said I could have my hair down as well and I liked that it swayed in the breeze. I took a big breathe as I left our room, Kira holding my hand as we walked to the common room. It felt funny to be in a diaper in public like this, but I was happy when no one seemed to care. Moreover, they seemed jealous of mine. I was wearing a teddy bear print one, and some of the other girls even asked if I had any extras. I giggled as we ran back to mine and Kira's room and they put them on. I'm happy Kira wasn't mad that we were kinda wasting them.

The party started with everyone coloring in trying to have the best picture, Kira running around taking photos and keeping everyone entertained. We all went to the beach and spent hours making huge sandcastles; some of the guys made a Mommy sandcastle and gave her huge tit, which made everyone laugh. It was such a fun night that I hadn't even realized what time it was by the time people started passing out on the beach or in the common room. I had been busy decorating a new paci with some of the other girls when I felt Kira come up behind me and playing with my hair.

"Wow, amazing skills you have little ones," Kira teased, but I knew she wasn't really teasing.

"Time for bed though, I've got to lock up the room now," she added, taking my hand and lifting up my arm making me stand. The other girls stacked their chairs loudly, making the three guys who had passed out on the couches wake up and slowly make their way back to their rooms.

"That was the best night ever, Mama!" I exclaimed as soon as we walked into our room. Kira smiled and picked a leaf out of my hair.

"I'm so happy you had fun baby. Mama did good," Kira said, reaching into the shower and turning it on.

"Shower and beddys baby girl," Kira added, taking off my clothes and diaper. She had changed me twice during the night as I wet my diaper not being able to hold all the drinks we were consuming. I knew that the moment I lay in bed I would be asleep and I guess Kira knew that too because as I dried myself off, she pulled a pull up on me quick and didn't bother dressing me in anything else as she tucked me into bed.

"Sweet dreams little princess, Mama loves you," Kira said, kissing my forehead as I fell asleep, holding onto her finger.

Alana's Sweet Baby

An MDLG and ABDL lesbian romance
about a baby girl who didn't know just
how into age play she was until her
Mommy's seductive introduction.

By Tina Moore

Chapter 1

"Yes baby, that's it," Alana moaned as the young French girl she had picked up at a less than savory back street fingered herself in front of Alana's greedy eyes. The girl, who Alana hadn't bothered learning the name of, reached for her cigarette that was burning out in the ashtray. Pouting as her hand was slapped away aggressively by Alana who refocused her camera lens. The night had been long with Alana having her fill with the boney girl before making her touch herself just the way Alana liked.

"Don't you dare fucking stop," she commanded, grabbing the girl's loosely curled auburn hair and kissing her passionately before pushing her head back down and watching her through her lens. The girl writhed on the bed of the cheap motel, rented by Alana for the sole purpose of capturing her youthful vulnerability.

"Cum for Mommy," Alana instructed,

throwing a couple of hundred dollar bills onto the girl's face.

"You're just a sweet little fuck toy aren't you baby girl," Alana said, narrowing her eyes as the girl began to arch her back and close her eyes. Alana slapped her tits, making her open her eyes again suddenly and nod her head, her sweet eyes looking for everything except what Alana was willing to give her. Alana moved around the head of the bed and took her panties off, sitting on the girl's face and riding her mouth as she photographed her pussy and thighs. The girl gasped, making Alana laugh and she lifted off her slightly allowing the girl to pant for air, her young ribs heaving and protruding under her soft skin as Alana tenderly ran her fingers over them.

"Such a pretty little thing," Alana said getting off the girl's face and kissing her mouth clean before untying her ankles and watching as the girl half cowered in the corner of the bed, unsure of what Alana wanted with her next.

"Come here," Alana said, rolling her eyes

and opening her arms to the girl who gladly crawled to her and snuggled into Alana's older body, getting enveloped by her large breasts.

"Suck," Alana said, rubbing her swollen nipple over the top of the girl's lips, smiling as she parted them instinctively and began suckling on the older woman. Alana lit a cigarette and inhaled deeply before she took her camera and started clicking again, making the girl look up at her, her wide eyes asking to be taken, her mouth full like the slut that she was.

Alana was 33 before she became an internet success. Before then, she had just been another photographer working a crappy day job while she tried to sell her art online. Photography was more than just art for Alana. It was a way to escape the disappointing world around her, where people shielded their true and most pure desires behind stressful jobs and mundane lifestyles. For Alana, the more well-known her art became, the easier it was for her to slip away from that kind of existence and into her world. A world where she could take women with the ferocity, she craved to express and without the guilt of enjoying a new woman when and where she wanted. With a steady stream of high paying clients funding her lifestyle, Alana was not surprised when an email came that offered her access to a successful young entrepreneur. A girl called Rosie. Rosie portrayed everything Alana hated about the world, but Alana had agreed to photograph Rosie after Rosie's people had said they would pay her to stay in one of the nicest hotels on the Upper East Side. Rosie was beautifully fake, with everything about her either altered or pretend. She was the definition of a millennial and had become famous for doing nothing but marketing herself and her lifestyle with a genius only a narcissist could pull off. Companies now gave her their product to get a mention on her accounts and Alana was to capture Rosie in a series of photos that were to be auctioned off at a charity event. When Rosie's people had asked her how long it would take Alana to do the series, she had lied and said three weeks. She knew it would take her less than two, but she wasn't about to let this little attention seeking bitch keep her from enjoying the city. Alana planned to finish the series as fast as she could so that she could spend the rest of her time finding a new muse. That thought excited her. The things she wanted to do to a sweet, young, dependent girl made her cunt drip with anticipation.

"Oh my god, look at how fantastic this is, this is lit!" Rosie squealed looking at Alana's page.

"It's like, sexy but serious," Rosie added. Alana just bit her tongue and tried to stay calm as she wondered what it would take to get Rosie to stop talking. She looked at Rosie with her perky tits and whitened teeth and smirked as she imagined smudging her indigo lipstick as she backhanded her across the face making her sparkling eyes water. She also found herself wondering what Rosie's pussy looked like if everything else she could see had been augmented. *I bet it's perfect;* she thought slowly closing the lid of her computer. Rosie pouted and looked at her with puppy dog eyes.

"If you want me to photograph you like that," Alana said nodding to her computer, "You'll have to take your clothes off," Alana continued. Rosie had selected a series of nude photos, and Alana smiled when Rosie nodded her head as though she had just been asked if she wanted syrup on her waffles. *Wow, it's nothing to her,* Alana thought watching Rosie. Today she was only going to do a few test shots to get a feel for the style Rosie wanted and sat back as Rosie began to take her clothes off in front of her. Rosie smiled at Alana as she pulled off her low cut singlet and folded it neatly, placing it down on the coffee table. She kicked off her heels and left them on the floor as she stood up and unbuttoned the top of her skirt.

"Does this mean I'm your muse?" Rosie said softly, for the first-time showing Alana a more vulnerable side. Rosie unzipped her skirt before tripping on her heels, stumbling backward. Alana involuntarily jumped to her feet and grabbed Rosie, pulling her body to hers and holding it there firmly with her hand grabbing Rosie's ass and the other snaking up her back holding the back of her head. What Alana didn't know was that this was the safest Rosie had ever felt, being held in the arms of the older, curvier woman.

"No, this means that I'm going to photograph all of this," Alana said almost lovingly, matching the softness in Rosie's voice before grabbing the hem of the skirt and pulling it off in one quick motion. Rosie gasped, feeling exposed for the first time in her 22 years and suddenly became shy standing only in her underwear in front of Alana. Letting her go, Alana smiled as the overconfident ball of energy turn into a shy, little girl in front of her eyes.

"You have to keep going sweetheart, you're not done yet," Alana said, finding her seat again and crossing her arms over her chest, enjoying the young girl's discomfort. Rosie just nodded as she slowly unclipped her black and red lace bra and placed it on top of her singlet, followed by her panties. Alana stood and took Rosie's hand as she passed, walking the naked girl through her own house and up to her bedroom.

"This is where you said you wanted it to be done yes?" Alana said to a silently nodding Rosie.

"Well?" Alana said raising her eyebrow and speaking more commandingly to Rosie, wanting more than just a nod. Alana looked at Rosie like she might devour her with her eyes, making Rosie swallow hard.

"Yes," Rosie replied, slightly pulling away from Alana and looking down to the ground.

"Uh huh sweetie, you're going to have to get used to me seeing you like this, or it'll be a long three weeks for you. Come on, lay down for me," Alana said gently laying Rosie down in the position she wanted her in. Going to her wardrobe, Alana smiled as she traced over the girl's lingerie, stopping when she saw a red lace panty and bra set. Coming back swinging the garments around on her finger, Alana threw them at Rosie.

"Put that on, I want to see something," Alana instructed as Rosie began to obey. Alana watched as Rosie dressed, her slender fingers adjusting the panties and pausing, unsure of what Alana wanted from her now. Alana pressed on Rosie's shoulders, making her lay back down as she got to work.

"There," Alana said in satisfaction as she placed a pillow under Rosie. She had positioned her so that she was on her tummy, leaning more to one side. She had taken red lipstick that was on Rosie's sideboard and carefully painted her lips, enjoying how Rosie blushed when Alana had winked at her. Alana had taken out Rosie's long brown hair and let it fall to its own accord and tilted her head up, making her mouth look ready to be fucked. Alana ran her hands over Rosie's slender body, taking in her curves.

"Stay still for me sweetie, I need you to hold that for a little while longer," Alana said seeing Rosie shift uncomfortably. Alana walked over to the bed and placed additional pillows around Rosie's hips, enjoying the subtle warmth that came from her thighs, to help support her. Alana felt the all too familiar stirring deep within her as Rosie pressed her head into Alana's palm when she cupped her face.

"Good girl," Alana said lovingly, looking into Rosie's eyes and stroking her cheek with her thumb, hating that she was getting wet with the control and proximity she had with the untouchable girl.

Chapter 2

Alana had two other photo sessions with Rosie and had enjoyed touching Rosie more and more with each shoot. Once Alana had made her sit straddling a pillow so that she could reach between Rosie's thighs and reposition it. Alana had taken the time to stroke Rosie's slit gently and felt her clit tingle, watching as Rosie looked away nervously, her face burning red but the wetness being easily felt on Alana's fingertips. Today, she had laid her on her back and draped a fur blanket over the top of her, having Rosie wrap her arms around her neck as Alana skillfully unhooked her bra. Today Rosie was too shy to strip in front of Alana, and she had begged to be covered. Alana had agreed, helping Rosie take off her bra and panties before bothering to ask if it was alright to do so, happy when Rosie moved so obediently for her. Alana felt herself become more and more drawn to Rosie, her long brown hair always sitting so perfectly and her come fuck me eyes always staring at Alana made her wet with desire.

"Come here, sweetheart, I want to show you what I've done," Alana said, smiling at Rosie, who grabbed a robe and quickly tied it in place. She didn't have her usual arrogance today, and Alana could almost swear she saw Rosie fight back the tears on more than one occasion. Rosie walked over to where Alana was sitting and placed the series of photos in front of her who looked at them carefully. She liked how Alana had captured her, but she knew they wouldn't sell. Alana had made her look innocent, and that wasn't what people wanted. They wanted the party girl, the one who dominated and teased the crowds. Rosie looked at her reflection in the photos and bit her bottom lip.

"They are beautiful, but they aren't going to work," she quietly said, making Alana frown.

"You said you wanted yourself captured in them, I did that," Alana questioned confused as to why Rosie didn't like them. Rosie took Alana's hand, making Alana flinch slightly and look at

Rosie in her eyes.

"You're the only person who has looked at me like that and been able to see this, and I wish you wouldn't Alana," Rosie said tilting her head to the photos on Alana's screen, making Alana smirk at the compliment.

"It's not my fault I see past all of this," Alana said gesturing to Rosie's body and then looking around the grand room they were sitting in. Rosie looked up and let her eyes roam around the room. The marble floors and gold fixtures reflected the light from the chandelier; the artwork on the walls did nothing to make the room cozier.

"I need the photos to be more like this," Rosie said, suddenly switching back to her soulless princess manner. She took out her phone and showed Alana a photo of her wearing a dress, sitting on a motorbike and looking seductively down a camera lens. Alana looked at the photo and looked back at Rosie, who had taken her hand away.

"You want me to turn you into a little slut?"

Alana asked, annoyed that Rosie had put her wall back up. Rosie laughed and got up, starting to walk towards the door.

"What? That's what you thought you'd be doing when you first got here, wasn't it?" Rosie said, leaving the room. Alana watched her as she left and turned back to look at the photo on Rosie's phone. *If she wants to be a slut, I'll make her a fucking slut*, Alana thought putting her laptop with the images of a doe-eyed Rosie in her satchel.

Alana only needed one shoot to get the images Rosie craved and even then had rushed it, annoyed that Rosie was determined to have the world believe something that wasn't true.

"We're done?" Rosie said, put out that the shoot was so fast, it had been less than an hour when Alana began putting her camera equipment away and tried to hide the smile that crept across her face.

"Yeah, baby girl, we are," she replied, looking up at Rosie and brushing her hair out of her eyes. Alana's loose ponytail allowed her wispy hair to fall out around her face, framing it elegantly. Alana came to sit on the bed she had left Rosie on and bit her bottom lip as she ran her fingers through Rosie's hair, taking a gamble on the young woman in front of her.

"I mean, I could stay?" Alana asked imagining how sweet Rosie would look like as her baby. The onesies she could put her in would, Alana guessed, take her less than an hour to get comfortable in. Rosie lifted her head and crawled her way into Alana's lap much to the excitement of the older woman.

"You don't know what you're getting yourself into sweetheart," Alana half laughed as she continued to feel Rosie's naked body against hers. Alana took the blanket that she had used to cover Rosie for the shoot and wrapped it around her as she felt Rosie's skin turn cold.

"Such a sweet baby. If I had known you were so sweet I would have tried to meet you earlier," Alana said knowing that she had to give the girl back but wishing she could take her home and keep her. Alana looked into Rosie's eyes and saw the baby trying to stay grown up, and Alana knew that their embraced needed to end before Rosie's heart attached itself to her the way only a little does.

"Come on, time to get dressed, you've got a lot of things to do today sweet baby," Alana said gently pushing Rosie from her arms and going back to packing up her equipment as Rosie stood and looked blankly at Alana before leaving the room to get dressed.

Alana spent the next few days editing the photos and was in the middle of editing them when her phone rang. She ignored it, letting it ring out, hoping to finish detailing the motorbike Rosie was sitting on before the end of the day, stopping angrily when her phone rang twice. She didn't bother to see who was on the other side before she answered.

"What?!" Alana yelled down the phone,

angry to be ripped out of her concentration. Her rage soon turned to concern when she heard Rosie crying on the other end.

"I'm sorry, I just didn't know how else to call," Rosie said, making Alana soften instantly.

"Hey, what's happened?" She asked, getting up from her computer and going out to the balcony. Alana lit a cigarette and blew smoke into the night air. She hadn't realized it was so late until this moment and had to crane her ears to hear Rosie as a police siren rang down the street.

"There was this meet and greet I had to go to, and I was meeting people and went backstage with one of the interviewers, and he got grabby. He told me that it didn't matter what I said, that no one would believe me anyway and that he could get me more coverage if I didn't refuse him," Rosie said crying into the phone. Alana frowned, she knew she was going to be drawn into Rosie's world, she knew that having a connection to her would mean she wouldn't be able to hide from the media like she had been enjoying, but she also knew that she couldn't deny the feelings she had for the girl.

"Can you come to my hotel? What did you do about the guy?" Alana asked, walking back inside and looking at the beautiful slut she had on her screen and shook her head.

"Yeah I can come, I know where you are. I told him to get fucked, but like still, I let him do some stuff before I told him that and like, just yuck," Rosie said, making Alana smiled at her choice of words.

"Well, I'll be waiting for you. Have you eaten?" Alana said hoping she wouldn't scare Rosie off.

"It's Wednesday, I don't eat on Wednesdays," Rosie said bluntly.

"Oh right sorry, I forgot," Alana said as she began to order a pizza online. Rosie had told her that BBQ chicken with pineapple was her favorite pizza during one of their photo shoots.

"It's OK. See you soon; I'm getting in a car now," Rosie said before quickly hanging up.

Half an hour later, Alana heard a knock on her hotel door and knew it would either be her pizza or Rosie, laughing when it was both.

"I've got your order, Miss," Rosie said, smiling softly at Alana. Alana raised an eyebrow at Rosie who just laughed and pushed past her.

"Have you got beer? It's past midnight so technically not Wednesday anymore," Rosie said, causing Alana to roll her eyes as she looked in the fridge, pulling out a six-pack.

"Yum. Did you order this for me?" Rosie asked, closing her eyes and chewing slowly.

"Maybe," Alana said opening two beers with her lighter and passing Rosie one.

"Thanks for this, I know you've got work to do. I just wanted to be somewhere; I don't know," Rosie said, turning to look at the photos Alana was in the process of completing.

"Safe?" Alana suggested draping a blanket over Rosie's shoulders. It was the middle of winter, and Rosie only had a light jacket on, thigh-high black suede boots and a short dress. In any other apartment that would have been more than enough, but Alana had turned the heating off, enjoying the cold air on her skin and being able to rug up indoors. Rosie pulled the blanket around her body and shivered as she nodded, looking at Alana with those same doe eyes that Alana had captured only days ago.

"Well, you're safe now, baby," Alana said, taking a slice of pizza and taking off the pineapple, putting it on Rosie's slice. Rosie looked up at Alana and Alana knew what was coming next.

"You don't have to do anything sweetie, I'm not like that guy," Alana said, stopping Rosie as she went to kiss her.

"I know you're not. But I've wanted to kiss you since I first saw you. Please?" Rosie said, placing her hand on Alana's thigh. Alana shifted uncomfortably.

"If you're going to kiss me, you'll have to do it like this," Alana said picking Rosie up swiftly and placing her on her lap, wrapping her arms around her and tilting her back slightly so that Rosie was being cradled in Alana's arms. She looked down at Rosie and rolled her body over slightly so that Rosie was pressed into Alana's chest and breathed with relief when she felt Rosie relax in her arms.

"Shh little one, you're safe now," Alana said as she felt Rosie start to cry. Rosie brought her arms up to her chest and gently pushed against Alana trying to get up, but Alana just gripped her tighter.

"Ugh ugh don't push Mommy away," Alana said soothingly, as she looked down into Rosie's eyes tenderly, watching a tear escape as Rosie gave in and melted into the embrace resting her head against Alana's generous breasts in surrender, sucking her thumb as she was rocked.

"This could easily be seen as sexual harassment Alana. You said you weren't like that guy," Rosie said with no real intention of ever calling her out on it.

"Do you feel harassed? Am I asking you do anything as he did? Or do you feel like you enjoy being cared for the way you need it? The way you dream to be taken cared of? Being in the arms of a Mommy who can see that you're just a little girl who needs to be looked after," Sabine replied knowingly, a smug smile spreading across her face as she unbuttoned her blouse, enjoying Rosie's fingertips tracing over the edge of her bra.

"You're lucky you read me well," Rosie whispered, wanting to stop the flood of emotions rushing her body as Alana pulled the top of her bra down and watched as Rosie began nursing instinctively.

"Ha, you're the easiest read sweet thing. Come on, tell Mommy what happened, not tonight, but before, from the beginning," Alana said gently, running her fingers through Rosie's hair and holding it back making her look up at her.

"I wouldn't know where to start Mommy," Rosie replied, shaking her head, letting her hair fall out of Alana's fingers. She dried her tears, got up, and rested against a wall. Alana stayed sitting on the sofa watching the girl she wanted so badly to own, struggle with her demons and exhaled in frustration.

"I've got you, nothing bad is going to happen to you now little one," Alana said as Rosie walked back to her and lay back down, getting gently rocked in Alana's loving arms.

Alana held Rosie through the night, feeding her pizza and watching as she got drunk in her arms, not wanting to be let go. As the night reached midnight, Alana carefully placed Rosie down in her bed and tucked in the blankets around the young girl's slender body. Coming to gently rest next to Rosie, Alana stroked her hair as she fell asleep, happy when Rosie cuddled into her curvier side as she slept. Alana wondered how she had so easily become so heavily caught up into Rosie's world, her last thought as her eyes finally shut.

"Good morning sweetheart," Alana said, coming into the bedroom with coffee and bagels. She walked to the balcony windows and opened them, peering down onto the street that had come to life underneath them. She smiled to herself, thinking of how the paparazzi would go crazy to know that Rosie was sleepily waking up in her bed. Alana looked back and saw Rosie open her eyes and blink slowly, looking around to try and find Alana.

"Hey," Rosie said, sitting up and watching Alana light a cigarette.

"Howdy," Alana replied winking at the starlet. She liked watching Rosie more than she wished she did and stayed out on the balcony as she watched her stretch her slim arms up and pull her hair into a messy ponytail. She had slept naked and walked her vulnerable body towards Alana, stopping when she got to the entrance to the balcony.

"Do you know how to make a million dollars in five seconds?" Rosie giggled taking Alana's cigarette and walking naked out onto the balcony, making Alana smirk.

"Get back in here," Alana laughed, pulling Rosie into her and holding her naked body, shielding her from the street and pushing her back inside.

"I know how to make a billion darling,"

Alana teased, pushing Rosie onto the bed and jumping on top of her, pinning her arms above her head. Rosie's playful laughs quietened, and she began breathing nervously, making Alana grind her teeth and hop off her.

"What are you going to do today?" Alana said, taking a coffee and sipping it while looking at Rosie.

"You," Rosie said, slipping off the bed and getting onto her knees, pulling Alana forward by the top of her skirt and pulling it up before Alana could stop her.

"Whoa hey," Alana said as she felt Rosie's tongue taste her through her panties.

"Oh, baby, you don't have to," Alana stuttered between breaths, spreading her thighs and placing her hand on the back of Rosie's head.

"It feels like you want me too," Rosie laughed before sucking on Alana's pussy lips and pulling her panties to the side, sliding her tongue up and down Alana's slit. Alana closed her eyes and rolled her head back; she hadn't thought Rosie would be so good.

"You're wet, Mommy," Rosie said. Alana suddenly opened her eyes and cupped Rosie's chin before looking at her angrily in the eyes.

"What did you just call me?" She demanded making Rosie try to cower away, Alana making it impossible by her grip.

"Mommy," Rosie whispered, looking down and going red.

"Fuck, good girl," Alana said, pushing Rosie's mouth back as she stood over her, pushing her hot cunt against the young girl's face.

"Lick Mommy's pussy baby girl," Alana said, reaching down and slapping Rosie's tits and flicking her nipples. Rosie dipped her tongue into Alana's pussy, moaning as she tasted her juices as Alana began to rub her clit.

"Fuck," Alana moaned slowly as she grabbed a handful of Rosie's hair and pulled her head back, taking her mouth off her creaming pussy.

"I can't baby I'm sorry," Alana said, gently

wiping her pussy juices off Rosie's mouth, kissing her tenderly and pulling her to her feet. Alana readjusted her panties and skirt and sat on the edge of the bed with a very confused Rosie.

"Um, do I suck?" Rosie asked nervously.

"Coz I've never fucked a girl before so like, I don't know what the go is," Rosie started to say, stopping when she saw Alana shake her head.

"No baby, you don't suck at all! I don't want to take advantage of you," Alana said, making Rosie roll her eyes.

"I wish you did," Rosie said, going over to where her clothes were laying and getting dressed.

"I suppose that I should be grateful that you are so respectful or whatever, but seriously, do you know how many people want to fuck me and you just turned me down like what the fuck," Rosie said. Alana let her rant and passed her a coffee as she walked towards the door.

"Do you think I don't want to fuck you? Is that what it felt like when I dripped in that pretty little mouth?" Alana said, taking Rosie by the hips and grinding into her making Rosie soften her angry eyes.

"Then why don't you want me?" Rosie whined, letting Alana rub her breasts against Rosie's face as she was cuddled.

"I do want you. Though anyone can have this little thing, I want it for keeps baby girl. So until you give it all to Mommy, you can play with everyone but me. Think about it," Alana said, groping Rosie's pussy as she spoke, making her a moaning mess in her hands before kissing the top of her head and gently pushing her out the door and closing it behind her. Alana took a breath and sighed as she shook her head in disbelief that she had firstly, fell for Rosie and secondly, stopped her slutty little mouth when she had been the best Alana had ever had in a long time.

Alana spent the rest of the day finishing Rosie's photos and getting multiple texts from Rosie in various positions. Her young firm body making Alana edit her image to capture Rosie like the slut she wanted to be.

"Stop it," Alana said when Rosie answered her phone.

"Stop what?" Rosie giggled down the phone, making Alana smile.

"Stop sending me photos of you trying to win the award for the biggest whore of the year," Alana said firmly.

"Yes Mommy," Rosie teased making Alana have more ideas than she wished she did.

"Oh, baby girl, you don't want to start this game with me. Mommy doesn't play nice," Alana warned making Rosie stop her giggling and go quiet on the phone.

"Yes, Mommy," was all that came after a few seconds, silence.

"I'm finished your photos. I think you'll like them; it's what you were after," Alana said, wanting to bring some professionalism back to the dynamic, but Rosie wasn't interested.

"What do you mean, you don't play nice?" She questioned making Alana roll her eyes.

"They are printed and framed to the specifications you requested, where am I dropping them off?" Alana said, ignoring Rosie's curiosity.

"That wasn't my question," Rosie replied. Alana thought for a minute before speaking again.

"You must be confused little one; Mommy doesn't answer to you, ever. Tell me where you need them dropped off now," Alana said sternly, taking Rosie by surprise.

"5th Ave, there's a hotel there, I'll get someone to text you the address, I don't know the name of it," Rosie said before hanging up the phone, put out that Alana wasn't letting her have her way.

Chapter 4

The second week of Alana's trip was coming to an end, and she knew two things. The first was that Rosie hadn't messaged or called her since she had turned her down and the second was that she was pretty sure she knew why. There had been newspaper articles written about it, morning TV programs talking about it and social media had blown up over it. The series had been shown to the public before the auction, and it had all but broken the internet. With its only aim to seduce and tease, the media had analyzed it as though it would cure cancer. The only commonality that tied everyone's opinions together was the intensity in their feeling. They either loved it, or they hated it, and they pleaded their cases with equal enthusiasm. Calling Alana's work a modern day masterpiece and a complete representation of a desperate millennial, Alana wondered how she would ever be able to move forward. She had stayed indoors, annoyed the paparazzi had been hounding her hotel since the piece had been unveiled.

Ordering room service for the third day in a row, Alana looked online to see if the photos were still trending when her phone rang.

"Hey, I was just thinking about you," Alana said before Rosie could speak.

"It's a bit crazy, right? I didn't think this would happen," Rosie said back, a smile escaping her voice. Alana was relieved that Rosie seemed unscathed by the brutal publicity.

"So how are you holding up?" Alana asked nervously.

"The only way I know how," Rosie replied, making Alana curious.

"Meaning?" Alana prompted. Rosie sighed as if she knew that Alana wouldn't approve of her coping methods.

"I've been partying ever since they were unveiled, I'm not even sure what day it is," Rosie said leaving out the parts where she had done more drugs than her body could hold, drank her bar dry and if it weren't for her very loyal security she would have had the paparazzi photos to prove it.

"Oh," Alana replied, unsure of what to say.

"Well, I'm glad you're alright. Why are you calling me?" She added, not wanting Rosie to think she was judging her.

"I wanted to see if you wanted to come over," Rosie laughed.

"For what? Partying? Not my scene," Alana said, enjoying Rosie's giggle down the phone.

"No, not so much of a party, as more of a, um, softer kind of time," Rosie said being very cryptic. Alana knew what Rosie wanted and gave a sideward smile as she thought.

"I don't know, from the sounds of things, you haven't been a very good girl," Alana said, hoping that she wasn't on the loudspeaker.

"Well maybe I do deserve a punishment then Mommy," Rosie replied, making Alana's eyes go wide.

"You   couldn't   handle   Mommy's

punishments baby girl," Alana said, teasing her.

"Oh please Mommy," Rosie said just before Alana hung up the phone. Sending Rosie a text instead, wanting her to read it over and over before she saw her.

Get in the shower and make sure you're clean for me. I want you naked in bed when I see you; your sheets better be clean too. Take out a toy you want to play with and have it laying at the end of your bed. I'm going to push you today sweet baby, love Mommy.

Alana was let into Rosie's house by her maid who received a generous tip making the maid look confused at Alana.

"For your discretion," Alana said, looking the maid in the eyes who just nodded her head and pointed upstairs. Alana climbed the marble stairwell and walked along the hallway to Rosie's room, opening the door slowly.

"I'm in here, Mommy," Rosie excitedly said when she saw Alana. Alana stopped and looked at

Rosie, enjoying how easy it had been to get her naked and willing to be fucked. Closing the door and locking it behind her, Alana slowly made her way to the bed, climbing on top and eyeing Rosie predatorily.

"What a cute little girl," Alana said as she stroked Rosie's face lovingly, making her gasp when she firmly slapped her cheek.

"I told you Mommy was going to push you today, sweetheart," Alana said, taking the pink bunny Rosie was cuddling and gave her red cheek kisses with it.

"Good thing bunny is here to kiss you better baby because Mommy isn't going to today," Alana said, getting up and going to her bag she had left at the door. She opened the bag, winking at Rosie who just giggled and took out two black silk ties and a strap-on.

"I wonder what fun I can have with these," Alana teased as she dropped the ties on Rosie's body and began to fasten the harness of the strap-on, enjoying the knowledge that Rosie would have to cum several times before it would fit her tight pussy. Alana took the ties and gently tied Rosie's ankles together, rubbing her freshly shaven cunt softly, parting her pussy lips and spitting on her clit before moving up to her wrists.

"So you want to play with your nipple clamps today little one?" Alana asked securing them onto Rosie, making her moan and squirm around.

"Oh, you thought I'd be gentle? Silly little girl, you aren't listening to Mommy, are you?" Alana said, placing her larger hand on Rosie's neck and squeezing until she was gasping.

"Start playing with yourself little one, you'll want to get nice and wet for Mommy or what I'll do to you will hurt even more," Alana said taking Rosie's writing hand and tying it above her head, gently slapping her tits until Rosie was playing with herself at a pace Alana was satisfied with.

"Good girl," Alana said, sitting back and stroking the big black dildo she had claimed as her own. The black silicon of the cock glistened as

Alana pushed it into Rosie's mouth, taking out her camera and photographing the compromised girl making her startle.

"Alana don't," Rosie said, pulling back and refusing her cock. Alana laughed and sat back and took photos of Rosie until she merely lay still on her back.

"These are just for me baby girl," Alana said, filling Rosie's mouth once again.

"Suck it, bitch," Alana commanded when Rosie tried to refuse her again, flicking the firm clamps on her nipples until she obeyed.

"Let me explain something to you, you pretty little slut, you're Mommy's plaything, and I am going to do whatever the fuck I want with you. If that means I want to take your photo, I'm going to fucking take your photo, and all that'll happen if you try to stop me is this," Alana said reaching behind her and slapping Rosie's pussy and roughly parted her pussy lips, fingering her with two fingers roughly as she screamed and moaned around Alana's cock.

"I know you'd take it. Little whores like you always do," Alana said as Rosie tried to match her thrusts, grinding into Alana's palm and sucking harder as Alana fucked her cunt and her mouth.

"Mommy I," Rosie started to say, stopping when Alana pulled out of her mouth and covered her lips with her hand.

"You'd better start with sorry Mommy baby girl," Alana said, pushing Rosie's head back firmly until her eyes began to water. Raising an eyebrow and waiting for a response, Rosie nodded as Alana took her hand away.

"Sorry Mommy," Rosie meekly said making Alana smile. She lay down next to Rosie and pulled her into her, making her arms and legs stretch.

"Mommy's sweet baby. You're not so naughty now are you sweet girl," Alana said, taking a paci gag and securing it around the back of Rosie's head.

"Do you remember the safe words or actions in this case, baby girl?" Alana asked Rosie as she stroked her hair and ran her fingernails up and down Rosie's back. Rosie smiled behind the gag and nodded her head before Alana kissed her forehead and placed her hand on her throat again.

"Good, then Mommy can get to work," Alana said, squeezing tightly on Rosie's throat and spitting into her hand. She began rubbing her cock again, slapping it against Rosie's cheek until she had covered both cheeks with her spit. Alana moved down to Rosie's thighs and gripped them firmly, pulling them apart before spitting on Rosie's already wet pussy. Alana smirked when she saw that Rosie had stopped playing with herself.

"Did I fucking say to stop?" Alana said using both hands to firmly slap Rosie's thighs until her handprints had made them burn red and Rosie squirm uncontrollably trying to escape.

"You're mine bitch, and you aren't going anywhere," Alana explained as she stretched Rosie's pussy and forcibly entered her, making her squeal and moan. Thrusting into her aggressively, Alana watched as the young girl became a hot mess in front of her, reminding her of the French girl she had used less than a month ago. Losing her train of thought, Alana shook her head and looked down at the famous girl's fuck doll-like body and reached for her un-tied wrist, deciding it was time to secure that as well.

"Come here, darling," Alana said, letting her affection for the girl escape her voice. But Rosie didn't notice; she was too busy having her fifth orgasm as Alana plowed her young cunt with a vengeance while she tied her wrist above her head. Alana couldn't care less how many orgasms Rosie had or if she even had any at all, Rosie's pleasure was of zero consequence to Alana, she was just there for Alana's pleasure. Alana smirked as she held Rosie's pelvis down, her hands on either side of the young girl's body and watched as her tummy was pushed out by the huge cock Alana was happily destroying her with the force she had used on Rosie at the beginning now less than necessary as her wet pussy took Alana's long strokes while she was slapped over and over.

Rosie's slender body turning red as Alana marked her soft skin.

"I want you to finish me baby girl," Alana said suddenly breaking her rhythm and pulling down the gag as she sat on top of Rosie's mouth as her last orgasm hit, shooting down Rosie's throat as she squirted taking Rosie by surprise.

"Swallow Mommy baby girl," Alana said lovingly while grinding deeply on Rosie's mouth, enjoying using her as if she were a common street whore.

Chapter 5

Alana woke up to Rosie's hair tickling her face, and she slowly opened her eyes letting them adjust to the moonlight streaming through the windows and felt the familiar hollow of her heart she tried so hard to fill. She lifted her arms to the ceiling and checked her phone. It was only 2:30 in the morning; she knew the bars and clubs would still be open and slowly crept out of bed as to not wake Rosie. Taking a cigarette and a bottle of whiskey from the nightstand, Alana made her way out to the balcony and into the cold air of the night. Watching the garden lights flicker and the blue lights of the lagoon style pool, Alana sat and watched the darkness. She could feel it. The evil she had outran but never been able to out-grow. The memories haunting her like the wind, always there, however calm or fierce. She popped the cork of the bottle and let it fall onto the floor as she tilted her head back to drink the liquid that did nothing but burn her throat before she lit her cigarette and blew the smoke into the night. The stars that she knew where there weren't seen from the cloudy night sky, and she wondered what would happen if she just stopped trying. What the sound would be like if she were to fall to the ground if anyone would miss her. Drinking again, she could feel the alcohol start to warm her body and pulse through her veins.

"What are you doing?" Rosie said, taking Alana by surprise and ripping her out of a memory she wished didn't belong to her.

"Nothing," Alana said, trying to hide her vulnerability, surprised when Rosie looked at her as though she saw it too.

"Mind if I join you?" Rosie asked seriously, taking the bottle gently from Alana's fingers.

"You can do whatever you want this is your house," Alana said, putting her guard up and making Rosie look at her with a seriousness Alana hadn't seen before.

"Do you want to share this with me?" Alana

asked, offering the cigarette to Rosie, who smiled and took a drag before giving it back.

"You know, they think I'm just this stupid rich kid that has everything I want," Rosie said, drinking deeply until she coughed and handed the bottle back to Alana.

"Aren't you?" Alana questioned playfully making Rosie laugh.

"No. I'm not stupid, and I have never got everything I want. I want peace, I've tried, but money can't buy that," Rosie replied, and Alana was surprised that they were having this conversation. *Maybe I fucked the fake out of her,* Alana thought to herself smirking as she remembered how Rosie had ridden her cock like a bitch on heat.

"I don't think you're stupid," Alana said, wondering where the conversation would go.

"I know you don't, that's why I'm here," Rosie said bluntly before looking Alana in the eye.

"Don't care what they say about you, do you?" Rosie questioned looking at Alana curiously referring to the mass media attention and criticism that had been placed on both of them like a crown of thorns. Alana tried to suppress her smirk before she looked up at Rosie.

"No, I don't. But I also don't want to be in the limelight like you do," Alana replied seeing that Rosie wasn't satisfied with her answer.

"But you were hiding before this, who are you hiding from?" Rosie pressed.

"Now why would I tell you that?" Alana teased pulling Rosie onto her lap and holding her tightly.

"Because I see it, I see you," Rosie whispered in Alana's ear almost bringing her to tears instantly.

"You surprise me little one. It's from a long time ago," Alana replied, burying her face into Rosie's sweet-smelling body, her warmth comforting Alana.

"And yet here you are," Rosie said, wrapping her arms around Alana's head, bringing her face into her breasts.

"You're such a baby," Rosie teased making Alana suddenly laugh before sitting back and wiping her tears away.

"You want to know what haunts me?" Alana said, reaching for her phone. Rosie got up and went to sit on the opposite chair and waited for Alana to find what she was looking for.

"Her name was Silva. We went to high school together. She was going to be a lawyer. I was going to be a doctor," Alana began before taking another sip of the whiskey. Alana passed her phone to Rosie, who looked at the girl, clearly younger than she was. Her youthful smile and carefree soul emanating from thc core of her being as she held her arms up to the sky and laughed with the universe. Rosie was surprised that such energy could be captured in a mere photo. She looked up from the phone and continued to sit quietly and gave Alana the time she needed to find the words to tell her story.

"She was my, my first, and if I'm honest, my only love," Alana said nervously looking at Rosie.

"It's OK; I knew this was never love," Rosie said, making Alana smile in relief.

"We were getting ready for our prom at her house when three men broke into the house," Alana said, stopping and looking blankly into the distance of the night. Rosie felt her stomach tighten because she already knew the rest of the story; most girls would.

"They had guns; we did what they said. By the time they left, Silva was hardly breathing, and I had to crawl to her neighbor's house to call the police because they had cut the electricity," Alana said stopping to look at Rosie who was looking at the ground.

"When I went back to the house, Silva had made her way to the front door. She kissed me goodbye, and I felt her last breath on my lips and watched as her lips smiled for the last time," Alana said as tears poured down her cheeks as she silently cried unstoppable tears. Rosie was speechless and dipped her head as the story so fucking familiar to hundreds of thousands of women was once again told by a broken heart who had to rebuild her life after someone tried to take it from her.

"When will they stop destroying us," Rosie said as tears fell from her our eyes and onto the tiles.

"I don't know sweetheart," Alana said, breathing in deeply as the air changed and began to warm, the sunrise lighting their faces.

"You made it," Rosie said, looking happily at Alana.

"What?" Alana asked, finishing off the whiskey.

"You made it through the night," Rosie said, standing up and walking over to Alana who held her like she was her life raft.

"For now," Alana said her tears welling up in her eyes again.

"Forever," Rosie said, kissing her tears away.

"I don't think I can take the pain forever, sweetheart," Alana replied, laughing in disbelief at the mountain she knew she was climbing.

"I'll help you," Rosie said, feeling her heart beat faster than she wished it would.

Chapter 6

"Well, what the fuck am I supposed to do with you now?" Alana playfully asked Rosie over breakfast only a few hours later. They had gone to a close by coffee shop and sat away from the windows. Rosie laughed to herself as she watched the other customers choose window seats without having to think of the headlines that would accompany their morning.

"I don't know, can you even see this going anywhere?" Rosie replied as she sipped her triple shot iced caramel Frappuccino. They sat in silence and watched the world around them with a distance like watching a movie. People were rushing in and impatiently waiting for their takeaway orders and others that were typing furiously on laptops with a pile of espresso cups collecting on their table. Alana watched as Rosie looked around at the happy couples stealing kisses in the morning sun and the newspaper delivery man dropping off the coffee shop's order.

"I have thought about retiring, you know," Rosie suddenly said over the sound of a loud coffee machine. The smell of burnt bread drifted towards them, and they laughed at the trainee who was frantically trying to fix his mistake.

"What would you do instead?" Alana asked, finishing her black coffee. Rosie just shrugged her shoulders.

"It's not like I do anything now anyway, I kinda just want to slip out of the limelight," Rosie explained. Alana understood why Rosie wanted to run away. If she had every public moment under constant criticism, she would also want to hide away. She hadn't truly noticed the pain in Rosie's eyes until this moment, and she wondered how she could carry such heavy sadness.

"You've done what you've wanted this far, why stop now?" Alana said, bringing a smile to Rosie's lips.

"Because a lot of people will lose a lot of money if I stop. I can hear the blackmail now,"

Rosie replied, motioning to the waitress before ordering another coffee.

"I made the mistake of creating a scandal the first time I wanted out, it backfired and flung me even further into the spotlight," Rosie laughed, Alana was happy she could see the humor in it.

"Like, what are you doing for the next few weeks?" Rosie suddenly said as the morning sun poured into the coffee shop. Alana smiled, excited to see what Rosie was planning.

"Nothing. Nothing that I can't palm off or put off, what did you have in mind?" Alana found herself saying. Rosie took a deep breath and held it before exhaling dramatically.

"Let's go, let's get the fuck out of here. You can work from anywhere, and it's not like we would run out of cash, let's go," Rosie said, taking Alana by surprise. Alana looked at Rosie and knew that she would leave with or without her, and she had to admit, life was a lot more fun with Rosie.

"OK," Alana replied as Rosie took her hand and held it with a shaky hand as tears started to pour down her face.

"It'll be alright little one," Alana said making Rosie laugh through her tears as she stood and held Alana's hand, walking through the coffee shop and fighting the urge to let go as people began to recognize her. Rosie's world turned in slow motion as she saw people begin to take out their phones and take photos of her and Alana, following them out onto the street. The excitement of the people who began to circle them made it difficult to walk, and Alana had to push people out of the way so they could make their way back to Rosie's mansion. Rosie gripped Alana's hand, but as a wave of paparazzi swarmed, Rosie felt Alana get swept out of her reach, and she was there, surrounded by strangers all clicking and yelling questions and opinions at her. Rosie frantically looked for Alana in the mass of people circling, turning around to try and find the hand that had steadied her.

"What?! What do you want from me?!" Rosie screamed as she saw Alana burst through the crowd knocking some people to the ground as she grabbed Rosie's hand once again and pulled her close kissing her forehead and grabbing a camera and throwing it onto the road before taking out her gun and pointing it to the crowd who backed up instantly.

"Fuck off, will you?" Alana calmly said while holding Rosie. They turned and begun to walk back along the street, toward the mansion that was a mere five blocks away.

"Where you going to use that?" Rosie quietly asked, still holding Alana's hand. Rosie hadn't realized Alana had or even carried a gun, but surprisingly it didn't scare her.

"Nope, there's no bullets in it," Alana laughed, making Rosie cuddle her arm as they turned the corner.

"Thanks, Mommy," Rosie said resting her head on Alana's shoulder as they walked, Alana winking at her as she felt the ache of her broken heart being put back together by the most unlikely of heroes.

"You used some very grown-up words back there baby," Alana said, referring to the vicious manner Rosie had spoken to the crowd only moments before.

"So did you," Rosie replied, kissing Alana's arm.

"Yes, but I don't think I like my little one speaking like that," Alana said, making Rosie laugh.

"Yours?" She questioned twirling out of Alana's arms and coming to stand in front of her.

"Oh, you don't feel claimed? That can be changed," Alana said, taking Rosie's hand firmly and walking her faster back down the street.

"What are you going to do, make me color some pictures or something?" Rosie said teasingly.

"No that would be so stupid, you're far too big for that, but you're not too big to be bent over my knee and spanked, diapered until you can't hold it anymore and bottle fed while Mommy gives you little kisses on your nose," Alana said making Rosie stop walking and look at her blankly.

"Really?" She asked, her world stopping as

she looked at Alana like she had just answered all of her deepest questions, shared her darkest secrets, and saw her in her truest form. Alana looked back at Rosie, wondering if this girl in front of her was someone she could commit too or not.

"Really," Alana said as Rosie jumped into her arms and kissed her mouth, forgetting the rules that she had lived by for the last three years.

Chapter 7

"Where do you want to go?" Rosie said, sitting on Alana's hotel bed, flicking through a list of countries on Alana's laptop.

"Honestly, I don't care. You can decide baby girl," Alana said, coming over to kiss Rosie before going back to packing her things.

"In Europe? Austria is nice this time of year?" Rosie asked Alana, who just nodded her head and kept packing. She had never been and was surprised how willing she was just to let go and jump into the mess that was the world with Rosie.

"Great, I'll just ring Jack," Rosie said, taking out her phone.

"Who's Jack?" Alana asked from the bathroom. She looked at herself in the mirror and wondered what Rosie saw in her. She was naturally beautiful, but the years of her life and the long nights of torment had worn their presence onto her face.

"My pilot," Rosie casually replied, making Alana laugh at herself and shake her head at how nonchalant Rosie was about flying private.

Alana tried to play it cool as they approached the private jet and bit her bottom lip to try and stop herself smiling like an idiot, but Rosie saw it all.

"Yeah, it is pretty cool, huh?" Rosie said as the car stopped. They got out, and Alana was impressed that Rosie had achieved so much of what most people deemed success. Alana followed Rosie over the tarmac and felt like she was in a movie as she climbed the stairs of the plane, reaching out and placing both her hands on Rosie's hips and pulled her back slightly.

"You're a clever girl," Alana whispered in Rosie's ear as she held her from behind making Rosie turn in her arms and kiss her passionately, running her fingers through Alana's thick black hair and giggling as Alana wrapped her arms around her waist as Rosie melted.

"Come on Mommy," Rosie whispered, making Alana smirk and let her go as they boarded the plane.

"This is insane; you do know that, right?" Alana said, walking up and down the aisle, holding Champaign in one hand and biting her other thumb. Rosie laughed and looked out the window. They had been flying for three hours and were over the ocean. The glistening blue looked like someone had dropped diamonds over the surface, and Rosie exhaled deeply catching Alana's attention.

"What is it?" She questioned coming to sit next to Rosi, who didn't bother to turn around but kept looking out the window. Alana put her glass down and reached out to turn Rosie's face to her.

"Hey," Alana said with concern as a tear rolled down Rosie's face.

"Nothing," Rosie replied, making Alana roll her eyes.

"Don't lie to Mommy," Alana said, making

Rosie laugh despite herself.

"What are we even doing?" Rosie said defeatedly. Alana thought for a minute. She was on the private jet of a 22-year-old who had convinced the world they should pay for her existence, on their way to Austria and said girl liked calling her Mommy.

"We are on a rather big adventure sweetheart," Alana said, stopping when she felt Rosie's hand reach for hers.

"I want to love you, Alana," Rosie said, sadly looking down.

"I know you do darling. I'm sorry I can't love you the way you want me too. But I can do this," Alana said, getting up and pulling Rosie up with her before laying her down on the sofa on the other side of the plane. Alana lay down next to Rosie and rested on her elbow, stroking Rosie's cheek and looking at her tenderly.

"I can look after you. I can hold you closer than you've ever been held and I can protect you with a ferociousness that even frightens me. I can promise you that I will stay as long as you want me and that my arms will always be open for you. You can trust me with this," Alana said as she placed her hand on Rosie's heart and looked down on her face before bending her head and kissing her gently.

"But I don't know how to rebuild the parts of me that feel," Alana stated honestly.

"And I would give those to you as well if I did sweetheart. You can have all of me that I still have left and you can trust that I won't leave you," Alana said, dropping her body to rest against Rosie's who snuggled into her.

"I love you, Alana," Rosie whispered as she held Alana's arm and traced the lines of her face, tracing her soft fingertips over Alana's lips and the bridge of her nose.

"You have all of me, sweetheart," Alana replied, her eyes smiling as she caught herself laughing.

"I can't believe this is happening. You are such a big girl for such a baby," Alana teased, bringing their conversation into a lighter note.

"So are you," Rosie said giggling as Alana scoffed.

"Don't think for a second I will not bend you over my knee and spank you right here sweetheart," Alana said, staring into Rosie's wild eyes. Rosie's gaze was full of daring and mischief as Alana decided it was time to remind her that just because she had some demons, didn't make her any less of Rosie's Mommy. Grabbing Rosie by her upper arm, Alana pulled her up and over her lap, pinning her down with her forearm.

"Don't make such a fuss or captain Jack might want to come and see what all the fuss is about baby girl," Alana said covering Rosie's mouth with her hand and rubbing her ass under her skirt.

"No panties, I should have just assumed," Alana laughed cupping her pussy from behind and teasing her clit as her moans where muffled.

"Such a wet and horny little one aren't you. That's how I like my girl, always ready and willing to be taken," Alana almost moaned, getting turned on as Rosie spread her thighs and reached back to spread her ass for Alana.

"Is that where you want it little one?" Alana asked, reaching into her bag and taking out a slim vibrator and pushing it into Rosie's mouth.

"Get it wet sugar," Alana commanded before spitting on it and sliding it into Rosie's ass and turning it on making Rosie dip her head forward and arch her back as Alana filled her.

"How am I supposed to keep it in there without you wearing any panties. Good thing Mommy is prepared isn't it baby girl," Alana said mostly to herself as Rosie was busy squirming on her lap. Alana took out a Chasity belt and slid it up Rosie's thighs before standing her up and locking it in place before Rosie knew what was happening.

"Mommy," Rosie whined and straddled Alana's soft thigh before rubbing herself on top of it trying to make her orgasm hit her like she craved.

"No, that's all you're getting little one, oh,

that and this," Alana said, taking a diaper out of her bag and making Rosie gasp.

"You didn't think you were so big that I'd leave you uncovered, did you?" Alana said, standing up and looking down at Rosie.

"Are you going to be a good girl for Mommy?" Alana asked, pulling on the top of the belt, making Rosie bite her bottom lip and nod her head with excitement in her eyes.

"Good, come here then baby girl," Alana said, pulling Rosie to the floor and putting the diaper over the top of the belt that was securing the vibrator.

"Pretty girl," Alana said, running her hands over the diapered girl in front of her.

"You know, I'll have to be out of this when we land Alana," Rosie said nervously breaking their play, worried about what the future held. Alana raised her eyebrow.

"Mommy," Alana corrected gently as she shook her head and pulled Rosie back down next to her.

"Of course, baby girl. You can trust Mommy," she added cradling Rosie in her arms.

Alana and Rosie rented a cabin in the mountains outside a small village in the Austrian Alps. Alana had taken to working in the mornings as Rosie slept, taking on online orders which helped to create a routine they enjoyed following. Rosie tied up her life, telling her people that she wouldn't be taking on any new products or endorsements and selling off three of her homes to buy herself out of two of her contracts she had with big clothing labels. The internet went wild with speculation as to what her mental state was but tucked away in the mountains with Alana had her more stable than she had ever been.

"Hi baby girl," Alana said coming into their bedroom to see that Rosie had woken up and was happily sucking on her paci and playing with the stuffies that despite Alana's best attempts, always seemed to make their way into their bed.

"I thought I told you to put these away last night?" Alana questioned playfully making Rosie giggle and roll around in bed.

"Come here little one," Alana said, placing her laptop down and getting back into bed with Rosie. It was winter, and the snow had fallen knee deep, making walking on the mountains difficult, so Alana and Rosie had taken to staying indoors, except for their shopping days.

"I think we need to go into town darling or you're little tummy will be hungry soon," Alana said running her hands over Rosie's fluffy white onesie and playfully biting her neck making Rosie giggle and push Alana away.

"Mommy!" Rosie squealed before Alana stopped and stood her up.

"Come on darling, Mommy needs to get you dressed so we can go," Alana said taking Rosie's hand and leading her to the cupboard, opening it up and looking at what she wanted Rosie in today.

"This will look cute," Alana said taking out red plaid winter trousers and black high-top ankle boots, a long sleeve white thermal top, and a black puffer jacket. Rosie shook her head no as Alana began to dress her, making Alana roll her eyes and grip Rosie's chin, forcing her to look at her in the eyes.

"No?" Alana questioned making Rosie look sideward and stop refusing.

"This one Mommy," Rosie said, pointing to a pair of pink pants instead.

"Please Mommy. Where are your manners, little one?" Alana said slapping Rosie's bottom firmly.

"That's not how you ask, and you know it. Don't be a bad girl for Mommy; you know what happens if you are a naughty baby girl," Alana said, taking out the cane she had used on Rosie a week earlier. Rosie began to suck her thumb, and Alana knew she would have no trouble with her for the rest of the day. Alana dressed Rosie, pulling her pants over her diaper and zipping up her jacket before she got herself dressed. They had been in Austria for a month and knowing they would only be here for another 3 weeks, Alana didn't buy the week supply of groceries she had done previously, instead she decided to only buy for a couple of days and settled with the plan that they would eat out for the rest of their stay.

"No put it back baby we don't need it," Alana said to Rosie who tried to put a big bag of candy in the shopping cart. Rosie pouted but obeyed forcing Alana to try and suppress her smile. She loved having Rosie as hers. It hadn't felt the way Alana had first thought it would. Rosie was different from her. With everyone else, she was the playful, cheeky slut who would be happily gaging to be fucked by anyone who wanted her. With Alana, she was calm, thoughtful, observant and sensual and Alana loved that Rosie had those qualities and that they were all hers.

"Sweetie?" Alana asked Rosie who was holding a magazine in her hands. Alana looked over Rosie's shoulder and saw what Rosie was looking at. *Young entrepreneur assumed dead*, read the headline with Rosie's photo under it.

"They think I'm dead?" Rosie said in a confused voice that Alana didn't know how to read. Alana waited for a response to come and held her breath in nervous anticipation.

"That is so rude!" Rosie laughed, putting the magazine down and walking off to get the milk Alana has told her to get. Alana smiled to herself as her heart was filled with pride at how far her baby girl had come. From the sensitive girl that was scared of the world to the woman who was comfortable in her skin and comfortable with what she needed to be happy.

Fuck. My turn, Alana thought as she got in the car and listened to Rosie's story about a dog she had just seen that was as big as a pony.

"What are you doing, Mommy?" Rosie asked coming up behind Alana who sat in the sunroom typing on her laptop. Rosie had gone for a walk that morning, and Alana took the time to begin to write about the things that haunted her. *If my baby can manage to sort her head out, maybe I can do the same*, Alana had thought while fucking Rosie the night before. Alana hadn't heard Rosie come back into the cabin and was startled, jumping and getting the hiccups which just made Rosie laugh.

"Mommy you are so silly, look, I got you a flower!" Rosie said, presenting the yellow petaled flower to Alana who bit her bottom lip.

"You're a little bit cute do you know that?" Alana said, pulling Rosie onto her lap and reading out the first paragraph she had written.

"She howled from the depths of her soul without regard for who could hear. The long journey to the top of the mountain had left her breathless, the pads of her paws sore and tender. 'Don't feel sorry for me,' she whispered to the small hedgehog who came out to see what the dark shaggy fur was that sat outside her burrow. 'Feel sorry for them,' she said, looking down the path she had just forged. Through stone and dirt, she had dug her path. It was deep, deep enough to hide a wolf as it made its way behind her and oh how they had. Snapping at her heels, biting down on her hunches they had only made her ascent faster, all the while trying to slow her down. And when she had finally reached the top, turning in one quick motion, she pushed them down the steep slope and watched as they tumbled and fell until she could sit safely on her perch. The hedgehog knew none of this; she hadn't come in on that chapter of the young wolf's story, she had only seen the victory and wondered why the wolf had refused to allow another on the top with her. 'Won't you get lonely?' She asked. 'No,' replied the wolf who turned to the rising moon and smiled as she saw a black figure moving towards her. 'I didn't climb this mountain for me, I climbed it for her,' the wolf said as another wolf greeted her and together they began to howl to the stars and moon that decorated the night's sky," Alana read, remaining silent and waiting when she finished seeing what Rosie would say.

"Silva?" Rosie asked. Alana liked that Rosie

never made her feel bad for still being in that room with Silva no matter where in the world she physically was, but this time, Rosie was wrong.

"No," Alana whispered, looking down and smiling to herself. For this first time, she had been able to feel a glimmer of something else. As though the door to her heart had been unlocked and left open, letting her move in and out of the space.

"Not this time. I want to love you," Alana said quietly as Rosie took her hand tenderly and kissed her cheek.

"I know you do," Rosie replied, her words not escaping Alana who laughed as Rosie replied with the same words Alana had only a month ago.

Chapter 9

"Mommy?" Rosie said, coming back into the cabin on the day they were meant to leave. Alana and Rosie had decided that it was best to head back to the States and build their new life together there. They had both decided that it was too complicated to try and stay in Austria and with Rosie's career slowing down they were both excited to get settled in New York. That's what Rosie thought was going to happen, but walking through the empty cabin, her heart began to scream words she didn't want to hear. Alana was gone. Her bags that had been packed near the door weren't there anymore, the toys that Rosie had left unpacked where all there except for the bunny that she often cuddled with, in Alana's arms and a letter was left on top of her suitcase.

I numbed it with everything that I could find darling — alcohol, sex, money, success. I stayed away from drugs; you've got to have your limits, right?! I see the sort of people who couldn't brace up, and I'm glad weakness was never an option for me, I don't think it's in my nature, but it is probably just a firm conditioning I refuse to shake. What do you want me to say? That I was sad, lonely, scared. That it felt like breathing for the first time when I would get lost in your touch and that nothing has made me feel as alive since. It is love I find so fucking painful; I'm very happy enjoying a girl for a while, but love is just too much for me to be able to let sink in. I knew I had a choice I knew I could have just let you go, but I wanted to let you love me, I wanted to love you, but it's just too painful. I'm sorry, baby girl, take care, Alana.

Rosie froze, speechless. She sat down next to her bags and cried for the first time in ten years, crying her heart out and feeling smaller and more worthless than she had ever felt in her life.

Alana had flown back to Paris and spent the next three weeks getting ritualistically drunk and looking up at the ceiling of a cheap hotel. The days of Rosie spun in her head, the days of Silva always interrupted them, hearing the sound of gunshots in her nightmares startling her awake.

"She's better off without me," Alana said out loud to herself as she stood and looked around her dark room for a bottle with anything left in it. The bunny she had taken from Rosie had long lost her scent of perfume and now reeked of bourbon and cigarettes. A knock came from the door, and Alana stumbled to the door, opening it slowly.

"Hi, you wanna let me in?" The woman the Alana had forgotten she had ordered hours before said, standing in front of her. Alana wiped her eyes and shrugged her shoulders and walked back into the bedroom and fell on the bed.

"Money is on the counter," Alana said, breathing deeply and drinking the last of the bourbon she had found. The woman thought for a minute before coming to sit on the bed with Alana.

"What the fuck is the matter with you?" She suddenly said making Alana's closed eyes open slowly.

"What?" Alana replied, unsure of what the woman was telling her.

"You're Alana Shummer aren't you? You are with Rosie. What the fuck are you doing here like this?" The woman said making Alana mad.

"I didn't pay for a fucking lecture, did I bitch?" She said, getting up to rest on her elbows.

"Well, it looks like you need one," The woman said going to the windows and drawing the curtains back making Alana squint.

"Tell me what the fuck has happened to get you like this?" The woman said, slapping Alana's face firmly when Alana started her rebuttal.

"Did I stutter, bitch?" The woman said confidently making Alana laugh.

"Guess not," Alana said, sobering up quickly and sitting up, crossing her legs and looking at the woman for the first time.

"I couldn't give her what she needed. She needed love; I couldn't give her that. She's better off without me, the end," Alana explained to the frowning woman.

"So are you finished lying to yourself?" The woman said, crossing her arms over her chest and waiting. Alana rolled her eyes and dramatically lay back down in bed.

"From what I've seen, Rosie had never been happier than when she was with you, didn't you guys go to some retreat or something together? You even protected her from the paparazzi. Have you seen how she's doing? She needs you more now than ever," The woman said piquing Alana's curiosity.

"What do you mean?" Alana asked, concern in her voice.

"She's been taken to hospital, she broke down on a talk show, and she just sat there, crying, it went viral," The woman said taking out her phone and finding the video of the interview Rosie came undone on. Handing it to Alana, Alana watched as the girl she had called hers cried as her heart broke in the most invasive manner possible.

"Why did you show me that?" Alana said quietly handing the woman her phone back.

"Because it looks like you could use more than just a fuck. You need a friend and a shower, come on," The woman said, taking Alana's hand and leading her into the shower, turning the water on and taking off Alana's clothes. The woman sat on the floor as Alana showered for the first time in days and watched as the bathroom steamed up as Alana let the hot water pour over her body.

"You can't burn out whatever it is that haunts you," The woman said, standing up and turning the water off. She passed Alana a towel as Alana reached for her packet of cigarettes.

"No," The woman said slapping Alana's hand away. Alana raised an eyebrow at the woman who just laughed.

"I said no," The woman repeated taking the cigarettes from the packet and breaking them in half.

"It's a filthy habit. You deserve better," The woman said to Alana who for the first time let someone have control over her.

"What am I even meant to say to her?"

Alana said as she got dressed in clean clothes and began cleaning the hotel room.

"Sorry might be a good start. I imagine you've shattered her trust so get ready for a backlash," The woman said watching as Alana tidied and began packing.

"I'm going to call her," Alana said more to herself than the woman who nodded her head and sat down on the couch.

"Um," Alana said wanting privacy and making the woman laugh as she got up and took the money from the counter.

"Good luck, darling. Be better," The woman said as she waved goodbye with thc envelope of cash Alana had set aside for her.

Alana took a deep breath before clicking on Rosie's name, her photo covering Alana's phone screen as she called.

"Hello?" Rosie's voice quietly said, her vulnerability making Alana lost for words.

"I'm sorry," Alana said, matching the quiet intensity of Rosie's voice. Silence echoed down the phone, but Rosie spoke first.

"You don't have to do this. I don't need you," she said, lying to herself.

"I know," Alana said, letting Rosie try and believe it.

"Then what do you want? Haven't you taken enough of me?" Rosie said, feeling anger begin to boil within her.

"I need help Rosie," Alana said, admitting to her flaws for the first time in her life.

"Well, there's an empty bed here next to mine," Rosie said, laughing despite herself.

"I'll be there in a day," Alana said excitedly.

"Rosie?" Alana quickly added.

"Yep," Rosie said defensively.

"I'm sorry I broke your heart. Let me try and fix it?" Alana asked, biting her tongue as she almost slipped on the words.

"I can't say if I'll stay, but I'll let you try," Rosie said hanging up the phone and placing her phone on her chest, breathing deeply as happy tears rolled down her cheeks.

"So, what am I supposed to do with you now?" Rosie said three weeks later upon seeing Alana standing in front of her. They had decided to meet at a back street art gallery after spending countless hours talking on the phone.

"Rosie," Alana said, becoming speechless and looked down at her feet, intimidated by the now powerful woman who stood in front of her.

"You had plenty to say before, do you want a pen and paper, would that be easier for you?!" Rosie angrily said, fire burning in her eyes, pain flooding her blood. Alana looked up and frowned.

"I never meant to hurt you," she said quietly only enraging Rosie.

"What the fuck did you think it would do? You come in, take me in, make me feel for the first time and then just bail?" Rosie yelled before walking out of the gallery, Alana in tow.

"I'm sorry!" Alana yelled back at her, causing Rosie to stop and turn on her heel.

"Yeah, I get that, what I don't get is why,"

Rosie said, pacing back and forth on the graveled driveway out the back of the gallery. Alana didn't know how to reply, so she just stood there, watching her life turn in slow motion.

"You need help Alana," Rosie said quietly, her expression changing from rage to love. She shook her head, and half laughed, surprised that she was able to have this kind of conversation.

"You need help, or anti-depressants or Jesus, just something, anything. I thought we were happy; I thought you were happy," Rosie said, stepping closer to Alana who felt littler than she had ever felt in her life.

"I know," Alana said softly, a tear escaping when she felt Rosie's hand on her cheek.

"Then let me help you, baby," Rosie said, making Alana laugh.

"You're still the baby, I don't care how sad I am I'm still your Mommy," Alana said without thinking, her eyes going wide as she heard what she had just said. Rosie thought for a moment before shaking her head no.

"You aren't anymore Alana, well, not yet anyway. Maybe in the future, but not right now. I need to be able to trust you again; I need you to be better," Rosie said despite wanting Alana to be hers again desperately. Alana nodded, understanding the situation before smiling a cheeky smile.

"Guess I better see a shrink or something then, I have big plans for you baby girl," Alana said, making Rosie laugh and hug her tightly.

"I don't want to love you like I do," Rosie whispered into Alana's chest as Alana held her. The sky turned dark as storm clouds came overhead and began lightly raining on the pair as they held each other, neither wanting to be the first to let go.

"Shall we go?" Rosie said to Alana, who nodded her head and slowly stepped back from Rosie, who just laughed.

"No I mean, shall we go back to mine. I don't want to be alone tonight," Rosie said holding out her hand beaming when Alana took her hand in hers and started running to her car as the sky suddenly burst, and large raindrops fell hard from the sky. Sitting wet in the car, Rosie reached over to wipe Alana's face catching her off guard.

"Hey," Alana laughed, becoming serious when she saw Rosie's face.

"I missed you. Will you get help?" She said as Alana turned the ignition and drove out of the car park.

"Yeah, I don't want to be that person for you or for me anymore. I near couldn't live with myself for those weeks. It got ugly," Alana confessed as Rosie took her hand in both of hers.

"How did you get out of it? Why did you want to come back to me?" Rosie questioned, looking out the window as Alana drove through the rain. Alana thought back to the night she had been given a reality check from the working girl she had paid and laughed, remembering how she had been ridiculously lovely.

"A friend talked me out of my bender. I'm grateful because after I learned that you weren't doing well like I had thought you would go without me, I realized I needed to come back," Alana said pulling over under a bridge and locking the doors.

"So you thought that I *needed* you?" Rosie said, crossing her arms over her chest and pouting.

"Well, didn't you?" Alana said amused and placing her hand on Rosie's thigh, slowly reaching under her skirt.

"Yes," Rosie said, feeling Alana stroke her pussy through her sheer panties.

"I thought so," Alana said grabbing at Rosie who moved to be straddling Alana's thighs as Alana put her seat back and held the back of Rosie's head as Rosie kissed her passionately, biting her lip hard.

"Ouch baby!" Alana yelled, making Rosie giggle.

"Now we are even," Rosie said, licking her lips, tasting Alana's blood. Alana raised an eyebrow and tried to get up but was stopped by Rosie, who placed her hand on Alana's chest and pushed her back.

"I'm in control today Mommy," Rosie said, taking two fist fulls of Alana's T-shirt and ripping it open from the top.

"Not if you are going to make me look like bears have attacked me," Alana said, rolling Rosie onto her back and tearing her panties off.

"Hey slow down, it's not as though I'm going anywhere," Rosie teased making Alana blush.

"Yeah sorry about that," Alana said, slowing down and kissing Rosie lovingly.

"I want you to be gentle with me, Mommy," Rosie whispered, enjoying the feel of Alana's full weight on top of her. Alana reached between Rosie's thighs and smiled as her wet pussy juices laced her fingers.

"You're always so ready baby girl," Alana said, sliding into Rosie and making her moan in pleasure. Rosie closed her eyes and bit her bottom lip before shaking her head and pushing Alana off.

"No, Mommy, I don't want to," Rosie said, her eyes looking afraid that Alana would be angry.

Alana took her fingers out of Rosie and looked at her with concern.

"Did I hurt you baby?" Alana asked, letting Rosie get up and move to the passenger seat, watching as she put her clothes back on.

"No, I just don't want sex, I kinda just want your cuddles right now," Rosie said, looking down and making Alana frown.

"You don't ever have to be worried about asking for what you need little one, come on let's get you home and settled so you can cuddle with Mommy," Alana said reaching for her jacket in the back seat.

"But first I think I need to cover up," Alana joked zipping her jacket up before she pulled out from under the bridge and back onto the road.

Alana smiled as she drove up the familiar driveway of Rosie's mansion home, stopping by the water fountain near the front door. It was late afternoon by the time they arrived, and Rosie had half fallen asleep on the ride home, reaching out of hold Alana's arm as she rested.

"Come one sleeping beauty," Alana said as she got out and walked around to Rosie's door. Opening it, Alana took off Rosie's seat belt and helped her out of the car before they made their way inside. Ignoring the maids who worked silently as Alana and Rosie walked through the house, they made their way to Rosie's bedroom and locked the door behind them.

"Finally!" Rosie said, falling onto her bed and closing her eyes.

"You need a shower little one, Mommy can't have you going to bed all dirty from the day," Alana said going into the bathroom and beginning to run Rosie a bath. Rosie got up and slowly made her way to the bathroom sitting on the edge of the bath as Alana undressed her.

"I thought you were a big girl little one, looks like you are a sweet baby when you are sleepy," Alana said stroking Rosie's cheeks with her thumbs. Rosie just nodded her head while looking up at Alana, raising her arms as Alana lifted her into the bath.

"Oh bubbles, Mommy that's nice," Rosie said splashing in the bath happily.

"I'm really happy to be here with you baby girl," Alana said, making Rosie smile a toothy grin and swim over to where Alana was sitting. She placed her head on Alana's lap, wetting her jeans slightly.

"I'm glad as well Mommy, I missed you, I need you," Rosie said lovingly before going back to splashing in the tub.

Alana watched Rosie until the water turned cold and got her out, drying her off and making her giggle as her toes where dried.

"Mommy," Rosie said as she balanced on one foot. Alana took her back into her room and sat Rosie down on the ottoman at the end of her bed.

"I did some shopping, Mommy," Rosie said, pointing to the cupboard. Alana walked over to see that Rosie had a collection of adult onesies and diapers, pacifiers and baby bottles.

"My my haven't you been busy baby girl," Alana said, running her fingers over the collection of diapers that Rosie had neatly stacked in her cupboard. Selecting the purple stripe one and a grey onesie Alana made her way back over to Rosie who looked nervous and excited at the same time.

"Are you going to lay down for Mommy?" Alana asked Rosie who was already resting on her elbows. Alana reached for the baby powder that Rosie passed her and rubbed it over Rosie's body, bending down to kiss the tip of her nose.

"Thank you for letting me be your Mommy baby girl," Alana said to Rosie who giggled and reached for her toes, getting gentle spanks on her thighs from Alana who pushed her legs back down.

"Keep your leggies down for Mommy little one," Alana said sticking the tabs of the diaper down and running her hands over the top of Rosie's diapered bottom as Rosie turned over and tried to tuck herself into bed.

"Not just yet little cuteness," Alana said, grabbing Rosie by the ankle and pulling her back so she could dress her in the onesie.

"You have to put your jammies on sweetheart," Alana said, dressing Rosie.

"And teethies," Alana laughed as Rosie pouted before getting a warning look from Alana.

"You haven't been punished by mommy yet, don't let it be tonight little one," Alana said, walking Rosie to the bathroom again.

"Mommy, am I done now?" Rosie begged turning the light off to the bathroom after she had cleaned her teeth for 3 minutes and not a second longer and looking at Alana pleadingly.

"Yes, little one, it's bedtime," Alana laughed,

taking Rosie's hand and pulling back her bed sheets.

"Mommy, are you coming in?" Rosie asked Alana, who took off her jacket.

"Mommy hasn't had a shower yet little one, can you stay up for five more minutes?" Alana asked, kicking off her boots and unzipping her jeans, revealing her red lace thong. Rosie smiled and nodded, enjoying the look of Alana's body and wanting it in bed with her.

Alana came back 20minutes later with just a towel around her waist, smiling at Rosie who was fast asleep. Alana threw the dry towel on the floor before climbing into bed with Rosie who opened her eyes and snuggled into Alana's arms, readjusting her position several times before Alana spoke to her.

"Shh baby girl Mommy is here," Alana said while holding Rosie and patting her back. Rosie murmured something Alana couldn't understand before she took a deep breath and fell back into her sleep. Alana stayed awake. Thinking about how close she had been to losing Rosie forever and held her tighter as she remembered how Rosie had looked at her with venom in her eyes earlier in the day. *That was close*, Alana thought stroking Rosie's hair out of her face and sighing in relief as she closed her eyes and went to sleep.

Alana and Rosie spent the next day locked up in Rosie's room not wanting to burst the bubble they had finally been able to create. With the wall length windows opened to the outdoor courtyard, Rosie had enjoyed a day spent rolling around in bed, relaxing in Alana's arms and playing in her little space.

"Baby, do you think we should leave the house today?" Alana asked as she got dressed, coming out from having a shower. Rosie shook her head at which Alana just smirked and went to her cupboard to pick out what she wanted to dress her in.

"Well that's alright, we are going to go out anyway," Alana replied, taking Rosie by the hand

and leading her to the bed.

"No Mommy," Rosie said, squirming on her back not wanting to be undressed. Alana stopped and thought for a moment before unbuckling the belt she had just secured to her hips. Slowly taking it off, she clapped the buckle into her hand before doubling the leather over.

"No, Mommy?" Alana questioned, jumping onto the bed to straddle Rosie who tried to push her off. Alana stayed firmly positioned on top of Rosie before lifting off her enough to turn her over and pin her down with her leg.

"Baby girl, do not say no to Mommy," Alana said calmly before striking Rosie on her diapered bottom. Rosie stopped resisting her and lay still, pouting and trying to fight back the tears. Knowing that Rosie's limits were easily reached, Alana let her up and turned her back to face her. She put her hands on either side of Rosie's cheeks and looked at her baby girl, lovingly.

"Don't say no to Mommy, do you understand me?" Alana said gently, opening her arms and holding onto Rosie tightly. Rosie buried her head in Alana's ample cleavage and nodded her head.

"Use your words baby girl, Mommy wants to hear it," Alana said, rocking her back and forth.

"Yes Mommy," Rosie said quietly, bringing her thumb up to suck only for it to be taken out of her mouth and replaced with a paci.

"Let Mommy dress you in something else baby," Alana said, going back to dressing a far more compliant Rosie. Alana chose a tight-fitting pull-up, a pair of high waisted jeans and a sleeveless button-down that gaped at the neck.

"Are you helping Mommy put on your sockies baby girl?" Alana asked as Rosie nodded and fiddled with one of her socks before Alana slid on heeled beige boots and finished the look with a lightweight trench coat.

"Very cute," Alana said as she pushed a black pacifier in Rosie's mouth and watched her in her little space while she got dressed.

"Where are we going, Mommy?" Rosie

asked as Alana put her hair up in a messy ponytail and checked her phone.

"Somewhere I think you'll like little one, come on," Alana said, holding out her hand to Rosie who excitedly jumped down from her bed and ran to hold Alana's hand.

Chapter 11

"Mommy, can you tell me now?" Rosie whispered into Alana's ear as they sat in the back of the town car that was driving them to the undisclosed location. Alana had seen the night before that there was a private party invite from one of her friends in an email and just knew that Rosie would love to go. The private parties of celebrities, Alana had learned were more scandalous than anything the tabloids could ever report, and this one was set to be the biggest event of the year.

"No sweetie," Alana said, pulling Rosie closer to her and rubbing her hand over the front of Rosie's pussy, her jeans muffling the crinkly sound of her pull up.

"Such a sweet baby girl," Alana said almost to herself, getting lost in the feeling of protective love that flowed through her instantly.

"I love you, Rosie," Alana said abruptly, the

words escaping before she could stop them, holding her breath as she heard what she had just said.

"I know Mommy," Rosie said, repositioning herself against Alana who was now cradling Rosie in her arms. The car stopped, and Alana got out slowly, taking in the lavish gardens of the property they were to spend the next couple of days. Alana had packed Rosie's bikini and a few other things she thought they might need in an over-night bag. She knew that these parties tended to last far longer than an evening. Rosie held Alana's hand as they walked up the path, hiding behind Alana when they waited at the front door.

"Is this the part where you sell me to the red light district?" Rosie said fearfully. Alana looked down and was amused by Rosie's imagination.

"No, sweetheart, we are going to a party," Alana replied, smiling as she saw Rosie's face light up.

"Oh cool," Rosie said, adopting her usual

confident manner and reaching out to knock on the door again. Banging loudly, Rosie impatiently stamped her foot but jumped as the door swung open.

"Hey cutie," Said a woman that Rosie knew instantly. Speechless, Rosie just grabbed on Alana's arm and turned, walking back down the steps of the mansions and onto the gravel driveway.

"What the fuck Alana?" Rosie yelled once she saw the door of the house shut. Alana rolled her eyes; annoyed Rosie was freaking out.

"What?" Alana replied. She had thought that Rosie would have liked to blow off some steam and was unsure of why Rosie was acting this way.

"Do you know who she is?!" Rosie squealed to Alana's amusement.

"Yes. And?" Alana asked not caring about who the IT girl was who had opened the door.

"She's just a naughty baby like you, darling. Didn't you know?" Alana said, making Rosie pout.

"I'm not naughty," she said, folding her

arms against her chest and stepping side to side unsure of how to process what she had just seen. The woman had been wearing a tight black t-shirt, white diaper, and thigh high rainbow socks. Her hair was pulled up into two messy pigtails, and the silver chained collar that hung around her neck had made Rosie wonder how her fragile looking body could hold such an object.

"You said it was a party!" Rosie said, shaking her head, trying to somehow make sense of this.

"It is, it's a party for Mommies and babies. Come on, you're silly," Alana said as Rosie sat down on the gravel.

"I don't wanna go, Mommy," Rosie said, looking up at Alana with a serious face that made Alana second guess if she was too mean making Rosie go.

"Well, what shall we do instead baby girl?" Alana said coming to sit down next to Rosie, who leaned over and rested her head on Alana's shoulder.

"Could we just go home please, Mommy?" Rosie said softly, taking Alana's hand and looking up at her with puppy dog eyes. Alana sighed and knew why Rosie didn't want to go in. Her whole world would end if the media got a hold of this information. The information that she was just a baby girl who needed Mommy to look after her. Alana stood up and held out her hand to Rosie, who took it eagerly and cuddled into Alana as they walked to where their car was.

"Thank you, Mommy," Rosie whispered as Alana buckled her into the car, tenderly reaching up and playing with Alana's hair making Alana smile at her lovingly.

"It's OK baby girl; Mommy is going to look after you always. I'm excited to see what games we play when we get home though little one. I have big plans for you tonight. And to get you ready, spread your legs for me," Alana instructed, waiting for Rosie to follow her request. Rosie obediently parted her thighs and gasped when Alana reached into her pull up and placed a vibrating egg against her clit just as their driver turned around the corner.

"Keep quiet little one, nobody wants to hear your moans," Alana said before kissing the top of Rosie's forehead. Alana walked around to the other side of the car and got in, holding Rosie's hand and enjoying her squirming and pressing her head against the back of the chair as the car drove over bumps and holes on the road, making her clit ache and her pussy wet.

"Mommy please," Rosie said the minute the door was shut behind them, making Alana laugh and rub Rosie over her pull up only adding to her frustration.

"Are you a horny little girl? Do you need Mommy to fuck you, baby?" Alana teased as she went to the bedroom followed by Rosie, who willingly let Alana push her onto the bed.

"Let me see baby," Alana said unzipping Rosie's jeans and reaching into her pull up only to push the vibrating egg into her pussy roughly.

"You'll take it one way or the other baby girl, Mommy is going to play rough with you tonight," Alana said going to the wooden chest they kept their sex toys in and took out a long black leather whip and a bit gag. Alana gently secured the gag behind Rosie's head, enjoying how she had to stretch her mouth wide to hold it.

"Such a pretty little slut," Alana said taking off Rosie's shirt and biting into her, making her wriggle, only stopping when Alana placed her hand on her neck and squeezed.

"No, don't move little one," Alana said, bringing her whip down on Rosie's tummy, making her bite down on the gag, Alana enjoying her muffled screams. Alana marked her until Rosie was only wincing with each strike and placing the whip down she took Rosie's pull up off. She took out the vibrator only to quickly replace it with her strap-on. She flipped Rosie and bucked her hips as she slapped her ass, making Rosie ride her deeply, Rosie's hands coming to rest on Alana's tits as she was fucked.

"Mommy wants to fuck you like I've paid you baby girl. Are you going to let Mommy have everything I want tonight?" Alana said to Rosie, who just nodded her head and matched Alana's thrusts.

"You'll take everything Mommy gives you baby girl, I told you I was going to enjoy you tonight darling," Alana said calmly as Rosie was fucked raw, her cries only encouraging Alana. As Rosie closed her eyes, Alana slowed her onslaught and took out the gag only to replace it with her cum covered strap.

"Suck you pussy juices clean off baby girl, such a dirty little girl, you'll say yes to anything won't you baby," Alana said, pushing her strap down Rosie's gaging throat. Suddenly taking it out of her mouth and releasing the firm grip she had on Rosie's head.

"I'm not finished with you yet sweetheart," Alana loving whispered in Rosie's ear as she kissed her neck and ran her finger-tips over Rosie's still warm tummy, the marks of Alana's whip clear and red on her Irish white skin. Alana walked out of the room, leaving Rosie to lay spent on her bed as she thought about how she had come so far, now being able to love a woman. *I know that there are other people out there that could give me something similar, maybe better in some instances even. But I want what she can give me. I can be little with her one minute and completely dominant in the next, and she can keep up. I'm free with her, it's nice. I like that she likes to control everything but that she listens to me and bends where I need and want her too. I like that I hate everyone but her, they are just so fucking boring and pointless.* Rosie's thought where interrupted by the huge object Alana had come back into the room with. A giant brown teddy bear with a long thick strap-on firmly attached from the inside made Rosie's mouth gaped open.

"Good, keep that pretty mouth open baby girl, you're going to play with teddy tonight," Alana said, putting the teddy's cock into her mouth, forcing it down her throat.

"Suck," Alana said slapping Rosie's face several times and pinching her nose as Rosie gaged and panted as her mouth was filled.

"Pretty little slut," Alana said affectionately watching Rosie service the teddy. Alana placed the bear in the middle of the bed and grabbed Rosie by a fistful of hair.

"Do you know how Mommy wants to watch you play tonight little girl?" Alana said with an evil laugh in her voice. Rosie nodded her head painfully as her hair pulled with every motion.

"Use your big girl words baby," Alana said, loosening her grip but spanking Rosie's ass.

"You want me to ride teddy?" Rosie questioned, getting a nod of approval from Alana who let her go and took a step back.

"Begin," Alana commanded, getting wet as she saw Rosie position herself over the teddy's cock. Impatient of Rosie's hesitation, Alana walked back over to the bed and pushed Rosie down by the shoulders, making her pussy full of the teddy's cock. Alana knew that the toy was stretching her by the sudden gasp of air the filled Rosie's lungs as the teddy was slammed into her. However, Alana enjoyed the grinding of Rosie's hips that followed, taking her whip and striking Rosie's ass several times.

"Fuck your teddy baby girl," Alana said as she began whipping Rosie again. Rosie lifted her hips off the cock to drop them down again panting as she bounced on her teddy fuck buddy.

"Fuck this is hotter than I had thought it would be," Alana said breathlessly, bending Rosie over the bear and pinning her down, making her feel the cock deeper inside of her.

"Mommy," Rosie said in the exhausted voice Alana had been waiting to hear.

"Just a little longer baby girl, you're not done just yet," Alana said coming behind her and guiding her lubed slim strap-on into Rosie's ass making her shake her hips. Alana held them firmly in place as she pushed into Rosie who continued to fuck her teddy until she lay spent over the large soft toy as Alana fucked her ass until she was satisfied Rosie would need a full day to recover.

"Cute little girl, I love it how you are so good for me," Alana said slowly sliding out of Rosie and pulling her limp body from the teddy who still had it's cock filling her pussy. Alana carried Rosie to the floor and rubbed cream over her red marks and wrapped her in her favorite snuggly blanket.

"Come to Mommy little one, let me give you all the cuddles," Alana said, picking up Rosie's bunny and smiling down at it.

"Bunny wants to give you kisses," Alana said as she lay down next to Rosie, playfully bopping Rosie on the nose with the toy.

"Mommy," Rosie said, exhaustion in her voice. Alana wrapped her arms around Rosie and squeezed her, holding her lovingly into the night.

Chapter 12

"What time is that interview you've got tonight, sweetheart?" Alana said, rolling over in bed and pulling Rosie to her. Rosie flinched, Alana had put her through a particularly painful session the night before, and she was still feeling it this morning.

"I don't even want to think about it, Mommy. They are going to want to talk about the movie and ask me if I'm dating someone and why I've been hiding on social media. I wish I could go up there and say I'm retiring," Rosie said playing with Alana's breasts as she cuddled on top of her. Alana ran her fingers through Rosie's somehow perfect bed hair and marveled at how stunning her baby girl was.

"Oh, Mommy's sweet girl wants to call it quits?" Alana teased making Rosie roll her eyes.

"Yes," Rosie said confidently causing Alana to laugh. Alana moved up the bed and sat up, keeping Rosie on her lap as she pat her bottom gently.

"You can say whatever the fuck you want sweetheart," Alana said, wishing she had a cigarette to smoke. It was these types of moments where she realized just how much she used to smoke after giving it up when Rosie started to have Asthma flare-ups the longer they stayed together. Quitting had caused Alana to gain a couple of pounds which had delighted Rosie to have something more to snuggle into and bigger tits for her to suck and play with.

"Well, now that I have your permission," Rosie laughed rolling off Alana and heading to the bathroom. Alana watched as she walked away, the marks on her back still present and the bruise on her neck beginning to show made Alana smile to herself.

Rosie was whisked away in the afternoon by her people who picked her up three hours before the interview was scheduled. Rosie had kept them waiting for an extra half hour as she let Alana change her back into a big girl after their morning of playing. Alana had decided she would stay in, opting for eating snacks and swimming in the pool while she waited for her sweet baby to return. She had moved into Rosie's mansion much to her amusement. She had thought it would be the other way around, but when Rosie pointed out that she was, in fact, a millionaire and that living in her home would make more sense because it was bigger and had more fun things to do than Alana's, Alana didn't feel like disputing the facts. They had been living here for almost five months, and in that time Alana liked that Rosie happily gave her full control over the domain. Alana had stayed working, taking on clients that had no idea of her relationship with the starlet but seeming to always have something to say about her. If Alana was honest, it was beginning to wear her thin. Having these people speak about her baby girl so negatively all the while being obsessed with her every move made Alana want to reveal the relationship every time.

Alana got out of the pool and dried off on the sunbed before turning on the TV to watch the interview. The media had hyped it with such intensity because it was going to go live and completely unedited.

Alana held her breath as she saw her baby girl walk onto the interviewing platform as she entered, stopping to wave to people and strike a few playful poses.

"Mommy's sweet baby," Alana said out loud as she sat down in the living room and crossed her legs on the sofa.

"So tonight we have the one and only Rosie Smith with us for her exclusive, reveal all interview about her debut film, juicy set secrets, and an apparent mystery lover," the female presenter began, gaining a predictable response of applause from the audience.

"Rosie, your latest gig, if you like, is that blockbusting movie, *Nowhere South*. Tell us, how did you land the role?" The interviewer asked as

Rosie nodded her head. Alana liked watching her body language, she knew Rosie didn't want to be there, she always bit both lips when she was trying to hurry up a lecture Alana was giving her and as Alana saw both her lips being bitten she laughed.

"Well, it's a funny story. I went to a party a few months ago, and by went I really mean, I walked up to the front door and then decided I'd rather stay at home with a special someone," Rosie said pausing and looking directly into the camera as Alana choked on the chips she was eating at the statement Rosie had just made. It hadn't only caused Alana to be surprised; the audience became hysterical with cheers, gasps, and applause.

"Then a few weeks after that, the host of the party called me up asking if I'd audition for the role of Jaz, I read the script and got the part," Rosie continued with a victorious smirk. The interviewer looked excited at where the interview was going yet stepped carefully as to gain the response she wanted.

"That is fantastic. Tell us more about this

mystery, man," she said, making Rosie smirk at her.

"I never said it was a man," Rosie replied quickly making the audience became hysterical all over again. Meanwhile, Alana was glued to the TV wondering how far she was going to go with all of this.

"I'm in a relationship with an older woman, I have been for almost a year," Rosie said triumphantly as she looked at the speechless interviewer who was clearing trying to think what questions she could ask next. Rosie waited until the applause died down before she spoke again.

"Is that what you all wanted? To leach onto my private life and suck me dry of insight and information?" Rosie began to say, a different tone falling over the audience.

"Well, is it?" Rosie prompted. Looking toward the interviewer, she began to speak candidly.

"You see, this is the thing about people knowing about your existence, I don't think you could even call it fame, it's just knowledge of you. They want to unpack everything you have, your life, your soul; it's almost like a drug for you people. You invade every part of my life, and it is never enough. You all have opinions about me and yet, you don't know anything about me, you only know what has either been shared as my social mask, my branding or what has been stolen from me. And the sad part about this is that it's not just me. You people do this to everyone you claim to love. It's not loving, it's an obsession, I'm the drug dealer to your addiction, and I came on today to let you know that I am not going to be supplying you anymore. From this December, I will be retiring. I deserve peace; I deserve a life that uplifts me, my relationship deserves it, and so does my Mommy," Rosie said before smiling directly at Alana who was in tears of joy as she watched Rosie stand, wave to the audience who were speechless and disappeared off the screen. Alana ran to the kitchen bench and grabbed her phone, frantically dialing Rosie's number.

"Hey Mommy," Rosie said, sounding like she had just offloaded the weight of the world.

"My sweet baby, come home to Mommy," Alana said lovingly causing Rosie to giggle.

"I'm already in the car," Rosie replied before hanging up, placing her phone down, closing her eyes and breathing for the first time in what felt like years.

I wandered out onto the beach, the soft, warm sand between my toes as I watched the morning rays rise over the ocean. When I think about all of the women I had used to curb the emptiness in my heart, it makes me laugh. It's not as though the world stopped turning or my blood was rushed with lust. It was a whisper in the night, a daring, a chance at something that was never meant to be tasted. Innocence is sexy, weakness is alluring, and nothing says take me like the eyes of a watcher, or was it just me. Rosebud lips parting with forced consent, it must have been fun. How many more times do you need to be honored and held in the highest regard before you understand that you are magnificent? You built an empire on every other brick they threw at you, you don't need to use this one as a cornerstone. You don't need to be so hard on yourself when all you have ever done is rise. Has there been anything you have started and not finished with such excellence that people think you are lucky? Have you ever backed down from a challenge? Haven't you fought every evil that dared stand against you? Please don't tell me that you've forgotten who you truly are, what I fucking made you?! I hadn't thought you'd be so easily confused. You see it, don't you when you look in the mirror? You see who you truly are. You were never weak, you were never scared, and you were certainly never meant to politely let them take from you for fun my darling. And yet here we are, going over the same thing we always do, aren't you sick of it? I know it makes your blood boil, I know it makes your soul ache, I know it makes you bare your teeth, wanting to fight. It's fucking meant to. It's meant to drive you; it's meant to pound your heart and *emanate protection and strength. You were never meant to be anything but an amazing light. You did it yesterday, didn't you? You did it last week, you do it every fucking day for them, and you can't figure out how to do it for yourself? What the hell are you waiting for? Is it too much? Do you burn too brightly for even you to handle? Is that why you yield to them? Why you kneel? Did you get told that your confidence was too offensive one time too many and start to give a fuck what those reptilian fuck dolls had to say? How dare you forget. How dare you try and challenge how I made you.*

Get very fucking comfortable with your light my darling; I'm not taking it away, the world needs you far too much for that. You need it far too much for that. Don't you know that when you let your soul roar it is heard for miles and felt over the seas? Don't you understand that I gave you this gift for a reason? There is no one else, so stop asking for the baton to be passed, it is yours, and you will rise with the weight of responsibility resting on your shoulders like the solider that you are. Don't be afraid of it. Have I not been here with you the whole time?

Rosie closed her laptop lid as she heard Alana's footsteps behind her coming from their back steps and out onto the sand.

"What are you doing, baby girl?" Alana asked, spreading her legs and sitting behind Rosie, pulling her back slightly and into her embrace.

"I'm just writing Mommy," Rosie replied as she showed Alana her work. Alana took the time to read it, stopping and thinking after the page had been read twice.

"This very deep baby girl, are you talking to yourself?" Alana asked, bending around to look Rosie in the eye. The waves of the cold ocean crashed down, and crabs ran across the white sand. Rosie watched them dig holes to hide from the morning sun before she spoke again.

"Yeah, I was. I was talking to myself like if the older me could talk to me now. I use to be so worried about what or who was talking about me, how they acted or reacted with the things I did. It was the game I was playing, but what I hadn't realized was that it was hurting me. Now speaking my truth was killing me, having people constantly invading my spaces just became way too much and honestly, if it hadn't had been for this last year, I don't even want to know what my life would have turned out like," Rosie said resting her head on Alana's shoulder. Alana stroked her hair and held her tight, she thought back on her life over the past year and agreed, she didn't want to think about how different it would have been without Rosie either.

"So, you like being my sweet girl then?" Alana said, taking the laptop away from her and placing it down next to where they were sitting. Rosie nodded, and Alana smiled as she took out a pacifier from her pocket and gently placed it in Rosie's mouth.

"Good, because I am not interested in having our life any other way," Alana said, picking Rosie up and taking her back inside.

Who is Tina Moore?

Tina Moore has enjoyed the lifestyle of a Mommy Domme for several years. She began exploring kink and BDSM in her youth and found her love of being a strict Mommy Domme in early 2000. Tina Moore is now an author of many MDLG and ABDL themed novels.

Having enjoyed many years in the kink community, Tina Moore combines these experiences with the sweet and naughty things her baby girl does to bring you tantalizing and salacious stories.

Follow her on:

Author Page on Amazon

Instagram @tinamoore.kdp

www.ingramcontent.com/pod-product-compliance
Lightning Source LLC
Chambersburg PA
CBHW030654190726
48286CB00001B/14